DAMNED ORCHARD

BRIAN HUNTER

I feel the need to begin here by stating that I approach my writing from a place of love.

A writer must craft elements of darkness and struggle into their work to give it honesty because that is the world we live in. No life is lived without pain. I find that I am driven by the contrast between that callous truth and the love which I pour into my work. I write what I write in spite of that darkness. My life is an affront to the cruelty of this world, and I hope my characters, who were created with love and written in sincerity, reflect that.

We still live in a place and time where good people acknowledge the injustice of this modern world and feel powerless to do anything about it; that is, sadly, by design. Yet I can attest that any one person can effect significant positive change in their world.

My writing is set in times and places that were unkind, unfair, and downright inhumane. The resilience of older generations, people born into strife and oppression, serves as the most incredible inspiration. The people in my life who have exemplified that resilience and strength were my influence for these stories. People who walk a path of nobility and kindness in spite of the world. It would be an injustice for me to ignore the harsh treatment many people endured before society made steps to better itself, and it would be hollow for me to write in a way that dances around that or ignores the fact that our world has not progressed nearly enough to make up for its legacy of hate.

While some people hold the opinion that it is wrong for a writer to speak on things they have not experienced due to race, creed, sexuality, or otherwise, I feel that path only leads to a place devoid of heartfelt discussion and rife with closed minds. I rebuke that notion in the strictest of terms.

So, from a place of love, I want to thank you for gritting your teeth and understanding the place for harsh words and cruelty within this particular tale and others. We remember to ensure we never regress.

~BRH

For Woodrow, the indefatigable.

~

Rushmore

Monday, July 20th, 1953

The ride to Custer, South Dakota, was easy. Comfortable coach seats on a couple of different railroads before taking a beautiful stainless fluted-side General Motors bus up the mountain. Mostly working-class folks on the seats around him, a few nicely dressed but mostly blue-collar types. The Greyhound eventually dropped Cam in front of an old-west type building on the corner of the main street, where a few tourists wandered about and the locals looked on. As with most pass-through towns in the Midwest, the locals tended to stand out compared to the folks just passing through. It was in their stance and the confidence that they weren't looking around at 'the sights,' just living their life. Custer had little claim to fame except for its proximity to a national monument—those goddamned stone heads-of-heads-of-state.

Cam showed up in boots and denim, a low profile indeed. He found his way into a café where he could purchase a very moist-looking pound cake and a cup of coffee. As he had expected, the lady behind the counter boxed and cupped his purchase 'to go' in cardboard and a paper cup. It was a quiet request for him to carry on, not settle down in the café. He'd thought to himself, *smells like spoiled milk in here anyway,* and he chuckled his way out the door. He had a thick skin his whole life and didn't let the narrow-mindedness of some folks ruin his day. Instead, he headed toward a small area behind the main street where he found a horse tie-down to sit on. In the sunshine of the day, he was able to see enough of the area to get the lay of the land. The grassy green area stretched the length of the town, and some railroad tracks in moderate disrepair told him that the city was once probably an exciting place. Now, it was just another bus stop near something a long-dead president stole from the native people. *Like most of this damn country…* he had thought.

Those new interstate highways are going to make mincemeat of the middle of the country, and give good folks all the more reason to leave and head west. He smiled at the thought.

In his luggage, which consisted of a green army-issue duffel bag and a thermos, he had his marching orders from Billy. The envelope had some copies of the police reports, as well as a few notes on whom might have something to say on the matter at hand. For some reason, the address of the man whose daughter went missing was not in the file. Cam knew the best place to find a man grieving over his missing child would be either his own home or the local bar. At this moment, Cam was a bit thirsty from the coffee and pound cake, which was every bit as good as he'd hoped. Moist, rich, and buttery. Fresh as could be. His sweet tooth sated, he threw away the cup and box and headed back to the main street to find a pub. With consideration for his Army-green duffel bag, he made sure also to have his dog tags dangling outside his shirt. Cameron had learned that one sure-fire way to claim whatever scrap of trust or respect he could was to remind people that Americans of all colors won the war. That subtle accessorizing had probably saved his ass and *definitely* earned him a free drink on more occasions than he could count.

It was well past noon, and the town's three bars were beginning to pick up business for the day. Walking into the bar near the East end, Cam entered slowly and set his bag down on the floor in a booth near the restrooms. Making his way to the counter, he aimed to inquire about his target. "Miss, I'd love a cold beer. Anything you choose, cold as you can make it." The older woman serving simply nodded and motioned for him to wait a moment while she poured it. The draft was golden and heady, given she used a cold mug from the freezer to hold it. It was a September day, but still hot enough to warrant a beer at peak heat. "Five o'clock somewhere, I suppose! Thank you, miss.' He tipped the brim of his gray baseball cap. 'May I ask you? I'm here looking for a friend. Do you know Nicholas Chambers?"

The woman had been half-listening, but on hearing the man's name, her ears perked up. "Sure, I know Nick, poor soul. You know his daughter went and ran off?" Cameron knew instantly he'd struck a chord.

"Oh no, ma'am, that's terrible. I hadn't heard! When did this happen?" He softened his voice and gently mimicked her friendly, sad tone.

"Oh, a while back, a month or more. He's a wreck, honest. I haven't seen him in weeks, but I sure do feel bad for the man. He ain't got many friends here, so bet he'll be glad to see you!"

Cam nodded in understanding. "I can't even imagine. A parent's love for their... It's just horrible. Any chance you could direct me to where I could find him? If it's no trouble..."

She paused and looked at Cam once over. "Maybe. Where did you say you knew Nick from?" She wasn't being rude, moreso protective. She clearly knew Nick well enough to wonder about the stranger standing there.

"I worked with him a ways back, lumber job a ways North of Seattle. Before I went to fight, of course, I knew he came back here for good, that's what he told me he was gonna do."

Her face softened. "You went off to war?" and Cam nodded gently. "I sure don't see many soldiers up this way, tell you what. Most of 'em stayed on the coasts when they got back, it seems."

"Well, miss, so did I! Bought myself a nice little house in Richmond, back in California. Sweet little place, and I got a nice white fence and all. Lucky to have come back, lucky for sure." His folksy tone set her guard down even further.

"Listen, finish your beer on me. Then, go over to the corner of the highway, can't miss the signs for Rushmore, see Mike in the western wear shop. Nick used to work that way, and I figure Mike might be able to point you in a direction where you'll find your friend. Oh, and send my regards if you see Nick, okay? Suuuuch a shame..." she drawled.

Cam's broad smile was now genuine. "I certainly will, ma'am." He downed his frosty pint where he stood, tipping his hat, which put a smile on her face. The dollar tip he set on the counter might have helped.

He departed swiftly and snatched his bag, waving goodbye over his shoulder. In the sunlight outside, the beer hit him just right, and he held his smile down the blocks toward Fifth Street. He passed a couple of local ranch types who tipped their hats to ladies in passing, and he noticed a few stores had carved buffalo statues in their windows. One of them was a smokehouse restaurant.

I wonder if that's any good... they're like cows, I think—just woolly.

He'd eaten some odd and desperation-driven things in his years, but never buffalo. The thought made him hungry, and he resolved to find dinner after visiting Mike.

Yeah… big ol' scruffy cows. I'm gonna eat one of those.

Reaching the store advertising 'Western Wear – Men & Women' on its broad glass windows, he took off his hat and stepped inside. Looking around, he saw several racks of clothes and rows of glass display cases filled with a wide range of manly gear, from flasks to belt buckles to fishhooks. He walked in a bit further and saw the one case that caught his eye, a deep and inside-lit case holding all manner of knives. He perused from one end, replete with small folding knives and a few Swiss Army knockoffs, to the far end, which had the more intimidating selection. One huge knife, about ten inches of blade length, rested on a thick and sturdy-looking leather sheath strapped up into a holster. It was an absolute brute of a blade, with leather laces to hold the holster tight to the body. Just then, a thin mustachioed man walked over to the case to greet Cameron.

"Howdy. How's them knives lookin' to you? See any that you gotta git?" His face was friendly.

"Thank you, sir, in fact, yes. I was looking at this big gal right down here." Cam pointed toward the glinting buck knife resting on its sheath.

"Why, that's a good one, son, you have some taste. Would you like to hold her?" and he opened the case, knowing Cam's answer would be yes.

Cam nodded and set his bag down on the floor. He leaned on the case with his hip, mimicking the body language of the thin man. As he was handed the knife, he could see its blade had a bluish tint that shone on some angles. "This is quite a tool, sir. I'd love to make it mine. Any chance you've got an under-shoulder holster for it?"

The man looked pleasantly surprised. "Well, now, you know your knives. Perfect place to keep a blade like this, if you wanna keep it somewhat concealed." Then his mustache frowned a bit as he looked over Cam. "You, uh… You sure you wanna be carryin' something this big, partner? Might get you bothered in the wrong places…" his tone sounded genuinely concerned.

Cam grinned a bit. "Sir, I simply plan on staying outta those places!" and he got a laugh out of the man.

"Well, that sure does simplify things, doesn't it? The price is on the tag. Holster included. How's that look to ya?" The price was high, but of no genuine concern to Cameron, who had already withdrawn the money from his pocket and was balancing the knife on one finger. The older man flashed him a bemused look and left toward the back rooms. Moments later, Cam could hear him speaking to someone else in the back, behind a tattered blanket dividing the rooms.

"Hey, would ya get me down a holster that'll fit this buck here? Gotta be a shoulder sling type. Paid for already."

Another, distinctly less-kind voice came back, "Get it yourself, I'm on lunch, dammit. Just use the ladder."

A minute later, the thin man returned with the blade holstered and ready for Cameron, who was holding out his hands, excited to receive his new toy.

"Thank you, sir, thank you very much! Listen, not to be a bother, but any chance you're Mike?" The thin man shook his head.

"I'm Curly. Mike's in the back, eating his lunch. Might be a while before he gets done, honest. You know him?"

Cam shook his head side-to-side. "Just know his name, lookin' for an old friend of mine, Nick Chambers. The kind lady over at the bar sent me this way." Curly handed Cam the knife in its sheath, with a bit of a polite bow. Cameron wasted no time and took off his outer shirt to strap the holster under his left arm.

"Well, sir, I'll let him know you're asking, but I work here only because Nick left; I never met the man. I heard he's been experiencing some unfortunate circumstances lately, which is sad news. Hope we can find him for you, bet the guy could use a friend these days. Beats being the town drunkard, anyway." Curly shook his head in disdain and left again toward the backroom. Cam thanked him and waited patiently.

This little town maybe ain't so bad… damn fine knife…

From the backroom, he could hear what seemed to be Curly and Mike talking in a low voice. It sounded as though Mike didn't want to be bothered, but Curly was a bit insistent in a very gentle way. "Just one minute, Mike, just go *help* the guy, would ya?"

"Shit. All right. Hang on." The gruff voice replied.

A bit of time passed after Curly stepped out onto the sales floor, nodding at Cam and holding up a finger to indicate 'just one moment.' A minute later, a large and strikingly unpleasant-looking man came out to the counters. He was still chewing and smelled of vinegar-soaked foods and cigarette smoke. He had a red rag in his hands and crumbs on his shirt. His furrowed brow was red from sunshine, his nose red from liquor.

"Okay, son, you looking for Nick? Huh. Tell me what-for, an' I'll decide if you need t'see him."

Cam knew this man was looking down at him in both senses of the word. Cam dropped his chin, slumped his shoulders, and gazed away toward the floor. He knew playing to the large man's ego would be his method of interrogation.

"Sir, yes. I'd like to find my friend, and the very nice woman at the last bar on the block said I might speak with you. She told me he's had a rough patch lately, sir, and I really would like to find him and see if I can't be of some help to him." He kept his tone soft and his hands resting at his sides, employing the most passive body language he could muster, knowing he could take this mountain of a man to the ground with minimal effort.

"Well, what good would *you* be? You don't look like much. Nick's got problems, y'see. The kid ran off. Folks seem to think he was being... *unkind* to her." The man was sneering a bit, though Cam paid no mind and instead glanced at Curly, who looked pained by Mike's derisive tone.

"Sir, I'm a reporter for my local newspaper, the *Seattle Coast Observer*, and I was sure hoping to write a story, imploring her to come home, seeing as the consensus is she's run away. Honest, buying this buck is the best part of my trip yet, and I'm hoping that you might help me keep things going well by helping me find my old friend." Cam pointed at the knife, now guarded under his overshirt.

"Oh, that's *you* bought that damned fancy knife? Haw-Haw...' the man laughed like a donkey. 'Okay, boy, I'll help you out. Least I can do, can't believe you didn't haggle on that buck... mostly your kind are too cheap for the good stuff anyway."

Cameron feigned a hurt look. Inside, he wanted to ball up a fist and knock this big bastard on his ass. He certainly *could.*

Seeming to find his manners somewhere under those chins, Mike continued, "I mean, you know, travelin' men... not... You know, uh..." Mike trailed off. Perhaps he'd realized it might be rude to insult a well-paying customer.

Mike shuffled off to the backroom again and emerged a short time later with a small scrap of paper. "There, Nick's house. Last place I got for him, though I don't imagine he's moved on just yet. Last I heard, he's been riding the buses and handing out fliers with her picture on 'em. Good luck to him, I s'pose. Now go on, git. You got what you needed."

"On my way, sir!"

Picking up his duffel bag, Cam slung it over his shoulder and nodded at Mike, then again more genuinely to Curly before he headed out the door. Looking down at the scrap of paper, he saw a phone number under the address. He took a breath and swiveled his head to get his bearings. The street was quiet, with just a few cars making their way through town or up the road toward Mount Rushmore and eventually Deadwood, another old cowboy town.

Across the street and down a block, he saw a payphone gleaming in the afternoon sun.

This is it. I hope the man's not out. I need to get back to civilized society.

He plunked some coins into the slot and rang the number. As it rang, he shifted his duffel around a bit. The new holster would need some breaking in. The phone rang a half-dozen times, and just before Cam reached out to get his coins returned, the line clicked open. A faint voice answered.

"Yeah?" The voice was quiet, but clearly male and older. Raspy.

"Nick Chambers, is that you?" Cam kept an even and friendly tone.

"Of course. You called *my* phone, didn't you?" Cam could hear that Mr. Chambers was inebriated.

"Sorry if I'm disturbing, sir. Cameron Mason calling. I'm a friend of William Bigsby's. You remember working with him? We should meet."

A sigh came across the line, and "gimme a sec." A minute passed, and the faint sound of ice cubes clinking in a swirling glass rang silvery tones through the handset. "I'm here. You have my address, I hope?"

"Sir, I surely do. Black Creek Road. I'll be there soon." Cam's reply was met with the click of a phone call ended. It wasn't rude; he could hear Chambers struggling to hold back emotion on the call. No affront taken.

Cam ducked back around the block and changed his traveling shirt for something a bit more business-like, behind the drug store. In a town this quiet, nobody was going to see him half-clad, nor would they care if they did. Afterward, he headed back around the block and caught the sole taxi he saw on the street. Not wanting any friction, he thought a little monetary lubrication would be a sound bet. Holding a significant five-dollar bill in front of the cab driver, he was beckoned into the rear seat without hesitation. The dress shirt and tie he'd donned couldn't have hurt. He'd slipped the knife into his bag.

The ride was short, perhaps five minutes. Cam asked the cabbie to please wait outside the house for an hour, and there were another five dollars in the deal. The driver nodded with a grin, and Cam's escape route was set. He was the sort of man who never walked into, nor drove into, a situation he couldn't walk out of—seeing as he had no idea what to expect from a man who sounded drunk already.

"Better safe than sorry."

As they arrived, Cam thanked the driver and slung his bag over his shoulder. He'd never leave that bag out of his sight, especially in unfriendly territory.

A knock at the door, and a somber, frail man answered. Cam supposed Chambers had been finding his meals in a bottle for a while now, and if he'd placed a healthy bet on it, Cam would have been right and richer. Chambers looked out of place in a lovely home, in a pleasant town, with a nice new Dodge in the driveway. Likely, none of it mattered to this broken and pitiful father. He had barely buttoned his shirt to meet Cam at the door, though the truth is, he'd been having trouble with the buttons due to his hands affecting the shakes. Cameron noticed immediately; it was common for men deep in the drink.

Chambers waved Cam inside, sat them down at the dining table, whereupon Cam placed his hands flat on the table. It was a subtle way of signaling calmness and attentiveness to the man. He'd been doing it for years since a superior taught Cameron the trick on-base during interrogation classes back in '43. It felt odd at first, but proved very useful in both disarming folks with its calm conveyance and even more so when others subconsciously mimicked the behavior. "The same way folks cross their arms with you, place your hands, and they'll do the same with hardly a realization that they're doing so." That's what the Colonel had said, and he was right.

"Nick, talk to me. Tell me what you know."

"I don't know ssshit." Chambers' words were slurred.

"You knew enough to get me here from Seattle. Tell me what you haven't told anyone else yet. Can you do that?"

"What makes you think I know anything that ain't in those papers?" Tears were welling up in the man's eyes as he motioned at the file Cameron had brought in.

"This town is small, Nick. *Real* small. I ain't from this area, but I know small towns. You gotta know more than you've been sharing so far, Nick. You can talk to me here. I won't breathe a bit of it to anyone. You have my word. I want to find your daughter."

"Her name was Cassie. You can say it, 'ssokay."

"Cassie? Beautiful name."

"Yeah. Cass-ee-oh-pee-ah. Like the constellation. I always loved that name.

Cam nodded. "We're going to find your Cassiopeia. I promise."

Chambers sat back, arms hanging at his sides, and opened up. "The *pigs*."

"The police?" Cam clarified.

"Police, yeah. The two state troopers picked Cassie up the day she went missing. I know who they are."

"Christ. You know them?" Cam was shocked, leaning back in his chair now. This was the fastest he'd ever cracked a case open!

"I *knew* them, pal. Passst-tense." His speech was slurred, but his eyes were wide.

"You gotta explain a little more, Nick. Tell me what you know. If you can?"

"They died, mister Mason, they're gone. I found out who it was who picked up my angel, and I tried to tell it to the Sheriff. He tells me, 'That's bullshit,' and kicks my ass out to the curb. The very next day? They get into a head-on collision with a drunk. Both of 'em in the same car, which ain't even normal, and...' he paused as he began to sob. He hung his head and continued. 'They were in the same car for no good reason and got killed by some drunk out on Highway 16, like amateurs. Same goddamn time, just when I knew I had somethin'... It's like I'm cursed, see? Can't get no clo-...*hic* ... closure." He stammered through a hiccup.

Nick's chest was heaving, and he was shaking from the stress of the situation and the booze eating up his nerves. "Car burned up, something real suspicious. Drunk didn't even remember the wreck. He took off on bail, and they got absolutely *nothing* for me. Said I'm a loon, said I made it all up for some revenge on the department for not chasing after Cassie. Threatened me to keep quiet or I get locked up again, for *bullshit AGAIN*." His weak fist pounded the table, and he cried his eyes red.

Cam leaned forward and clasped his hands. "I am so sorry, sir. I truly am. I'm not here to upset you, I'm here to *help* you. There's a chance your baby girl is still out there, alive and well. You need to get it together and help me find her or figure out why it happened. You gotta dump that poison down the drain and get your head clear, Nick. Can you do that? Do it for Cassie?" he motioned to the bottle the man was nearly finished with, some cheap bourbon with a half-missing label.

The words seemed to knock some sense into Nick. He sat upright now, pressed his hands into his eyes, and took a long, almost exasperated sigh. He then stood directly up like a puppet whose strings were held aloft, grabbed the bottle, and walked it to the sink. He dumped the contents directly down the drain, almost mechanical in his movements. "You can leave. I gotta get dry. Come back tomorrow, same time. I'll be waiting… I'll be sober. I've got a list. I've got a whole list and it's got names and… you'll see." His back was still turned as he waved his hand, beckoning Cam to leave. It was apparent that the man was embarrassed by his emotional state, and Cam knew it would do him no good to press the poor man any further today.

On his way out, Cam placed a hand on Nick's shoulder. "I'll be back, and we *will* find your girl. I know it. Thank you for giving me a chance." He walked out and departed in the cab without another word. The cab was waiting.

The ride to town gave him some time to think about where to turn next, how to flip this investigation, and not stagnate on the bullshit police reports. He knew it was going to be a tough one because the local cops were almost certainly involved. Yet, if his gut was right, a cover-up of that size told him two things: the law in this town was bought to some degree, and the tree must go way up if they can snuff two staties without hesitation. Someone or something *big* was involved here.

What if that drunk just imagined some of that? Any of it? What if he's been in the bottle so long his memory ain't serving him anymore?

The thought crossed his mind that a conspiracy might be unreasonable, that the whole thing could simply be bad goddamned luck, but he set his mind to prove that theory or find bodies in the process.

Cam's jaw clenched tight as he pictured the little girl, ten years old, being picked up by policemen and trusting them. Going along with the lawmen, as parents teach their children to do. Thinking everything will be all right, thinking they're protecting her. He wondered at what point trust became fear, at what point this child saw their captors for what they were. The idea put a knot in his throat, and he shut the thought out of his mind just as the cab rolled to a stop at the same corner he'd used the phone booth earlier. It wasn't fate; there simply weren't many street corners in this shabby little town.

"Here's your spot, bud. Where's that extra bill?" Cam handed the man another five dollars, too goddamn much money for so little work. Still, he was paying for the *insurance* of the cabbie who had stayed around earlier.

"Thanks, pal. I'll call dispatch if I need a ride out of here!" He offered and shouldered his bag as he stepped out of the car.

"I won't hold my breath…" the driver grumbled, shifting the car into gear and idling off.

With no set place in mind to stay and feeling out of place in that dusty little town, Cam knew he'd either need to find a friendly room and board or take his chances with the local motel. The former seemed tiresome, so he set foot back down the road toward a Motor Inn he had seen on their drive. As he shortly arrived, he saw two good signs: a neon sign proclaiming "Vacancy" and an empty lot. He knew he'd likely find a room if he played a professional and waved a few greenbacks in the face of whoever ran the place. It was after dusk now, and he was hoping the night clerk would be a bit more lenient than some prior places he'd been asked to vacate in similar little towns.

Setting his mind on getting his way, he straightened his shirt and went inside. Behind the dull oak-and-tile countertop, a friendly smile greeted him. The smile belonged to a sweet-faced, possibly college-aged native girl with an impressive green stone necklace, looking festive but a bit silly on her slight frame.

"Good evening… uh, sir, will you be staying with us?"

Without hesitation, Cameron laid some cash on the counter and asked, "If you'll have me?"

She pointed sheepishly to a small sign on the wall that read *ALL ARE WELCOME - JESUS LOVES YOU* and nodded rapidly.

"Oh, that's kindly. Is this a sundown town?" he asked, an unnerving question as always.

She shook her head and sheepishly replied, "No, too many tourists. Rushmore. Maybe before that. I don't know."

He shrugged and set his bag down. With a warm smile, he assured her, "Yes indeed, we take our graces where we find them, don't we? I'd need the room for a couple of nights or more. I appreciate you, little miss."

She smiled back and turned to select a room key from the oak cabinet on the wall.

Friendly face… I hope it isn't the last around here.

Cam was sure to thank her graciously for the room and leave her a generous dollar in gratuity. Once seated on the bed in his room, the cool air sapped the last of his will to do anything but lie down on the threadbare orange duvet.

With a sigh as he sprawled out flat on his back, he chided himself, "Oh hell… just a few minutes… need a damn bath."

Sobering Up

Tuesday, July 21st, 1953

Coffee… coffee and chow. Then you get to work, old man.

Having not unpacked the night before, a quick shower and a change into fresh jeans and a plain white cotton shirt had him feeling light and ready to depart. He had no wish to punish his back by lugging the bag around town for a second warm day. Instead, he opened the drawstrings and removed three things: his new buck knife, which he diligently holstered under his left arm, his beat-up sheepskin wallet, which held a few forms of identification (several of which were less than genuine), and his blue denim shirt, which he thought would be appropriate in the dusty cow-town. After a brief stop at the inn's front office to inquire about *friendly* eateries, Cam took the proprietor's advice and headed for a café at the far end of town. He'd brought the case file along for something to read until the clock neared three and he could head for Nick's house once more.

The café was small and quaint; the decorations had a French Country feel with a Midwestern accent. It was a bit of a jumble, but probably the best they could do out here in the middle of nowhere, considering the recent price hikes in the Sears catalogs.

It could be worse; better than eating in the alley anyway…

The man chose a back corner table and settled into breakfast with eggs and toast, a slab of ham, and more cups of coffee than he could recall. The newspaper was slim but fascinating. In these small towns, one might learn about something as trivial as a broken shed window or the status of a well-liked pastor's troublesome hip. Mainly, the pages were adorned with local advertisements, as this was a tourist town, and every little shopkeeper wanted to make sure he had some steady foot traffic from all the rubes getting off the buses or arriving packed together in a shiny, overloaded sedan with screaming kids and matching plaid luggage pouring out of the trunk. Still, the kitschy and charming positivity of the local rag kept him entertained, and he found himself poring over the advertisements. It was no Time magazine, but it held his interest and let him get his food settled before he undertook the task of rereading the horrors in the envelope sitting there next to his plate, caked in drying egg yolk.

Maybe I could use a new coat, looks like a good sale. Shit, I don't need a new jacket. Especially not one that makes me look like I belong around these hick towns. How about some boots…

Around noon, he saw a scowling woman behind the serving window glancing his way. He realized he was sitting there occupying a booth at lunchtime without being a lunch customer. He remedied that by ordering half a turkey sandwich and some soup, which he knew would go cold. However, he was comfortable and had no intention of going out in the sun without a good reason. He had hours to kill and nowhere else to be.

After a few bites of the sandwich, Cam took to the task at hand; he made sure to hold the reading materials behind the folder so as not to shock any passersby heading to the toilet, with his copies of the police evidentiary photographs that were, at best, grisly, some downright shocking. Two hours passed as he sat and read the brief twice cover to cover, finding many passages in the police reports to be so oversimplified in tone that he wasn't able to decide whether the police involved were simpletons or accomplices. Hence, he had to assume the latter. Past cases where abuse of authority was in play had instilled in him a healthy skepticism when it came to badges.

By two o'clock, he'd compiled a list of questions he would ask Nick, point-blank. Also, in his mind, he'd worked out a story he'd stick to should he get hemmed up in his investigation. On this assignment, he was still Cameron Mason, but today Cameron Mason was an investigative reporter for the *Seattle North-City Herald*.

Nobody had ever pointed out that Herald, which hadn't existed in decades, but if they ever called the phone number on Cam's card, they'd reach his publishing supervisor, Gary Glenn (one of many aliases for Billy, and a 'tell' for Billy to play along should anyone call up to ask any questions). The reporter was a persona Cam had employed several times in his investigations away from Seattle, finding folks often loved the idea of getting their thoughts and opinions into a newspaper. As Billy mused frequently, "ego is a gateway to answers".

Time passed as he nibbled at the sandwich and watched the oils congeal on top of the soup. Families and folks passed by, with very few stopping in, and most of those few were looking to grab a quick bite for the road on their way up to see Rushmore. On their way to worship that massive stone idolatry dedicated to men who did both great and terrible things, but somehow attained a saintly reverence among all the little sheep flying their flags.

If these suckers knew what we were doing every time we sent soldiers somewhere we didn't belong, maybe they wouldn't be so proud.

With a sneer, he realized the negativity and cynicism wouldn't get him anywhere, so he pushed the thought away. Opening his wallet, Cam counted his business cards and wondered if they would hold water in the small town of Custer, South Dakota. His mind painted an image of someone needing to wait in line for the town's sole payphone to try and verify his story. The thought brought him a chuckle.

No, sir, nobody knows, and I'd bet my wages nobody cares.

The skinny watch on his wrist was nearing three, so he finished the sandwich and abandoned the soup as he packed up his business, excited to get on with this damned case. The disdain he held for working cases like this certainly struck a nerve, but he forged ahead, knowing that *someone* needed to do the right thing and find answers in this sad turn of events. Somebody had to account for all of these children. Somebody had to care.

Nick Chambers seemed like a good but wounded man, needing some closure at the very least. Same as all the distraught parents before him. In the best-case scenario, Cam would catch a trail and find the kid. That thought brought him a bit of comfort, the idea of reuniting that broken man with his only child.

Christ, I hope that's where this is headed.

Cam held onto that wish for the duration of the cab ride up to Nick's, and it helped him relax in preparation for what was to be a friendly but serious interrogation with Mr. Chambers.

The clock on the dashboard of the Ford sedan showed 3:42, a bit early but close enough. Cam paid the cab to wait five minutes before departing to ensure a ride home if Nick was away. Walking up the steps, he arranged the folder a bit and ran a comb through his short hair, clearing his throat and clasping the folder. The knife felt awkward in his armpit.

His knuckles rattled the door, then he paused for a few moments. Not hearing any sounds inside, he glanced back at the driveway. Nick's sedan was there, dusty and one tire perilously close to flat. He knocked again, louder. No response. This seemed odd since he was expected, so Cam thought he'd better look around a little harder before departing. Walking around the back of the house, he could peer in through the lace curtains a bit. Seeing the state of the place, he knew *something* must have gone wrong. The kitchen table was on its side, papers strewn about in the kitchen and down the hallway. Cam bolted back to the cab just as the driver was pulling away, so Cam shouted, "Hey, man, don't leave just yet!" The driver braked and parked, stepping out.

"What's going on? I was headed out…"

Cam sneered a bit, "That wasn't five minutes, man. Just stay a spell. Listen, Nick's a friend, and I'm not sure he's OK. I'll give you ten dollars to sit here and wait for a bit, okay, sir?"

The cabbie looked around, nervous. He seemed unsure of the deal. "You know this guy well? I drive him home from at least two bars a week; he's a drunkard."

Cam reached into his wallet, taking out a $10 bill and his business card as a reporter. "Listen, it's okay. He's supposed to be here. I just need you to wait, please. Help me out. I'm a friend. I'm here to help him get right."

The mention of Cam being a career man seemed to put the driver at ease. He took the card and the money and stood with his hands on his hips. "I'll give you a few minutes, sure. Just don't get me involved in any bull-crap, son. This ain't my job."

These crusty hicks are getting on my nerves…

Cam nodded and turned back to the house. He saw the old leaded-paint door and frame and knew he could pop the door latch with a little force. Opening his denim shirt a few buttons, he withdrew the buck knife and jammed it between the doorframe and door, in the brass striker plates. With the butt of his hand, he struck the end of the hilt and twisted it with his other hand. The torquing force popped the lock, and the door swung open. The smell in the house was musty, and a knot set into his gut as he imagined what he was about to find. Deftly sheathing the knife, he beckoned the driver to come closer. The man walked up the path and stood at the doorway.

"Please give me two shakes, sir. Thanks for keeping watch. I'm lucky that the door was open! I'm just going to check on my friend, okay?" The driver nodded, still holding the business card and the $10 bill in his hand.

Cam stepped into the house, holding the hilt of that buck, ready to defend himself. He could see that the kitchen and living room were clear. Stepping into the hallway, he slowly pushed open the doors to the rooms. Nobody was in the first two rooms, which was a relief to him. Now his mind played the scenario that Nick was out, and Cam was currently breaking in… not a fun scenario, but better than the rest. The following two rooms were clear as well, and Cam relaxed a notch. Taking a breath in relief, he turned and shouted over his shoulder to the driver, "Man, I feel foolish, looks like he isn't here!" while he used his open palm to open the last door at the end of the hall. As he turned to look into the bathroom, a wave of putrid stink and humidity struck him in the face.

The scene was appalling. In a blink, he ascertained two things: the nude, contorted body of Nick Chambers was lying in the bathtub, cradling a shotgun, *sans head*. One leg hung over the ledge of the tub. That bottle of whisky with half a label was tucked neatly under the arm of the hairy, motionless corpse, implying that the man had taken his life after finishing a gallon of cheap booze. However, Cam knew that the same bottle was empty the day before, not owing to this man taking his life. Now, all the pink hues departed this husk, and the clammy skin turned blue wherever blood settled. The bowels and bladder had voided into the tub. His clothes were hanging on a peg on the wall; he'd seemingly been preparing for a bath when he met this fate.

They just… they snuffed him… dear god.

Cam *knew* it was a setup, and now he knew he would be either deep in the muck with local police and investigators (where his cover would be blown quick), or he could take a big step back and walk away as though nothing had happened. The only other person involved was the cab driver outside, who didn't know a thing about the corpse stinking up that once-fine house.

Cam turned on his heel and shut the door behind him. He took two long strides before he drew a breath, and by then he was nearly out of the hallway. Taking out his handkerchief, he wiped his face and slowly paced out of the hall. He took one more deep, slow breath as he got to the front door. There he found the cab driver waiting with arms folded, looking bored and peering about inside.

"No, sir, he's just not here. Guess I must have been worried for nothing! I'll need a ride back to town, s'pose I can give him a call later."

The driver shrugged, tucking the money and business card away in his back pocket. "Guess so. That ten gets you back to town and more if you need it. Been slow lately, tourists ain't around like in season." As his geniality signaled he was none the wiser about the grisly scene in the quiet home, he continued, "Nice gettin' a little extra from you too, chief. I do appreciate it." The pair walked back to the Ford and headed back into town. It took all of Cam's effort not to show any sign that he was in a hurry to get the hell out of there.

No reason for me to stick around, Nick ain't giving me any answers now. Can't muss about tryin' to find that list of his, either. His stomach quivered in excitement and disgust.

After the driver dropped Cam off at the Motor Inn, he knew he'd better get out of town before anything else occurred; he knew it was only a matter of time before whoever killed Nick Chambers would come looking to tie up loose ends, and Cam had no interest in getting tied up. Much to his chagrin, the little lady at the front desk informed him that the next bus out of town would arrive the following morning.

I'd better give Billy a ring. He won't like how this unfolded. Hell, I don't like how this unfolded. South Goddamn Dakota. I need to get the hell out of here.

Wyatt Earp

Wednesday, July 22nd, 1953

A gentle knock at the door of his room woke the aging gumshoe, peeling his face from the pillow as his sweat stuck to the cheap fabric. He responded with a sneer and a couple of blue words mumbled into the air as he wiped a little saliva from his cheek. Then the idea crossed his mind that it might be that sweet little gal from the office coming to bring him a message from a missed call. He had had the intention of checking in earlier in the day, but the day got away from him. Slipping on his boots and wrapping his robe around himself, he shuffled toward the door with a smile forced upon his face.

I could use a little good news as much as I could use some good sleep. This fucking case is bedraggling.

Just as he lashed the belt of his robe and cinched it, he swung the door open to find a sour-faced, very perturbed-looking State Trooper standing there at the door.

"Are you the dumb sonofabitch who's been poking around about this and that?"

Cameron let out a heaving sigh and shrugged his shoulders.

"I'm not awake enough to tell you my middle name, much less know what you're talking about. Do you know what time it is? No disrespect, Officer. Honest."

"I'm a lawman. It doesn't matter what time it is. Put your fucking pants on, Johnny. We're going for a ride."

The man had truncated the slur, 'Melon Johnny'. It was a bastardization of Neapolitan Italian *mulignane,* or eggplant—just another vile word soft-brained men used to hold other men down.

Cam looked down at his barely clad self, feeling a draft come up underneath his robe. He felt exposed in more ways than one as he peered around the cop's shoulder and saw the cop's partner leaning against their dark, shiny sedan with his hand on his holstered weapon.

This could be ugly. Better play it light.

"Suppose I need a bit more than pants, sir, but give me two minutes to get myself presentable and take a piss, and we can go anywhere you want."

So he did just that. Slacks and shoes, a shirt and a coat, keys and three crinkled dollars he had left on the dresser the day prior. Conveniently, he forgot his wallet in his other pants as he dressed. Forcing the most cheerful grin he could muster under the circumstances, Cam shuffled out the door and locked it behind him.

"I'm all yours. Say, what's this all about?"

The man who had been leaning against the car had opened a rear door and was beckoning for Cam to join them.

"You don't have questions, boy. We've got questions, and you've got answers. That's how this works tonight. Got it?"

The man's leathery face told of years of nicotine and alcohol abuse. His hair was slicked back and shiny, but Cameron couldn't know if it was brown or black. He supposed it would probably be jet black, judging by the man's slight East Coast accent and his use of an Italian slur earlier. Trying his best to keep from baring his proverbial fangs, Cam nodded and hunched his shoulders down, shoving his hands into his pockets, feigning to kick a rock as he treaded toward the car across the gravel driveway.

"Shucks, I just got to sleep a short while ago. I'm sorry if I kept you boys. Sometimes my snoring doesn't wake me up, so I hope you weren't waiting at the door too long."

The man who had knocked on the door scoffed at the idea.

"I didn't hear any snoring in there. But you sure do look tired, old man. Get in the car."

Leaning on his polite acquiescence, Cam nodded and, without a word, slunk into the backseat of the sedan. Both of the lawmen slid into the front seat and slammed the doors shut. The driver lit up a cheap cigarette without rolling down his window.

Rude sonofa…

The man in the passenger seat peered over his shoulder at Cameron and sneered, then turned to his partner and gave him the nod for them to proceed. It was clear he was the one in charge, having waited by the car because the cop with less seniority got to knock on the door where somebody might greet them with a high-velocity lead injection.

Once underway, they drove for about 15 minutes south and away. They had turned on the radio, and it was big band, so at least that and the comfort of the warm Chevrolet and that broad rear seat were something to appreciate in an otherwise tense situation. Cam watched the scenery shift from scrubby trees into a more jagged landscape and a lot more Rough hillside. He knew he would bide his time and volunteer nothing. If they had a question, he would answer it honestly, but there was no point in giving them any rope to hang him with. At a certain point, the road opened up a bit into a sort of pastoral area, and Cam took the opportunity to take stock of any little roads or mile markers they might pass. He saw one sign that he swore said 'Jupiter Creek,' but he may have misread it, as the headlights didn't really favor the cheap tin signs marking the little side roads.

As the road split off at a highway intersection, they pulled into a dirt lot behind what appeared to be a storage yard for farm equipment. There were various implements scattered about, including large trailers and tractor attachments, but no other vehicles.

The passenger was the first to speak.

"Okay, boy, let's have it. What the hell are you doing, skulking around here? Why am I getting calls about some colored man poking around where he shouldn't be?"

Taking a deep breath to wash the tension and nerves out of his voice, Cameron let out a long sigh and stared out the window toward the adjacent forestry. He'd lay the bullshit on *thick* for these dolts.

"I'm just a reporter trying to earn his keep, do some good. Help an old friend who has lost his kid, help a man with a demon in a bottle. You know what he's been up to, just drinkin' himself silly every day. I aimed to help him find some respite, that's all. Last I checked, that was the Christian way. I'd love to give my boss's contact information to you, but this time of night, I don't trust anyone's going to answer the phone."

Sneers shot back and forth between the duo of dunces. The boss was the first to dig in.

"Yeah, that's what we heard. That's what you've been telling people. But we want to know why you show up, and then Nick Chambers goes off suck-starting his 12-gauge. What did you say to him? How did you end up at his house?"

Cam plastered on his besk look of shock, letting his jaw hang open.

"He WHAT now? He went an' —" he faked choking on his spittle as he peered out the window, wincing.

The driver taunted him, "Oh come on, you got those dog tags. You ain't new to a little blood, are you, son?"

Cam bit his cheek hard enough to invite misty eyes to the party.

"Jesus Mary and Joseph, that damned fool. That damned heartbroken fool…"

The boss wasn't buying it. He turned and reached back, poking Cameron in the forehead, angling for whatever truth would satisfy him.

"You ain't old friends with Nick Chambers, though, are ya? I knew Nick from ranch hand days way back. He was no fan of mixing races, no, sir. And here you are, acting like you go way back. It stinks, so I say you have *one* chance to own up to the truth or we're gonna have to—"

Cam leaned back and cut him off with his Hail Mary.

"Fine, fine. Shit. His little girl is the reason. That's it. His child went missing a while back, and he reached out to a couple of private investigators who specialize in missing persons cases. My boss has his agency out in Seattle; he gave me the case. As I understand it, through a sort of game of telephone, someone at the Bureau passed him a file, knowing that he was soft enough to take on some hard luck cases here and there. I'm just a road man. I get the shit cases, the stuff that comes up dry for too long."

The man behind the wheel was watching Cameron like a hawk through the rearview mirror, which he had tilted downward to see Cameron's face; Cam was settled down into the seat, good and low. It wasn't a case of bad posture; more so, it was Cam wanting to be able to kick the hell out of the back of that seat if one of them got squirrely. With a good bit of force, you could kick the seatback forward and maybe even pin a guy against the steering wheel or dashboard. That was the only way he knew he might be able to steal a couple of seconds to get out of the car and get clear if they were to draw on him.

Thank god they skipped the handcuffs…

"Yeah, we know about his little girl. She ran off, probably out there sucking pricks at a truck stop somewhere in Fresno or Houston or some other shithole. We told him as much, but he didn't want to hear it."

Cam wanted to spit at the vile image the man had put into his head.

"I think she was a little young for that."

His interrogator in the passenger seat snickered at the comment, which made Cam even more perturbed.

"Haw-haw! You'd be surprised, or maybe not… I hear them colored girls get goin' nice and young. Niiiiice and young."

Cam was chewing on his cheek to keep his tongue from loosing, putting that filthy sonofabitch in his place.

"Listen, I'm just doing my job. I don't know Nick, and we weren't friends. But that man… he was a mess. You know it, and I know it."

The boss thot back, "Yeah, well, Nick's been a mess for a long time. His wife was a mess. A tramp, a weedhead from Carson City. No surprise her kid ended up on the same road. What I want to know is why some big-city shitheel thinks he can come up here and try and solve some big mystery when the case has been closed and we have all the answers we need. Ain't no mystery for you here, boy."

Cam considered a different approach here.

"I'm sorry, sir. I probably should have liaised with your Department. Anyway, Nick didn't even want to talk to me. He basically shoved me off, and he was shit-faced drunk, so anything he said sounded loony anyway."

"Oh yeah? What did he say?"

"I can't say word-for-word, but he told me some tall tale about how he knew his little girl had been snatched up and sold off. Said he knew it had been happening before, happened in other places too. It sounded like he had just made it up to convince himself that he wasn't a deadbeat father who ran off his baby girl, just like he ran off his wife."

The rude man snorted and struck up another foul, cheap cigarette before butting in.

"Yeah, and if that little girl is anything like his wife, yeah, she's definitely turning tricks at a truck stop somewhere right now. We get a lot of that on the high roads. That interstate road plan of Eisenhower's… that'll make it even easier for 'em! Imagine spreading your legs in Poughkipsee on Tuesday and San Francisco on a Saturday. What a world!" The driver guffawed and slapped the steering wheel.

"I don't know about that," Cam responded with a shrug.

The boss and primary interrogator didn't look so convinced.

"So you're telling me you got nothing out of Nick, and now he's a pile of meat, and you're just hanging around? It seems to me that you've got your answers, and you should probably hit the road… While we let you."

Ahhhh. There it is.

"Listen, sir, officer, I'm sorry, patrolman. Look, I don't even know your names."

"Fletcher and Ellis."

Cam nodded along, "Oh, Ellis. Yeah, Ellis Island. Italian, yeah?"

The driver turned over his shoulder and blew a puff of acrid smoke in Cameron's face.

"Yeah, my father came over and he had to change our last name to something more American-sounding to make sure he could get a job before one of you fucking coloreds took it out from under him."

Last chance to charm these shitbags.

"I'm sure your father was a hard worker. My great-grandfather was a stoneworker. That's how we got Mason, Cameron Mason. I'm named after him. He wasn't much to look at either!" He forced a chuckle and felt a smidge of the tension leave the car.

The interrogator pulled out a piece of chewing gum and put it in his mouth. Then another, and then, surprisingly, yet another. He was chewing on a wad of gum like a cow chews its cud. Dribble escaped the corner of his lip while he sneered and stared down his nose at Cameron.

"So you ain't got any more business here in South Dakota?"

The chewing and chawing were incessant.

"No, sir, not a bit. I need to get my tired bones back to Seattle. This isn't really my sort of place. It's far too nice for me."

"Huh. Nice… right. So you're going to get back on that Greyhound bus and you're going to leave our town in peace, right?"

"I would have left already, sir, but the bus doesn't come except in the mid-mornings."

Cam's nerves were wracked. He knew what was probably going to happen next, and he really hoped to avoid it.

"You'd better pray that bus shows up bright and early to haul your narrow ass back where you're wanted if there is such a place. Otherwise, me and Ellis? We're going to scoop you up again and see if you like the slop they serve down in county."

Cam leaned forward a bit, eyebrows raised and eyes down.

"Hand on the Bible, sir. I'm headed out of town first thing in the morning. I don't want anything to do with whatever business is going on here. I've got my answers, and my boss isn't going to make another dime on this case, so the job's done. It's over."

The driver unbuckled his lap belt and turned back to Cameron once again.

That sounds like a plan, Johnny. How about you step out of the car with me for just a minute? I have something I want to show you.

Here it comes.

Cameron knew that there were just enough eyes on him that these boys weren't going to put him in the dirt. He also knew that they had no reason *not* to tune him up just for being what he is.

"Listen, I feel like there's some way we can avoid this. I feel like you boys could even just let me out here, and I could walk until my feet bleed, but I will find my way back and get on that bus. Please?"

It was too late. Both of the cops had already stepped out of the car, and Cameron knew that he had to swallow his pride and take his licks. He had done it before, and he was prepared to do it again. He took a moment to check his surroundings and saw that no cars were passing, but dawn was starting to break. It carried a slight blue haze, and he could hear, through the sound of blood rushing in his ears, the chirping of birds in the nearby tree line. From the corner of his eye, he could see both of the highway patrolmen standing some 10 feet away from the car. Ellis was cracking his knuckles. Fletcher had his thumbs hooked in his belt nonchalantly as though he had done this a hundred times.

You stupid old man. You don't have any backup out here. You should have raised hell. You shouldn't have gotten in the car. You shouldn't have let them drive you this far. There's no way you can walk back in time and make that bus. They're looking for an excuse to punish you. You've got to give them some reason to take you back to town or at least somewhere close…

He stewed while the boys outside the car waited impatiently.

Chambers.

Trying to hide that wry smile that often accompanied a good idea, Cameron slipped out of the back seat and felt his heels dig into the gravel and dirt of the rough lot. He stepped one step away from the car and shut the door behind him, but then stepped back and leaned his backside against the sedan. Raising his hands, he pleaded with them.

"Boys, I know you want to knock me around a bit, and I understand it. I came here acting like I own the place, and I've got penance to pay for that, but I've got something that I think you boys want, and I'm willing to trade it for a ride back to town after."

With a chortle, the Italian asked, "After what?"

"I don't know, man. I see you boys have a little steam to blow off, and I'll give one of you a free shot. But after that, at least let me take you back to Nick Chambers' place. He had something that you might want to see. Something that wasn't any use to me, but might be some use to you boys."

"Why don't you tell us what you think might be of use to us, and I'll let you know how much of a beating it's going to spare you."

His hands still up in the air, Cameron shook his head. "No, sir, I don't know exactly, but if we go there, I can help you find it. I'm a gumshoe, remember? I've always been keen on finding stuff. You'll see. I'm in a real bad position here, and you boys could always just thump me on Nick Chambers' porch if you wanted to, but I feel like maybe you won't be in the mood if I give you something real useful.

Fletcher stepped forward, clenching his fists. "Why don't we just beat it out of you?"

"I'm an old man. You can beat me later. Come on. Two big, strong lawmen like yourselves worried about little old me? When you could be having hot coffee instead?"

Ellis fired up another of those goddamn stinking cigarettes.

"I dunno, Fletch. Maybe he's right. We can kick his teeth in later, but for now, maybe we've got something we could take back to—"

His partner cut him off.

"Quiet down, Ellis. I'm two steps ahead of you. Let's get going. I need a cup of coffee anyway. Get back in the car, Mason." He thumbed toward Cam, who obliged immediately, letting out a sigh of relief. Fletcher was grumbling to himself while Ellis was just mindlessly puffing away on his cigarette, as he spun the wheel and put them on the road back toward Custer.

Short of town after having taken a back road they had not taken before, they arrived at Nick Chambers' place. There was crime scene tape across the front door, and what appeared to be an unmarked patrol car parked on the paltry lawn.

Leaning forward and squinting over the dashboard at the car in the driveway, Fletcher let out a curse. "Goddamn Clark."

Ellis parked the Chevrolet right behind the '48 Mercury Sedan and threw it into park.

"Johnny Boy, you keep your mouth shut and you play along and you might not be spitting out your teeth when we finish up here. Capiche?"

Cameron nodded and let himself out of the sedan. Fletcher put up his hand to indicate that Ellis and Cameron should wait by the car.

"I'll go talk to Clark. I'll send him on his way. It's early and there's no chance that fat fuck hasn't eaten already, but maybe I'll buy him breakfast anyway."

With that, he headed into the house while Ellis struck up another cigarette. "Want one?" He inquired of Cam.

Cam shrugged, declining. "I'm trying to lay off. Been smoking since my first deployment. V-A doc said I should cut them out."

"Oh yeah? My doc says it's just fine. And I tell you, I never felt better than after I had a fag. Been smoking since I was twelve. I ain't stopping anytime soon."

Under his breath, Cameron mumbled, "Lord, please hurry."

A couple of minutes later, Fletcher came out of the house, and just behind him came a portly middle-aged man in a disheveled shirt and jeans, not the highway patrol browns these boys were wearing.

Cameron smiled and waved at him, offering, "Hello, Mr. Clark!"

Ellis kicked Cam in the shin, chiding him, "Shut yer trap."

"Sorry, sir."

Moments later, Cameron was inside the house alone with the two highway patrolmen. The stink was rising. That home smelled like death. Nobody had bothered to clean up the mess that Nick Chambers left behind. Just a bathtub smeared with shit and piss, still bits of brain and skull on the wall; it was putrid.

"All right, Detective,' Ellis offered, 'Show us what you wanted to show us."

He shoved Cameron into the living room. Cam did his best to stay off the defensive, for now.

"Okay, okay. When I spoke to him on the phone, he had a list. He said he had a list of names. I don't know what names, and I don't know what for. But, it's no use to me anyway. Like I said, no money in it. And, I figure, if he had some sort of vendetta against the police, like he said. Well then, some names might be on there that you don't want on somebody's mind, especially when they come around clearing the place out. Family, I mean, they might misconstrue. You know what I'm getting at."

Ellis nodded, still smoking. Fletcher sat back against the kitchen counter and waved his hand in a sweeping gesture.

"Okay, Sam Spade. Get to work. Find me that Maltese Falcon before I finish my coffee, and I'll personally drop your raggedy ass at the bus station."

Fletcher turned to the coffee maker on the counter and started preparing a pot.

"You got it, boys, I'm on it. Thank you. I mean that. Gonna start at the other end of the house and work my way back here."

Ellis nodded, shooing him away, barking, "Well, get to it then, boy!" as he scratched his genitals.

South Dakota's finest. Hmmph.

Cam trod down the hall that smelled like fetid death. He held his breath, but some of it still slipped in past his nostrils. He started in the bedroom at the end of the hall, opening a window before he began to dig around.

Come on, Nick. I know you had to have something. I don't know just what, but if there's a chance your little list can get me out of hot water, then I'm begging you. Please tell me you hid it well enough that whoever gave you that haircut didn't find it before they cleared out.

He got busy searching everything in the room and the little closet: behind shelved books, under pillows, between mattresses, inside shirt pockets, under shoe insoles. It took him three or four minutes to clear that room. Nick didn't have much.

The next room was the missing daughter's room.

Cassiopeia Chambers. Nine years old. Christ.

A lump formed in Cameron's throat the size of a grapefruit as he looked over the sad, dusty decay of memories that would be lost forever. Happy moments, the love of a father. These little bright outfits folded up neatly on that little white cubby shelf next to a stuffed pony that looked crudely stitched like something you win at a county fair. He had to stomach it. He paused at the doorway, and he could hear the coffee pot burbling now. It would only be a few minutes before that jackboot Fletcher would be drinking his cup down.

Come on. I know you loved her. I know she was your world. Please tell me there's something here. I saw the way it destroyed you. I think I saw maybe the man you once were. I know she didn't just up and leave. There's love in this room. Good stories. Come on, Nick.

He took to thumbing through the pages of several little paperboard-clad diaries on her desk. He rifled through a couple of drawers of art supplies. There were some decent little paintings in there. Trees and squirrels, rays of sunshine. The sort of beauty that can only come from a crayon in a tiny clenched fist.

He came to the last little bookshelf. There was nothing. This room was empty. He heard the clinking of a mug echoing from the kitchen, and he could smell Ellis smoking another goddamn foul, cheap cigarette.

Have some respect, you fucking donkey.

Giving up on that room, he turned to the bathroom. He could almost see the green waves of stink emanating from the doorway, and he was hesitant to go in. Still, he knew that there was a good chance whatever happened with Nick was sudden, and there was a chance that Nick's prized possession, evidence against the bastard who took his daughter, might have been close at hand right up til the end.

He darted back into Nick's room and grabbed a moth-eaten white cotton shirt from the drawers. As he stepped into the bathroom, he wrapped that shirt around his face and grabbed a bottle of cologne from the cabinet next to the door. He sprayed a couple of spritzes onto the shirt over his face, knowing that it would only slightly mask the permeating, rotting meat and shit stink that filled the room.

Fuck.

He checked around underneath the sink and in the cabinet. Nothing there. No secret door behind the mirror. Nothing under the bath mat. Nothing in the stack of towels stacked nearby behind the bathtub and sprinkled with brain matter and crusted blood. Cameron had to punch himself in the thigh a couple of times to distract himself from vomiting. His hands would never be *truly* clean after this moment. He slid his hands between the towels one by one. Six towels. Nothing in between. Nothing was folded among them.

Come on, Nick. If you sobered up, you had to know this was a possibility. Did you hear them coming? Did you undress yourself for a bath, or was there a barrel aimed at your head? Goddammit, Chambers.

He turned to leave the room, dejected, but then paused just inside. Turning back toward the bathtub, he stepped over to it gingerly and clenched his fists, squinting against the searing smell of the cologne and the stench of mortis seeping through the shirt.

Final resting place. Maybe not just for you, huh?

He placed the bath mat over the edge of the tub, upside down, so he could lean against it without getting any of that muck on himself. Kneeling, he reached across the tub and down the far side. It was a narrow gap, but just wide enough for him to get a couple of fingers down there. He worked it from left to right, his palms sliding against the crust of dried blood and flesh.

THERE!

He felt the corner of an envelope there behind the bathtub. Ever so carefully, he pinched it between two fingertips and slowly lifted it up and out from behind the tub. It was a plain brown envelope, like an interoffice envelope. It had a bunch of names written on it, and then they were scribbled out badly enough that he couldn't really make out any of the names on the envelope. He stood up and stepped back from the tub, wiping his hands on one of the better towels before peeling open the envelope.

"Whatcha got there, buddy?" Fletcher inquired from behind him.

God. Dammit.

"I don't know, sir. It's just an envelope and there's something inside, but I haven't opened it. I was coming to hand it to you straight away."

"Sure you were. Sure. Well, let's have a look."

Fletcher snatched it from Cameron's hand and took it back out into the living room. Cameron followed behind a few paces. Fletcher tossed his coffee mug into the kitchen sink and slapped Ellis on the arm, beckoning him to follow. They both walked out onto the porch, leaving Cameron standing in the kitchen. He supposed it would be better to let them be.

Fletcher opened the envelope; that much Cameron could see. He didn't show what was on the paper to Ellis, but some color drained from Fletcher's face while he read what was written there. It was agonizing for Cameron to watch a clue grow legs and walk away, but it was just fine by him if it meant he could keep his teeth.

For a flash, Cameron thought about darting out the front door, but he thought better of it, knowing that he would be on foot and they would catch him easily in that damn Chevrolet.

"You boys find what you needed?" He asked loudly, hoping to get a response.

Much to his surprise, the men simply exchanged a couple of words back and forth that he couldn't quite make out, and they hurried off the porch to their sedan. Cameron stayed static there in the kitchen, waiting for the next shoe to drop. It didn't. He heard the ignition crank on that eight-cylinder engine, and he heard the car peel out of the driveway in a hurry, sending rocks and dirt up in a rooster tail.

They had left him behind!

"Heh. Ha… hahahaaaa!"

Cameron laughed out loud at the sheer insanity of it all. Now a bundle of nerves and shaking with adrenaline, Cameron spoke to himself, and nobody in the kitchen could hear him, while the coffee pot burbled and roiled.

"Guess they decided I wasn't worth another thought. I wonder who's on that list. I wonder how deep that root goes. Two crooked cops are one thing, but two *scared* crooked cops… fuck. Billy is going to kick my ass. No. He can kiss it. I'm getting the fuck out of South

Dakota."

Cam took a swig of coffee, swallowing a lump of guilt at how callous this all was. A man dead, a child stolen in the night, a second-tier private dick in the wrong town, narrowly escaping a lynching. He hadn't slept for shit, and now his nose and throat were soaked in the stench of cologne and day-old corpse leavings. He felt like a run-down piece of roadkill. All the same, he started the walk back toward town. The only good thing that happened on this day occurred shortly up the road. He held out a thumb, and nobody stopped, but then he remembered he had those three crinkled-up dollar bills in his pocket. Every time he heard a car coming past, he would wave those three dollars in the air. It took five tries, but on the sixth, a box truck painted up for a moving company pulled over and let him buy a ride back into town. He thanked the driver after their wordless, short trip, and the moment his feet hit the pavement in downtown Custer, Cam sprinted for the little inn where his belongings had been left the night before.

"Okay, old man, time to make haste. The open road is calling!" he joked to himself.

Sweating, Cam bundled up his clothes into his bags, checked out of the Inn, and walked back to the town's main intersection to wait for the next bus in *any* direction. Seated quietly on the bus stop bench and wringing his hands together, he promptly came to two decisions. Firstly, he resolved never to bring another witness into something that could end up an ordeal without keeping a close eye on their safety. Secondly, he would see this goddamned case through to the end no matter what happens. The thought that someone would kill a man to cover their tracks did not bode well for the fate of the little girl, and that made Cameron downright *pissed*. A fire in his gut had replaced the unease.

Better keep my head down and get gone before I call Billy. No coincidence they offed Chambers the day I arrived, no way. I'd give my left pinky toe to read the names in that fucking envelope. Maybe it was more than names. Perhaps it was evidence. Maybe it was Abraham Lincoln's autograph. I've got nothing to show for my work here, except that we now know it's bigger than we thought.

As Cam sat looking across the street at the Western Wear store where he'd bought his blade, he noticed a portrait in black-and-white in the window. The gold leaf regaled that "The infamous Wyatt Earp Shopped here!" and the caricature of the famous outlaw was dashing and handsome. Cam was unimpressed. The look on Wyatt Earp's face… it was so cocky. It taunted him. Cam grumbled at the portrait under his breath, "The hell do you know? What should I have done?"

The guilt over Mr. Chambers' sad end was like a grit of sand in his teeth.

I did what I could. Couldn't have gone any other way. Doesn't mean I'm giving up on the little one.

The wild-west icon's smirking portrait offered no reply, only a cynical stare and one raised eyebrow.

…fuckin' hate cowboys, anyway. At that moment, the Greyhound bus pulled up curbside, blocking his view of Earp. Across the street, two young boys fired off cap guns as they chased each other gleefully.

"South Dakota can kiss my ass…" Cam sneered as he stepped onto the bus.

Cold Case

Wednesday, October 14^{th,} 1953

"Pink… fucking… yarn."

Cam Mason grumbled the words at himself, an admonishment.

"Couldn't help yourself tugging at some pink yarn stickin' outta the dirt, and you end up manacled to a pipe floatin' toward death. You simple *bastard*." He'd practically spit the words out, furious and frustrated at his stupidity, at the dire circumstance said stupidity had caused. He was alone; there was nobody else there to chastise him.

Rattling his steel shackles against the frigid and scaly pipe in the dark room sent a clatter of noise through the hollow, riveted walls of the old fishing trawler. The rattle died off against the cacophony of rain pelting the hull. He could feel the sway of the boat under his ass, where the damp floor stole his body heat.

"Now *what* are we gonna do about all this?" No answer came, only the dull crunch of a keel bottoming out, rattling the old bones of the boat like rocks in a tin box. It rattled Cameron plenty, too.

Listing. Broadside now…

The waves twisted the hull in the water, his equilibrium warring with the horizon of the far wall as his feet dug in. Teeth clenched, his snarky inner monologue replayed the realization in no uncertain terms.

Nobody is piloting this fucking dinghy. We're… no. I'm adrift—just me and my coffin.

This sent a knot into his gut and a quiver in his bowels.

You're gonna die out here, old man…

The voice taunted him. It was his own, but apart, like someone whispering too close into his ear. It was inside, but eerily distant.

"No way you let them drown you like a rat, no way. Get your bearings goddammit,' he shouted, fighting that voice inside that was so sure he was as good as dead; 'get your bearings, you dumb sonofabitch!"

Shaking his head and clenching his fists, he leaned into the pipe and stood up as tall as he could. His hair brushed the low ceiling. The light entering the room through a six-inch porthole was hardly enough to make out the walls and the floor, much less anything of use. His hands fastened behind him, he leaned forward and back as the boat swayed in the current.

He leaned forward and donkey-kicked the pipe. It was steadfast. "Aww, c'mon now." He kicked again. A rattle in the wall clamps, but the pipe was as rigid as ever. He kicked a dozen more times, and all it did was make him more sure that he was stuck, that this piece of shit hollow metal pipe might be his end. He'd often supposed it would be a much smaller metal pipe and an accompanying projectile.

Wonder if drowning is worse than being shot… rather not find out today…

The boat rocked left and right; he could feel the churning water dashing against the vessel as it floated along. The water was so rough that the bow didn't keep her straight. The storm outside roiled on, and the rain was near deafening. The boat was spinning in the water when it lurched so hard it knocked Cam off his feet and to his knees. The steely shriek of a keel dragging across rocks echoed through the hull again, before the surging storm waters shoved the boat half-sideways and shouldered it back into the rushing current.

Gotta take the hurt, old man. You gotta take the hurt or you're a dead man. This thing is going down.

With steely resolve, Cam crouched down and waited for the next sway of the boat away from the wall he was chained against. Grimacing, he knew what he had to do.

"Do it, Cam. DO IT!" The boat rocked toward the far wall, and with that, he sprang up and forward away from his cuffs, hoping to break loose from the pipe.

RUNTCH

The manacle fractured his left wrist, and a shard of bone came jutting through skin and scraping against the steel cuff like a house key on cement.

"OH YOU FU- F- FUCKIN *BASTARD!*" Cam howled in pain as the blood ran down his wrist and the cold steel struck a hot nerve in the torn flesh. Still, he was detained.

You're going to die soon.

"No… NOT a goddamn CHANCE' he shouted aloud, his thoughts now his primary opponent. 'I'm not DONE!"

A few labored breaths, and Cam found his resolve, pausing before he made another attempt to free himself. Head lolling and chin on his chest, he closed his eyes and ignored the damage. The pain seized his arm like a vice, but he knew real pain well enough to work through it.

"God, Allah, Yahweh, if any of you old bastards are up there, I'm only gonna ask *once*. I need a little more time. Just gotta… I can't leave that little girl lyin' out there in the mud. I can't leave without doing one good thing. Give me just a little more time, I'm *begging* you."

Silent for a few breaths, he hoped to hear something besides the rain pummeling the decaying wood and rusted steel of the death trap surrounding him. He hoped the floor would stop rocking, the blood would stop running out of his decimated hand.

No reprieve came.

Okay, I get it. You're all too busy. If I make it outta here, I did it on my own. I'm sorry for askin'…

Grasping the pipe with his good hand and placing one foot forward, he leaned his right shoulder on the wall to steady himself as the floor undulated like flowing lava, with his weight taut on the pipe. He went back to mule-kicking that goddamn metal stick that had him pinned. Ten kicks. Twenty. After fifty kicks, his leg cramped up, but he didn't care. A hundred kicks went by in as many seconds, his hip and leg ached like the time his chute opened only halfway over the Rhein and dropped him like a stone in six feet of water. He counted the kicks precisely; it kept his mind off the failure in his body—the excruciating sensation of bone against steel.

One hundred three…

He felt a rattle again in the ceiling bracket that had held the pipe so well thus far.

Come on, you fucker. One hundred four…

The rattle grew into a clank. Something that sounded like a rivet plinked to the floor in the darkness.

CRUNCH

The boat hull struck something in the water, sending Cam tumbling to his knees again as the vessel pivoted violently. It felt like a car crash, immense and heavy, the colossal impact dulled only by the slowness of the boat spinning in the water's drag. The undulation sent bile up to his mouth. His right shoulder had taken the brunt of the wrenching impact and was quickly weakening his right-hand grip, which held on to the pipe, while his broken left hand dangled like it was already dead, like a sign of things to come.

Okay, you old rag doll, break this goddamn thing, and you get to live with all this pain.

A smirk formed on his face through the tears and stabbing pains wracking his body. He stood halfway, putting every bit of power he had left into those kicks.

Five. He kicked again, harder. *SIX.* The pipe rattled just a bit louder this time.

Shit. Shitshitshit… okay, this is the ONE, Cam. This is it.

He released the pipe with his right hand and grasped his mangled left wrist to support it, his shoulders screaming in hot agony, and his chest muscles tearing like old shoestrings.

One hundred… SEVEN! He kicked the pipe with all of his force, falling backward into it as his boot slipped on his blood.

CLUNK

The pipe broke away from its support and sheared at the fitting close to the ceiling. It now bowed away from the wall, but only a foot or so. Cam was sprawled out on his side, arms still cuffed around the pipe behind him. In the darkness, the crooked talisman loomed over him, a stake pinning him down.

"Fuck you," he murmured and sprang upright. Hiking his grip up to his mid-back and standing on his toes, Cam took a deep breath and leaned forward away from the wall. Despite the slick blood covering the pipe, his one good hand's grip held fast. For a moment, he was suspended in the air, leaning forward like an alluring wood carving mermaid on the prow of some old pirate ship, his arms drawn back and his chest held out proudly.

Shit.

The boat lulled in the water for a moment as he waited, as though it were pensively awaiting the outcome.

The pipe stayed, but only for a few moments. The old leaden metal finally gave out under his lean hundred-sixty-something pounds, slowly bending and letting him fall to the wet floor on his stomach with a wet *plop* like a cartoon gag. His face came to rest on the wood planks as the boat heaved and pulsated underneath, the rain never relenting. For what felt like an eternity, he closed his eyes, taking in the cold of the floor and the sounds of the rain outside. Rushing water splashed and slapped at the hull, and a flash of lightning flickered outside.

He wanted to taste the rain.

Wriggling free from the pipe, he regained his footing. After standing at the porthole for two breaths, he could see the river raging around his vessel. He saw the moonlit levee embankment, another flash of lightning, and, some distance downriver, the abutments of a bridge.

"Ah, hell. Get OFF this boat, Cameron!"

Yanking the door open with his hands still fastened behind him, he stood now on the deck of the ship as it undulated toward the black skeleton of a steel bridge over the Sacramento River. Thick cast-cement columns backlit by a dim sky held up the arched spine of the bridge, and he blinked rain out of his eyes as he assessed. This boat was headed *directly* for one of those thirty-foot abutments. Cam knew he couldn't swim with his hands restrained and his body exhausted, so he had only one option.

Float, you old bastard. C'mon, get to shore. Come on…

His feet stayed fast; terror was only slightly outweighed by his survival instinct.

"I said you need to FLOAT!" He screamed and sucked in a deep breath before leaping off the side of the boat.

The wintery water stabbed his body with countless cruel needles, but only for a moment. Another jolt of adrenaline surged through his chest sharply, sending the body's equivalent of high-test gasoline into his veins. Cam rolled over underwater and went limp, desperately holding in the breath he'd captured. For a moment, he felt the water grasp him and keep him in suspension like the hands of the reaper were clasped upon him.

Just wait… he reminded himself as the boat drifted away from overhead. After the shadow receded and a glint of moonlight shone through the murky water, he could feel the current taking him. He bounced off some debris or rock, but it was just his hip. All he could feel now was the cold. The cold and his wrist. That goddamn shackle. His legs flailed in the water like a dead frog in a flushing toilet.

Hold. Hold it. Just wait…

Deep under the water, this battered man existed in a moment away from time, squeezed his eyes like fight-ready fists, and *remembered*. His favorite moment. A memory. The fading recollections that had intertwined to some degree after so many years. This memory was *warm*, dream-like, a drug in itself.

A diminutive and curly-haired little girl floating in a cheap plastic pool on green grass, sunshine bearing down on Cameron's neck and back as he cradled her head and fat little thighs while she held her breath in that meager shallow water. She was pinching her nose tight and wriggling in his hands. Bubbles surrounded her, and her hair swirled around in the water like seagrass, soft and rhythmic. It danced to and fro as her little feet kicked instinctively. It echoed Cam's childhood baptism, which was carried out in a field, in a water basin, surrounded by people he'd never known nor had an opportunity to meet. He still enjoyed the retelling as a child; his mother was *so* enthusiastic in her bedtime storytelling. And he held his baby girl… no baptism, just old-fashioned summertime fun and giggling.

Tilting his daughter's little head up, she spat out the metallic-tasting garden hose water and cooed, "Papa, did I do it? Did I go *swimming*?"

"Almost, lil' miss, almost. But before you swim, you gotta *float*. And that's what you did, just perfect."

She sat up in the slippery wading pool and splashed with her hands, so her papa tickled her ribs, sending her into a laughing fit. Her little tummy jiggled, and her perfect, happy cheeks enchanted him, made him feel alive. The sun was no match for the golden rays of that tiny smile. Tiny button nose and little nibbling teeth, and those diminutive ears that stuck out under her silky hair. Water droplets clung to the lobes of her ears and jiggled back and forth with her cherubic laughter.

The shore. Get to shore.

Cam opened his eyes and grimaced at the stingingly cold water, yet he was thankful his breath held steadfastly. Floating toward the surface, he could see lightning igniting across the sky above him. The murky water couldn't drown out that, couldn't drown out his hope. He *refused* to relent.

Another day. You take another day.

The stale air whooshed out of his lungs just as he breached the surface and gasped for life. With another flash of lightning, he could see the boat overturned, its hull dragging with a crackling groan against the bridge abutment. The river was carrying Cameron toward the wreckage at a rather rapid pace. With new breath in his lungs, Cam took to kicking, a wriggling backstroke to make his way to the closer shore. His hands were bound, but his spirit was determined. Against floes of detritus and branches from fallen trees churning through the water, against the current that knew not the way it surrounded and quenched in its folds, against muscles seizing and clenching in the icy water… Cameron Mason fought like hell. His legs kicked and thrashed as he wrenched his arms behind him to-and-fro just to keep his chest aimed at the sky. The raindrops stung his eyes as he looked up, craning his neck back between breaths to keep the levee shore in sight. It was but a few meters away, and it felt like *forever*.

Still, the storm-swollen water, the debris, and all the pain in the world were no match for a man driven by a will to live stronger than he'd known in decades. The will to outlast the world, if only to do one small act of good before his number was up. Every bit of bone and sinew and piss and vinegar drove that man to survive.

The stubborn bastard washed up against the shore, coughing and puking up the muddy, earthen storm waters he'd swallowed in his struggle, but he was alive. He spat up bile and filthy water as he coughed up a laugh in the face of the fates.

"I- *kaff* … I'm still HERE you fuckin' SHITHEADS!" He screamed with a rasp into the stormy night sky.

Muscles shuddered and spasmed with acid and exhaustion as he lay his face into wet, pebbled sand. He met the earth with his forehead like reuniting with a long-lost lover. Mud and dirt mashed into his nose and mouth, in between his teeth as he sobbed and spat in the soil as his body trembled with manic shakes of adrenaline owing to the ordeal and, of course, to his injuries. He knew the tremors would subside soon enough, just as they had when he stood in the cold rubble of small towns ravaged by artillery during his time in the Second World War. Those moments were anything but silent. Now, the patter of raindrops on his wet clothing was tiny drumbeats echoing in his waterlogged ears.

The rain was warm to his skin as he was just barely this side of hypothermia. It washed away blood and grit, pain and tears. It felt like a kiss, a grace. He rested there until his sobbing subsided, lying on his flank and face still half buried in the mud. He fell out of consciousness for a short while, limp and alone on that levee as water lapped at his feet.

When he came to, he hadn't moved an inch. His right eye was pasted shut with mud, but he rolled back and let the rain remedy that as his thoughts fell back into organization. Eventually, Cam felt the strength to stand; he turned his body up from the levee earth and looked toward the horizon. A small light atop the bridge, which almost sent him to a watery grave, now serenely blinked at a breath's pace, fading in and out. Cam sat there in the mud, still feeling his heartbeat in his throat, while trees of lightning flashed across the sky. Each white-hot strike was immense, its tendrils and spine spanning the breadth of the county. Perhaps the whole Sacramento Valley. Within those bright bolts, Cam spotted a small outcropping on the bridge abutment nearest him; it was the operator's booth of the old iron drawbridge.

"Any port in a storm…" Cam joked to himself as he clambered to his feet. "Okay. Be right there."

Good People

Friday, October 16th

"Pink yarn?"

"Pink yarn."

Billy Bigsby let a disappointed sigh escape his chest, but it sounded like he had turned his head away from the phone receiver.

"It was just so out of place, John… that poor woman told me every little thing about her baby girl. About that sweater she was wearing, that woman was *so* certain I would find her little angel just sitting on a bench somewhere, sunshine on her face, in that hand-knit sweater. Bright pink, like a flower, she said."

Without trying, Cameron could still vividly see the thick tassel of bright easter-Sunday-pink yarn dancing in the cold breeze in the shadow of that derelict Fruehauf freight trailer; he could feel the grit under his fingernails after he dug up some gravel while tugging at the thread. He could still feel the diminutive, cold hand poking from that ragged sweater sleeve, clasped limply in his own, just before he was cold-cocked from behind.

Billy's voice snapped him out of the memory.

"Skulking around some plot in the middle-of-fuckin'-nowhere and you come across the only piece of hard evidence we found, tangible proof in months that these missing children aren't just runaways or census mistakes… and now we are forced to assume it's going to be gone… I'm sorry, *she* is going to be moved before we can get anybody out there who we can trust to unearth that little child." There was a hint of melancholy in Billy's voice; Cameron knew that Billy had a vested emotional interest in this case by now.

All this work and nothing to show for it. Damn.

"Yeah, Billy. I'm sorry. I figured as much. I also figured I'd better hitch up that little trailer you bought me and get out of town before those local thugs figure out I didn't go down with the ship like a good sailor. If I didn't have to find a doc and get my wrist plastered in town, I might've been able to sneak back out there myself and do right by the child, maybe bring this whole thing into the light."

"Don't be silly, Cam, you're liable to get yourself tied up to another goddamn boat. Maybe one with stronger pipes, and then where would we be? You've got to watch out for yourself, seeing as I don't have anyone I can send out there to do it for you, or I would've done it. Christsakes, you're not there to kick down doors... you're a colored man in the wrong part of the world, Cam. You're there to sneak, to find things. I can't guarantee your *safety* from here, dammit. You're not in the Army anymore, remember?"

"If I were worried about safety, I wouldn't have taken your job offer, Billy."

"We have *friends* who do the heavy lifting. Friends with badges. That's all I'm saying, old man. You're there because you're goddamn *smart*. You need rest, and you need to *think*. That's all I'm asking. Say, how are you liking that little canned ham?"

Cam bit his tongue and let Billy's chastising roll over him.

He's right.

"The trailer? I like it just fine. I sure wish it had a water closet, but I suppose it's comfortable otherwise. I'm no stranger to making do when I have to use the crapper."

"Fair enough. They call it a camper, you gotta live like you're out camping. Just don't fish with the same bucket! Speaking of Johns, what say you head up North and pay a little visit to John Talbot? Give you a chance to recuperate and get him filled in, I might just have you boys trading places. Doesn't seem like that little town is a safe place for... ah..."

"Colored folk? Not unless you're a ranch hand."

Cameron had known going into all this that he would be in unfriendly places. He knew before he ever took a cent from Billy that working as a private investigator wouldn't be easy. He knew damn well he was too old to go out into the world kicking ass to get his answers, and that he would have to work twice as hard and twice as long to see any success that a white man in his position might have.

After a long silence, Billy offered, "I know how things were in the service, and I know how things must be out there. I also know you are too stubborn to give up, and I know that I can't make it any easier."

"Maybe I don't want easy. I would have stayed in the service if I wanted it *easy*.

Billy chuckled into the handset. " There isn't much about the Army that a man could call easy. Did you forget I was there?"

"I remember you getting thrown in the brig for disappearing a whole damn week; they found you buttoned up in some brothel with a box of cigars and enough bourbon to drown a battalion."

"And a redhead."

"*Aaaaaaaand* a redhead," Cameron echoed, mocking Billy for the way he always ended that same damn story.

"Sure, Cam, maybe I had it easier than some since my father made sure I never saw battle… but you were so good with your team, you and Irish and Gabriel and Par-… ah, hell. Listen, if we're going to open old wounds, you'd better make your way up here to Seattle, and we can do it over a bottle. Hop in that little truck and get your leathery ass up to John Talbot's house, see me when your arm heals up. Until then, I expect you to enjoy a paid vacation."

Cam smirked, knowing there was a string. There's always a string.

"And you need me to…"

Billy sighed; you could almost hear the shrug over the handset. "… and put John on the right track so he can follow in your footsteps down there on the river, maybe get a bit further."

"But I'm not off the case, right? You're not taking that away from me, are you?"

"For Pete's sake, have you ever known me to put anyone out on the curb? No, sir, I've got other plans for Cam Mason. If anyone's going to solve this thing, it's not going to be out there in Sacramento, not since you likely spooked those bastards. If anything else is going to develop, it's going to be somewhere we don't expect. Maybe John can find something on those trucks, maybe not. We know what to look for now."

"Then I'll give your regards to John when I get up to Portland…"

"No need, Cam. He's sitting here in my office. Drive safe, pal."

Cam grunted 'mm-hmm' into the handset of the payphone before resting it back on the hooks. Stepping out into the sunlight, he looked across the street where his little yellow truck sat in the sun with its matching yellow-and-white camper, parked curbside in front of the California state capital. A beautiful, sprawling lawn surrounded the capital building. Horseback police slowly trod around the building, with white columns at every entrance, and a line-of-sight view of the broad boulevard that made up the heart of the city. Domed-roof courthouses took up another city block adjacent, and the manicured lawns were covered in fallen oak leaves.

Pretty place… lovely garden.

As he darted across the street back to his truck, he looked up and caught a glimpse through one of the Capitol's paned windows: stodgy old men standing around, shaking hands, and accomplishing nothing.

Goddamn politicians.

~

October 18th

"Just park it anywhere!" John shouted, jogging down the broad driveway and waving to Cameron.

Tapping on the brakes, Cameron looked around and saw the perfect patch of dirt to back his little trailer into. John's house was small, with perhaps two bedrooms and no garage. The plot, however, could be described as sizable. Rickety fences lined the property, while the front lot was more dirt than a lawn. Still, from the road, Cameron had seen that the house had a pleasant backyard with a few oak trees and some evergreens lining the fence where the property abutted some sprawling farmland. It looked to be a few acres all in all.

Reaching across with his right hand to open the vent window in the door, Cameron shouted out to John, "You got it, let me drop this heap here, and then I need the water closet!" He had been holding it for perhaps a hundred miles simply because there were no good service stops along the way that looked friendly.

He shifted the old truck in the park, killing that rumbling V-8 engine and withdrawing the little brass key. John opened his door from the outside and offered him a hand.

"It can't be an easy drive one-armed. I imagine you could use an aspirin and a cold drink."

Cam took John's hand and lurched out of the truck, with a half-smile shooting back, "Don't mention drinks until I've relieved myself, or are you fuckin' with me?"

As Cam strode hurriedly toward the house, John shouted after him, "Yes, sir, big tall glass of lemonade! All you can drink!" and trailed off into laughter.

A few minutes later and many ounces lighter, Cameron joined John out on the home's little porch facing the road. John was sitting there with a grin on his face and a pitcher of lemonade.

"Sorry for teasing you, I haven't seen you in ages. To be honest, you look a little worse for wear, Cam."

Cam snorted, eyeing the pitcher covered in condensation. He withdrew a tin of cigarillos from his pants pocket before sitting down while letting out an old-man grunt.

"If there's one thing I love about you, John, it's that you're honest. I must look like ten pounds of horseshit in a five-pound sack. Two days' drive on cold coffee and stale jerky will do that to a man."

"Oh, you're a tough old goat, and the weather's been nice. I'm sure it wasn't too terrible a drive, especially since you get to sleep where you want." John nodded toward the little camper.

"I suppose you're right, but I'm still a bit busted up after my run-in with those sheriffs back in Isleton."

"Crooked country cops… isn't that an American tradition?" John asked as he poured a tall glass and handed it to his weary friend.

"I'm not too fond of *those* American traditions. I'm of the mind that this country could use some progress. Maybe just a softer boot on my neck. You want tradition? Bake me an apple pie."

John winced at the comment and didn't respond, staring thoughtfully into his glass as Cameron lit a small cigar and held it in his swollen, purple fingers, which hung out the end of a dirty, scratchy cast that appeared barely good enough for hurt livestock.

"I'm sorry, I'm a guest in your house, and here I am complaining. I feel like I'm being… what's that word? *Boorish.*" Cameron winked at John, knowing that John's parents were English and it was a common term on the other side of the pond. He'd also heard it in those silly trans-Atlantic accents in the cinema.

"Not in the least, Cam. If anyone's got a right to gripe, it's you. I think Billy felt pretty bad about how things turned out down there. In fact, I don't believe it… I know it. He said as much to me just the other day.

"And what else did he say?" Cameron inquired, puffing on his cigar.

"He said he would get me up to snuff on the details, on everything you found. I suppose he's having me head down there to follow up on those trucks, and maybe speak to one or two more families of those missing kids between Sacramento and Stockton. See if we overlooked anything, maybe bring something to light now that we know how they are moving the little ones."

"Well, that's still a stalemate. I heard that some blue-and-white striped freight trucks were seen around the time those kids went missing, and that no major trucking companies operating in the Sacramento Valley paint their trucks in that color scheme. None I can find, anyway. One worker at the farms, an old Chinese? He remembered the trucks and said they were too shiny. Said they had markings on the door, looked like new cabover trucks. Like a White or a Freightliner."

"That'll make it easier to find them, I bet…"

"*Hmph.* I put on my best professional voice and rang up the State police at every inspection Point in California, and not *one* of them I spoke to could recall seeing those trucks or at least recognizing them. Worse yet, the only description I got of a possible perpetrator in all this is a 'fat man in coveralls, five o'clock shadow and smoking a cigarette'… fuck me if that doesn't describe half the people in that county."

John rocked forward in his chair and pulled a flask out of his back pocket, dousing some golden liquor onto the ice floating in his lemonade.

"Sounds like we know more than we did a month ago, and that's thanks to you. I think we should fire up the barbecue out back and maybe break out some bigger cigars, we've got the place to ourselves for a while… the little lady is back in Connecticut with her family for a while."

Cameron held out his glass, and John poured a generous float of liquor on top. "Young man, that sounds a bit open-ended. Everything all right with the wife?"

Feigning a half-smile, John nodded and looked out to the horizon as he responded in an almost practiced way, "I love my wife, and I want her to be happy. Right now, she's happy when she's away. Lets me focus on work, anyway."

"Mmm-hmm." Cam sipped the float of liquor from the glass, then helped himself to another dousing of what he thought *must* be Kentucky bourbon, judging by the bite.

~

October 28th

BANG

The revolver kicked like a mule in Cam's hand. The round whizzed past the Coke bottle and out into the field, hitting the ground with a zinggg, perhaps a quarter of a mile away.

"Jee-zus *Christ*, John! What sorta bullets are you putting in this thing? I didn't know they made cannons you could holster!"

John cackled madly at the sky and raised his pistol, firing one-handed at the bottle some twenty yards away.

BANG

...

SKRSSHHT

The Coke bottle on Cameron's end of the fence exploded into a million pieces of glitter.

"See, now *that* is how it's done, my friend. I know a guy out in Grants Pass who makes these rounds; he calls them tree-cutters. I always stock up when I'm out in the mountains. Quite a kick, huh?"

Raising his barrel again, Cameron nodded with the biggest grin plastered across his face.

"Quite!"

BANG

...

RUNTCHHH

The branches of one of the small evergreens planted at the edge of the property blew apart into splinters and detritus as the lead tore through its trunk.

"You missed, old man!" John teased.

"What do you mean I missed? You called these things tree-cutters!" Cam retorted.

John shook his head, firing the last three rounds in his pistol and taking out two of the five bottles still posted along the fence rails.

"What did my tree ever do to you, Cam?" He holstered his emptied revolver and turned to his friend, still grinning from the excitement of firing such formidable weapons.

"Just practicing, and I think a tree looks more like a man than a Coke bottle, anyway. I promise not to murder any more of your beautiful backyard if you're gonna be so *sensitive*."

"Cam, smaller targets take *skill*. Practice. I don't spend bullets for fun! Well, not *just* for fun."

He handed the revolver to John, having earlier declined the leather belt and holster John had offered him. John opened the barrel of the gun into the palm of his hand, pouring out empty shells and a couple of unspent rounds. Cameron continued, "Looks like I'm getting my cast removed come next week. You ready for what's next? I know Billy wants to send you back down there now that we've had a little bit of breathing room, see if you can suss out anything else."

John shrugged, looking out at the horizon for a spell before he responded, "I think Billy's just trying to keep me busy. Keep me from losing it, being alone out here. I think he worries about me. Helped me buy this place, you know. Said it was for all my hard work, but... I haven't been working much lately."

As they walked back to the house, Cam offered in all seriousness, "You seem a little lost, John." John didn't reply.

They plunked down on the porch with some cold tea.

"I don't mean to be a stick in the mud, Cam. It's been nice catching up with you, and I know you needed the rest. Maybe it's just lucky timing."

"There's nothing lucky about your marriage troubles, John. You know, I really tried to make it work with Lizzy after we lost my... after things changed. Feels like a lifetime ago... hell, it *was* a lifetime ago. She left for a fresh start, and I got pissed, so I joined the Army. There was no glue gonna put us back together. But... for a while, we *tried*."

"She's a fine woman. I meant what I said. I want her to be happy. With all this traveling and putting myself in harm's way, I've been doing it for near a dozen years, I think she's just fed up with it. Maybe she deserves somebody who can be here with her. Maybe I should get a real job and stop playing detective like I'm some Philip Marlow. I'm not even very good at this, and you know it."

Cam thought about that for a bit, choosing his words carefully and thinking about his own life, comparing it to John Talbot's.

"Nobody knows better than you what you've got to do as a man. If you were asking for my opinion, which I believe you might be, I would say you need to try to save what you can. Nothin' in this world is important as family."

"She's all the family I've *got*, Cam. We talked about having a...' he caught himself, cleared his throat, and changed tone, 'well... we've talked about doing a lot of things."

"Then it's even more important."

"I know. I know that. But... what about the case? What about you?"

"I don't have any family left, John. Just a few old friends. Good people to be sure, but... not much to lose. Just me and my truck."

"You're going all-in on this case, aren't you, Cam? I could see that in your eyes when you called the boss the other day. You've been itching to leave since you arrived."

"It's the only purpose I've got left. No choice… I'm all in." Cam grumbled. No more words were shared in the evening air.

The sun set like a fire upon the horizon, burning as far as the eye could see.

Cabin Fever

Wednesday, September 14th, 1955

Two years had passed in a blink for this greying, determined old cus. From day one, this case had made Cam Mason's nights a bit bleak; all those nights, the moon seemed to hide away from him, the darkness lit instead by all these wicked, burning eyes here on Earth. Two years of sneaking about and living these short, false lives looking for clues… too many months chasing ghosts, seeking answers from people who refused to hear questions. It could instill paranoia in an unprepared man. Private eye work was thankless; a man's heart needed to be steeled against despair on a long, cold case. Cynical Cam Mason lived in distrust of the world by clear-minded choice.

While Cam was a thoughtful man, the extent of what he might encounter had until this very moment hardly been realized. He'd spent days on buses, weeks in seedy hotels, months on long winding roads, and occasionally a few nerve-wracking moments standing face-to-face with proper villains in an attempt to suss out an explanation for what was adding up to be *dozens* of missing immigrant children. A lonely path to walk when society couldn't care to remember the names, all the little faces. Nights of quiet, countless midnights so very still you'd think god never invented the cricket.

Yet at this moment, Cameron's ears rang with the echo of a procession of close-range gunfire. His shoulder ached from the impact the sawed-off twelve-gauge sent like the strike of a sledgehammer through his outstretched arm. He could now smell the stench of all that wickedness, and it was no triumph. His gut was twitching, his breath held in like it were his last, his asshole still clenched tight from the shock of an unexpected gunfight.

He glanced over his right shoulder, the path of the bullets the opponent had fired, but luckily met with nothing vital, just the adjacent tree line. The sound of munitions volleyed past one's ears had the strange effect of making a man acutely aware of his mortality; Cam had experienced that on several occasions in his travels. He'd never expected a friend to be the one pulling the trigger. In a blink, it was Cam's *instinct* that had ended the other man's life, not Cam's *intention*.

Cam's breath finally expelled in the cool night air, his face wet with blood-spatter and his gun-wielding arm aching post-event as it always did. In a panic, his instincts had set him on his heels, raised his shotgun to level, pulled the trigger into that darkness... he didn't know whom he'd fired upon before the muzzle flash. It took him a blink of an eye afterward to realize he knew well the man he'd just ended with a single barrel.

You dumb sonofabitch, it didn't have to go this way!

The jarring truth and sudden gore of what he had just done were muted by the shadow he cast through the doorway under the porch lamp, his silhouette struck across the warm husk of what was once a brother of sorts. A man Cam had known since before he had a single gray hair. He let out a breath and relaxed his grip on the worn-smooth wood buttstock of the gun as he lowered it, its hot barrel sizzling against the sweat and oil impregnating the leather of the low-slung leg holster.

The dim light of the moon cast through the wisps of smoke still silently pouring out of the end of the barrel. It was a dirty, lithe smoke akin to that of pipe tobacco. The snakes of silver and black unfurling toward the floorboards recalled moments he'd been in combat, where the little details would stand out to the mind's eye in a surreal and perfect focus. Cameron had always figured it was the brain's way of taking the attention off the grisly reality of things, or perhaps mute the shocking and fracturing events that would so-often send men home twitching, angry at the world.

He thought back to his friend Gabriel, whose return from war to civilization left a wake of loss and confusion that nearly cost him everything he cared for. In the end, Cam had carried *that* man from freedom to cold shackles to salvation, and he'd have done the same for this dead man at his feet.

The long shadows from the porch light were framed so perfectly by the doorway. Just then, was Cam to be judged by his own shadow? He might seem a giant. In reality, this unassuming and gentle-faced man was subtly trying now to disappear in that shadow, to pay no mind to the hot death spattered across him. Quiet returned as the ringing in his ears faded, yet he had not moved an inch in what felt like ages. His knees stiff, his body called out for reprieve. It had in truth been only the count of a few heartbeats, but that's no good clock to count by.

Get your nerve, dammit. You did what needed doing. Get your shit together, old man.

Kicking Steve Hardigan's boot, he gazed at the body through misty eyes.

Maybe we could have fixed this? Coulda walked it all back. You dumb sonofabitch!

In the silence, he could now make out the grotesque and lurching sound of warm blood and fluids creeping out of a soft form. Steam rose into the cold air, escaping this body from holes not put there by his maker. The sound was of the end of life, and perhaps the end of some aspect of Cameron's own. He shuddered at the noise; the buckle of his shotgun sling rattled a bit from the shiver that shook right through his boots and into the hardwood floor of the cabin.

He reached out his left hand, his right hand still clutching the heavy weapon. On the wall, he found a small light switch button under his fingertips. With a press of his finger, he sent electricity to the only light in the room, a flimsy metal-shade lamp dangling from the ceiling. The light focused in the center of the room and over the corpse, over the glistening wounds of Hardigan's body, almost as if to *shame* Cameron for causing such a mess and highlighting his sins like a stage light.

With his jaw clenched and chin held firm in place, Cam's eyes darted back and forth, scanning the room. The dusty, barely stocked shelves looked like a poor man's pantry; this was a hunting cabin. Two sinks were side-by-side on the far wall, mismatched, of course. One of them showed signs of age and decay around the backboard, presumably from the sink used to clean the game that was killed. There was a broken couch slumped against the left wall, a small side table holding up a large empty ceramic mug that was lying on its side. The round table in the middle of the room was strewn with papers. No notable adornments on the walls, save an out-of-date 1954 calendar proudly displaying a brunette pinup model, boldly labeled "Miss June" in block lettering over a smiling blonde with a comically thin waist, now over a year out of date. Perhaps the occupants had left that very month, not returning since, or maybe they simply cared so little for the passage of time in the outside world that nobody took the time to change it.

No, thought Cam, *she's just so pretty they didn't have the heart to change it*. He was probably right.

Turning on his heel, he faced right. The canary-yellow-and-rust refrigerator was leaning slightly to one side, partly sunk into the decaying wood floor due to condensation and spilled water, which was rotting away at the timber underneath. Its door was a bit ajar, and it made no sound, unlike a running refrigerator. Cam was curious as to why someone would own a refrigerator, which was *rare* in these parts, that was not refrigerating.

With a deep breath of fresh air near the doorway, he finally sheathed the shotgun back into its holster. Stiff back and dry tongue aching for relief, Cam stepped over Hardigan's feet and toward the fridge. There were a few clean-looking towels resting on the edge of the counter next to the refrigerator, so he took one of the towels out of the stack and used it to wipe Hardigan's blood from his face. He tossed the rag in the sink, feeling disgusted at the blood sprayed across his clothes.

You must look like death, Cam.

He turned back to the fridge, still curious. Unsheathing his buck knife from its leather holster under his coat, Cam gripped the hilt firmly and used the flat of the blade to open the dingy door.

Under the light dimly cast across the room, he could see several large, perhaps gallon-sized jars of dark liquid. Beads of condensation reflected the light, and he figured it must've been kept cold until relatively recently. The humid room air was quickly warming, perhaps spoiling whatever might be in those containers. He'd seen moonshine in such a container before, but there was no moonshine on earth as dark as this. It was nearly black. He placed the knife under one side of the container and twisted it to provide leverage and tilt the jar; just as he suspected, the liquid inside slowly tumbled to one side, with a viscosity similar to that of oil. Small pieces of something soft bobbed to the surface within. Disgusted, he yanked his knife back. The jar tipped back before falling on its side and rolling right off the shelf, whereupon it shattered across the floor.

Oh Christ, what a mess... Cam lurched back as the spill spread toward his feet.

The red brine was coarse, unclean. Now, among the glass lay a few, perhaps a half-dozen, small animal organs. None of them was larger than a fist.

That smell, the fuckin'- This is a hunting shed, Cam. Relax.

Now he recalled what looked too much like a pelvic bone he'd seen protruding from the ash pile outside the cabin when he'd arrived, the *reason* he'd approached the door with his gun drawn—another shudder down his spine and a twist of the stomach.

It's gotta be animals: just deer or some shit.

Unable to resist acting on his curiosity, Cam stepped over the spilled mess and pried open the freezer door with his blade. The door swung wide, releasing a putrid stench into the room. Inside were neatly stacked, brown butcher paper-wrapped meats. Most were thoroughly soaked through with fluids of various colors; whatever was in the wraps had been rotting for quite some time. The air from the icebox was tangy and dense.

Cam spun on his heel, slamming the round yellow doors shut as he faced back into the room. The long, chrome door handles clattered as they latched. The lamplight still shone on Hardigan, the room cast in its dim glow. Cam scowled at this mess more than what he'd found in the fridge. Clenching his jaw helped keep him from vomiting, but only barely. He steeled his resolve by choosing to be mad about everything now.

Okay, fat man, you tried to smoke me. We ain't friends anymore. Guess they're gonna find you like this... undignified. Seems that's all you deserve.

Despite the stench from the icebox and the mess of a fresh body bleeding and shitting itself onto the floor, Cam was thankful that he wasn't forced to work in *total* darkness. He'd spent three lonely nights in those unmapped woods searching for this hideout, so the lamp was a small grace. Slowly pacing back to the body by the door, which was splayed out facing the roof timbers, Cam set his knife down on the newspaper that was scattered across the dining table.

His deft hands rifled through the pockets of Hardigan's body. He withdrew a wallet and checked its contents. Nothing special, just a thin wallet with a South Dakota driving license and enough money to buy a sandwich and a soda. Cam checked the vest pockets; nothing but clove gum and a pair of buckshot shells. He grasped the shoulders and turned the body onto its side, reaching into the back pockets. Cam was careful with his reach as the body had voided its bowels, as they all do. In one pocket, just a comb. Stepping over the body, Cam shoved the body to the other side and searched the back pocket. His fingers felt something cold; he removed it with two fingertips, narrowly avoiding the mess.

While he shuffled the body around, he chastised his old pal aloud.

"You *heard* me, I called out for you! You must've known it was me. You tried to take me out? You dumb sonofa… just lay there and don't cause any more fuss."

He withdrew an old cigarette lighter. It was a nice copper-and-silver lighter, with a thumbwheel on the top corner and a trigger on the side to lift the wick cover. On the underside, the stampings of its brand were worn away from too many years of burnishing by pocket change. Memories of Hardigan casually lighting his cheap cigarettes came to mind. Warm memories from a time long since passed. He shook them off, tried to avoid humanizing this body in its current state, after what he had just done.

Having found no cigarettes, Cam flicked the thumbwheel, but only sparks came out; no flame arose.

Why you carryin' around a dead lighter and no smokes? Guess you won't miss it. Christ, I could use a smoke…

Feeling somewhat overwhelmed by it all as the adrenaline wore off, Cam sat down at the mess of a dining table. Silence and stillness hung in the air, save for the tick of the clock on the wall. His first thought was thankfulness that the ringing in his ears had mainly subsided; that shotgun always took its toll on him that way. If it weren't for the unmatched utility, Cam would have replaced it in his arsenal years ago. A dozen or more tussles ended in his favor with that weapon in his clutches, and the unpleasant aftermath from using it, he supposed, was worth the cost.

Now, he waited for his legs to become steady as he sat there holding the lighter. Hoping to distract himself from the mess around him, he fingernail-picked the bottom plate off, sliding out the cartridge holding the wick and the cotton wadding, which soaked up and held lighter fluid.

Gotta fill these things. I have some fluid in the glove box…

With a keen eye, he saw that something was stuffed into the little tin tub next to the square of cotton. He used his knife's point to pry out what looked like a stone. With a bit of leverage, he brought to light an object that initially confused him. It looked almost like a small, white carrot. He held it to the light and rolled it over.

This is a—

His stomach now succumbed to the shock of the evening and clenched up as he doubled over, vomiting onto the table and across the newspaper. He leaned over the floor for a minute and cleared his throat, spitting and cursing until he regained his composure. Using his clean handkerchief, he wiped away tears from his eyes. Insides still in knots, he had nothing left to heave up. The air was putrid, but his legs still felt too weak to stand.

With a scowl and bleary eyes, he lifted the small bone to the light. It was thin and delicate—a finger, perhaps, or a toe.

This belonged to a child.

As he inspected it closer, he could see faint markings on one side. It looked almost as if a word had been etched there—three rough shapes, like carved Vs, all slightly different.

No, that doesn't make sense…

He wrapped the little, terrible keepsake in his handkerchief and tucked it away in his vest pocket. Sitting there, breathing foul odors and staring up at the ceiling beams, he cursed himself for being too weak to stand.

Don't go soft now, old man. There's work to be done. Man up, get your shit together!

Through sheer will, Cameron stood up and spat out more gut acid across the floor. He spent a while peering into the kitchen cabinets, checking under the couch cushions. Everything in the cabin had a good layer of dust on it, save for the body and the fresh pile of stomach contents that he left. There was nothing else useful here, though Cameron silently hated the idea that he was barely further along in his investigation after taking Hardigan's life.

Looming over the body once more, Cam said a small prayer under his breath. Sheathing his knife, he turned out the light and walked out the door. Closing the front door would do little good, as he'd kicked it damn near off the hinges when he had arrived. He figured that now, if he left it open, wildlife might smell what was inside and make a fine mess of it before anyone found the grisly scene.

Nearly reaching his truck, Cam paused for a moment as an idea took him. A terrible, but useful idea. He walked right back into the cabin and turned on the light. He picked up the wallet he'd removed from the dead man's pocket, slipping it into his back pocket. He retrieved a knotty blue blanket from the couch and placed it over Hardigan's head with a gentle and respectful hand. Standing over the body at the knees, he steadied himself and aimed his shotgun once more.

With another deafening *BANG*, his trusty shotgun took away any passerby or policeman's ability to identify the man without going to great lengths.

Feeling deeply regretful about the night's turn of events, Cam slapped the light switch off and walked out.

Rough roads

As Cameron walked in the moonlight down the path where he had stowed his truck, he could feel beads of sweat dripping down his forehead and lower back. At this moment, he was wishing he had brought some cool water on his trip. It was only a mile or so, but he was shaken up by what he'd just left behind in the cabin and was feeling desperately unwell.

After what felt like forever, Cam saw the comforting sight of his tired, beat-up 1937 Plymouth pickup sitting in the gravel path with the moonlight reflecting off the fading paint and trim. Her yellow paint set her out in the woods and was a welcome reprieve like no other. He'd been to nearly hell and back in that truck, and the years and miles showed on her as much as they did on him. The door creaked slightly as it opened, greeting him.

He reached into the dash and retrieved a red-and-white tin of cigarettes. This one, in particular, was painted to resemble a pack from his favorite brand, but it reminded him of the Army-issued cigarette boxes they'd been given while he was deployed. Tapping on the side of the tin, he could hear maybe a half-dozen smokes loosely rustling about in the box.

Plenty to make the drive back. Don't smoke 'em all, Cam. Get your head cool.

Leaning on the hood of the truck, he hung his head and shuddered as the image of that now-deceased man on the floor occupied his mind. He stood there for a while, letting the smoke fill his lungs, feeling the clothes sticking to his body. He could smell the blood on his shirt, mixing with the silty smoke.

After lighting a second smoke, he had to force himself to stand up from leaning on the cold hood. The old bench seat springs groaned as he slid onto the well-worn brown leather. The cigarette still hung from his lips. Unbuttoning his shirt, he took off his necklace chain that held two things: a dog tag from his service, and the key to the old truck. Once or twice, he'd been in a situation where someone tried to get his keys away from him. He figured it was about the last place someone might look; he loved that old truck and hated the idea of losing it to some lucky kid after a rotten row on a job. He pushed the key into the ignition but paused for a moment. Something bothered him now, something from inside the cabin. He didn't want to risk going back and getting caught up further; he'd have to work from memory. His habit of talking out loud to work out his issues had, over the years, become Cam talking out his problems with the old truck. He'd pat her dashboard a bit and slump in the seat to relax, or even lie sideways on the seat and stare at the old tattered headliner while he worked his way through a problem.

The moonlight was reflecting off his hood, and he half-smiled at the sight of his lovely hood ornament. He'd pulled it off another wrecked car in a junkyard and bolted it right on, giving his little truck a shining and rather well-endowed winged angel leading the way wherever they went. It was his first pleasant sight of the evening, and he chose to focus on that as he fired up the engine and slowly drove down the gravel drive back toward the main road. A few yards down the slope, Cam lit another cheap cigarette from the embers of the last one. Cranking the window down as he idled along, he let the fresh evening air clear out the smoke, sweat, and gasoline fumes from the jerry can on the floor of the truck. His hands were shaking, though he couldn't tell if it was from the nicotine or the near-death experience.

Some three miles had passed, and he finally reached the paved county road. He'd been driving with parking lamps only to avoid being spotted. Rolling to a quiet stop, he came to a halt a few yards shy of the main road and turned off his lights altogether. The Chrysler engine purred quietly while he waited. Not wanting to be seen by any other passing cars, he sat there for perhaps five minutes to ensure the road was clear and quiet. His patience proved valuable as he saw headlights coming from maybe a mile away. Shifting the truck into reverse, he backed up a hundred yards up the hill past the treeline. Shutting the engine off, he waited. Smoke rose from his barely smoldering cigarette that he'd had to relight a few times already; cheap tobacco didn't always burn well, but he hadn't paid for them anyway. He'd claimed them from a lost-and-found bin at a roughneck bar outside Cle Elum some weeks back, tossed them in his tin, and hardly smoked any since.

After a couple of minutes, he saw through the forest those headlights putter past on the main road; they were heading west.

"All right, we're going East," he said to the truck as he started the engine once more. She roared back to life, and he ran his hand along the cold steel dash. The direction didn't matter much; this was eastern Washington State, and it was very much farm country. There were always north-south and east-west county roads to be found if you were patient. He needed to go North, but he could waste a few miles East and make it up on a different road West for the tail end. Better than taking a backtrack route, better than being followed.

Since his discovery at the cabin, he understood that wrapping up the case soon would not be an option. Neither would involving the police, as the deceased, Steve Hardigan, happened to be a volunteer Sheriff who had recently retired from the Washington State Troopers. No, involving the police was a poor choice at the moment and would remain so until he had some proof of what was going on.

Gotta get on the line with Billy. Sure, I got some leads, but with Hardigan dead? It's gonna fall on his partners if I can find 'em. Gotta hash this all out and find another tree to bark up.

With the main road now quiet, he pulled out the cracked white plastic dash knob for the headlights and drove out onto the main road. The stars in the sky were lovely and bright, with only a low fog in the distance where Cam knew there was a body of water. He'd passed a reservoir earlier in his travels and thought about how nice it might be to take a day and just fish the waters here. His truck was barely above idle, humming like a Singer sewing machine as he made his way over the hills and curves of the road. With a long drive through the night ahead, he threw his cigarette butt in the ashtray and reached once again into the glove box for a lonely, cheap cigar that had been rolling around in there for days. As he lit the foot and took a gentle puff, his mind flashed what he saw in that cabin, the strangest thing; the scoring, or etching, on that little finger bone. It set his jaw to a clench. Looked almost like Roman Numerals, or something similarly angular.

Those jars were holding organs… looked small, maybe game. Maybe…. ah, hell. How would I know anyway?

Needing a distraction, he thought about how he ended up in such a pile of shit. Knowing that this newest revelation of a State Trooper's involvement in disappearing folks must be related to the case that set him on this path, the missing children, he knew he needed to clear his head make some sense of why he just pulled the trigger on a man whose wedding he had attended, a man who was now going cold in a puddle of himself.

Goddammit, Steve, you knew it was me. You must've known, and you tried to pop me anyway. What could be worth that? Who the hell did you become?.

Cam's mind looked back a bit further, just slightly more than two years. The case that started all this awful course of events, the sad story that convinced him to drop everything and dedicate himself to seeking some closure for some very unlucky folks. He set his focus on replaying the events as best he could, to what led him here. Perhaps he could recall something to guide him further in his investigation? Smoke saturated the cab of the truck as his memories started playing like an old projector on a tattered movie screen.

July 20th, it was... '53, yeah... I remember that goddamn mess. Cam vividly recalled the start of this whole ordeal.

~

Monday, July 20th, 1953

Cam's phone had been ringing off the hook for two days. He'd had a fever, some crap flu the boys at the navy bar down in Alameda had been passing around. With his voice returning enough to answer the phone, he snatched the receiver off the wall, nearly pulling the base off its hooks. His patience had worn thin listening to the ringing from the bedroom all weekend. He cleared his throat and spit a wad of phlegm down the kitchen sink, then barked into the receiver, "The hell do you want? Been calling me for two days! This is an unlisted number, goddammit!" The other line was silent for a moment.

"Cam, it's Bigsby. We need you." Cameron stood up straight and nearly cracked a smile.

"Billy, goddammit, shoulda *known* it was you. Okay, okay. Sorry that I yelled at you, man. What's going on where you don't have anyone else to call? Not that I don't miss you, of course."

"Oh, now I'm flattered, pal. I tell ya, I've already called everyone! Nobody's loose; everyone is playing house or some silly business. Even Irish wasn't picking up!"

Cam let out a chuckle. "Yeah, Shay ain't gonna pick up, man. I talked to him a few weeks back; he's on a vacation of sorts. Went home, in fact. Said he needed to get away from his lady problems for a while. You ask me, sounds like she ain't really his lady... but that's not my business, anyway. So what's the job, Billy? Something on the beach, I hope?"

Billy laughed at the idea. "Cam, you live in California. Aren't you surrounded by beaches?"

"Well yeah, but nobody's paying me to go to 'em right now...." And that sent Billy into stitches on the other line. Cam had needed a laugh after his weekend of sweaty sheets, sickness, and self-pity.

"Honestly, I didn't want to call you in on this one, Cam; it's a bit rough around the edges. I mean to say it's vetted and there's money here, but it's also in some nasty territory. Not your kind of folks."

Cam knew what he meant; a lot of jobs were in areas where a colored man could not be as effective an investigator as a white man. Cam liked to stay near the coasts; it seemed to him that there had been a lot more decent folks who stayed out of the middle of the states.

"Billy, I'll take what you've got and do my best. I can't leave you in the wind; I owe you. What's the job? Don't hold back, pal."

"All right, all right. I won't keep you waiting. I got a call last week about some shifty business in the Dakotas. A couple of folks got hemmed up there, and their kids went missing while they sat in jail for what appear to be falsified charges. Minor stuff, really. It's as if someone went out of their way to pick fights with these folks and ensured it went south for them. A local attorney is stonewalling the cases when I try to dig, but I managed to get a hold of one of the folks who needs help. They told me that the local law took him in for public nuisance, after a bar fight that he insists he had no part in starting. Of course, he's a single father after his wife passed from a nasty accident, so it was just him and his daughter. The local law took her from the neighbors, citing the safety of the child as the reason. But it gets strange, Cam."

"...Strange?"

"*Real* strange. Cops who picked the kid up said she was going to a group home, just a cot-and-milk spot, until her father got released from county jail. It should have been an easy thing, group homes in every state these days, after the war... so, the father convinces a pal to pay his bail and gets him out after a week. The state has no record of the girl, nor does it have a record of the uniformed officers who picked her up. Like she just vanished, gone. Now the poor bastard can't go anywhere but sit at home and wait for the phone to ring; he's a damned mess. He found me by calling an attorney he knew from Chicago, who happened to land on my desk by chance, since the boys in suits are currently focused on bigger fish. They throw me a bone now and then. He's lucky they did because at this point he's got no shred of evidence, and it's likely he won't find her unless we get involved, Cam."

Cameron stood there in silence for a short time, processing the whole thing. "So this guy got cleared of charges?"

"Totally. It's like someone up high wanted the whole business to go away, hoping this guy might go away himself. Honest, I think they might have planned on getting him killed in that fight from the sound of it. Guns were drawn and all. We might be walking in on something worse than a simple kidnapping, anyway."

"How's that, Billy?"

"Well, I ran down some missing persons cases in the area, looking for a pattern. Guess what?"

"I don't wanna guess, man."

"Well, he isn't the only one missing a kid. I found three more cases where folks' children have simply up and disappeared, no trace. No investigations, or nothing further than a page of the missing persons ledger. All of 'em in the last decade. Of course, the local boys have the folks convinced that the kids ran off, but witnesses are saying otherwise in two of the cases, and in the third, well…" he trailed off.

"Billy? In the third, what?"

"Well, in the third case, they found the kid. A young boy. He was found, deceased, in a granary out near where he went missing, maybe a few weeks later."

"So?"

"So the kid was missing his hands. Clean gone, Cam. Just taken off. Coroner's report surmised wild animals must've gnawed off the hands postmortem, but I bribed— er, paid a county clerk to send over the full-fat file on it. The pictures don't lie, Cam. They were taken off mechanically. Something sharp."

"Dammit, Bigsby. God damn it." Cam was disgusted and disappointed. "You know I hate this shit, man. You *know* why, too." Without saying directly, he reminded Billy that he didn't work with kids' cases, not ever. Billy knew the story, knew damn well why those didn't sit right with Cam.

"I'm sorry, Cam. If there were anyone else, I'd lean on them, but… you're the best I've got. And this little girl might still be alive, pal. I feel like we gotta help, even if we don't want to. I know you don't like these jobs, and I'm sorry, okay?"

"Sorry. Yeah. Okay, man. O-kay. I'll work it. But, you gotta send me some info and front me my travel costs. South Dakota? You sure are sending me into the shit here, Billy."

"I mailed it Monday. Should be there tomorrow."

"You're an asshole, Billy."

"Love you too, Mason."

Cam hung up the phone with a grimace.

The next few days were spent packing, then Cam riding two trains and a bus out to a little town in South Dakota. The city of Custer, South Dakota, had a small population and one long-distance bus roll in daily. Didn't matter that it was due just south of the town that held the Mount Rushmore monument, Abe Lincoln's civil-rights-championing face and all, the city (and much of the state) still held hostilities against folks who weren't 'local' types. Cameron would be no exception.

~

Old memories faded now, but the feelings they carried stayed pinned to Cameron Mason's heart for quite a while.

The winding road carried Cam and his trusty pickup down the valley road toward his motel hideaway, not far from the Snake River, which cut a convoluted path across the corner of Southeastern Washington State through the little scrappy towns south of Pullman, the only city big enough to be printed on the cheap gas station maps. As he traveled, Cam saw hand-painted signs dotting the landscape; his headlights were too dim to light them up properly. A few were legible, with white backgrounds and some lovely bordered lettering for crisp apples and other fruits and vegetables. The local farms sold at the markets, sure, but most small farms sold locally. Out here, one could practically fill a pantry at the little roadside farmstands littering the state for pocket change. It had a sort of charm that made people stick around sometimes, even farmhands who knew they could make more money in California often made their way in Washington because it was charming in a way.

The Columbia River's connections and tributaries cut their paths through the state in undulating and often breathtaking ways. Cam thought about how his old friend Gabe used to talk about a few childhood trips through the area, how much it had meant to him. Gabe was a good man whose ordeals, about a decade back, had culminated in the capture of a madman who was slaughtering folks in alleyways in New York. Gabe had worked a smidgen for Billy in the years since, but Cam liked to think of it as retirement.

With the moon shining bright in the sky, Cam gripped the steering wheel tightly and shifted his focus to the drive. He'd had enough of old friends this night.

Tick Tock

It was half after too-goddamn-late. Some miles up, Cam came across a familiar numbered county road, taking him North. He had cause to return to his motel, recollect himself, clean up, and hopefully take some rest. He kept his mind off the cabin he'd left behind, the body, and the bones. Miles passed, and he smoked the last three cigarettes to the point where his throat ached and his hands shook from the nicotine. The smoking kept him awake; a long haul was hard for a man who hadn't slept an hour in the past two days. After twenty miles of dead-straight road that had nearly lulled him into dreamland, he came upon the small, sad motel that he'd been calling home for two weeks now.

Practically stumbling out of the truck, Cameron stretched his legs and rolled his head to unkink his neck. The old truck had its share of charm, but it sure wasn't in the seat springs. Tossing the gas can from the front seat into the otherwise empty truck bed made a CLUNK that half-startled him, and he realized it was too late to be fumbling about for the sake of the other guests at the motel. Quietly walking, almost tiptoeing across the gravel, he made his way to room number six. He practically snuck inside for fear of making any jarring sounds. He didn't want to wake anyone and be seen wearing a holstered shotgun and spattered in blood. He went in deftly and cautiously, making sure nobody was waiting to get the jump on him.

Wouldn't be the first time.

The place was quiet, hot. Empty. Catching a glimpse of his reflection in the bathroom mirror, he laughed a bit.

I look like a goddamn cowboy.

He sneered at his reflection and gave it the finger. The sound of the whisky uncorking brought him a sense-memory and soon after, a warm sensation in his mouth. Those cigarettes had his mouth aching for a drink, any drink, and he was set on punishing that sore throat with some old-fashioned Kentucky rye whiskey. He'd said on many an occasion, "The only good things ever to come outta the south were blues and booze." He was damn sure of it. Two shots later, he was almost ready to dig back into the case.

No sleep until you chew on this a bit and let those aspirin kick in, you old goat.

Seated at the table, after spending much of his drive recounting the Custer case, he remembered the story of the little boy who went missing back before he took on this damned case. More specifically, the boy was missing his hands.

"Good Christ, there's… that little boy from the silo, could this be his?" In his disgust, there was a flicker of hope that there might be some answers among all this hurt.

It's the sort of thing any man would rather forget, but that wasn't a luxury for this man, who was wholly dedicated to solving a case, no matter how deep or murky the waters got. He reached into his pocket and withdrew the handkerchief, but simply set it on the table. He'd need a few drinks before he could bring that nasty thing out again.

He stared at the clock on the wall of the motel kitchenette. The hands were white against a black face, unusual and almost beautiful. It was just shy of two-fifty in the morning, and the clock hands were struck in V-shapes that resembled a smile. Moreso, a V-shape that resembled the markings on the tiny artifact he had secured in his handkerchief.

Chrissakes, it's not a letter, it's a time? The idea struck him.

He looked closer at the etchings, some shallow and some deeper. On the table, he saw a pencil peeking out from under the newspaper. He picked it up, flicked the rubber dust off the eraser end. His face scrunched up in disgust as he unwrapped the handkerchief and held the bone to the light, but he persisted. Taking the side of the pencil's lead, he rubbed it slowly across the etchings. The tiny grooves did their job, catching enough lead to burnish their etchings dark against the stark white bone. He could make out four shapes, sort of a V-L-V, and of all four, the most extended etching was vertical.

This is a code, it's a clock!

"Two… Four or five… three?' he said to himself. 'February fifth, maybe fifty-three… is that a four?"

He looked closer at the grooves, now shining silvery under the light, holding up the edge of a newspaper sheet to better gauge the angles. Then, he copied them, much larger, on an envelope from the pile on the table.

"No… It's five-three. Two, five, three."

Cam talked to himself to work out a problem, not just in the truck. In the service, he was teased mercilessly by a few men who knew how self-conscious he was of that little quirk. Yet, here in the silence, this time it felt good to put some voice in the air. The coppery and earthy smell of the blood on his coat he'd draped on his chair, was warming and becoming putrid. But at this moment, Cameron Mason was oblivious to the whole awful scene. All he cared about now was to crack the case. This sick code wasn't proof, but it was evidence for goddamned sure.

Yeah, coincidences happen, but not like this. The date is so close to when the photos of the little boy they found were taken. I remember the images; he looked so stiff, not even scared, with his eyes closed. Goddammit…

Mulling over the possibilities and paying plenty of attention to the rye, this man sat in near silence, listening to the rhythmic sound of the clock ticking its hours away on the wall. He felt a lump in his throat, and he knew what was bothering him.

Closing his eyes, he spoke aloud to his old friend Steve Hardigan. Not the Hardigan lying there unidentifiable tonight, but instead, he talked to the friend he *remembered*. The man whose wedding he had attended joyfully, the man who used to take Cam and Billy and sometimes even Shay on fishing trips, the man who would volunteer at the youth center in town. He spoke of the *idea* of the man, the construct of what he believed his old friend to be.

"I miss you, you bastard. I miss your wife; I miss your eggnog. I knew you'd lost your way, and I'm damn sorry that I let it get this far. Billy, he heard some things, and when he told me what you were into, I didn't want to believe it. To be honest, I still don't, either. What happened to you?' he asked rhetorically, not expecting an answer, 'just give me something to work with? If I can't clear your name, maybe we can still get your soul headed in the right direction. I'm so sorry…"

As the whisky was warming his senses and dropping his guard, Cam's cynicism took hold of the notion of it all.

"The hell does it mean, why would a man who did something so evil need to remember the date?' he questioned the air, 'Just doesn't make sense, no sir."

Almost without looking, he slammed the shot of whiskey and

splashed another into the glass, his thumb over the mouth of the bottle to meter it out. Just now, he wished he weren't alone in this dreary kitchen, hunched over some lost soul's stolen bits. Knocking back the shot, he could feel the fire in his belly becoming an aching in his arms, and he knew he was beyond exhausted. With a solemn and short prayer over the remains, he wrapped it up diligently and placed it on the top of the icebox. It was time to sleep; he was overdue for a few days of rest. Taking the bottle by the neck, he stumbled toward the bed as he downed one last swig. This night, he slept in absolute stillness.

~

Waking after ten, getting out of bed brought an ache in Cam's shoulders and a hollow in his stomach. He cracked open the icebox and swigged the last of his roadside fruit-stand apple juice straight from the bottle as he stood staring at the old coat caked in dried blood. He'd draped it over a chair, but the weight of it pulled it to the ground in a pile overnight. He supposed he was far enough now from the cabin that it wouldn't be suspicious to the maid if he asked her to have it cleaned. After all, he'd checked in as a deer hunter, and that can be messy, handy cover for sometimes less virtuous things.

Cam started the day with a call to the offices of William Bigsby, back in that beautiful old high-rise in Seattle. Billy had bragged about having 'a view and a view,' hinting that what's out the window might be equaled in beauty by the sweet girl taking calls in the front office. This day, she'd answered the phone, only to inform Cameron that "Mr. Bigsby is on the road today, but he's going to leave word for you tomorrow, so be sure to call back in the morning, okay?' and Cam was happy with that.

Two years into this case, Billy hardly went a month without tracking down some witness or uncovering some fudged police report for Cam. Not that Cam had been on the road for the entire two years, but when something came up big enough to warrant travel, Billy would get Cam on the road and set him to the clues. Billy was less apt to do fieldwork, not for some reverence of the boss/employee relationship but for the simple fact that he had no legs.

It was a sad and funny story, one that Billy was happy to tell whenever he had a few too many pints or a strong cup of joe. Pretty much any time, really. The story goes he'd taken a bet against a cousin of his about someday climbing a famous Canadian mountain before departing for the war, and returning from said war with one leg wasn't going to stop him from making good on that bet. Billy was a consummate athlete in his youth, so he decided being one-legged wouldn't hold him back from completing such a 'silly' challenge as *climbing an ice-covered mountain!* Yet upon his championing the summit and besting his (admittedly a bit overweight) cousin, he developed some damnable frostbite on his remaining leg that neither of them could fix on the mountain. By the time he'd returned, it was just in time to save the leg at the knee and put Billy in a wheelchair for the rest of his days. "I hate crutches, can't carry a damn coffee!" he would bark every time someone suggested it. He wasn't the sort to let it slow him down, though. He was a motivated man and a model of self-sufficiency, and Cameron admired that.

Now, Cam sat on the stoop of his motel room while it was still cool enough to collect his memories about the remainder of that South Dakota trip, which had gotten him so personally involved in this case.

Miss Hardigan

September 15th 1955

It was a very pleasant Thursday and merely a three-day drive from home for Cam, but he shook off the idea of heading back. Hardigan was going cold, and so was the trail. Cam dressed keenly and went outside to stretch his legs a bit, where he ruminated with a cigar on the tailgate of his truck for a while. He was a mite sour about being stuck in such a shithole with so few leads to follow, without the safety of the wealth of information Billy would usually provide before sending Cam into any new situation. Billy only had Hardigan as a lead. Of course, Cam knew whatever nefarious shit Hardigan was up to might still be sussed out.

Still gotta call Billy and get him to revisit the case… get more case details about that missing boy, Cam figured. *Work down the chain on the old 'five W's' … Whom, What, Where, When, and the all-important Why. First-day detective work. Simple as can be, old man.*

Puffing his cigar and watching diminutive birds dance around on the telephone pole wire, which hung lazily over the cracked and dusty road, Cam decided on his next move.

I can dig into Hardigan's involvement… small-time, like digging with a spade. Gotta dig slow and quiet, no shovel—just little stupid piles of dirt. Work the ground and hope nobody finds Hardigan.

Another mouth of sweet, oaken smoke.

Yeah, that's the only way. Tread lightly.

The body he left would be damned hard to identify as Hardigan. Cam knew that Hardigan's disappearance would likely be treated as a missing person case and would go nowhere unless someone knew about the cabin or until someone figured it out, like Cam had. He hadn't seen evidence of anyone else residing in the cabin, so with any luck, the scene itself wouldn't be discovered any time soon.

Don't want to be caught on a limb… I gotta pay a visit to the wife. Haven't seen her in a spell… Hope she doesn't mind.

More smoke swirled around his tongue as he worked it out. The cigar was. Getting bitter, oily.

I can just pop in to see her, use my visit as a cover for some poking around town. Keep it quick. She's probably still a… nope, don't even think it, you old cus.

It was mid-morning before Cam left for town. Hardigan lived some forty miles away in a decent suburb with his wife, in a diminutive railroad town with a blue-collar population and plenty of dirt for Cam to dig. The trip wouldn't be arduous, but Cam decided to gear up as he might find himself away from his room for more than a day or two. He puttered the Plymouth over to the gas station and parked at the only pump. A friendly, clean-uniformed attendant came to meet him after lightly jogging across the concrete. The man was clean-shaven, but his hair looked like a blind man had cut it; he might've been assumed a hobo if it weren't for his uniform.

"Check the oil for you?" the man inquired as he neared the car, resting his palm on the fender for a moment.

"Sure, that'd be kind of you," Cam replied, still sitting in his truck. He tipped his hat toward the attendant, who beamed back through the dirty windshield before lifting the hood.

After a quiet moment, the man closed the hood. His face was washed in confusion, nearly scowling, at what he had seen under the hood. Cam drummed his thumbs on the steering wheel, waiting for the attendant. The confused man opened the hood again and set the hood prop so it stayed up high. He leaned over to the side so he could see Cam's face. This was always Cam's favorite part.

"Uh, sir, you know this ain't the right engine?" in a manner that implied he thought Cam might be unaware of what was motivating the rusty truck.

Dressed in tweed and looking clean as a whistle, Cameron swung open his driver's door and stepped one foot out as he leaned over the roof of the truck casually. "Seems not." The attendant looked back toward the engine, then again at Cam. "Ain't this one of them new Chryslers though? A Hemi-head?"

Cam chuckled a bit. "Yessir, good eye!"

A pursed frown creased the attendant's chin as he blurted out, "But

…um …*why*?"

"Suppose I needed a bit more get-up-and-go?"

The confusing engine in question was a brand-new Chrysler Hemi Firepower V8, glinting in the midday sun, its flecked gold-painted block and chromed valve covers gleaming like a diamond in a dog turd. Three hundred and thirty-one cubic inches of rumbling power hiding in the vehicular equivalent of a dented wheelbarrow. Its spark plugs lined up in a row down the center of each brilliant, shiny valve cover, nearly grazing the narrow hood panels of the old truck. A matching bright-gold cylindrical air filter adorning the carburetor sucked in enough breath to let the monster of a power plant spit fire out the tailpipes, or damn near it. This particular type of engine was recently quite famous for both winning races and powering air-raid sirens all across the nation. It was heavily publicized in magazines like Popular Mechanics, as well as in TV ads that Chrysler paid thousands of dollars to run in prime time. Still, it was a damned odd sight under the hood of any but the newest and most luxurious Chryslers and DeSotos.

"I ain't never seen one, honestly. Didn't figure I'd see one under the hood of a… uh… *work* truck, y'know." His politeness was refreshing. Cam knew luxury cars were uncommon in rural areas and figured he'd tell the man the story of how such an out-of-place drivetrain ended up there.

"I know she looks like a boot full of piss, funny story there… I blew a head gasket on that miserly Chrysler flathead on a long haul up a steep grade, towing a shitty tin boat. We were trying to make time getting up the grapevine out of Los Angeles and ended up nearly crawling back to a tow yard. Blowin' smoke and water out the whole time! Couldn't stand to lose the truck since I bought her new, had a friend back home keep her through the war. It was all I had to come home to."

The attendant chimed in, "You served, huh?"

Cam nodded and lifted his dog tags from under his shirt and tie.

"Yes, sir, I put in my time… anyway, thanks to the yellow pages, I found a wrecker yard down in LA, not far from where I was. When I pulled up, I swear the old codger laughed at my truck. Hurt my feelings! I showed him the lint in my wallet but offered him half my fishing haul to let me pull a flathead six-cylinder outta the yard. Dime a dozen."

"And you pulled *this*?"

His incredulity was warranted, and it goaded Cameron on.

"Come to find some starlet had rolled her '53, with that very engine, and the car was a total loss, see, but the guts were just fine! Old boy had been planning on saving it, but when they delivered him a folded-up flag instead of his son, well… seems his plans changed."

"My brother didn't come back, neither."

A somber beat was shared between them, while crows cawed from the field adjacent. It was a mournful song.

"Sorry for that, my friend. Too many lost, good cause or not. Well, this mechanic, I gave him a box of Cubans I had picked up in Mexicali and shared a few of my stories… all the while, he dropped her frame and welded this big, beautifully insane motor under the hood. Damn genius, my new pal Randall. I've got to see him again soon, come to think of it. Pretty fine job he did, yeah?"

The story had enthralled the mechanic, and he offered a wistful half-smile. He leaned on the radiator. "Well, I know enough to keep her purring, you don't mind if I take a bit and check your timing and your plugs and such? Don't see many of these 'round here."

Cameron patted him on the shoulder. "Sir, I'd appreciate it more than I can say. I'll head in and wash up a bit, yeah?" The attendant was already back under the hood and stretched an arm out with a 'thumbs up.'

"Get yerself a coffee, gonna be a few ticks!"

Cam took the time to step away toward the service office, where he found a still-steaming pot of coffee on the table near the chairs reserved for folks having their vehicles serviced. It was a polite gesture he wasn't going to overlook, and so he filled one of the neatly stacked small paper cups to the brim with the dark caramel-colored roast. He'd not been a coffee drinker much in his youth, but now, reaching his fifties, a cup of coffee could give him a bit more reason to find his way out of bed. Sauntering back to the fuel pumps and careful to avoid spilling any of the brew, he saw the mechanic just finishing up checking his maintenance checklist. The man was grinning, clearly a car nut and someone who appreciated a little horsepower.

"All set, sir, everything's now looking fine and right as rain. If you're meaning to fill your tank, the service is on the house. Deal?"

Cam looked down at the small pile of spark plugs on the floor and knew he was getting a fine deal. "Tell you what, this is some damn good coffee. Go ahead and fill those jerry cans up, too, and use the high-test!"

He made a cheers motion with the cup, "I'm sure glad I brought her by."

"You bet! It's my place, I'm Larry. Been here thirty years, come next year. You feel free to come through any time!"

Larry was quick to fill the tank and the fuel cans and turned back to ask Cam, "No offense, really, but what do you need such a monster of a motor for in this old farm truck? Like driving Frankenstein's monster! Are you one of those hot-rodders I've seen in the movies?"

Cam laughed and almost spat out a bit of coffee. "Oh no, sometimes I just want to go a bit faster than the next guy."

Larry nodded again and finished topping off the jerry cans. Cam paid him and tipped a whole dollar, along with a good, long handshake, before heading up the road.

Startin' to like it up here, Gabe. Your dreamland, the 'Pacific Northwest'… maybe I get it… he sighed contentedly before striking up another smoke.

~

After an hour of ambling over lovely roads and bombing through valleys with windows rolled down to let in the cool fall air, Cam reached the manicured lawns and smoothly paved streets of the suburb where Hardigan and his beautiful wife had made a home some years back. He parked two blocks shy of Hardigan's house on the corner of a side street that had a half-dozen neatly painted houses, each with lush green lawns. In his rearview, Cam saw the mountains looming over the town in a picturesque little vignette.

Not wanting to worry about his nerves, Cam had reached under the seat and spent a few minutes lightening the flask he kept tucked away. He had to be mentally ready to greet Caroline Hardigan and pretend as though he hadn't just ended the life of her husband, not twenty hours prior. No matter how righteous Cameron was, no matter what good reason he had for his actions, sitting here about to walk into the man's home? The guilt and nerves had his hands jittery and his guts in a vice.

Cameron hadn't felt such a weight in some time. He knew exactly the last time he was so nerve-wracked, standing over the closed casket of his daughter about twenty years ago. The lump in his throat was washed down with another swig, and the only reassurance he could give himself.

Simmer down, Cam… that was another man, another life. Ain't your fault, ain't your burden.

He was nearly ready to step out of his truck when Caroline Hardigan came bounding out of her front door.

"Ah, shit!" He spilled a little booze on his lap as he slumped low into the seat and watched.

She looked just as he remembered from the silver-framed wedding photo Cam had at home on his mantle. Bittersweet memories came flooding back, no matter how hard he fought. The photo, the way he felt that day. The picture was gleeful and candid. He'd been playfully holding up a corner of her flowing train in jest, with her making a theatric 'shocked' face and a nearby Steve Hardigan feigning a heart attack over the scene. It looked like a silly advertisement from a cheeky magazine.

That was a beautiful goddamn wedding. Gorgeous bride, and a pillar of a groom… Why'd you go and muck it all up, Steve? You dumb sonofabitch…

Caroline Hardigan was wearing a bright blue dress and a white summer hat. Her fair skin glowed in the sun; she turned back with a twirl to wait for a man exiting the house just behind her. Cam's heart nearly skipped a beat as he recognized the man to be one of the state troopers he'd seen with Steven Hardigan in a photo. He saw that the man was James Corker, another trooper. Cam could see his red nose from a distance and was positive this was the man he'd been seeking at the cabin the night prior.

Cam withdrew Billy's file from under the passenger seat, carefully lifting a photo from under a paper clip. In the photo were three state troopers standing in front of a highway car, all matching uniforms and each man holding their hat over their heart. Hardigan was standing tall in the middle, a man named Corker to Hardigan's left and an unknown trooper to his right. That photo was what led Cam to the cabin, owing to a keen-eyed truck stop waitress in the tiny town of Colton, an hour down the highway from Pullman. Cam had been looking for Corker that night, but Hardigan was never Cam's target. Cam had been intentionally avoiding Hardigan so as not to sour the case—just an unfortunate turn of events.

Are you willing to take out another crooked cop, Cam? He thought. Cameron was no stranger to bending or breaking laws in the name of enforcing true justice. "Laws protect men in power; oftentimes, true justice means taking that power away irrespective of the law." A lecturer had suggested that on many occasions during Cam's college studies before the war, often in reference to some political coup involving a deposed dictator. Cam had loved the idea of it, the service of *true* justice.

If Corker's a shitheel and Steve was too, wonder if... how... Caroline's wrapped up in it?

Worry gave way to skepticism as Cam realized Caroline and James were smiling and chatting, looking familiar and pleasant. Corker looked like a regular sort, not a man sneaking around abducting children. Cam's mind was whirring with the details of the case, and he no longer felt those jitters about seeing Caroline. His fists gripped the steering wheel tightly, and he felt a thump in his veins. Heat. The warmth of confidence, of excitement. Forward movement on the case. He set aside the idea of following Corker, knowing the man was a local and wouldn't be hard to find. Still waving to Caroline, Corker got into a brown Studebaker and rolled off down the road.

Two things caught Cam's attention. First, he noticed Corker adjusting his belt and tucking his shirt, which was out of place. Then, he looked at Caroline and noted she was very subtly adjusting her garters and slip skirt.

"Oh, you sly motherfucker, Jimmy Corker," he whispered.

He just *knew* the two had just been involved in something seedy. He knew he might later leverage this observation to extract information from Caroline, even if it made him feel like scum.

I'm gonna get you, Jimmy.

He sprang out of the truck and casually strolled to the house where Caroline was still on the lawn, watching Corker drive down the road. She had her arms crossed and was wavering in place as though she'd been drinking.

"Caroline!' Cam shouted when he was a lawn away, 'Caroline, I would know your ivory bones anywhere!" She spun around, and a flash of confusion on her face quickly melted into cheer.

"Cameron!' she shouted back as she threw her arms up in excitement, 'Cameron, you dog! I can NOT believe you're here, on my doorstep! Where have you *been*? Where's your old truck?"

She scanned the street. Anyone who knew Cam knew he'd likely be buried in that truck. "Is that you parked way down yonder?"

He rushed up and hugged her tightly. She returned the hug like a lifelong friend. "Yes, ma'am, it is! I had your address a bit mixed up, but I found you anyway!" Their embrace was tight and friendly. He could smell the gin on her breath, nearly seeping from her pores.

Must have been quite a morning… or quite a long night.

She released her hug and stepped back to size him up. "That's fate, isn't it? We were meant to meet again, you know. I haven't seen you in what, maybe a half dozen years? You're looking lean and mean as ever, Cam."

He stepped back and clasped her hands like a gentleman courter. "Shit, just about a dozen. I was passing west heading to Seattle, thought I'd take a detour and say hello. I've been missing you and Steve; I hoped I'd catch up with you all. Lost the number a while back, and had some bad luck for a while. But enough about me, how are you? Where's the old man?"

His affection for her was genuine, and she lapped it up. The pliability of a person full of romance and gin was nothing short of surprising. He knew he couldn't judge her for being a little lush. Life was hard, always the needling of good hurt and bad hurt… a little vice eased it either way. Moreso, he felt like shit for asking after Steve, but he had to play the role.

"Oh, he's been out a few days on some hunting trip. Took the week, in fact. You aren't going to catch him this trip… no bother. Why don't you come inside for a cold drink, and let's catch up? Have you got the time?"

He looked at his bare right wrist, checking an imaginary watch, "Looks like I got *plenty.*"

She led him by the hand into the house. Just inside the threshold, she took off her hat and shoes and pushed him onto a couch in a playful manner. Cam saw a bit of white residue on the table and immediately knew it had been one *hell* of a night for her and Jimmy Corker.

"Looks like I missed the party!' he commented, as she walked to the kitchen. 'You sure have a nice place here, you guys have been doing really well. I'm happy for you." He scanned the room as he talked.

Her voice rang back from the kitchen, "Just a bit of entertaining. Of course, I miss Steve when he's gone, and he is gone a whole lot these days…"

Her voice trailed off a bit before she stepped back in with some lemonade on a lovely silver tray. Setting the tray down, she sat next to Cam with her hip right up against his.

"You look like you could use something stiff, Cam."

Caroline, in another life, I might have said the same to you…

He scooted over a bit, regaining some small space between their bodies. "I think I'm good so with lemonade, little lady, but who knows how the day's gonna go.' He winked at her. It was clear that he had the goods to interrogate her a bit without being too obvious. 'So Steve's out camping? Er, hunting?"

She looked down a bit. "Yeah, he's on a few trips every month now. He has a cabin he shares with his friends, but won't invite me. Says it's *for the boys*. Won't take me even when I pout!" and she stuck out her lower lip as an example.

"He's a dummy. I'd take you to all sorts of lovely places if it were my place to do that. This lemonade looks mighty cold!" and he took a gulp that emptied half the glass.

She smiled and proclaimed, "It's frozen! I buy it at the grocer in a can! Just add water. Or, you know, whatever." She motioned toward the considerable dry bar across the living room.

He glanced over the gleaming bottles as she laid her hand on his thigh. He chose to ignore it for the time being.

"Saw your pal heading out, looked almost like a guy Steve said he worked with. Jimmy *something*…" and with that, his interrogation had begun.

He turned back to her, and she was staring intently at him. "Cam, you have such beautiful eyes. Where did you get those eyes?"

If he weren't so richly complexioned, she might have caught him blushing a bit. "My mother was half-Italian, a lovely woman. My old man was a bear, no beauty, just brawn. I know I got all my looks from my mother!"

She laughed loudly. He clinked their glasses and finished the lemonade, waggling the glass to imply he'd like more. She was a dutiful host and sprang up to refill his glass. From this angle, as she walked toward the kitchen, Cam felt a pang of guilt at his primal instincts. He also saw just why Corker had been so inclined to visit his friend & coworker's wife outside of everyday social graces. Ignoring the instincts, Cam leaned back into the plush couch and focused on the mission. He needed to probe more about Steve's affairs.

"What's been going on with Steve, then? He hasn't rung me up in a year or two. A bit sad about that, Caroline. I know you're a busy pair…"

She returned from the kitchen with lemonade that was now clearly a good portion of gin, judging by the washed-out color of it. She sat down, looking a bit flustered. "He's been too busy for *both* of us, Cam."

She swigged her drink and slumped her shoulders, gazing into her glass after a long sigh.

"Remember that day? The wedding? It was amazing, so perfect. He was so fit and happy, and I was…' she thought for a moment, 'I was just so hopeful. I never met a man like that back home, and well, he certainly gave me a lot more attention when I was young. You know, we met when I was fourteen?"

Cam held his tongue on his opinions. "Yeah, I recall. You were a lovely bride, eighteen years old, right?"

She took a swig and wistfully replied, "Seventeen. He made me lie to the preacher for the appearances and all."

"Caroline, I've known that man for a long time. We played football together in high school. Sometimes he just needs a little time… or a little talkin' to. I know we ain't best friends, you and I, but I do care about you. I want you both happy and healthy, and you don't really look either…' He clasped her hand again, 'Any chance you know how I might get hold of him while I'm in town? I could try and talk a bit of sense into him."

She began to cry and picked up a cocktail napkin to dry her eyes. "Not much sense left in that man, Cam. He doesn't want me anyway."

His curiosity overshadowed his empathy. "Now what are you talking about, Caroline? What man wouldn't want a girl like you?"

"He doesn't want me, he wants someone younger. I'm thirty-two years old now, and I'm all washed up, Cam. He was talking up girls at the bar, trying to get somewhere. He'd even taken off his ring and secreted it away! I only know because the owner of that bar and I go to church on Sundays, and that old man is one of the decent ones. He told me the truth, Cam. Steve's been out there catting around and I'm stuck here, the housewife of the god-damned *year*!' She threw her glass across the room, where it bounced off a sofa without shattering. The futility of it seemed to madden her. 'I'm *sick* of it, Cam. Honest, I'm just lonely and sick of it! He treats me like property!" She was now fully bawling into that wet little napkin.

Cam leaned over and hugged her tightly. "Sweet girl, *no*. Don't go down that road. You've got a lot to offer. Any man with his marbles could see that… and I think you know you got plenty of options. So why not make some changes? Go back to Missouri, see your mom and pop, and see where they ended up. They gotta be missing you anyway!" His words were genuine, and she hugged him back for a long time while her crying subsided.

"Cam, you're right. I just need to get away for a while, just get my head straight. You really think he'd let me go for a while?"

The scene of the last time he saw Steve Hardigan crept into the little projector in Cam's head. With his eyes closed, he simply responded, "I know he would."

They embraced for a while longer. Cam silently choked with guilt over what he had been forced to do, how he'd likely ruined what was left of this little lady's happy life. She was all broken up about Steve, and she'd *never* get closure on that. He'd broken her heart and disappeared.

Guilt-ridden, Cam sat up and gripped her shoulders as she wiped away tears that had somewhat spilled down onto her alabaster cleavage and blue dress. "Caroline, I'm going to do two things. Firstly, I'm giving you bus fare and some travel money. You're gonna give your parents a visit and take some time away from this place. You need that.' He looked toward the half-drank dry bar and the evidence of lines of cocaine on the table. 'Nextly, I'm going to track down Steve and talk with him about all this. You just pack up and leave a note, and I'll bear the brunt of whatever happens when he gets the news, okay? I'm gonna handle this so you can get some time to yourself. Get your heart right, and your head too if you're able." He motioned to the cocaine on the table.

The talk of freedom seemed to bring her relief. She nodded, drying more tears. She quietly got up and went to the kitchen for a moment, returning with two glasses of water. Sitting down again, across from him on a separate couch, she quietly asked, "You promise not to tell him about me and James? I don't want to get that man in trouble. He's been nothing but kind to me; in fact, he seems to dislike my husband quite a bit. I feel like he's been sticking around just for me. Leave him out of all this, okay?"

Cam took the water and had a deep drink. "I *promise*, little lady." He meant it, but in a way she would never understand.

"Tell me you'll do one more thing, then. Okay?" Cam asked, patting her on the knee. She shook her head up and down mildly, trying to dry her eyes.

"Just leave with what you can't leave behind, and don't turn back. Don't look back at all, just go home and wait for him. Until he comes around and makes this right, you just live your life, okay?" He hoped she understood what he meant.

I'll circle back in a few months and break the news, get the house settled, and such. She needs this right now.

"If I don't see him again, I'd be okay with that, Cam. Honest. He's not a good man like you."

Cam's guilt had slid away a bit, but with her compliment, it came right back in a knot under his Adam's apple. He stood up and reached into his wallet. Sifting through his modest road money, he withdrew enough to get her back home safe and fed. He was aware of the irony that a good bit of it had been drawn from her dead husband's wallet. He folded the bills and placed them in her hand, clasping it shut.

She looked at her palm. "It's a lot. I don't need that much, Cam."

He closed his eyes and shook his head sternly. "You take it, I'll get mine back from Steve when I tan his rear for being so bad to you. Now go, pack. Leave him a short note and don't look back, okay, Caroline? You'll hear from him, or you'll hear from me. I know how to find your folks."

She smiled a bit. "I've gotta get at this… You take care of yourself, Cam. I don't know if I'd have the guts to do this if you weren't pushing me." She walked him to the door, and they exchanged pleasantries like the last half hour hadn't happened. She sent him off with a soft kiss on the cheek, and yet again, this woman had Cameron Mason blushing.

Why's it gotta be so complicated…

Trudging back to his truck, he felt a wave of both relief and remorse. He hoped that her slide into sin and debauchery had been abated as long as she got on that damn bus. Cam felt in no mood to dig today, so he left town with a heavy heart and drove home, trying to count the falling leaves, trying to keep his mind off it all for a while.

When he arrived back at the motel, it was getting toward dusk, and the air was warm and humid. Cam stripped to his shorts and undershirt in the room to do some Army-style exercises using the furniture and a heavy jug of water. He hadn't exercised much in the last few months, but he kept a good build and a flat stomach, and that was a point of pride for him. After his workout, he sat on the edge of the bed and timed his heart rate as he measured his breaths. He could feel the blood in his limbs washing away stiffness in his fingers. The place smelled of sweat and aftershave, but he was too tired to do more than open a window pane.

The red glow of the 'vacancy' sign shone through curtains flowing in the shifting night air. Grunting as he stood, Cam showered before he realized he'd not yet eaten. Finding the small café next to the motel still open was quite a relief. He ordered a ham sandwich and a buttered

potato to take back to his room, eating it over the sink like a bum.
Get some sleep, old man. You're gonna feel better tomorrow.

The Boss

Friday, September 16th

The cracked window he'd left open had let a chill into the room that set him shivering as he got out of bed. The heat had been turned off, and Cameron had slept on top of the bed, disturbing the bedding only a bit. After that exercise, he'd felt like a furnace the night before. With dawn came, as always, the intermittent sound of trucks sweeping past on the narrow road and the clatter of his room neighbors packing hastily to get back on the road, as most folks at the Motor Inn were one-night-stay travelers. Cam woke with a splash of water on his face and a couple of aspirin. He regretted drinking the prior day, but only for the foolishness of drinking on an empty stomach.

Cam took a walk to the dusty street corner where a phone booth gleamed in the sun. He dialed up Billy Bigsby just as he'd been instructed to do by that man's sweet receptionist the morning prior. With a cigarette hanging out of his left hand, Cam plunked some nickels into the phone and dialed a number he'd memorized better than his own. One and a half rings later, the lovely young lady on the other end greeted him. She had been awaiting his call. Apparently, so was Bigsby. She transferred Cameron with haste. Billy picked up in a half ring.

"Cam? What's the good word, pal?"

Cam let out a sigh and responded with the truth. "Well, Billy, it's good and bad. Should I start from the top?" Billy simply responded with "mmm-hmmm" from his mouthful of what Cam guessed was coffee. "Okay, then. Get a pen if you need one." Cam gave him a moment to shuffle around for a pen and paper. Billy didn't need the moment; he just grunted as if to say 'Go ahead'. Billy had a penchant for taking notes, a quirk Cam appreciated about the man.

Fastidious as always. Tedious, too. In a good way. That's what Shay called 'im…

"Okay, Billy. It's a mess. So, I get to the little pit stop you sent me to, that little burger stop in Uniontown. Went in with open eyes and came across your man's contact. He pointed me to the same place you did, the Hall of Records. Came out with quite a few names; I've already sent you an envelope with those files so that you can attach them. Simple stuff, just the local notes on the county and state missing persons' reports. Not much there, we didn't expect much."

Billy sighed, "We sure didn't. Still, I'm looking at the file and I see a couple of lists with names here. Scrambled as usual," He took another sip.

"I'll get to that. I dug into the little coincidence you brought up—the movement of similar cases from South Dakota to Washington and into Northern Oregon this past year. I came up with seven cases in twenty-five months, Billy. Every one of them filed, every one of them unsolved. You read the cases, and all the work was done right. Files are thin, and interviews are short. As you expected, none of them came up with any leads or motivation, just some damn vanished kids. That is, except for one file."

"Oh yeah? Which?" Billy sounded like he was leaning into the phone. Cam took a drag before continuing.

"Back to the Chambers case, Billy. Before he died, Chambers told me he'd found the cops that picked up his little girl, said he knew who they were, and then boom… they ended up dead the day after he ran crying to the sheriff. When I went back to Custer a few weeks later, I got stonewalled over all of it. I thought for a while that the sheriff *himself* might've been part of all of this muck, but it swerved hard left on me."

"How so? Nice to hear we're still on that lead after two years…" the scribbling in his notebooks whispered across the warm tones of the bell telephone lines.

Cam continued, with emphasis. "The old man, that sheriff, he sang like a bird when someone from the feds called him up… *someone* who happened to know the right questions to ask." Cam was implying it was himself calling, and Billy knew it. They'd been doing phone impersonation interrogation tactics for years, and it had gotten them farther than any strong-arm or wiretapping could have. Everyone wants to impress the higher-ups, and there's *always* someone higher up.

"Once I got him talking, it was like a Catholic confession. He spilled to me how Chambers came to him with some silly story about cops carrying off kids, but it seems Chambers had names. Specifically, Ivers and McMaster. Two long-time troopers who had been working in the Dakotas for years. Anyway, the Sheriff said that he had mentioned it at a poker game that night. Next day, the word is that those troopers ended up in a real nasty wreck that claimed both their lives."

"Some wreck…" Billy chimed in.

"Smelled like a cover-up, and the cherry on top? That sheriff asked me for *protection!*"

Bigsby retorted, "Well, Mister Federal Bureau, did you promise him any?"

Cam just laughed into the handset. "Seriously, he sounded spooked. All I could do was offer to look into it. Guess what he gave me?"

"I hate guessing, Cam." More writing scratches in the background.

"He gave me *names*. All the big shots playin' poker with him that night."

"I see. And you sent me that list, too?"

"Billy, you know I did. Last name on the blue list." Billy was holding a small blue scrap of paper with eight names arranged in a column, each listing only the first and last name. He compared it to another piece of paper, a key that the two had devised. The first and last names were scrambled, based on the month and year. It was simple for Billy to rearrange the first and last names into their correct places, but anyone who happened across the list without the key might as well be pointing at random names in the phone book.

"Okay, Billy, last name on your list there. That old boy, he's the one I'm squarely lookin' at now."

Billy was quiet for a moment. "But, that's… isn't that the…?"

"Yessir, it is. The District Attorney who oversaw the missing person cases in South Dakota, and found jack-diddly for leads. Oh, and take one guess who just moved to Washington in the past couple of years? New career and all."

"Goddammit, Cam. You sure know how to root out some bullshit, don't you?"

Cam covered the phone as he had a good laugh at Billy's rare use of foul language. "Sure do. You pay me to, don't you? So here's the deal. I figured out who that cat's social circle was with a bit of calling around. Turns out, he was in a hunting club with a few guys, including an old pal of mine from California, back before I joined up. So I tracked down a few of them, all of 'em thinking they had some judge on the line. A couple of them pointed me toward the DA, but one name on the list I didn't touch just yet."

Billy interjected, "Your old friend. Hardy? No… Hardigan. Am I right?"

Cam shot back, "You're exactly right. Steve Hardigan. The man I thought would be a good friend to have behind a badge. I had to be sure he was part of it, or *damn* sure he wasn't."

Clicking his tongue, Billy grumbled a guttural 'hmmmmmmph' and paused to hear the news, good or bad. From his interjection, he seemed to foresee that it was bad.

"Yeah. Shame is, he *was*. Somehow. Flashed a pic of Steve and his pals around, came up with a handful of leads. I thought I was following his pal Corker, another trooper, to someplace good and nowhere. It went left, Billy. Steve Hardigan tried to take me down. Christ, I'm tellin' you he was a different man than I knew, different altogether. Must have been deep in it."

"And where's the Hardy Boy now?"

"Ah… yeah. That's the hard left turn. Steve made a bad choice for both of us, but things landed in my favor. I'll catch you up on those details off the wires."

They would talk cases and leads all day, but Billy always had a policy of never discussing the real heavy stuff or anything criminal over the phone. His ties to the Bureau had Billy ever-cautious that there might be somebody listening in at any given time. "It's only paranoia if they aren't out to get you!" he'd quip, and his boys understood.

"So sounds like you have a couple more leads to, uh… run down before you get to the top?"

"Sure do, sir. I'll do the diligence, as always. But, I'm gonna need some time off after this one. A real break, Billy."

"Okay, Cam. Anything. You know best, I'm just the operator. Just keep me posted, and I'll run some names myself. Check back in a couple of days?"

"Sure thing, Billy. Be good." Cam ended the phone call, lighting a cigarette with a cupped hand and wearing a furrowed, frustrated scowl.

He knew Billy would run the names on the list, sure, but his connections and investigators had a habit of finding threads most men might not see. Subversive things, old associations, and older debts were brought to light in many a case that Billy Bigsby had worked. He had stopped major crimes, shed light on fraud, and even ended a minor Russian incursion onto American soil. Work to be proud of, whether or not the world ever knew of it. It was a fantastic thing, Cam had joked to himself, *how this desk jockey with no legs could do so much damn legwork.*

Still, Cam had no idea why Billy was grinding so hard on a case nobody was paying for. As far as Cam knew, Billy hadn't found another client in the case since Paul Chambers. No matter, Cameron Mason would march on and find a way through the case like always. The least he could do, after he might have been the cause of Chambers losing his life to a forgery of a suicide. Billy had deep enough pockets, and Cam knew Billy might just care more about the truth than the red ink.

Regardless, it was time to track down the new lead: Trooper Jimmy Corker, the skinniest gigolo Cameron had seen this side of Texas. The idea of that red-nosed featherweight making headway with a beauty like Caroline, Cam shook his head at the thought.

After taking a final drag and heeling the butt into the asphalt, the slightly bedraggled man trudged back toward the Motor Inn to gear up. It could be a long couple of days figuring out the schedule of this homewrecking cus, never mind the likely need for a stern interrogation.

Snatched

Friday, September 16th

Three hours later, Cameron had arrived in town dressed arguably like a farmhand in his denim and flannel, staking out the local hole-in-the-wall State Trooper station from a dirty little bar across the street. He'd noted the brown Studebaker in the back lot on a walk-around and knew it might be a good number of hours before he saw any man's hide needing tanning. So, he sat patiently in a window booth with a cola and waited. He'd tipped well enough to buy him a lack of disruption.

Hours passed as he ticked away the methods of questioning he'd use on his target. He intended to work through the investigation without further unnecessary bloodshed, but to do so, he would need to be a very careful jailor. Once he took this gangly prick Corker captive, it would be a tough job not to be harsh with him. That is, of course, unless it was certain Corker wasn't directly involved. If he was? Cam resolved to take a more heavy-handed approach. As he swirled the two paltry remaining ice cubes around the cheap plastic cup left behind by the cola he'd overpaid for, he thought about some of the dirty tricks Uncle Sam had taught him for extracting information from folks (mostly Germans) in the decades prior. There were several shockingly different levels of interrogation in which he was both trained and well-experienced. His preference was a simple blindfold-and-spook tactic, but that was meant for civilians and children. Recalling the words of his staff Sergeant, some five years into his service, "men can take a beatin' longer and meaner because a grown man better understands the consequences that can come with surviving," which proved to be true most of the time.

The next level of interrogation often involved a mild application of brass knuckles or a fistful of lead pipe, and some thick tape to minimize the mess. Above that, some typical workbench implements, alongside a lead-acid battery. Above even *that*, well... Cam did not need to think about the *heavy* stuff just yet. Nevertheless, Corker might be at the root of this whole mess. If that were the case? He'd need a bedside priest with a strong constitution by the time Cam was finished with him.

Did that make Cam a bad person? He had been told a hundred times that it was a *necessary* evil. He was simply someone's right hand, and Cam stayed on the good side of justice if it meant turning down work or stopping a case cold. Not every interrogation was righteous, meaning oftentimes he'd have to make a call back to Seattle to inform his boss of such a finding. In those cases, Billy would simply find "nothing of use" for the client, occasionally stonewalling them with masterful bullshittery and fake leads for them to chase off the meter. Billy would do his best to a point, considering a good quarter or third of their contract work was handed down from some bureau or agency with a D.C. Address. It wasn't always labeled as such, but they *knew*. Billy had too many visitors with dark suits and black briefcases.

He'd offered Billy Bigsby his thoughts on the matter once. "It's like the damn Mafia Billy, but instead of some old Italian? It's a blue-suited politician in the back of a stretch Cadillac. Bet the government ain't gonna use contractors like you forever, someday they'll be so dirty they'll just send their boys and you'll be outta business."

"Cam, on that day? On *that* day, we retire to a porch somewhere and smoke some of those cigars you're always toting around. We'll ring up the boys and make a soiree of it. I can't work forever, sure, but maybe I can't be the one to call it quits. Time will tell!"

The sleuth's cola was fully warm now, and he had no stomach for the last bit of it. The sun was setting soon, and he'd need a keen eye for moving on Corker, so he bought a cheap beer and nursed it for nearly an hour this time. Just as his patience was growing short, Cam's target strutted out of the side door of the local station in the same suit he'd had on the prior day. It was disheveled, and his gait informed Cam the man was either drunk or damn tired.

"Guess it doesn't pay to be out late catting around, pal... Caroline could do better, anyway," he whispered to nobody as he slid out of the booth. Minutes later, he was tooling down a few narrow roads with his eye on the ruby-red oval taillights of the old Studebaker sedan. The going was slow, and he correctly figured the man had opted for the cheap six-cylinder flathead as the hills took the little brown car a bit of work to surmount. You could hear the exhaust note sputter before Corker would downshift to second gear to amble over the roads. Rural Washington's hill-laden countryside was no place for a gutless grocery-getter if you wanted to outrun someone.

The slow pace of the drive helped Cam mull over the questions he had for this unfortunate, oblivious man slowly loping down the road just ahead. A blinker activated; Corker was turning down a gravel road to what looked like a small private property nestled in the trees. It correlated with the county road address in Corker's phone book entry, which Cam had looked up in the bar's yellow pages. Cam watched the Studebaker turn off the country road, but to ensure Corker was unaware of his tail, Cam continued down the road a good half-mile before turning around to get closer.

As Cam approached the driveway, he parked the '37 up around a curve where it could not be seen from the house. He cut the engine and hopped out, grabbing his gloves and a roll of tape from the bed of the truck. Calmly striding across the road, he made his way into the woods that surrounded Corker's place. With his hat brim low and his collar flipped up, he snuck around the back of the property, keeping an eye on the house. A modest yellow cottage-style home, and, judging by the windows at ground level, a brick basement, which was uncommon for this area. A stroke of luck! One light could be seen from outside the house, in the kitchen. Corker could be heard washing dishes and whistling the opening song of 'Dragnet'. Cam was dead-silent in his approach, but nearly let out a chortle at the irony of it.

He could see Corker walk out of the room, so Cam took this moment to sneak across the patchy lawn toward the back of the house. Now, he crouched under the windowsill of the kitchen and waited. His patience wore thin as minutes passed, and his knees started to ache; he was as relieved as could be to hear a toilet flush. Hard-soled shoes audibly shuffled back into the kitchen, and the man gathered up what Cam assumed was an early dinner, taking it into another room and clicking the light as he left the kitchen. A few moments of quiet hung in the air before the faint sound of a radio could be heard.

O-Kay, mister Corker. Settle in and doze off like a good boy.

Still avoiding the noisy crackle of sticks and leaves, Cam crept around the right side of the home and stopped under the next windowsill. He reached into his back pocket and pulled out a drugstore makeup mirror. This little instrument was one of his most effective tools in subterfuge; on many occasions, it allowed him to check in windows and around corners where he'd have otherwise been spotted.

The first window was a dark room; *all clear,* he assured himself. He half-crawled to the next window, hat held in one hand and mirror in the other. Judging by its smaller size, higher placement, and frosted glass, Cam knew this was the bathroom where Corker had already finished his business, so Cam proceeded. The third window was the jackpot. Lace curtains let him clearly see Corker leaning back in a large armchair, his arms casually folded behind his head, with the radio playing some brassy tunes.

Cam held steady and monitored Corker for a minute or more, seeing no movement. He crept back a foot and stepped away from the window, letting him rest his aching knees from the crouching. Using the mirror, he peeked at the edge of the window again. The man was dead-still; either relaxing or asleep, so Cam knew it was a good time to make his move. He noted Corker was still wearing his shoes; he'd be heard if he walked on the plank wood floors as Cam snuck into the house.

Perfect. Almost too easy.

Slowly, silently, Cameron Mason slipped the mirror into his pocket and shuffled toward the back door, which led into the kitchen. The screen door was locked, so Cam simply cut a slit into the thin screen and reached in to unlock the little metal J-hook. Another stroke of luck; the inner doorknob was also unlocked. Cam walked right into the kitchen as though he belonged there. The kitchen was dark, but just enough moonlight shone in that Cam could see the basement door, facing toward the back door. It was slightly ajar, and the basement stairs started just inside the doorframe. Cam had put away his knife and pulled his hat back on his head.

If he were caught, he could simply play dumb and claim he'd been lost in the woods and was looking for a telephone. Such an excuse had worked in a similar investigation the year before. In fact, Cam almost smirked now at the thought of bringing out the old "play dumb" routine again. They thought he was a waiter, just another colored man walking around the service hallway of a hotel. That was the night he recovered a stolen painting worth more than a dealership full of shiny new Hudsons.

Dumb sonsofbitches never suspected a thing...

Now, as he stealthily tiptoed into the hallway and toward Corker's living room, he heard the faint sound of snoring. Arriving in the living room behind the recliner, Cam's lanky frame cast a shadow behind him across a wall of dusty photos and knick-knacks on little hooks. He loomed over Corker, still dozing, and took two slow breaths. A half-eaten tray of reheated frozen dinner sat cold on a folding tray next to the chair. It smelled of pepper and pork fat.

You're gonna hate this, Jimmy. Hope you enjoyed that meal. Dunno how you could, though—nasty shit.

Deftly, he slipped on a pair of cowhide gloves, which gave him a grip like a vice and kept him from getting marks and nicks in a scuffle. From his back pockets, he withdrew a drawstring potato sack and a roll of heavy tape. He slowly peeled two strips of tape off the roll and stuck them to his thigh, stuffing the roll back into his pocket before stepping closer. Steadying himself, Cam placed his feet shoulder-width apart and leaned forward in a boxer's stance; he'd need to be fast and sure-footed to ensure the capture went smoothly. One long, slow breath in, then slowly released, helped steel his nerves just like when they taught him sharpshooting in basic training. Then, he smiled at the sound of another long, comfortable snore from the slight man in the chair.

Be smooth, old man, be smooth. He's a sitting duck.

In a swift motion, standing fully behind the chair, Cam shoved the potato sack over the sleeping man's head. He then pulled the drawstring, which cinched the sack around Corker's neck. With his right hand, he pressed Corker down into the chair by the chest. Corker immediately awoke, but in a state of pure confusion.

Folks are never ready for waking up in a bag.

Corker's legs kicked straight out and knocked over the flimsy folding table that held aloft that wretched plate of slop that landed so hard it spattered the drapes in mincemeat. Corker's arms shot straight outward as if to catch himself from falling, chest still held down firmly by his assailant. It was like holding down a panicked dog. Corker was now grasping at the hood, looking for a way out.

Cam snatched both of Corker's wrists with one strong hand, wrenching the poor bastard's arms upward and back over his head just like he'd been relaxing before. He clamped Corker's arms up against his stomach with one arm and pulled a strip of tape off his thigh for Corker's wrists, holding them tight. Now he could pin Corker into the chair with his left hand and cover his mouth with his right hand.

The whole motion of things had only taken some four seconds. Cam held steadfast while his captive prey caught his bearings. After a few panicked, muffled wails, Cameron knew Corker was just about awake enough to understand what had happened.

Corker began to plead, but it was muffled by the gloved hand of his assailant. Half-awake and terrified, Corker bit down hard into Cam's hand. The thick cowhide glove protected Cam's palm long enough to pull back and punch one quick jab into Corker's exposed ribs. With a squeal and a sharp exhale, Corker sputtered and coughed, now unable to catch his breath enough to yell again. His legs shook and spasmed against the chair, one shoe falling off in the tumult.

Cam grunted, "Stay quiet, goddammit!" in a gruff voice that sounded nothing like his own.

Corker was struggling a bit, Cam repeated, "*Quiet*, or I'll hit you again."

Corker stopped wriggling and slowly nodded his head in understanding, still whimpering from the pain in his ribs. Cam lifted the burlap a bit and placed a strip of tape on Corker's mouth before tugging the sack back down and drawing it closed.

Corker was now fully captive, a rag doll in a cheap suit.

You look fuckin' sad, Jimmy.

Still, Cam felt no guilt, merely pity.

Cam snatched Corker up by the wrists and his belt, swinging him over the side of the chair onto the floor, whereupon he dragged the man back into the kitchen. The hooded form remained quiet, likely knowing he was helpless. Perhaps the tape over his mouth helped remind him of that fact. His pained whimpers subsided, though he could not see nor hear his attacker. Cam had made sure of that by trying on the burlap sack in his motel room to be sure.

In the still-dark kitchen, Cam was now kneeling on Corker and holding his bound arms outstretched. He had one knee on the man's chest and one shin flat on the floor. Cam put on his gruff voice again, as he would throughout this whole ordeal, in order to avoid being recognized later. It was an old trick. The radio still offered up some soft tunes in the other room.

"Nod your head if you understand your situation," he barked. The man nodded his head fervently.

"Is there anyone else coming?"

The sack swayed side-to-side.

"I'm not gonna kill you, but we are going to *talk*. You understand?"

Another up-and-down nod.

Cam lifted Corker and stood him up straight, holding his taped hands behind his head, his elbow's crook nestled around Corker's throat. The man was panting heavily through his nose, the tape on his mouth held steadfastly.

"We're going downstairs."

Cam had dragged Corker half-stumbling into that basement, kicked his feet out from under him, then taped his wrists to a support beam in the center of the room.

"I don't have much to take, the radio's pretty new..." Corker pleaded.

Corker was defeated, captured, and very clearly acquiesced to his vulnerable position. Cam doffed his hat onto a nearby broom handle and sat down on a small wood crate. He sighed, looking over the pathetic little man practically trussed up like a Thanksgiving turkey on the cold basement floor. His gruff voice sounded even more gravely in the balmy air. He was also doing his best to hide his mild accent as he spoke.

"We got a mutual friend, so I'm gonna ask some things and you're gonna answer. Later, I'm gonna let you go. If you lie to me, I'll know it... and I'll hit you again. Worse. Understood?"

In the dim light coming down from the old glass ceiling bulb, the burlap sack lolled in agreement. Cam reached over to loosen the drawstring and, from underneath, peeled off the tape from Corker's mouth. He let the bag fall back into place over Corker's chin and sat back down on the crate.

"You know about the kids. I wanna know what you know."

Corker was quiet. He shifted around a bit.

"TALK!" Cam barked.

"I don't know any kids... whose kids?" Corker unwisely responded.

Cam stood up and walked toward the helpless man. He placed his heel on the man's groin, but put no pressure yet. Corker squealed a bit in surprise. "Speak up, Slim. The kids who went *missing*." His tone was intense.

Sniffling and stifling a sobbing cry, Corker shuffled around a bit more. "How do you know about that?" Cam stepped back a bit and removed his heel.

"Good, you aren't as dumb as you look. I know things. It's my job.' His throat dry from growling the words out, he continued, 'And it's my job to find out *more*. Talk."

Corker's breathing was rapid, and he was nervous.

"I know a little. I know where they went, but I never asked why. Just please…"

His attempt at begging was cut off by Cameron's heel back on the groin.

"Corky, you're starting to slip up. Just cut the shit and tell me what you *do* know. Tell me how you know it, too. Details could save your future kids…"

He dug his heel in a bit. Corker made a choked, gurgling sound and nodded once more.

Jimmy Corker cleared his throat and spoke up, the burlap muffling his words.

"Okay, okay. I'll tell you all of it… just back up and lemme… let me just have a *breath*, you louse!" He sounded defeated. Any man in his situation would be.

Cam poked him in the ribs.

"What did you mean you never asked *why*?"

Corker took a long breath and spat out his words with ire, "Because I didn't want to know. I like living, you know?"

Cam shot back, "Assume I *don't* know. Explain it to me, like I was a child."

Cam was impatient for answers. The sacked man sighed and replied, "Because the last two guys who knew anything and tried to use it ended up dead. Those troopers back in South Dakota. They knew too much. Got 'em killed, you know. Fuck, I knew Ives from church!" He sounded sincere.

"Oh, yeah?' Cam coaxed him on, 'You don't seem like the church type!"

"They said it was an accident, but that was *horse*shit!" Corker spat out.

Losing his patience, Cam poked Corker hard in the forehead through the burlap.

"Like. I. Was. A. *Child.*"

Corker was struggling to swallow through his tight throat.

"I, uh… I didn't suspect it, 'til some voice on the phone said I'd get the same treatment if I ever squealed. 'Closed-casket, ' he said. Like I have a mug worth looking at anyway… but I still like living more than I care about anyone else. Yeah, I'm selfish, sure. Why wouldn't I be? Nobody ever did *me* any favors…" he trailed off.

The outside air was cool, but the two men breathed a thick moisture in the cellar, and its one little window was fogging. Sweat glistened on Cameron's forehead, and he knew that his own discomfort was making him impatient. He leaned back a bit, reached into his pocket, and withdrew a paper pack of smokes. He'd forgotten the tin at the motel. Tapping one end and taking a deep, long exhale, he stuck a bent cigarette into the corner of his mouth and struck a match. At the sound, his captive company's head cocked to one side in the burlap sack.

Cameron grunted, "Need one?"

Corker let out a huff, "Sure do. Guess you never know when it's going to be your last."

Cam stifled a laugh.

Good and scared.

Lifting the bottom of the burlap sack, Cam tightened the drawstring so it was resting at the bridge of Corker's nose. In this downcast light, it seemed dramatic—a caricature of a medieval executioner. Cameron had to make sure he would not be recognized and ideally not accurately described in any way. He stuck a crooked cigarette between Corker's lips and struck another wood match. The man drew in what Cameron was sure must be the most prolonged drag he had ever seen.

"Save your lungs, you got more *talkin'* to do, Jimmy."

Corker was silently sucking on the cigarette like a straw.

Time to shift tactics.

The captor put away the smokes and sat down, stretching his interlaced fingers out in front of him and loosening the laces on his heavy boots to let his aching feet rest a bit.

"Corker, I'm gonna be straight with you. I know about the district attorney. You're going to tell me what you know about that, and it better line up with what I know. You're a smart guy, and if we can get through this without you pissing your pants or pissing me off, you'll catch the next radio news hour. Just know that this is what I *do*, and I will go right through anyone at any time to get what I want. If you help me, those slugs won't be breathing enough to make any more midnight calls to your house… understand?"

Corker was nearly done with the cigarette.

"Yeah, I understand. Fuck you for that rib shot, but I appreciate your honesty."

He spat out the butt of his finished cigarette onto the floor next to his leg.

Cameron took the last drag of his own and put it out under the toe of his boot.

"Let's talk about that DA O'Rourke. Fill me in on your part in his operation."

Corker shuffled around a bit and relaxed his body, as relaxed as a man can be when his hands are strung up above him.

"Short story. What I heard, I heard directly from O'Rourke himself, unfortunately. He caught me taking envelopes a while back and hauled me in, gave me a nasty side job. Seems he figured I was dirtier than I am… on account of Steve talking me up. Steve was *terrified* of O'Rourke. Steve warned me too, telling me this guy was the real thing —the kind to put the screws to anyone in his way, man, woman, or child. He doesn't care. Of course, I played along because I'm a goddamn fool. Figured I could get something big out of the deal."

Cam kicked his foot and inquired gruffly, "What did you get?"

"This shitty bungalow, and that stupid fucking car. The miserly fuck bought me the six-cylinder, you believe that? I mean it's got overdrive but… anyway, by the time he had me running those little kids upstate, I was in too deep to back out."

"Sad story, heard it a hundred times. You seem smarter than that nonsense, slim."

"Well, everyone else was in. Maybe I don't like feeling left out, ya know? Anyway, I'm out. Been out a while. I got really sick, goddamn cancer was eating me up. Lost all my meat, just look at me. I'm skin and bones. I'm a desk guy now. Hardly do nothin' but clerical work and phones."

Sneering, Cam grunted out, "Seen worse. Dachau, for one…"

Corked paused and considered that statement.

"Well, that's a horrifying example, but it says something about you… soldier. *Humph.* So like I was sayin', those docs tell me I nearly died, but you can't be good hired muscle if you ain't got any, right? So O'Rourke cut me out. Fuck, they cut out half'a my bowels too. I ain't had a real steak in a year. I can hardly finish one of those tin-foil airline dinners. I miss a steak… fuck, I miss a lot of things…" he mused.

Cam remained silent but kicked Jimmy in the shin, which invited

Corker to continue.

"Fine, fine… what I know is, this DA doesn't play nice. He doesn't care if you have a badge or otherwise. He's one of those old-school types, and I've personally seen him pistol-whip a man half-brain-dead for missing a delivery time. O'Rourke has a shiny badge that's polished with blood… he shot some Mexican for looking at him sideways after a poker game. Finished his beer and planted a scrubbed pistol on the poor bastard."

"And got away clean, I assume."

"You bet. Made sure we *all* knew it was an open-and-shut case. Fucker made the papers for that one!"

"Sounds like he needs worse than a burlap bag and a cigarette."

Cam reminded Corker subtly that he was still being interrogated.

"Maybe… he has some important friends who like some real foul entertainment. People who run this state, higher up even."

They don't need trucks to move kids locally… maybe this wimp really doesn't know.

"Is that it? Just a bunch of badges doin' the nasty with these stolen kids? Throw 'em away when they've finished?"

The thought turned Cam's spit dry in pure disgust at his callousness. The imagery was pervasive, shrill in his mind as he spat the words. He wanted to vomit.

"No, no… that was what Steve thought, but I don't think so…' Corker replied, sounding defeated, 'that can't be it. Some of those kids go to the border, and some of them ain't breathing when they do. Depends on the day, on the ask."

Corker cleared his throat and spat on the floor.

"The *ask*?"

"The orders."

"Orders from *who*? I doubt O'Rourke was calling you on that telephone upstairs."

"Fuck, I never knew. Why would they tell me? I got out, and I plan to stay out. See, if you go looking for trouble with O'Rourke? You are *sure* to find it, and it's going to be more than you can handle. What in the world are you going to do, tough guy? All alone with your tobacco and your tough guy voice. If you were a lawman, you'd have brought me in. Bunch of malarkey!"

Cameron snorted at the projected emasculation.

"I got all I need to take care of business, the only reason I'm grilling you about this in the comfort of your own basement, as opposed to a ditch in those woods, is because of that mutual friend."

Corker let out a confident, unsettling chortle like one of those mechanized fortune-tellers at an arcade.

"I figured. How is she?"

Cameron was taken aback.

"She?"

Corker knotted up and down slowly.

"Yeah, you know. Little blue dress, likes to party?"

Cameron felt a brief flutter and a pang of something like panic in his stomach. He was not fond of surprises. Corker clearly had information Cameron didn't anticipate, which threw a sizeable wrench in the gears of the interrogation.

"How did you guess?"

Corker crossed his legs for comfort and let out a long sigh.

"You're not so clever, mister. You still smell like her perfume. Are you smarter about going after the *real* bad guys? Or are you going to show your hand before you get a chance to take on O'Rourke?"

Circumstances had taken a turn. Cameron had no way of anticipating that Corker would be *so* about his wits. Worse, Caroline was not the best judge of character, and Cam was unsure if he could trust Corker as far as he could throw him. In his current state, Corker wouldn't be that hard to throw. Like a nervous tic, Cam pulled out his buck knife and slowly rolled its handle over in his hand.

Dammit. If you ain't gonna bury this little shrimp, you better be ready to get outta town fast.

"Corker, if you have such serious misgivings about O'Rourke, you're not working on his level. You say you want to help me make this world a better place? Make sure you ain't lookin' over your shoulder in case I fail?"

Corker sat silent, baiting some offerings from his captor.

"I may not be as smart as you, Jimmy, but I'm a better man. I'm going to do this thing, even if it gets gruesome. I don't wanna have to tie you up tighter and leave your ass down here for the roaches to pick at."

Corker raised his covered head as though some divine idea had just struck him. "It's not like I have you by the balls, pal. I won't be much good to you in a fight. I don't have much fight left in me these days, but I've got some things I could certainly do my part to protect. Rather not end up a hobo, anyway. Tell you what, fire me up another one of those cigarettes and I will tell you *everything*—every last bit. In the end, you can leave me be or finish me off if you think I've been bullshitting you. How's that?"

Cameron withdrew a hand-rolled for Corker.

"You got yourself a deal, Slim. If you behave? I might even take off the sack. Smells like an ass crack anyway," he snickered as he stuck the smoke in Corker's maw and sparked the end.

"Okay, okay… sit back, soldier boy, and keep up. Picture me a few years back. Eager, and bigger than I am now. Maybe a few more hairs. Picture a kid who grew up with a father in the clink and a mother standing on corners in Pittsburgh to keep milk in the icebox. Picture a kid with a big chip on his shoulder, if you can. A mean kid, a bad seed, grown into a meaner man. Before I knew better, I thought the world owed me something… and I was gonna take it. Just had to find someone willing to put me to work."

"Did you know the first lawmen were slave patrols? No surprise you wanted to be a police officer."

"Hey fuck you, first of all,' Corker retorted through the smoke; 'I ain't that sort. I grew up with colored kids too… I hate everyone, no matter their color!"

"Fine, I'll hush. You talk."

"Well, I found someone to put me to work. Not long after I got my badge, either. Sure, I put the hurt on a few people, but I never killed any man who didn't draw down on me first."

"You never put your hands on a kid?"

"Ah, hell, I mean… sometimes they'd act up. You gotta keep those little boys in line, they don't speak English sometimes, and they have so much bravado… they weren't all so small. The bigger kids you gotta lay into a bit, just to let 'em know who's in charge."

"Not in my experience."

"Yeah, well, it worked for me. Anyway, the boss wanted us to keep those kids alive and healthy. I'd give them a bucket, some food, and a little jug of water or milk. Maybe better treatment than they got on the farm, some of 'em… I swear, I figured they were selling these kids to people who wanted kids. At first, that seemed all right by me, since I was dealt such a shit hand. Almost felt *righteous*. Thought they'd be seeing a better life… at least until…"

Corker's head hung as he trailed off.

"Until what?" Cam prodded him.

"Until they started handing them off in a trunk. Cold."

"And you never had a hand in *that*? Just an errand boy, huh?"

Corker took his time answering, puffing on the cigarette and shifting his legs slightly.

"I think that evil set into me, rotted me from the inside. Gave me the cancer. Took everything else. O'Rourke let me live outta pity. Or maybe he just wanted to watch me rot into a grave so he could give that fucking car to the next asshole with a grudge against the world."

Cam saw the need to shift gears. He was curious about Hardigan's involvement, but didn't want to implicate himself. "There's no way you are the only local involved in this mess. Any other troopers have their hands in this?"

Corker nodded again, slowly, almost solemnly. "Yeah, one other guy. Steve Hardigan. Big mean son of a gun. He's been in this longer than me, and he stayed in. I think this business of treating kids like dogs, it messed him up worse than me... it fucked him up pretty bad."

"But not sick like you."

"In his head. Sick. Demented. Like something broke inside him."

He took another long, deep breath and continued. "When I got roped in, they set me up to spend some time with him. Sure, I already knew him from work and such. He showed me a few things, like how to move the kids around and where to stash them. O'Rourke has a few places around the county, quiet little places. Hell, O'Rourke bought that big man Hardigan a hunting cabin! They spent weekends up there. I don't know what they were up to. I wasn't invited unless I was delivering. The way Hardigan used to talk, that place is built on a pile of bones."

Cam saw the image of those skeletal remains in the smoke wafting across the room: the ash pits of Dachau, an acre of dirt dotted with piles of shoes.

Maybe I did the right thing. Chrissakes...

"Hardigan was out there... he talked about people like they were animals, he'd crack wise about fresh kill. I fuckin' *hated* my time with Steve. He wasn't like that when we were new on the force. He used to seem like a decent guy. Maybe it was all bluster, but I think he had a screw loose... hey, who am I to judge?" He let out an uneasy laugh.

Cameron had his answer, in a way. Not wanting to seem caught up on Hardigan, he changed the subject.

"He's on my list. Now, who else?"

Corker shook his head. "I never really met anyone else; mostly it would be anonymous. You get a call, and you follow the instructions. Somebody you don't know comes by later and does their part. I think that was O'Rourke's way of keeping anybody from putting things together. As far as I could figure, these kids were getting sold like property. Dry goods. For what, to whom, I never knew."

"And you didn't *want* to know, right?" Cameron interjected.

Corker let the cigarette fall from his mouth onto the floor and took a deep sigh. It was enough of a response.

The two talked on for a bit longer. Cameron had taken out a small notepad for names and dates, and other notes that might prove helpful. Something like an hour had passed, and Cameron had still been mindlessly playing with his buck knife. Without a word, he reached over and sliced through the tape binding Corker's wrists to the support beam, then sat back down. Corker rubbed his raw wrists but didn't reach for the hood. Without being able to see, he turned his head toward his captor and inquired, "Sounds like I'm in your favor, huh?"

Cameron tapped his blade on the crate, thinking, "We will see about that."

"I don't *know* you; you can walk out right now, and I would never say a word."

"Oh?"

Corker shifted his weight and turned toward Cam, still seated and still lolling his head in deference.

"I mean, they're gonna find you. It's a small town, it's a small group of folks who have everything to lose. They'll find you if you're poking around."

"Maybe, Jimmy. Maybe not. This isn't my first dance."

"Sure. The thing is, all of this evil? I have been pushing this out of my head and trying to forget… trying for over a year now. I took to the bottle, and look where that got me? Nearly dead. All I got now is a little bit of joy in my life and a whole freight car of guilt. I have a right to life, just like everyone else, but those kids… those kids had a right to life too, and I know that there's no way I can make up for all the things I've done wrong. The only way I can maybe find some peace is if I do something good… if I do something righteous to keep that from happening again to somebody else's kids."

His breath was heavy, and Cameron could see that he was upset, maybe crying under that burlap.

Corker pleaded, "I'll help you. I mean, if you trust me enough to let me. Might be able to help you come out of this alive. What do you say to that, stranger?"

He knows I'm not gonna kill him. He coulda let me walk out… I could use an ally.

Cam decided it would be wise for him to keep this man in his pocket. He stood up and took a long, drawn breath of the stale air. He withdrew the cigarettes and the small matchbox, tossing them onto the floor next to Corker's leg. Corker reached out blindly and fumbled around until he found the pack.

"Slim, you might end up being of some use to me. Today, I'm going to walk out that door, and you're going to forget we talked. Not a word. Don't ask about me, don't leave this nasty basement until you smoke at least two more of those. Keep your ear out for the phone, and when I need you, I'll be calling. Until then, I know you've got some sins to atone for, and I believe you will get your chance. Go to church, and stay outta the bottle."

Corker nodded his head and breathed a sigh of relief.

With his loosened bootlaces dragging on the floor, Cameron lurched back up the dark stairway and through the kitchen. He was drained, hoarse throat from disguising his voice for what felt like an eternity. His work set out before him, he began to lay plans on how to catch the son of a bitch at the top of all this.

I'm gonna come back to Jimmy and vet whatever I find. Maybe I'll twist it a little so I can test him. Everything he said lines up with what I saw at the cabin. Good start, but he ain't proven yet. O'Rourke ain't gonna be held to account in the courts… this is all on you, old man. This is gonna get nasty.

As he ambled down the highway and back to the dilapidated Motor Inn, he entertained himself with the thought of how happy this would make the boss.

Billy loves this shit.

City Hall

Saturday, September 17th

Cam woke up and sat straight up in bed. He had slept soundly and, for once, could clearly remember his dream. Rubbing the sleep from his eyes, he recounted the dream as best he could, which was short but far from simple.

The dream was vivid, black and white, much like the photograph he carried of O'Rourke and his company. Everything in heavy contrast. Vision shaky, lending a twitchy, violent motion to everything. Like a movie missing frames. Cam was himself standing over the edge of a vast pit dug into the soft ground of some unknown forest, the ground littered with slender birch trees and crunchy pale leaves. He tossed a cigarette butt down into the pit, where a pallid hand midair unceremoniously caught it, extinguished between fingertips. He remembered the eyes, the eyes that reflected no light at all. They were strained, fraught with anger and fear. The gyrating figure barked some instructions; unclear words—nonsense, but in the context of the dream, they had made perfect sense. The air tasted like gasoline. O'Rourke took shape as he contorted into the belly of the hole he had himself dug, arms folded like Bela Lugosi's vampire... Cam spat on the soil, and O'Rourke dissolved away into the dirt like so much ash in a rainstorm.

Cameron's neck crackled and crunched like dry twigs as he contorted his neck and looked down; a shovel was gripped tightly in his strong left hand. He felt the texture of the wood. It had deep striations in the swollen fibers and was rubbed nearly smooth in two places, where two hands had arduously worn away what was once a sinewy and mighty tree limb into almost a toothpick. He recalled placing his hands in the well-worn grooves as so many clearly had before, lurching forward and using the trusty shovel to sling modest mounds of dirt into the hole. As each shovel-full of soft dirt collected in the makeshift grave, it grew in size as it fell into the void.

He could feel his heels sinking into the dirt, but it was soft. Cool. Comforting. Even as the roots began to pierce his skin, writhing and wrapping around the bones of his bare feet.

A few effortless swings of the shovel and he had nearly filled the entire pit. He recalled wiping the sweat off his brow as the sun crept in between the leaves above in scattered but very linear rays. Everything was a washed silver tone, except now he looked at his hands to see that they were rough and bleeding a rich and glistening red from the effort. Moonlight gleamed off them like a polished gemstone. His vision dimmed, like looking through murky river water. He felt a knot in his stomach, dropped the shovel, and winced in the dream as he shut his eyes tight.

Sitting up in a state of confusion, he tried to understand the symbolism of the bloody hands, the digging.

That goddamned pink yarn. Her little hand… You're in it now, and you're gonna make a mess of things, old man.

He groaned at the days ahead and forced his creaking bones out of bed with a grunt.

Breathing the steam of a near-scalding shower, he hung his head to let the hot water run over the back of his neck. He thought about how many times he had come across graves himself, in wartime. He'd always felt the tranquility of a quiet plot in cool soil was a grace.

No… a respectable death wouldn't suit this bastard.

He wouldn't just take O'Rourke down, no. He would try and make some restitution come from all of this. He knew that man was powerful, and with power often comes wealth. No, he wouldn't just put O'Rourke six feet under. He would *take* from the man first. Some sort of Robin Hood, some shadow of Lady Justice, trying to balance the scales in a horrifying and too-far-gone odyssey of tragedy and loss.

Soon after, Cameron was traversing the nearby county road back toward a diner he'd spotted last time he was headed down to Walla-Walla. It was a rundown place, but the counters looked clean. He'd seen white and colored folk sitting at that counter eating, so he didn't bother to consult his little book to know it was a safe place.

Today was no different, much to his pleasure. The diner was teeming with folks eating and chatting, all colors and creeds. Farmhands sat next to men in two-piece suits, all vying for a refill of coffee or a little more catsup. Today, he sat in a booth and watched a flock of stupid little birds peck at the grass lining the highway. He cleaned his plate of the pancake special and downed three cups of coffee, leaving a decent gratuity, before using the payphone outside to make a call back to Seattle.

"Billy, it's your favorite leathery old goat."

"Now, Cameron, you're not *that* leathery. Maybe suede. What's the good news?"

"We're getting places. Not good news, but… at least it's *something*. We still gotta catch up on that bad scene, but for today I'll just fill you in on the basics."

"Hell, progress is progress. We're doing good work, Cam… even on the days we're spinning our wheels. What have you got?" Billy was always an optimist, especially in the face of time. He was patient to a fault when it came to these drawn-out cases.

"I caught a fish and it sang. Good song, too. Might help me get my hook into another fish, the big one. So that little minnow is back in the pond."

Cam spent a few minutes explaining to Billy in carefully coded terms what he had found and accomplished up to this point, and what the plan forward was. Billy was excited at the prospect of an end to this case, invested as he was. Cameron understood that to mean that Billy had been bankrolling the entire job. Almost two years' salary at this point. All along, Cam had a suspicion that somebody involved was paying Billy to get this job done. Now, he felt half guilty about his expenses along the way, knowing that they were coming directly from his friend's pocket.

"I'm not sure if you're tryin' to motivate me, Billy, or get me to stop spending so much."

"Cam, if you were doing anything I didn't want done? I certainly wouldn't have waited two years to tell you. Just follow the case, work the leads, and bring this thing to a close. Not for the money, Cam. For the kids. Please…"

Cam had to stop for a moment and let that soak in. Billy's heart was in this, too, no matter how remote. It felt damn good to hear.

"For the kids… and our souls, Billy. For mine."

"You're doing better than me, you old goat. We both have things to atone for."

They said their goodbyes, and Cameron headed into town, dressed in his nicest three-piece suit. Green Fields, a city that began as a railroad spur near a single orchard, had grown into a population of approximately eight thousand people and several industries. The 'Fields' portion of the name was a bit misleading, as it was nestled in a valley. The town center was tiny, perhaps just three blocks of old brick and mortar buildings; a few original log buildings also survived. Cam adored the colorful and charming little buildings, all decorated with flowers and benches, and gold letter signs in nearly every window.

Living in California for many years, Cam had seen firsthand how money and progress often overlooked history. Too many buildings in California were being demolished in favor of something newer and taller. And, in Cameron's opinion, something cheap and ugly as well.

No spit-and-toilet-tissue buildings here. Rustic. Yeah, that's the word.

He found a cozy alley for the truck and walked around the central city block. It was a sunny, cool Saturday, and folks were meandering about, visiting the little storefronts and buying groceries for Sunday dinners. He spotted City Hall and walked on past, seeing its door open and the banker's hours painted on the door glass.

Open on a Saturday? Lucky me. Would hate to sit on my duff all weekend. That bed ain't exactly luxurious…

Cam continued the walk to see what else was around. There were three eateries, one laundromat, two hardware and sundry shops, and one little theater with a "FOR SALE" sign in the window. The modest marquee overhead had a few letters left behind spelling out nonsense.

Guess they don't care much for the arts here.

He had brought a phony, though reasonably good quality, Washington driver's license that listed him as Cameron *Wilson*. The fictitious Cam Wilson was an associate editor for a defunct newspaper in Seattle, which never printed pages again. Of course, if you asked him, Mr. Wilson would reply, 'The Seattle Park-Times Gazette is a *vital* newspaper that is serving its communities well. ' He'd recite that with confidence. Which communities? He hoped nobody asked. For the sake of a thorough cover, the Gazette's phone number rang through to the fifth phone in Billy's office high up in Smith Tower, looking over downtown Seattle.

After standing around a bit and observing the little stretch of small-town charm through the blue smoke of a cheap cigar, Cam made his way toward the diminutive city hall. A sweetly decorated brick building with green and purple accents, he nodded at the few folks standing outside smoking as he walked in with confidence. A petite, dark-haired woman at the clerk's desk was in a friendly disposition, and upon presenting his business card, she was happy to help. The brass nameplate in front of her was oxidized, but stamped in bold lettering.

ANNA MCGOVERN - CLERK

"What can I assist you with today, sir?" she asked with a kind smile. Cam rested his briefcase on the tile floor and stepped to her desk, leaning over the marble ledge just a nose.

"Mornin' miss… *McGovern*, I see. Cam Wilson, glorified reporter, if you ask my boss…" he offered with his most charming grin, tipping the brim of his hat before removing it to be polite. Sliding his hand-trimmed business card across the counter, she barely glanced at it.

"I'm out here working up a column on notable figures in the region, a bit of a fluff piece. Made my way to your desk after my managing editor heard that you have a rising star in District Attorney Wallace O'Rourke. Any chance you know ol' Wally?"

Her expression warmed from friendly to comfortable in a flash.

"Of course I do, sugar, *every*body knows Wallace O'Rourke!" She replied with a broad wave of her hand toward everyone and no one in particular.

"He's up for elections soon again, I'm sure you've seen the signs out there on a few of our lawns. Ask around, he's done a lot of great work out here. Taking care of a lot of the…" she hesitated for a moment, clearly wanting to remain as polite as possible, "…the little *problems* we have had in our little community recently. In fact, the whole county went for him with *seventy-one percent* support last election, and I don't see it going anywhere but up if he chooses to run again. He hasn't been around here as long as some, but he's done real good."

Christ, she's layin' it on thick. Maybe that's part of the job… perhaps he's a good fella, or maybe she just ain't lookin' to change careers.

Cameron had to force another genial smile.

"Well, all I know is he came out here from the Midwest and has quite the record. Honestly, I'd like more history on the man, as I don't want this to be a strictly political piece. You know, some folks get upset at that sort of one-sided writing. We do our best to stay on the fence back at the Gazette," he offered with clasped hands as though he were at communion, and she seemed perhaps just a bit charmed.

"Well, I can lead you back into the archives with some pointers to do your research, and when you are done, I could tell you a little more about the man himself, as he spends a lot of time here with the mayor. For now, I need to attend to the desk as it's the busy hour."

Cameron looked over his right shoulder, then his left. He was alone with her in the lobby. Regardless, he smiled and nodded again. "I sure would appreciate that, miss."

She thumbed through some record drawers, pulling index cards that would lead Cameron to the appropriate records in their back hall. Many of these small towns would hoard every newspaper and official document in perpetuity, as such a small media sphere didn't produce enough for them to warrant throwing anything away. In fact, he noted how their records room was a bit paltry compared to some far smaller towns he'd visited. Cam hung his coat and hat before he diligently went to work combing through the drawers full of the last few years' newspapers.

Hours passed; the reading was heavy and the information sparse. As far as the sleuth could suss out? O'Rourke had relocated to the area a few years prior, having taken over the family business, a fruit packing company located not too far away on an offshoot of the Snake River west of Green Fields, connected to the Columbia River. Three years ago, the incumbent DA was embroiled in a scandal involving a young candy striper and accusations of impropriety; that DA stepped down and relocated somewhere East. At the time, the vox populi called for fresh blood, and O'Rourke just *happened* to be in the right place at the right time.

I don't like coincidences. Luck is one thing, but c'mon now...

Cam recalled something his father had said once, after throwing down a newspaper and folding his arms in a huff, he'd exclaimed, "Special elections never benefit the people... guess in our case that means they're just like *regular* elections!" His father was a jovial man, though his humor was born from truth. Even in his youth, Cameron knew that he would never be happy with his station in a country that thought of his family and his people as unworthy because of a trait that was out of their control—hated for the color of their skin. He missed his father; he pined for that unflappable optimism.

Pop would've loved to see me now, all gussied up and maybe making a difference. Lizzy too...

Upon exhausting his reading on O'Rourke, Cam turned his attention to that fruit-packing plant. It was reportedly one of the older and more established plants. There had been some troubles there over the past 40 years or so, regarding a few industrial accidents taking the lives of workers, and, subsequently, a few reports of missing children. Children who were here without papers, and therefore nearly invisible to the law. Even the newspaper had come to the supposition that the children had run away for a better opportunity, but Cameron knew better. He knew no seven-year-old would travel with their family to a strange place and abandon everything they know on a whim. He knew that the local folks, farmers and laborers primarily, likely couldn't care less about a few missing kids, as there were hundreds of migrants working their properties annually, whose names they didn't even care to know.

What are the chances they'd even care about a fieldhand gone missing at the end of the day, much less the kin of a fieldhand? Life ain't got much value at the bottom of the barrel.

Cameron sat there, starting to get that sinking feeling again. He had stumbled upon what was perhaps an even bigger conspiracy than he had suspected. He saw no coincidence that O'Rourke, a man he knew was abducting and sometimes taking the lives of children, had been adjacent to similar reports and disappearances in his young adulthood. In all his years dealing with bad people, Cameron knew that it usually started in youth, not later in life, as in Hardigan's case. *That* one still threw him for a loop.

With his notepad nearly full of names, dates, and locations, Cameron decided it was time to step back from the fact-finding and conduct a bit of a hard-soled investigation. He packed up the little briefcase and took himself back out into the reception area. He was disappointed to see a young man seated behind a counter, where not long before, he had been flirting with that lovely Miss McGovern. He tipped his hat towards the man, who, upon seeing Cameron, looked somewhat surprised.

"Howdy. I'm all finished up, sir." He smiled at the young man.

The man shot back, "Sir, I'm not sure who you are… *where* did you come from?"

Cameron reached into his pocket and drew another business card.

"My apologies. I've been in that records room for quite some time. That nice woman had set me up back there with what I needed. Here are your index cards, and I'm all finished," he repeated as he handed back all the record cards he had been given earlier.

The man's face looked relieved and a bit embarrassed. "I'm so sorry, sir. I knew you were back there; I just didn't expect you to be… I already have your card here!" He sheepishly held up Cameron's first business card.

Cameron was annoyed but disguised it well.

"Thank you kindly, sir. I'll keep this one, and you keep that one! That nice little lady said she had a little more information for me. Any word on when she might be back?"

The young man shook his head. "She went home for the day, perhaps try tomorrow."

Cameron plopped his hat back on his head, tipping the brim towards the young man as he turned and exited. He knew he had enough information to start and would rather not be seen in the office again. Billy's voice was constantly chirping wisdom from the back of his head, and this one rang oh so true: "The less that folks see of you, the less they think of you". He meant simply *don't be memorable.*

Strutting his way back toward where he'd parked, Cam paused at the cardstock and trinket store next door. He popped his head in the door. Upon seeing a silver-haired shopkeeper behind the counter reading a newspaper and looking thoroughly bored, Cam inquired, "Pardon, sir, how far is the drive to the Rainbow Packing plant?"

The octogenarian shifted his gaze up and rumpled his brow as he took a moment to think, and replied thoughtfully as he half-folded the paper and thumbed toward his right.

"At the next corner that-a-way *without* the stop sign, take that road North for fifteen minutes if you drive easy. That'll put you there, can't miss the signs. It's on the river-side." The man adjusted his glasses on the bridge of his nose and returned to his reading. Cameron gave a quick nod of thanks and departed.

Hurrying back to the truck, Cam checked his watch and saw that it was nearly three in the afternoon.

With any luck, I have some time before everybody goes home for the day, as long as I'm there by four… damn farmers and their early hours. Good chance to dig a little bit about the O'Rourke family, maybe they'll be interested in having our exalted newspaper publish something kind about them. Rich folk love that shit.

When he got back to the truck, Cam grabbed his lunch pail from behind the bench seat and tossed it onto the passenger seat, whispering under his breath, "15 minutes to eat. Damn." he munched on that half-stale bread and salami as he rolled up the bumpy highway, planning his con job in silence.

Family Business

Up hills and over dales, the perky little truck bounced and jostled on its squeaky springs.

Central-Eastern Washington was known for a few key things. Spectacular fall colors? Certainly. Rolling hills lavished in brilliant fall colors? Absolutely. Friendly, neighborly folks always open-armed to their fellow man? Eh… not so much. Small towns dotting rural landscapes tend to be a bit closed-minded, to say the least.

More worrisome, the Klan presence in these areas was still strong.

Over the years, Cam had developed a knack for spotting the folks who might not brush him off. So, Cam made a game of it. He'd watch for a flash in their eyes, the eye roll, or that leery squint folks do when they don't like the smell of something. It's a visceral reaction, and Cam would catch that split-second of a tell in their face. If they looked kindly, no sign of *disdain*, he'd press on. If that recoil started to show? He'd just as happily turn around and wave goodbye before they had a chance to say anything at all. He often wondered if he was wrong for judging so quickly.

Hasn't let me down yet, and I don't owe them a damn thing.

Among the winding curves and short stretches of one-lane blacktop, Cam managed to scarf down his food. After some fourteen minutes by his watch, he came to a sweeping bend in the road that opened toward the river; on his right spanned a shallow river several dozen feet wide, rolling on past. On his left, elevated railroad tracks were winding through this valley along with the river. There he was in between, itching to crack this damn case yet juxtaposed by a deep yearning to go lie down in the tall grass and watch the clouds roll by, instead.

The shrill hoot of a whistle shattered his daydream. From West and behind came chuffing and lurching a smallish steam locomotive hauling a train of about a dozen fruit-packing refrigerated boxcars. He was having trouble watching the road and also keeping an eye on the fast-approaching train in his rearview mirror! He supposed he should just let the train catch up to him, and then he could pace it and get a better view. Since his childhood, Cameron had been enamored with the railroads. He had seen some beautiful passenger trains in his youth, as his father would often take them down to the railway station in Oakland, and they would watch people come and go. Trains met at that station from all around, and trolleys came and went, headed for Alameda and San Francisco over the bridge. His family had not been wealthy, and his father had made a point to find some enriching activities that would keep Cam out of trouble. Kids do tend to enjoy trouble.

It's strange to think Pop was born before cars were on the roads. I wonder what the world was like for folks who had the railroad, a couple of horses, and their feet. No, thank you. I'll keep my V-8!

Patting the dashboard and grinning, he let off the gas a bit. The oily black steam locomotive in all of its huffing-and-puffing glory charged up beside the Plymouth. Smoke billowed from the stack over the nose, and he could see shimmering heat waves emanating off its body against the blue sky. The engineer waved toward him with a leather-gloved hand, the other hand resting on a big red lever.

Cam reached his left hand out the window and, placing his fist in the air, made a tugging motion that signaled to the conductor he would like to hear the whistle. The conductor nodded and smiled, reaching up and grabbing a chain that traversed the window frame.

Cam could see him pull that line taut, and with a burst of steam from the boiler, the cacophony of that shrill steam whistle rang throughout the little valley. Cam eased the gas a little and caught the locomotive's pace; he was now traveling alongside on this beautifully winding road next to a winding creek. Golden leaves on sparse trees whizzed past behind the train, and hillsides covered in lush greenery surrounded it.

At this moment, Cam wished he had a camera, but he knew a mental picture would be plenty. He slowed down a bit and let the train pass so he could see the caboose. The boxcars ambled on past; some had colorful railroad monads six feet tall on each side. One was a goat on a hill, and another car's herald looked like the Korean flag. Yet most were orange cars plastered with six-foot-tall paintings of orange groves and sturdy crates, strong men carrying them toward a rising sun.

These cars were also billboards.

Then, the caboose caught up to him. This far back on the train, most of the noise now was clacking iron wheels and the jostle of their massive couplers clanking against each other. The caboose was unusual in its crisp and clean appearance, shining almost like it had just been painted. It was a bright, sunflower-yellow, and he could see the brakeman sitting in one of the corner chairs, smoking a pipe, ignoring the rough undulations of the track that danced the car around him.

Oh boy, he looks cozy.

It seemed like the perfect place to be right now, and Cameron was envious. With a smile and a wave, he slowed his truck back down to a more reasonable speed, and the train kept on chugging ahead. Of course, Cam knew he was headed in the right direction, as this train was likely headed to a packing plant to drop off its refrigerator cars, known as *reefers.*

Just a few more minutes of the road, he came to what seemed to be something of a clearing in the hillsides where the river continued almost dead straight north. He saw the train up ahead, slightly to the west; it looked as though it had come nearly to a stop and was barely chuffing any smoke. On the right, he sought a modest but still somewhat sprawling facility of three warehouses surrounded by stacks upon stacks of fruit crates. Some were adorned with decorative paper advertisements marking the farms that would supply the fruit. He loved that artwork, with its diverse brands and silly names, as well as the beautiful drawings of the valley. It was really something, and he saw much of that in his trips around the Sacramento Valley over the past few years. Of course, with much of California farming becoming more industrialized, you saw less of the folks moving little crates and more of the big cabover trucks rolling along filled with ice and fruit.

As the rickety Plymouth pulled into the lot where most of the other vehicles seemed to be parked, he had driven past most of the packing plant. He couldn't miss the sizeable block lettering on the roofline of each warehouse; RAINBOW FRUIT PACKING

This was clearly in the right place, and the workday was almost done. Cam parked and grabbed his briefcase, heading toward what he thought might be the office. A simple blue door stood alone on the side of one of the warehouses.

As he made his way to the door and reached for the handle, he heard a voice behind him: "Can I help you, stranger?"

Cam turned with a smile plastered on his face, extending his hand to whomever it might be.

"Cam Wilson, sir. I'm with the paper out in Seattle!"

The man standing in front of him was a portly and hard-laboring sort, with tan skin and his dirty hands placed squarely on his hips. He was wearing dusty gray coveralls, the same as those of several men nearby who were loading pallets onto the back of an old GM pickup. He looked Cameron up and down, and seeing Cameron was a fit and nicely dressed man in a city suit, he nodded and extended his hand.

"Finley Bailey, pleased to meet you. Where can I aim ya?"

Cameron shook his head vigorously and responded, "Well, you look like a man who knows what's going on around here. Sure is a beautiful place you have here. I didn't expect such a nice drive. The boss sent me out this way for an article we're working on about the hard-working folks out here in the farmland; we're doing a Sunday back-pager. Big spread. Any interest in helping me out?"

Cameron's geniality was finely tuned, and the man was clearly susceptible. His brow relaxed from a furrow, and he grinned as he patted Cameron on the shoulder and led him into the office, offering a firm handshake like an old friend.

"C'mon in, mister Wilson, I'd be much obliged. We sure don't get a lot of press out here, well, not the last few years. Say, this is gonna be *good* press, right?"

Cameron smiled and nodded, "Well, of course! There's no such thing as bad press, Finley!"

Finley walked over to the small coffee table in the corner. The drip pot looked ancient. Finley poured the two of them a cup anyway. To Cam's surprise, his first sip was pleasant. It was cold, sure, but that's better than lukewarm.

The stout fellow sat Cam down in a cozy and well-worn fabric chair, Finley himself sitting across the desk in a leather office chair.

"The coffee is much appreciated. Helps me wash down lunch, anyway. Tell me, how long have you been working here at Rainbow?"

Amidst organizing papers and stacking them aside on the desk, Finley replied, "Honest, some days I forget. I think it's been about 20 years now, yeah, should be 19 or 20—long time. My folks moved up here after the stock market crashed. My father was a truck driver, and this was a waypoint on his route. He loved those big trucks. Loved the mountains. Hell, I never much liked driving."

Cam chuckled, "The way folks drive these days, can't blame ya!"

Finley nodded and swigged a sip, offering "Sure, sure… anyway, I'd rather be playin' in the dirt!"

Cameron smiled warmly, "I know the feeling. I grew up in the Midwest myself. My father was no farmer, but he certainly knew how to pick a spot for a picnic. I've been in Seattle for a few years, and boy, I love my trips out this way."

The farmer took another sip of coffee and swished it around in his mouth before swallowing, "Seattle… ain't got much use for the city. Well, what can I tell you? You can get our fruit in Seattle, so you must be here for some stories. What led you to Rainbow? Surely there are bigger packers and farms between here and there."

Cameron nodded and understood that it was time to get down to business.

"Honestly, my boss wants a feel-good piece that is focused on local agriculture, family stuff. Not the consolidated farms. I was reading up at City Hall on the region… seems like Rainbow is a pretty storied place. The local District Attorney owns Rainbow?"

"Yes, sir, Mr. O'Rourke came out here and took over when his papa passed. It was sad, sure, I knew that man most of my life… but his son is doing just fine. We've been growing our operation and picking up new business, and I don't see a stop to it. We've had these rainy seasons, keeping everything good and fertile. It's been a good few years."

Cameron was taking notes and nodding. Glancing up from his notepad, he asked dryly, "What can you tell me about O'Rourke? What kind of man is he to work for?"

Finley stewed on the question for a minute.

"Honestly, I hardly see the man. Met him a couple of times. Don't think he likes the dirt much; he always comes in these nice suits, and I've never seen the man anywhere but the office. Not my business, he knows what he's doing just the same. He pays men like me to handle the hard work."

Cameron thought it was interesting that somebody so *dirty* might be so fastidious. He made a note of it in a corner of his page and circled it twice. He looked back up at his host and decided to dig in a little bit.

"I hear that, Mister Bailey! On the books, this is a nice place, and the people in town seem to know it in a good light. Somebody mentioned you had some troubles concerning some missing folks… some kids?"

The question clearly put Finley Bailey off, and he scowled a bit, looking down into his nearly empty mug.

"Suppose we had some troubles, had a few folks walk off the job, and a couple of runaway kids. These people come up from Mexico and Texas and such... seasonally, of course. A few of them went and made some noise about their kids running off, but I've seen plenty of folks just up and leave for their reasons without having to think there was some foul play."

"Sure, folks are free to come and go! Plenty of work out here for those migrant families." Cam interjected.

"Rightly so! This is a great place filled with kind people. Don't want anyone thinking I said otherwise. Ain't got *nothing* to do with Rainbow or Mister O'Rourke."

The man returned to gazing down into his mug. Cam knew guilt when he saw it.

"Let's just focus on the good things, Finley. A Sunday piece, it needs to be positive. We save all the bad news for the weekdays!"

His lightheartedness drew a breath of relief from Bailey, who stood and went for a second cup of cold coffee, which he gulped down in a single breath. He turned back a Cameron with a smile.

"I appreciate that. There's nothing newsworthy in this cramped little office. How about I take you through the facility?"

Cam stood up and handed his mug back to the man.

"Sounds like a great idea!"

The two went on a stroll out of the office and toward the river. They walked the premises for a bit, Finley pointing out some equipment and a few interesting notes about the facility and the way they pack fruit.

"It's a grid, really. Side to side and top to bottom. They don't get squashed because they all share their burden, sorta like grains of salt!"

"Must help that you keep it cold, too, yeah?"

"Oh, sure. Fresher that way, too. Those warehouses are damn chilly!"

It was all rather hum-drum, but Cam penned away with notes. In reality, he was writing in chicken scratch while taking in the layout. Finley was somewhat oblivious, leading Cameron around and loudly praising all the different aspects of the facility, from the offload ramps that they built to meet the railroad to the gravel yard where they serviced all the harvesting equipment.

"See, the main orchard itself is just a short way up the road. This valley's littered with farms! It all rolls downhill, so to speak, and ends up here where we ship it off with pride."

After a half-hour of milling about and getting his shoes dusty, Cam was ready to snoop around a bit. They had gone full circle and ended up back at the office. Cam placed his hand on Finley's shoulder.

"Sir, this is fine work. You sure do have a lot to be proud of here. I think you've given me a lot to write about. My best interview to date!"

The man hooked his thumbs in the straps of his overalls and smiled broadly.

"You really think so? I've never been chatted up about the work, not like this."

Cameron nodded in approval and shook his hand.

"Oh, absolutely. Say, do you mind if I take one last look so I can make a few sketches?"

Finley waved his hand, "No problem at all. You take your time, and just make sure you don't bother too many of the hands. They're hourly wage... I don't think I can afford you interviewing *everyone!*" He laughed deeply and slapped his knee, having amused himself greatly.

Cameron chuckled, "Promise I'll stay out of their way and head out in a blink, don't you worry, Mr. Bailey!"

~

In the shade of a small stand of ochre-leafed trees not far from Rainbow Packing, Cam sat himself down at a rickety table a stone's throw from the river. The wind was picking up a bit.

Some rest won't kill me.

Withdrawing a cigarillo from his coat, Cam struck a match and held it to the end with his eyes closed, listening to the rustle of the foliage over his head.

Cam's mind was far away. In place, in time.

"That's the secret, pal, you gotta toast the foot. Even on the cheap smokes. That's the thing."

It was 1942 again, and a hand was on his shoulder. He looked up to see a tall, stout, young-faced private standing just behind him. Cam had been sitting on his helmet a few yards from the makeshift walls of their base of operations, nestled in the foothills, not far from the battlefront. The chill in the air stung his cheeks.

"Warm the foot, huh? I could use *my* feet warmed, private. Damned canvas boots!" Cam shot back, joking.

"Oh, I don't offer those services... but if we don't bomb the brothel tomorrow when we take that little town? I bet you'll have the chance. No, sir, you *toast* the foot. That's the smoking end, the correct term. Did you know all the flavor of a cigar is in the wrapper?"

While he was talking, Gabe tossed his helmet into the grass next to Cam and sat down, facing the same blue twilight on the horizon.

"I'll give that a try, sure. Never really thought about that before, but it makes sense. Marshall, right? Cam Mason."

"Oh, I know who you are, sir. You've got a bit of a reputation. Nobody in my tent has anything better to do than gossip. Someone taught me the same, you know, about cigars. The day after I got here. Hell, you believe I never had a cup of coffee until I joined the service?"

"Ah, you're a young cus, bet you never nee-"

"-ver needed it!" Gabe replied, finishing Cam's sentence.

"Ha! So maybe I'm old *and* wise." Cam smirked as he said it, feeling half-right.

Gabe kicked a few rocks out from under his boot heels and stretched his legs out, groaning.

"Cots are for shit. Worn out and rusty. How's yours? I hear your scouting detachment gets a bit of special treatment around here."

Cam chuckled and grinned at Gabe, puffing a wisp of cigar smoke in his direction.

"Maybe a bit, but that's cause we don't get shit-else out there on forward operations besides what we can carry. Have you seen any action yet?"

With a deep sigh, Gabe replied wistfully, "A bit, but nothing useful. Wish I was doing something a little… a little *bigger*, you know?"

A jeep rumbled past, and they both held their breath as its tired engine spat out a trail of blue smoke. The driver was unaware he was dive-bombing a couple of soldiers trying to enjoy the air. After it cleared, Cam dropped his shirt collar down from his mouth and chuffed his cigar to get the cherry hot again.

"So you're a patriot. Bet you signed up on day one. Fight *the good fight*. Sound about right?

Gabe stuffed his hands in his pockets to ward off the chilly air.

"Anything to get outta there. See the world. More than I knew from the magazines and such, anyway. Why'd you join up, sir?"

Chewing on the end of his stogie, Cam mulled the question for a moment. "Suppose it was the only thing that made sense. Heard what those flyboys were doing out at Tuskeegee, and I guess… I guess I saw some purpose in it. Not all of it, but… it made more sense than staying home."

"Sounds righteous enough. Maybe someday you'll have a chance to save *my* skin like these stories I've heard. I can repay you with quality cigars and a tin foot-bath! They sell 'em at Montgomery Ward's…"

"Be careful, son, I sent home a private with a rotten trench-foot last week, Campbell lost three toes a month back… and you might be next!"

Cam punched Gabe's arm, and laughed as Gabe fell off his helmet onto the soft ground laughing, "Ha! Good luck. I'm no good if you don't feed me. I do better close to base camp."

"Okay, you damn pack mule, I'll bring some extra jerky and a couple of these smokes. Deal?"

He handed the cigarillo tin to Gabe, then his lighter.

"Throw in a good double ration of coffee and I'm your guy, Lieutenant Mason."

"Shit, kid, just call me Cam. And shut up, just look at that view. Doesn't get much prettier here."

They sat back and watched the stars disappear into the blue twilight.

~

The burning match hit Cam's fingertips, snapping him back to reality. He'd drifted off into the memory, just long enough for the ache in his back to set in. He looked skyward and saw the wind rattling the trees. The dry leaves rustled against each other like the sound of crumpling a newspaper broadsheet. Matchbook still in hand, he stood up and decided to walk the property once more before heading home.

No sense in wasting the day. I could use a little more information, at the very least.

After a long walk along the river, Cam came upon the packing houses, finding most folks had gone for the day. There were still a few laborers in the warehouses; he could hear their voices inside and the sound of pallet jacks rolling around on concrete floors. He kept walking. A bit further down the road, as he was rounding the last warehouse, he found an older man sitting in the shade of the building's awning. The man was smoking a hand-rolled cigarette. His freckled brown skin wrinkled at the corners of his eyes and mouth. Cam thought he looked like a kind soul.

"¿Cómo te llamo?" Cam offered, inquiring about the man's name.

"[Salvador. Speak Spanish, eh?" the man responded, his accent thick.

"[Enough to say hello, perhaps a little more.]"

"[Ah! Some is better than none. Sit with me?]" Salvador offered with a gesture.

Cam leaned against the corrugated steel wall and slid down onto his rear, with the groan of an old man falling into his favorite armchair.

"[Thank you, Salvador. I'm Cameron. I'm a newspaper man.]"

"Mucho gusto," Salvador replied cheerfully and went back to watching the smoke slither down his hand from the small cigarette.

"[Have you been here long, Salvador?]"

"[Since before dawn. Long day. They are all long days.]"

With a chuckle, Cam rephrased his question. "[How long have you been a *worker* at Rainbow, friend? Many years?]"

Smirking, Salvador implied he'd been ribbing Cam. "[Oh, sure, long time. Twenty-nine years gone now.]"

Without saying a word, Cam opened his notebook to one of the last pages, handing it to Salvador. The man put his smoke out in the gravel and read the page, mumbling to himself as he worked down the list of names.

"Mariela… Lucinda… Delgado… Angél. Pe…. *Pedro Garza.*"

With each name, Salvador's brow furrowed a bit more.

"[Why do you show me this?]" the old man inquired, brow furrowed in concern.

He handed the notebook back to Cameron, who tucked it away before answering.

"[Some of them left here, left Rainbow. They never *arrived* anywhere.]"

Salvador shifted his weight to stand up as he replied, "[I don't know anything. I've got to—]"

Cam took his arm, firmly but with a gaze that pleaded empathy. He nodded toward the ground, pleading "lo siento, lo siento… un momento, *please?*"

Reluctantly, Salvador sat back down and rocked his head back against the wall.

"[We do not talk about that.]"

"[I see, but I am not here for Rainbow. I came to help.]"

In English, Salvador grunted, "Nobody helps. Gringo, negro, nobody helps. Why you?"

"[Salvador, these niños, niñas… they are missing many places. I follow, I seek them, for two years. I read, I learn español…]— Solo para encontrar a las niñas"

Shaking his head, the old man replied, "[The little children are gone. The parents are gone, no more work.]" "Terminado."

Cam placed his hand on Salvador's shoulder and pleaded. "[This happened many places. Good men are looking. Do you know where they went? Who took them?]"

"[Good men. Hmmph. Boss says the children have run off. Three little ones, too small to run away. No, they did not leave. Taken. *Disappeared*.]"

Cam sat back and pulled out his dog tags from behind his collar, raising them for Salvador to see. They looked dull and worn, much like Cameron felt at the moment. The sun was setting soon.

"[Many children, Salvador.] Dozens. California, Washington, Oregon, South Dakota."

Salvador put up a hand to stop him. "The world… your country is not kind, Mister Cameron. Men do nothing. Soldier. I know you have *seen*."

Cam took out his notebook and flipped to a page where John Talbot had sketched the trucks Cam had been searching for in Isleton two years prior. The little pencil sketch had been filled in with crayon where the blue colors should be. John was no artist, but Cam had little else to go on.

"[Ves… estos camiones?]' Cam repeated in English, unsure of the proper translation, 'Have you seen these trucks, Salvador?"

Dusting off his hands, Salvador took the notebook once more and turned it sideways to look at the sketch. With a deep breath and letting it out in a huff between his teeth, Salvador nodded his head and tossed the notebook back in Cameron's lap.

"[Your trucks come. They get gas, stop quickly. Maybe five times, maybe more. No loading.]"

Cam took Salvador's arm and they stood up together, nearly embracing.

"No cargo? They don't take fruit? Ah…" he had to think about the translation before asking again rather shabbily, "Ellos no… toman cajas? Nada?"

Salvador thought about the words for a moment. It was obvious Cam's Spanish was lacking. "Never. Only truck I see that never take or brings boxes." Salvador responded, head on a swivel, looking for anyone who might be eavesdropping.

"Leaving north every time."

"Then I go North. Salvador, you are a good man. You will see me again, friend. I'll be—' he recalled what he hoped were the right words just as he shook Salvador's hand, '...*volveré con buenas palabras*. I'll see you again with good news."

Cameron left Salvador there in the shade, briskly walking back to the lot where he'd parked. After reaching the truck, he took a moment to let the feeling of adrenaline wash over him as he clutched the steering wheel tightly. His hands were almost shaking, his armpits soaked. Excitement.

"Christ. I gotta find a *phone.*"

Casing a Joint

Dusk was creeping over the horizon as Cam made his call over to Seattle. Just as he suspected, Billy was in the office 'working late'. The reality is that Billy was sitting in the office, drinking Scotch and reading magazines. Like any manager, work was not something this man spent much time doing. His specialty was establishing connections, securing favors, and cultivating 'owes-you-ones' with valuable people. From the payphone, Cam both briefed Billy on the new information and put his old friend to task. The plan was for Billy to make inquiries with Rainbow's local police department about the missing persons' cases, taking along a friend who happened to be a federal investigator interested in closing the case. As always, Billy had his connections, and luckily, someone in a very legitimate position was willing to vouch for him if things escalated.

Throughout the call, Billy seemed distracted, and Cam inquired why. "What's got you off in dreamland, man? I thought this was interesting to you," he teased. Billy replied as expected. "Just business, buddy. Listen, I wasn't gonna tell you, I promised not to say anything...' A change in tone accompanied his pause, now more somber when he continued, 'We got Shay back in town a couple of days ago. I gave him your number and filled him in on the details. He's gonna be reaching out to you, okay?"

Cam was as pleased as punch. "Well, hell, I miss the guy just like you. Can't wait to catch up with the man!"

"Maybe, he's had a rough one. His mother passed away, okay? So tread lightly, that's all. You know how Shay can be sometimes. Sorta... *eccentric.*"

"His momma? That wonderful lady mailed us so many sweet things when we were deployed. You shoulda seen it, Billy, the candy and the magazines… she must've been a real special old gal." There was a quiet moment, something of a moment of silence.

"…must've been, yeah. He could use a friend, and I know you boys go back. Just let me know if he seems straight, if he's ready for work. Okay?"

Billy's concern was well-founded. Shamus "Shay" Hayes had a propensity for diving headlong into the bottle and losing his way when the going got tough. Cam knew he owed his life to Shay at least a couple of times over and was going to do his best to cheer the man up. He made a mental note to check in with the office at the motor inn a few times a day until Shay reached out.

Billy, the perpetual businessman, directed the conversation back to the work at hand. He and Cameron discussed possible outcomes and how best to approach the job. With one good, strong lead, the options were few and clear. Cam offered to check back the following evening on the day's progress after some reconnaissance on O'Rourke, with Billy agreeing to do his part. They ended the call with the usual pleasantries. Cam's mood was still a bit elevated; he would be happy to see Shay despite the bad news.

Cam found himself at the small sink in his room to mix up a cocktail with his half-empty bottle of bourbon and a bottle of ginger ale. He'd stopped on the way home for a bit of dry goods, enough for a few days. He knew that he would be eating on the road for a stakeout, which meant bread, cheese, dried meats, and a thermos full of coffee, with an empty milk jug to use as needed.

He'd done enough stake-outs to know the tricks. At his local upholstery shop back in Richmond, he had insisted on getting the thickest, smoothest cowhide bench seat he could afford for his little knockaround Plymouth. Had it stuffed like the couches of royalty, and he *almost* looked forward to spending a good part of the day off his feet in that well-cushioned truck cab.

A few days prior, while looking up Corker's home, Cam had also managed to find an address for O'Rourke in that phone book. At the time, he wondered why anyone would want to be found so easily. Not the bastards, though. He knew the best way for a guilty person to seem innocent was to hide in plain sight.

The drive back into town was a pleasure; this late in the year, the leaves were turning. He needed a warm coat against the morning chill, so he put on his leather jacket over a thick denim shirt and two cotton shirts. His dusty and weather-beaten wide-brimmed Western hat topped off the ensemble, and he tipped the visor down in the truck to keep the morning sun out of his eyes. Much like many mornings, he warmed up his hands by lighting up a thick cigar, palming it in alternating hands as he drove. After a short while, the heater in the truck kicked in, and he had plenty of hot air at his feet and across the dashboard's defroster vents. That big V-8 engine certainly pumped plenty of warmth when you drove her in low gear.

At a reasonably early hour, he had arrived at the home of his target.

Nice house. Too big. Wonder if it's got a basement.

With a good view from a short way up the block, he parked in a place where he could see a lot of the property but stay relatively out of sight. He loved a cold morning stakeout, fogged up the windows of the truck, and he could not be seen from outside, except perhaps for a silhouette. He took off his hat and sat low in the seat, using the back of his hand to swipe a small, clear view through the humidity that had silvered the windshield. He wiped away the edges so he had the perfect view of just the house and lawn, a little house-shaped opening in the fogged glass.

The O'Rourke family clearly had been wealthy people. He silently wondered whether they were all as bad as old Wally. He wondered whether the family wealth perhaps came from nefarious things like stealing kids and selling them, or if it was just the one black sheep son-of-a-bitch whom Cam was here to stake out.

Plenty of families got their money selling slaves and stealing land… guess if you look back far enough, any family would have a skeleton in the closet.

Ruminating over his disdain for a man he'd never met, Cam brought his notebook and a sharp pencil. One of the things he enjoyed doing, despite never having any formal training or much direction since his young school years, was sketching architecture. This particular home was very out of place here; a New England-style brick colonial home, replete with the Ivy and the white picket fence that one might see in upstate New York or Massachusetts. He took a breath and let out a long sigh, steadying his hand a bit after the coffee from a cafe on the edge of town. Cigar in mouth and pencil in one hand, a glove on the other, he raised his knee as a table and began sketching the estate. That was what this home was, an *estate*.

Maybe I'll have myself an estate someday. I don't see the need for the space… I wonder if Gabe's place in Chicago is nice like this. That woman probably has them livin' in a dream home from LIFE magazine… lucky cus. And the GAMS on that Lindy. Shit. I miss that big lunk.

In the back of his mind, he knew such a beautiful home might not survive the absolute hell he was likely to put this bastard through. His sketch was a bit solemn, as part of Cameron's grand plan was possibly to burn this lovely house down to embers, bringing O'Rourke into a frothing panic.

In his years of subterfuge during the war, Cam had learned that it was easier to blindside and trap somebody when they were otherwise occupied with a terrible event. He recalled one mission where he and his unit had snuck out to a village not far from the battlefront in France. They were on orders to recon and, if possible, capture a commander in one of Hitler's SS commands (of which there were nearly too many to keep track; Germans sure had a knack for bureaucracy). When they arrived at the occupied building, it appeared to be heavily fortified, so they set to clearing the place of personnel with incendiary devices to set the main house alight. Men panicked and failed to extinguish the flames, and were easily sniped while fleeing for their lives. The screams and shouts, and raging inferno covered the sounds of the gunfire. When Cam's unit charged through the back door, they cleared the building to find the commander in question. He'd been rocked awake and choked with smoke, terrified out of his mind... running around in the buff and pleading for help. The man had thrown sense out the window, and in his panic, he was easily bagged for delivery back to the unit, gagged and shivering in the cold night air.

That bare-naked Nazi ended up being an asset for the Allied forces, but mysteriously, the man himself didn't survive his interrogations. Cam was told he 'ran out of intel, then ran out of breath; heart gave out.' Sure, it seemed cold at the time, but after another brutal year at war? Cam *understood* why they'd snuffed the bastard. Cameron himself had not been present for that interrogation, but the men who extracted the commander's tactical knowledge saved hundreds or likely thousands of the Allied forces' lives. They were also the men who had trained Cameron to interrogate a captive.

Cam quietly counted his blessings for their tutelage every time he had to lay hands on somebody in such a situation. Despite how ugly such business could be, he wasn't a man who minded getting his hands dirty, and he knew where to draw the line depending on the severity of the situation. Cameron had taken a few lives in his days, but each life he had taken had always been in the defense or protection of others. Rarely just his own.

His mind was wandering a bit, though the sketch was nearly complete. Tall, slender evergreens lined the property, and a looming, bluish-green forested mountain covered the horizon behind. His picturesque view through the small patch of clear window was enough to help him lay down a sketch that he was actually proud of. Looking at the sketch and admiring his shading work on the roof, his eye was drawn up to somebody leaving the property. In an instant, he recognized the man to be O'Rourke himself from the photograph. Of course, the photo was a few years old, and O'Rourke looked a bit heavier and more tired, but it was indeed him.

Okay, you sonofabitch, let's see what you're up to.

With O'Rourke departing, Cam had two distinct options. The easy option? Stay put and watch the place for other individuals coming and going. No other way to know if Wally's going to be alone later. The harder option? Tail the man without being spotted. Right now, Cam was prepared to take either route, so he pulled out a nickel and flipped it up in the air. It bounced off the cloth headliner of the truck and fell flat down into his palm, heads up.

Looks like we're following.

At that very moment, as Cameron went to tuck the nickel in his shirt pocket, he was taken by surprise by the sound of a hand slapping the roof of his pickup. The nickel fell under his seat. He glanced over his left shoulder and saw no one at the window. He looked over his right shoulder just as the passenger door swung open wide! He nearly swung a fist at his good friend Shay Hayes, leaning into the truck and grinning like the Cheshire cat from the children's books.

"Goddammit, Shay!"

Old Friend

"You nearly gave me a stroke!"

Cameron's voice was loud enough to wake the neighborhood.

In his cheerful but slightly muddled Irish lilt, Shay Hayes put his finger to his lips and loudly whispered, "Hush, Cam, you're on a stake-out, yeh? You'll give up the gig!"

Shay chuckled as he took to plucking the front bench seat clear to make way for his tailored duff.

The old man was near speechless.

"What in the blue hell are you doing here, buddy? You were supposed to *call!* I'm in the middle of serious shit here, youngster."

Climbing into the cab of the truck, Shay chortled while he shoved paper wrappers, cigar bands and the (thankfully still empty) glass milk jug onto the floor.

"Billy-boy insisted that I come visit my good friend, but *I* insisted I make it a surprise!" he had a mischievous smile, "In fact, he tried to talk me out of it. I said to him, 'And who are you to keep me from my one true love?' So he told me what you're up to!"

He poked Cameron in the ribs, teasing him like a juvenile brother.

"Oh, not with that shit again. I... seriously, Irish, I'm on a stakeout!! You remember what that means, don't you? Stop poking me!"

Cameron's temper was not short, but Shay always loved to press his buttons.

"Of course I remember. You sat here for *how many* hours watching this place just to see the man drive off? You used to be all action! I think you're getting soft, old boy," he poked Cameron in the stomach this time.

Cameron swatted his hand away and scowled, though he was holding back laughter.

"Just… just get in and sit the hell down, you're going to ruin this! Hey, that's my jug. Don't come in here like you own the place! You drive me crazy with that shit," he started picking up his things off the floor and fastidiously arranging them on the seat between them.

Shay was bouncing in the seat like he'd had a pot of coffee.

"Don't fuss about the jug, let's go get some food. You can take a piss there. *Jeeeeeezus*, this is the same truck!?! I wasn't sure at first…you've been driving this heap for getting on 20 years, are you ever going to give her up?"

Cameron knew that Shay secretly adored the old Plymouth and was just giving him a hard time. Cam fired up the ignition, put his hat back on, and turned his attention toward the road. Through half-clenched teeth, he chortled and said with a wry smile, "You're buyin' breakfast, slim."

Not long after, the two were settled into a cozy booth at one of the local diners. Shay had popped in beforehand to make sure it was *friendly*. A roadside establishment with welcoming signage on the door that told Cam it was a good choice. Shay had nabbed the booth first, while Cameron took his time in the john. The two had received some sideways glances on the way in, given Shay's flamboyant appearance in a perfectly fitted twill suit, with a bowler hat on his clean-cut head. His accompanying a colored man was probably the *least* of people's concerns.

Coffee made its way to their table, and Shay was fanning himself with a menu after doffing his coat and loosing the buttons on his vest. "These little restaurants, they're always far too warm. In all my travels, I never could figure out why they keep these places so warm. Nobody likes to eat when they're sweating!"

Cameron didn't look up from his coffee when he replied, "Cheap. They're just cheap. Not every place has air-conditioning like the city, and the kitchens are hot as hell."

Shay mulled it over a bit, "I suppose you're right. I've been in Seattle too long. In fact, going home was just the reprieve I needed. It's a beautiful season; everything is flourishing, lush, and green. I think that's supposed to be my favorite color, isn't it? He was poking at the stereotype about the Irish, but Cameron remembered seeing him wear *plenty* of green.

"Shay, if you didn't want to wear so much green, why the *hell* did you join the army?"

The well-dressed man smiled a devilish smile and replied, "The guns! Oh, and that delicious food!" It was a ridiculous answer from an absurd man.

Cam peered around for a bit as he lowered his voice. "You know I'm glad you're here, Shay. We need to talk about this job." Shay looked up at him from over the brim of the menu.

"We do, sure, but not here. No, my man, we have much to discuss somewhere quieter," he offered with a knowing wink.

Their waitress came just then and jotted down their order. Shay was his usual charming self and bargained for a side of bacon in exchange for the toast. She teased him, "It's only because you could stand to put some meat on those bones!"

Cam swigged his coffee while Shay chatted the lass up a bit before she departed for the kitchen.

"Cam, I can't stay long. In fact, Billy has me on my way out toward Chicago for some strange stuff. You know he likes to send me on all the wild goose chases, but I insisted on coming through to see you. You're still my brother, you know. He told me about what you may be up against here, the challenges you may face. I think I could help. But we've only got the day. So let's have a good morning before I kick your ass this afternoon!"

Cameron simply replied, "Fair enough. Tell me about your trip. I heard some news… but I'd rather hear it from you."

Shay took a deep swig of coffee and cleared his throat.

"I suppose you're inferring about me Ma. You'd be right, it's news in a way. Perhaps not how I wanted to spend my trip home, but it's not all bad, my friend."

Cameron shook his head and offered, "Well, I'm sorry either way. If you want to talk about it-" but Shay cut him off.

"Actually, in a way, I suppose I do. She was a grand lady, that's without question. Perfect? Heavens no, but I don't suppose anybody is. We all have our flaws, Cam. I'm blessed that I could visit her before the end, it helped me put some things in perspective, you know? Last of my family, and all. I feel a bit like a dangling thread now… loose. 'A bit in the breeze,' as she said… words I had never heard her speak 'til that day. She could see me, Cam. Not as her baby, but as a man. Grown, weary. Last of the Hayes clan."

The waitress had arrived at the table with their breakfast, which consisted of ham and eggs with seasoned potatoes. They had ordered the same, as they often did. Cam buttered his toast, and Shay dove right in for the bacon.

Shay continued with a mouth half-full, "Truly, I don't want to get too philosophical or naught, yeh? It's simply that you know I don't have a lot of memories from way back."

"We don't all get much of a childhood…" Cam winced as memories of his talks with his father, talks of slavery and hardship, talks of their family tree, somber memories of how many branches were broken so young.

Shay replied, "Sure, I suppose yes. I suppose that's what I mean. Listen, my sweet Ma went out in a good way. Peaceful. She knew it was her time, and she only had one thing to pass along to me."

Cameron raised an eyebrow, asking, "What did she say?"

"She told me she loved me, and she said… I s'pose in very near words as she was speaking the old language… that I best find my coming years leaving behind all of the violence. She told me I had peace and real goodness in my heart, and I simply needed to follow that. She'd not wanted me to be a soldier, but she knew I couldn't be swayed back in my youth."

Cameron was quiet for a few moments, thinking of the words to respond. They both ate a bit, and Cameron finally spoke up.

"My old man asked the same of me. I just… I needed a fresh start, and it was the only thing knocking at my door. Not surprised she didn't want her sole surviving son running off to war. Might've told you the same myself if I hadn't met you in a goddamn *trench*. You told me once she didn't know all of it; Did she mean the war? Or maybe what you've been up to *since*?"

Shay nodded and waved his fork a bit to ask for a pause. After a swallow, "She cursed my name for joining the service… but not that, no. I'm certain she meant this gumshoe bit I've been playing at. I believe she knew, though I had never told her…. This work we do, my friend, it's not always right. I think perhaps it's about time for me to retire the ol' billy club and bare-knuckle. I'm getting old for it anyway."

Cameron laughed hard, and bits of food came out of his mouth. He looked at his friend with a curious eye, "Shay, you look not one day older than when we met. Hell, you're still in fighting shape. Look at me, I can't keep these hairs from going gray. I'm just… tired. I think my knees started making noise. What in the world are you talking about, *old*? You could do nearly anything. You could start a whole new life today and settle down with a pension."

Shay looked a bit dejected at his friend's mistaking him. "I'm plenty aged, but that's not the point. She's right, you know. If we don't stop to seek some peace, I don't like where all this is headed. You remember, Gabriel, he…" and he ended his sentence, shaking his head. Neither man spoke for some time, and Cameron was losing his appetite.

Cameron turned to the simple white clock above the beautiful pastry case. Ten-fifty-five in the morning. He hung his head for another moment and reached into his pocket, withdrawing his beaten-up flask. As he locked eyes with Shay, he took a deep swig. Though Shay started to speak, Cameron cut him off, "It's 5:00 p.m. somewhere, slim."

The duo finished breakfast with hardly another word. Shay ate like a man in his twenties, famished as always. Cameron pushed the food around with his fork and took a few more bites. The conversation had ended on a low note. After the check was settled and the two were back at the truck, both men stopped at the doors, and Shay ran his hand along the roof of the Plymouth.

"I really do love this thing."

Cameron smiled, "I'm not puttin' you in my will just yet, sonny. Hey, let's take a beat. Somewhere we can stretch our legs. I saw a fine little spot a ways back."

Shay nodded, and they embarked into the rolling hills.

On the ride, Shay opened up Cameron's notepad. He saw names, dates, special little sideline notes about people who might be fibbing, or places that might be significant in the investigation. Cameron was a private investigator, sure, but he was still also a soldier. Shay could see that some of the notes were instructions from Billy, and others were references to specific tactical maneuvers or interrogation tactics. He took a deep sigh of breath and turned the page, expecting more disheartening facts about the deceased and Cameron's skepticism in just about everyone and everything. Instead, as the little pickup rambled down the old highway, Shay turned the page to a beautiful and surprising sketch he had made just that morning. Shay recognized the house Cameron had been watching over.

"Cam, you bloody genius, this is beautiful. I mean to say, you've got a real talent!"

Shay was being genuine, and for Cameron, it was the highest praise he had received in a long, solitary while. He continued, "Where did you learn to draw like this? A clunky old tank like you!"

With a balled-up fist, he tapped Cameron on the shoulder. He was joking, but Cam's face was stern. In all seriousness, Shay rested the notepad down on his leg and turned to Cameron.

"I'm sorry, old friend, if I've struck a nerve."

Cameron was quiet for a few minutes, navigating down the old tree-lined road. He finally spoke up, "My daughter. I used to draw with my daughter."

Shay was both elated to hear Cam open up. He began rambling on, "Why, I never knew you had a little one! Oh, that's fantastic! Why haven't I ever heard you mention her? If she's like her father, she must be quite a talent. Say now, what are you doing on the road? You should be retired so you can focus on bein' a family man! Christ, I'm gon' to speak with Billy about gettin' you a vacation."

Shay turned his attention back to the drawing. The geometry was crisp, and the gentle strokes that make up the trees could have easily been mistaken for an old print photograph.

Cameron gripped the steering will tightly and took a deep breath. "I can't see my daughter, Shay. She's passed."

Shay looked back up at him with the most pallid, ghastly look on his face as he processed Cameron's words.

Closing the note pad and folding his hands on his lap, "I'm so sorry, I'm so sorry. I had no idea, I would never have said…" and his voice trailed off a bit. He had known Cameron for over a decade and had never heard of this aspect of Cameron's life before.

Cam glanced at Shay, whose face was painted in remorse. Still gripping the wheel and facing the road, he did his best to smooth out the awkward moment.

"It was a long time ago, no harm, Shay. You haven't stepped on any land mines here. It's… I just don't talk about that. I haven't for a long time."

"Cameron, I won't bring it up again. But, if you would do me the grace of telling me what happened? I've never heard you talk of family, save a brief rumble about that ex of yours. Always supposed you were just private."

Despite his awkward insistence on knowing more, Cameron knew that Shay was processing this new information about his long-time friend and genuinely was concerned about what had happened. Cam swallowed the lump in his throat and pulled the truck over onto a gravel shoulder right alongside the wide river. He gazed off into the running water and spoke.

"Abigail, that was her name. Abigail Lailah Mason. My beautiful little girl. We had her young, Lizzy and I. Elizabeth. Shit, we were kids ourselves, barely out of high school. Lizzy had gotten pregnant. I wasn't working; we were trying to avoid a pregnancy, but little Abigail had other ideas. Can't say it wasn't my fault, anyway. And that child, oh lord, she was in a hurry… she came early, kicking like hell. I remember pacing curbside at that hospital ward for the better part of 22 hours. A whole day had flown past, and Lizzy was just dyin' to get it over with and hold her baby. I must've bummed fifty cigarettes waitin' for news, Lizzy was… she was a little slender, and that can be risky if… well, anyway, Abigail was born late that night. It was magic, Shay. We had a great room; my pops had some connections at the hospital, and they put us up in the good ward. Not in the lesser rooms like they usually sequester us folks. If they'll have us at all."

"Suppose I do, yeh." Shay sat there, watching the river with Cam. His old friend was teary-eyed, but the resolve and stoicism chiseled into his face were like a Renaissance painting.

Cam took a long breath and relaxed his grip on the wheel.

"We were watching the stars. Lizzy was in terrible pain, but we just counted those stars. We got to nearly a hundred, I was markin' the window with a felt tip pen for each one, but finally Abigail must've told her it was time. From then on, it was just… *easy*. Baby wanted out as much as Lizzy wanted her out, and when she came into the world, she was perfect and still and smiling. Smiling! Man, I kid you not. I grew up twenty years in those twenty short minutes. It was magic… felt like magic, anyway. Elizabeth's doctor, a real kind sort, Jewish, I think. He told me a story from his *old* country. A story about an Angel, born at night. Lailah. So, little Abigail Lailah Mason. That baby was absolutely *everything* to me, Shamus."

The two men faced forward and sat quiet for some time. Cameron had shut off the engine, and the only sounds were the rushing water and the chirping of a few forest birds. Shay knew better than to spoil this time; he had never seen Cameron be anything but strong. He had no idea how to proceed. So, he realized it was best to let Cameron take his time.

Cameron took his hat off, resting it on the shift knob where it lazily swung back and forth. He placed his hands on his lap as though he were in church. Staring down at his belt buckle, he continued. "It was wonderful, but it was tough. I chose to raise my family in California because I knew that's where she would have the most opportunities. Folks there had some pretty fine ideas about equality, about justice. About color. Lizzy didn't want to be away from her parents back in Mississippi, of course, but I didn't care. I insisted on it, I *insisted* that we try and make a better life for ourselves. You know how this world can be. They say it's changing, but I'm still waitin'… been waiting my whole damn life, Shay."

The lump in his throat had returned to strain his voice, but he spoke on.

"I had six wonderful years with my lil' babygirl. She was perfect, every hair on her head. Artistic and talented. Her mother, Elizabeth, was the best mother ever to hold a child. It was like a dream—a different life. We had Abby's friends over; it was her birthday party. Seven years old! She was shorter than the rest of her class, and they all loved her, watched out for her. I remember it was so odd seein' her in school with black and Oriental and white babies, all just smiling and learning." His eyes misted, and he took a moment to watch the river.

Shay breathed a sigh and murmured, "*Beag*. It's… It's an old Irish word for *small*, me Ma used to call me that when I was in nappies."

Cam smirked slightly and cleared his throat before continuing. He was choked up, wistful.

"My little babygirl… little *beag*. Huh. I like that. We were throwing her party, and I was inside, while Lizzy was in the backyard. Nobody could find Abigail for the cake. We called her out; we thought she was playing a hiding game. Man, we looked everywhere—closets, basement, the whole place. We…" he paused, tears rolling down his face now. Shay handed him a crisp white pocket square.

Cam sucked in air through his teeth, looking for some sensation that would ease the tautness in his face.

"Lizzy bet me she was hiding in the sedan. Abigail loved that back seat; all her toys were back there. I was herding the littles in the backyard when I heard the worst sound I've ever heard. Lizzy ran out, and she found our baby there in the street. Abby was runnin' after her ball, and some fool driving too fast in his Packard… She was— Lizzy wailed like a banshee. I could hear her heart break, I just *knew*."

Shay reached over and clasped his hand on Cameron's shoulder. He did the best he could to let his friend know that enough had been said. Cameron looked pale, but his eyes were clear, still filled with fury after all these years. Shay could see his hands clenched in his lap, steely fists, and understood at that very moment how such a beautiful and loving father might end up a cold and stoic killer, a world away. Another life, another man. Shay understood that pain, and he swallowed his words, sitting there in silence with his brother.

After a short while had passed and the tension in the air had become less palpable, Cameron raised his chin and cleared his throat. He fired up the Plymouth and put his hat back squarely on his head. Readjusting in his seat, the once again stoic man continued his drive up the narrow old lanes. Without saying a word, he withdrew that paper pack of cigarettes from the glove box. Pulling out two sticks, he handed one to Shay, and Shay returned the favor by bringing out his brass side-wheel lighter (quite an antique), which he used to give Cameron a light before lighting his own. If you could count on one thing, you could always hedge your bets that Shay would be polite in nearly any situation. Hell, he had even been polite in battle.

Cameron nodded in appreciation and lit his smoke, never taking his eyes off the road.

As they climbed up a bit of a hill, Cameron turned off the pike and parked the truck on a scenic vista. It was a beautiful place, but very sparse. As the men stepped out, they each looked around, finding no signs of life or civilization in that little remote valley. A line of trees blocked the road. Here, they could stretch their legs and talk more.

Shay used another handkerchief to dust off the front fender and headlight on his side, sitting on it and crossing his ankles. The curvy fenders were relatively comfortable, if not a bit chilly through wool slacks. Cameron folded his arms, and they leaned back comfortably on the nose of the truck. A hawk flew by overhead, then circled down to catch some unseen prey in the beautiful valley where the river had long since cut its path.

"I really appreciate you coming through, Shay. Boy, we sure have seen some things," he nodded toward the breathtaking panorama in front of them.

Shay nodded and took a drag before offering, "Honestly, after I talked to Billy and he told me how deep all this had gotten, you see, I felt an obligation, old boy. I know how seriously you have met all this responsibility, and now I know why…" he paused a bit, counting his words. "I *feel* that I know a bit better why you haven't taken a rest, and why you haven't been home in nearly a year. I understand it, maybe I disagree with it… But I understand. The littles. The wee ones who haven't got anyone. They've… well, they've got you now. Whether they know it yet or nae."

Cameron nodded solemnly. He unfolded his arms and hitched his thumbs into his belt loops, relaxing his shoulders slightly. "I've got to do this, I can't explain it, but I need to see this thing through. It's all I know, it's all I can think about. I've held these photographs, I've stood in the bedrooms of little children snatched away. The corners in leaky lean-tos where a simple man with leather hands can't bring himself to toss away that old straw bed or a flour-sack doll. I'm getting old, Shay. If I can do one good thing before I give up and sallow on my porch? It needs to be *this*." His serious tone implied how far the man might be willing to go.

"Cam, Cam. Jesus, pal, haven't seen this darkness in you in ages, it's a bit frightening. Do you know that? You are the *only* man I've ever been afraid of. I've seen you out there, in combat; you're a beast. You put yourself in harm's way many a time, more so than me or any other man in that damnable war. Do you know that nobody thought you would make it? A whisper of a mission, and you would grab a rank of men and head for the hills. You were unstoppable. And do you know what?"

Cam shrugged a bit and grunted, "What?"

"The only thing that can stop you, old boy, is you *yourself*. You've got to make a choice one of these days to take your foot off the gas. Honestly, it's a wee bit scary even now. I notice how your eyes narrow when you work. I've seen that look, and I know how far you are going to take this. I know how far you are willing to go, anyway."

Cameron sneered just a bit; it might have been the start of a smile. "I'm gonna get this son of a bitch, I'm gonna put an end to all of it. Are you gonna help?"

Shay didn't want to respond directly; this was a conversation, not a bludgeoning. "Just… just think of the options. I know the easy thing is to put a bit of lead in this fool and throw him in the bog, but what about the other way?"

Cameron cocked his head to one side, turning to Shay.

"Other way?" he was being snide.

"You know it, Cam. You know, we don't always have to go in guns a-blazing like this was some battle. Do you remember that lesson we got in '43, that mission in Austria?"

Cameron shrugged again, "Barely."

"We had to pull those boys out of the net in that little shabby town on the hillside. Remember, they got yanked off the train and hemmed up by the local goose-steppers?"

Cameron nodded silently, recalling the mission as if it were an episode of a serial radio drama.

Shay continued with a soft voice, "It wouldn't have served well to go in and put all those folks in their graves, of course not. So we loot the fuckers. We take their stash and drop a stack of American dollars on the desk. Made the fuckers think their commander was selling out to the Americans."

"Those fools strung up their *captain!*" Cam burst out laughing.

"And when they were busy spending those American dollars on whores and liquor, we sprung our boys and got them off that mountain *safely.* And only the bad guys lost, not a single shot fired. Sometimes… you have to be clever to *really* win."

Cameron had folded his arms again and laughed at the idea. His body language spoke to his satisfaction at the long-forgotten memory.

"So listen, Cam, all we have to do here is hang the bastard out to dry. You don't need to add to that tally of yours; Lord knows it's high enough. Think about it, who's the most clever bastard I ever met?"

Cameron smiled, still gazing off at the rushing waters. "Probably *yourself*, but that ain't saying much." He poked Shay in the ribs.

Shay put his hand on his chest in mock surprise. "…me? I'm insulted! Of course, it's true, but I'm insulted all the same! It's *you*, you daft bastard. It's always been you, right there behind me!" he patted Cameron on the back, and they shared a belly laugh that echoed across the valley.

Cameron turned to him. "I'm a dog after a bone, ain't I? Hell, I'm drinking a bottle or two a week. God damn it, man. You might be right for once."

"I know I'm right. Ma was right, and she was wise." Shay paused for a moment to clear his throat, a bit of somber emotion in the words that followed. "If you don't stop throwing yourself at this, you may not see the forest for the trees. Use that damned big brain of yours, find a better way. Everybody who knows you is worried. Gabe and Lindy are worried. We've seen too much death and destruction, the lot of us. There's a more righteous path, and I've watched you walk it. No ego, no sacrifice, just righteousness. It's nary too late to make a fresh start, and by Christ, if anybody needs it? It's you, Cameron Fucking Mason."

Cam paused and cocked his head, "Gabe is worried about me?"

"We talked a month ago. He's doing rather well, you know. Considering all that he went through…"

"How's he seem? Is he… does he remember? Does he remember what I did to him?"

"Gabe remembers you saving him from that hospital, arm-in-arm with Lindy. He remembers you're his *brother*, and he loves you accordingly. And he's fine, fried-egg brains and all. Aye, he's a touch sillier than he used to be, but maybe that's for the best. Billy has him doing recon again if you can believe it… Don't you owe it to him to stick around a little longer? Don't you owe it to *all* of us?"

Cameron heaved a heavy breath and let the mist in his eyes dry a bit before responding. This man standing next to him, despite being born on the other side of the world, was perhaps his closest friend left alive.

Left alive.

The thought resonated with him deeply. He understood that there was no ego or authority in the voice of his old friend; it was all honesty, altruism, and genuine concern. In his mind, Cam tried to make a quick count of the people whom he had left to care for him, and he could not make a list beyond this little world, beyond Billy and John and Gabe and Lindy. Shay, of course. Not another name, not another soul. Not another face flashed before his eyes. In that moment, he felt very alone, yet more connected to this silly Irish lad than to anybody else in his life, or anybody in nearly a countless number of days. He knew Shay was right, to the core of his being.

Cameron stood up, dusted off the back of his pants, and walked over to the precipice of the scenic vista. He stretched his arms out wide, palms stretched open, almost in a crucified position. From the depths of his stomach, he bellowed a great and mighty shout, a war cry against all of his past wrongdoing. All of the anger and all of the gut-wrenching resentment he held, what had been driving him to insomnia and alcoholism… he released all of that turmoil into the air until he was out of breath and his throat took on a rasp. The deep and booming shout echoed across the rocky and moss-laden valley walls.

His arms dropped to his side, he slumped forward a bit, and took a new breath. The cool air filled his lungs, sending electric tingles into his limbs and digits. He felt invigorated, almost elated. This burden that had pushed him so very deep into the depths of himself felt lifted away.

He turned now to Shay, and from the corner of his eye, he caught a glimpse of a very old, very frail man standing before him in that same woolen suit. He blinked hard, and his eyes cleared. There stood his dapper and handsome young friend, and Cam said nothing of the trick his eyes had just played on him.

"You're a strange man, Hayes—one of a kind. I miss how it used to be. You're right about all of it. Goddammit." He walked back toward the truck as Shay pulled a slender gold flask out of his pocket. He flicked the small spout open and reached out to offer it to Cam.

"The old country stuff, pal. Just a nip should coax the day along. We've got planning to do."

Cam smiled widely at his brother-in-arms and toasted to the sky as he enjoyed a bit of the caramel-colored grog. He felt it splash warm across his tongue, then dissipate in his palate. Hardly an effort to swallow, it was nearly effervescent. Not quite a liquor, not precisely a spirit. With a slightly confused look, Cam handed the flask back to Shay.

Shay took his own sip, slipped the flask away, and flippantly appeased Cam's confusion with "Nothing else like it, yeah? Now let's get to work. We've got a plan to hatch."

They climbed back into the truck, the engine rumbling to life with a flick of the key worn nearly toothless. Shay was correct; there was work to be done.

Renewal

Sunday, September 18th

The morning sun crept in through the cheap motel curtains, casting a gentle glow across Cam's face, waking him. He sat up and swung his legs over the edge, expecting the usual ache and creak. Instead, he felt strange. At first, it was almost numbness. In a moment, the blood rushed to his feet, and he felt invigorated. His legs were taut, almost sinewy. He stretched his arms out wide and instinctively reached for his left shoulder, which gave him trouble every morning. Not this morning, no. His fingers met an old scar he could no longer feel, piercing that old, damaged nerve in his neck. He brought his hands to the front, balling up fists that felt like iron shipyard chain links. His fingers dug into his palms, his arms firm, and his muscles packed with energy. He stood up, shaking off a disoriented feeling. His step was almost spring-loaded. The floor beneath his feet was plush carpet on cement. On other days, his arches ached at meeting the floor. Today, his heels barely touched the rug as he strode over to the mirror. In nothing but shorts, he scrutinized himself in the old mirror that hung crookedly on the door. Its silver backing had oxidized, giving a haunting image to its observer.

"Huh. How about that…"

He saw his own mouth agape, not in tired slack but in surprise. The body was the same, his old scars and hard-earned flat stomach still there, but he could almost see the slightest changes. His skin felt tight, nearly youthful. He felt light in his bones. He smiled at his own visage and saw the familiar Cam Mason of years past, grinning back with perfect teeth as usual, but the corners of his eyes were a few wrinkles shy of his years. In his half-awake state, he pressed his palms into his eyes, trying to rub away the sleep.

Murmuring to himself, he mused, 'Haven't slept so good since...' but without an answer for himself, the thought trailed off.

Opening the tap to a hot shower was the day's first duty. His body felt awake; now it was time to get the mind going. A long, hot shower often got all the gears turning. He stood there among the steam-fogged pink tiles and recounted the night. He and Shay had spent the day over a notepad, drawing up the plan. Shay had only the day to spare and jumped on a bus in town the prior night—orders from Billy. Cam didn't mind; he wanted to get back to building a case on O'Rourke. It would be far simpler now, after Shay helped Cam create a surefire plan to open the book of O'Rourke's wicked deeds to the world.

The details of the plan came to life in Cam's mind, each piece like a mechanized part of the machine that was this brilliant, yet flawed, plan. Cam knew he had a significant amount of work cut out for himself. It would be no simple feat to set a trap that only O'Rourke himself could spring.

He stopped at the Motor Inn's musty office and ate a terribly stale pastry from the bread basket on the welcome desk. The woman minding the office graciously let him fill his thermos with their pot of weak, warm coffee for five cents. It was all he had time for right now.

He headed into town in a decent brown suit, replete with a spiffy driving cap Shay had gifted him some years back. It was a houndstooth newsboy hat, and Cam rather liked the cut of the cap on his square-jawed face. With his notepad on the front seat of the truck, he tore out the page with the O'Rourke plan and tucked that into his pocket. The notepad got stuffed under the seat, and he was off. Half a tank of gas would do for the day; he had business to attend to in town, and it wasn't too far a drive.

On his arrival back at City Hall, the sweet dark-haired woman was at the desk yet again. She waved at him as he arrived through the plate-glass doors. He tipped his dapper hat to her as he walked into the small and marble-rich lobby. They exchanged pleasantries, and she inquired what brought him back.

"You were here plenty the other day, nearly half a day! What's got you so interested that you came back to see me, cowboy?"

She winked a bit at the well-dressed man standing there.

"Miss, I'm not here for much. Just a bit of follow-up is all. May I spend a little time with the land records?"

She looked at him curiously.

"Not very exciting stuff, you know. Old dusty deeds?"

He smiled with zeal and leaned forward onto the counter.

"Honest, there are plenty of things I'd rather be doin'… but my editor says he wants more history in the piece, and I gotta walk before I can run if I ever want a corner desk over Pike's Place market, see?"

She leaned a bit further in herself.

"I hear it's a swell place to take a… wife? Girlfriend?"

Her eyes swept over his hands. Strong, steady. Not a ring in sight.

Cam was flattered, despite her being a bit outside his usual taste in romantic pursuits. He reached over the edge of the desk, taking her by the hand. "Little miss, you should see it. All the lights shine out through the fog, a harbor full of business and hustle; it's really something. Best dining in Seattle, too…"

Her hand clasped his briefly before she realized her surroundings and withdrew to her typewriter, cheeks blushing. Cam knew the signs; she just might be utterly *smitten*.

"You'd better get all your work done so that you can see to other pursuits, don't you think?" as she stood up and showed him the way to the records room, perhaps only twenty feet away. She strolled and swayed a bit. He was thoroughly amused, though feeling a pang of guilt for leading on a woman, as he was.

With a nod, he left her at the door and sealed himself into that dusty room behind the old wooden horizontal-split door. They call them 'barn doors,' but this was lovely shiny oak, even if a bit utilitarian by design. He supposed it must have, long ago, been a combination of a door and a reception window before the growth in the area slowed down, and they just swung the top half of the door shut and turned out the lights.

Opening the first drawer, he saw enough of their filing system to find what he needed. Files were arranged by decade, then by name. Last name, or business name. He spent the next two hours slowly combing through The O's for O'Rourke, and the R's for Rainbow. Along the way, he found a few notes for related business ventures and named family members on a few deeds that lent some variety to his hunt for O's and R's. In all, he'd carried seventeen folders out of that room. The numbers had grown when he sussed out the name of the landholding company O'Rourke's father built on paper to keep things away from lawyers and trusts. Hours well spent, but now his stomach was rumbling a bit, and his heels told him it was a good time to sit a spell. Finding a desk in the corner, he flung open his notepad to a blank page and got to copying. It took another hour of knuckle-dulling writing as he took names, locations, chain-of-ownership information, and more from those seventeen files. His pencil needed a half-dozen sharpening rounds as he churned through the stack.

You think you're untouchable, but you just ain't met the man willing to reach out and touch you yet, Wally. Think you're luck is about to change.

Finally finished, he leaned back into the chair. He saw a handwritten sign taped over the desk that visitors ought to "Leave files on desk for clerk to file away". He thought it would be better if he handled that himself; seeing as the O'Rourke family outright owned a good chunk of the county and its employment, it would be best if nobody knew just what this reporter was investigating. So, he tidied up and filed everything as perfectly as he'd found it.

Sauntering out into the lobby again, he found his friend seated idly at her desk. As she sprang up to meet him, he set down his things and stuffed his hands in his pockets. "Miss McGovern, a sight for my tired eyes! How are you?"

"I'm as well as I need to be, though we could always make a day better!"

She presented her hand in a slight curtsy, clearly trying to be funny. He took her hand and kissed it in the most southern-gentleman way he could muster. "I'm Cam-"

"I saved your card!' She exclaimed, 'I might need the services of a big shot reporter someday, Mr. Wilson!"

He shook his finger a bit. "So *formal*! You're welcome to call me Cam.' She seemed a bit weary, and he decided to take advantage of some local insight while he could; 'May I ask, Miss McGovern, if I can treat you to lunch? I have a few details I'd love to get *just right* before I send it up to my editor."

Her flush cheeks drew taut with a shy grin, "Cam, I'd enjoy that, but I've got things to attend to as of now. Can we make a date tomorrow?" He nodded agreeably.

Nice to see a smile 'round here… how can I say no to a date?

"I'll await tomorrow. Say noon. For today, suppose I'd better get back to the typewriter, deadlines approach!" as he strode out of the clerk's office.

She waved goodbye and watched him as he walked down the hall and out the door. It was endearing, and Cam thought it best to escape before he had to marry the girl. Small-town customs, you know.

His trusty notepad in hand, he made his way to a payphone. Dialing up Jimmy Corker, he rested his head against the payphone's glass side. Three rings, four. On the fifth, he reached to hang up when he heard a staccato "Yeahwhat" through the phone.

Lowering his voice as he lifted the receiver back up to his ear, "Corker. It's your new boss."

The line was quiet, then Corker responded.

"Shit. I hoped that was a bad dream, til I coughed up a lung the next morning. What the hell were those cheapskate smokes? Don't answer that. I'm busy anyway. Whaddya want?" Cam was calling James Corker at work, and Corker was still a State Trooper, desk job though it may be. Cam needed to play it safe for Corker's sake.

Cam smiled as he had drawn out another pack of the same hand-rolled pure tobacco leaf cigarettes and lit the end right then. They were a special smoke he'd bought a half-dozen packs of at a rest stop on a Wyoming Indian reservation a few weeks prior, but Corker was right, it wasn't important.

"I got a list of places. I'm gonna read off. You're gonna tell me if you did any of your 'special' work for O'Rourke at any of these places. Yes or no answers, okay buddy?" and prepared his pencil.

Corker hesitantly answered "Sure," and waited for the list.

Cam took a good drag of his smoke and began reading off locations he'd found under the past and present ownership of the O'Rourke family.

"Warehouses at the packing plant," he asked.

Corker sighed, "No"

"Family home up on Round Hill Road"

The reply came, "No."

"Docks near the grainery way down on Highway Twelve"

"Nope" from Corker.

"Old firehouse in the east end of town" … Corker hesitated, then replied, "Nothing pertinent to your situation."

"Motel up in Brasserton"

"Once or twice," the man replied. "Finish your list".

The two continued down the list, and all of the answers came back negative. Cam knew that Corker wasn't going to volunteer much over the phone. He chewed on his tongue and took another drag of his cigarette.

"Okay, yes or no answers on this. If I press O'Rourke on the motel, am I gonna get anywhere?"

"Yes. Plenty far." Corker was a bit more forthcoming than Cam had expected.

"Okay. Is that where he kept those kids when you were running them?"

The line was quiet for a bit of time.

"Once, yeah. That's it." Corker was speaking in a hushed tone to avoid being overheard.

Cam prodded a bit further.

"Will there be anything there if I go lookin' myself?"

Silence again, for maybe half a minute.

"Probably. I don't know. Just tread lightly, pal."

Cam knew he could press for more info, but didn't want to get too deep in the questions right now.

"Okay. I'll dig. You think about anywhere else I need to be, and I'll call you at home soon for that list." Corker was again quiet on the other line, but eventually replied with a defeated-sounding "yeahsure".

Cam hung up and was rather pleased he had found the first necessary piece of leverage he would need to put O'Rourke into a corner. The plan was actually quite simple. He turned back to the Plymouth down the street, ambling and reviewing the notes he and Shay had made the prior night. He was at step one, and that was okay. Step one, specifically, was to catalog and amass some compelling information that might incriminate a man like O'Rourke. The more daunting task would be proving anything, but our man smiled as he knew Wallace O'Rourke would be the one to prove plenty. Cam's day was made, as he had a starting point. Aiming his truck toward the motor inn, he drove slowly and planned his disguise.

This is going to be fun.

Mid-afternoon arrived, and Cam walked out of his room into the sun. He'd unrolled his blue railroad-style coveralls, legs bearing stains from bearing grease he'd found in a service cabinet on his last trip on the Great Northern Railway's luxurious Empire Builder train, that grease smeared on the pants replete with some toothpaste and melted chocolate bar wiped onto his otherwise-clean boots to mimic paint spatters.

He looked down at the pants and remembered the awkward moment he got caught by a Pullman porter on that train, in the middle of rubbing the coveralls on a few fittings underneath one of the passenger cars. They'd stopped in some dusty town in Minnesota and had a layover where Cam needed to prepare his disguise. He recalls the old Pullman Porter catching him doing the dirtying deed between the sleeper cars; after raising an eyebrow, then checking over his shoulders to see the coast was clear, the man waved Cameron to 'hurry up' and even led Cam into the railcar attendants' restroom to wash his hands afterward. It was unspoken that folks of a particular kind took to looking after each other, especially in often unfriendly territory. That was a hell of a mission, and the last time Cam had seen Chicago… before the mess in New York with Gabriel. Chicago was a mess in its own right, but damned pretty as a skyline.

Wonder if that Porter lives in those silly little Pullman houses outside Chicago. Fucking company towns. They should have hung that robber baron.

Hopping into the truck and heading South, Cam set his sights on doing some investigating at O'Rourke's motel down in Brasserton, an unincorporated pit-stop on the way to Spokane. The hour-long drive soothed as the cool air streamed into the open vent windows. September had more than halfway passed, and he made a quiet promise to himself he'd try to be back on his own doorstep by the first of October. He thought about Hallowe'en, the decorations he loved, such as paper bats and hanging toy skeletons. It reminded him that, deep in his rucksack, was buried a piece of actual human bone, and it soured him on the idea of hanging a skeleton this year.

He felt an overwhelming urge to rid himself of that piece of evil right then, but he knew he couldn't just yet. The single, small but haunting piece of evidence was enough to refocus his mind back on the drive, back on his plan. He'd need a lot of luck and a little help if he were going to pin this rich and powerful bastard to the dirt.

Well before the close of business, he arrived at the Motel. He looked up at the dilapidated sign, "Five Stars Motel". Apparently, they had a skewed idea of what 'five stars' meant. This place was dingy, dirty. As he pulled up, he saw mildew in the wall paint and rot in the eaves & window frames. It wasn't an inviting place by any measure, and he wondered if that was part of the plan to deter people. He looked around and saw no vehicles in the lot aside from his own and an old spoke-wheeled Chevrolet rusting away on deflated tires. Still, for some reason, the "No Vacancy" sign was lit. It was damn odd. His eye caught some movement on the far side of the property. An older man, maybe 70 years of age, was walking along the back fence with a handful of garden hose. Cam saw this as an opportunity.

He hopped out and walked straight over to the old man, extending his hand first. "Howdy, sir! Can you help me?"

The old man turned halfway to Cam and muttered, "We're full, son, an' we don't let rooms for single men, 'specially not spades," as he went back to walking toward the back property.

Cam let his hand down, receiving no handshake. He wouldn't be deterred. "Sir, I'm here to work. Mister O'Rourke sent me out, sir." He was beaming his most friendly grin.

The old man stopped, turning again. "Work? What the hell is Wallace sending me help for now? This place is already falling apart, and he sends me help *now*. Shit." He spat onto the ground near Cam's feet.

Cam would not be turned away so easily. "Sir, I'm here for the windows. Just that, sir. Winter's coming, and… you know, it gets cold, sir."

The incredulous look on the old man's face was priceless. "*Windows?* I've got bigger problems. Come back with some paint!"

"Sir,' came politely, 'I only know windows, really. I've been working on his other properties for a while, and well… windows are the first place rot sets in, ya know that, sir? So, I'm supposed to come and check it all out and get him an estimate on them all. I wouldn't want to keep the boss waiting, you know, sir?" Cam was doing an impression of a young man he once knew, who used the word 'sir' like it was a breath between words. His reasoning had been, 'they can't say you're rude if you say *sir* just enough times!' and it had sent Cam into stitches. Right now, the thought of that silly young man trying to shake every damn hand he could had Cam stifling a laugh.

"What do you need from *me*, son?" The man sneered.

"Sir, just some keys, sir. That's all, sir! Won't take but an hour, sir! Just gotta check 'em so I know what parts and such to bring when we do the whole job." Cam leaned forward with a hand outstretched.

"You'd better be done by six, I leave at *six sharp*. When you're done, I expect a full list so I can check your work. Don't fuck it up and don't steal nothin' because I'll *know*." He dug into his pocket, handing Cam a ring of master keys.

Cam smiled a big, grateful smile.

"Sir, you ain't gotta worry about me. I'll do good work, sir! Thank you!" and he walked off, getting twenty feet before waving back and hollering again, "Thank you, sir!" to amuse himself.

As he neared the first room in the old red-roofed C-shaped motel. It was 1A. The center wing of rooms started with 1B, and the third wing on the far right started with 1C. Cam reached the door of 1A and just as he began to knock, the old man shot back loudly, "Stay outta 2C, that's closed!" and his tone was rather insistent. Cam waved back and shouted, "Yes, sir, you got it, boss!" and continued on his way. He knocked, entering after there was no response.

Way to spll those beans, old-timer.

In room 1A, the detective was immediately bored. He pulled back the shades and saw, yep, frame rot. Easy. Likely, all the rooms would need windows. He would jot notes on each window to make sure he was "doing the work" and not to raise any suspicion. Sitting on the edge of the bed, he looked down at his boots. He laughed aloud at the sight, nice boots covered in chocolate and toothpaste, looking like hell. He sarcastically wondered if he should spit-shine them or simply lick them clean. The thought was ridiculous, and his chuckling made him need to take a piss. In the restroom while he waited for the last two drops, he looked to his right—the back window in the shower.

Aluminum frame, painted shut—broken crank. Crack in the pane. Needs replacement.

After he flushed and finished annotating the windows' state of disrepair, he wondered if he should just retire right there and take up window replacement. Business would be great here. Except nobody was paying, and he was technically committing a misdemeanor. 'No worries,' he mused; 'nobody's gonna pay for shit after I get O'Rourke tossed into a penitentiary.' He moved on to room 2A.

The process continued, with each room being checked and the windows being glanced at. Some of the rooms were musty, and most of them appeared to have not been slept in for months. The moths had eaten half a curtain in 3B, and 4A might have been a real crime scene not too long ago. *Who else uses chalk on carpet? Shit, maybe kids. Kids get bored…* the thought echoed in his bored skull.

Finally, his time to shine had come. 1C got a knock, no answer. Inside the room, everything was clean, looking almost unused. The TV still had a sticker on the knob from the sales floor. The thought occurred to him that if someone were using any room anywhere for harboring abductees? They'd likely keep the adjacent rooms empty.

"Smart… ugly, but smart," he muttered to the still air in the room.

Finally, his opportunity to dig in deep. He opened the door and walked out of 1C. Looking around and seeing nobody, he put the master key into the door for 2C. It didn't turn.

"Shit", he thought.

He looked at the ring and saw two other, less-worn keys. Trying the first, it didn't fit. Looking around and feeling a bit nervous, he tried the second, smaller key. It didn't turn. In a bit of desperation, he wiggled the key a bit. With a small click, the knob turned. He let out a sigh of relief and slid into the room. Closing the door behind him, he turned to face the room. What faced him there shocked him so much that he dropped his keys and backed into the closed door, almost reaching for the knob.

The scene wasn't gruesome, no. It was, in fact, relatively spotless. The walls were a pleasant shade of pink, and the curtains were of a decidedly pleasant white lace. The carpet was fresh and still had vacuum patterns in it.

What shocked Cameron upon entering the room was its contents. The bed was covered in stuffed animals. Teddy bears, tigers, giraffes. The lampshades were circus scenes and brightly decorated, casting gay light onto the walls. There was no television; instead, a small blue wooden table where every children's board game he'd ever seen was stacked. The far wall was the worst of them all. He walked closer, seeing his reflections in a dozen round funhouse mirrors.

Those mirrors were the polished chrome lids of candy jars, each of them reflecting his visage in a warped and circular fashion. Each jar held a candy; one was brimming with licorice, and another was filled with plastic-wrapped hard candies. Each of them was full or nearly so, and there was another shelf below with stacks upon stacks of the most delicious boxes and bagged confections Cameron had ever seen.

Cinnamon rounds, licorice, taffy drops, chocolate kisses… Christ…

This room was a literal child's dream, a cornucopia of all the things one might need to keep a young child amused long enough that they may not miss home, may not cry for mama… may not say no when you ask them to touch something, do something crude that they do not yet fully understand. It was a black-hearted nightmare wrapped in crepe paper and a bow.

Cam felt sick to his stomach, and a knot in his gut told him to check the room and get the hell out of there. He turned and deadbolted the door, so it could not be opened from outside even with a key. His instincts were ablaze, Cam ignored the ponies and pillows. He lifted the mattress but found nothing underneath.

Rubber sheets. Like a hospital.

Cringing, he dropped the mattress and turned away. He checked the nightstands; nothing ominous, just a Bible and a half dozen small, pastel-illustrated children's books.

He went into the bathroom next. It was a flawless, perfect white. Every surface was glossy porcelain or tile, and the whole room was clean enough to eat off. Behind the shower curtain, nothing but an empty shower without a window. A bar of soap. He dragged his fingers along a wall. The grout was waxed.

Nothing sticks… nothing soaks in. No blood, no mess, they can just… oh god.

Feeling green in the face, he finally turned to the medicine cabinet and swung open the mirrored door. Inside were colorful bottles of pills. It almost looked like candy. As he peered into each little container, he recognized a few of the pills. Pain medication. Pain medication and Quaaludes… sedatives for unruly children, children who resisted. Pain medication for children who misbehaved, who were taught a lesson… or for more nefarious reasons, reasons Cam did not want to think through.

His instincts now were to burn the place down, to set it ablaze and walk away without looking back. He sat on the corner of the bed and mulled over the options for a moment. He realized that it would be up to him to ensure this grotesque lair was shown to the world... he couldn't destroy part of the evidence that would guarantee O'Rourke never see the light of day again.

Stick to the PLAN, old man.

Standing up, he checked out the curtain. The unpleasant codger who'd handed him the keys was nowhere to be seen. Sneaking out of the door, Cam stepped out of the room and closed the door behind him. He turned to use the key to re-lock the door.

At that very moment, the old man walked around a corner from the rear property, three rooms over and perhaps thirty feet away. Cam had just secured the lock and knew that he could play dumb on this one.

The snarling old man barked at him, "Hey! Told your lazy ass to stay outta 2C, galdurnit!" His words were slurred, and Cam could tell the old fart had been drinking. Cam swung around to him, beaming again.

"Sir, I'm sorry! I don't read too good, sir! Anyway, see, I didn't go inside; this key doesn't open the door, sir. I'll just wrap up and leave you be, sir." His heart was beating fast as the excitement and jitters of almost being caught ran their course.

The look Cam received matched that of men who had aimed to take his life in battle. It was a look of disdain and ill intent. The old man spat again and proclaimed, "You damn Johnnies never listen. Get the hell outta here, it's six o'clock. Gimme that damn list and I'll call the boss myself tomorrow. I'll be sure to give him your name as well. What did you say your name was?"

Cam tore off the list of windows he'd inspected and smiled wryly. "It's Charlie, sir. Charlie Ford. Thank you, sir!" The old man didn't bat an eye at the fake name. Cam placed the note into the dirty, crusty hand of the attendant. He received no thanks and walked back to his truck, stifling a breath of relief to himself.

Dusty old shitheel... fix your damn windows yourself!

He'd gotten half a mile down the road when the adrenaline wore off and that knot returned to his stomach. He thought about the things he'd seen in that room, thinking about the nefarious intent behind so much of it despite the dreamlike design of everything.

What a goddamn nightmare. A horror show. And they don't know... why would the children understand? They just... they're coming from nothing, and then they're in that place, and they must... oh my god.

He reached down under the seat for his big flask and then remembered Shay's face, chiding him and reminding him that vice won't bring him closer to any closure. With that pang of guilt, Cam stuffed the flask back under the seat unopened. He took out his pack of cigarettes, held them in his hand. Looking down, he thought to himself *I feel better… I feel right for once… why would I poison that?* And he crushed the cigarettes into a mess before tossing the pack out onto the road.

His taillights faded into small red jewels on the horizon as he made his way down the road toward his own cheap, run-down motel. He knew it would be a long few days ahead. For some odd reason, his bones missed that creaky, lumpy Motor Inn bed very much.

Full Plate

Monday, September 19th

Daybreak brought Mr. Mason another pleasant waking. His staying off the drink and smoke, he deduced to himself during a long and hot shower, must be what has him feeling so refreshed and invigorated. *Shay must've seen I needed to clear my head. Miss him already.*

Off to a good start, he picked a northern connecting road. That is, of course, after a pit stop at a trucker' waylay restaurant to fill up the thermos to the brim with piping hot black coffee. He skipped breakfast, planning for a hearty lunch with his new friend from City Hall. He had no plans of conquest with her; he simply saw an opportunity to make a new acquaintance and perhaps glean some less-than-public information on O'Rourke's dealings in the area. He'd need to tread softly there, as he didn't want to raise suspicion beyond what a curious out-of-town newsman might deserve.

Shit. Maybe she's playing me like a fiddle. What if I'm not so clever? Guess we'll know soon enough.

His plan today was to take a trip to the Rainbow Orchard and see if he might be able to use the place in the coming maneuvers. His credentials were already somewhat vetted by Johnny, the old-timer who ran the packing plant. As long as he played dumb and didn't ask any tough questions, Cam figured he should be fine.

Rolling up to the orchard, he saw countless well-manicured rows covering a substantial number of acres. Trees sprawled up and over rolling hillsides, in perfect grids and lines. Plenty of space between the rows of apple trees to drive through, which he may need later. He'd also timed the trip from the orchard back to the main county road in case things went sideways; he counted six miles from the orchard to the closest payphone, where he could hike out if his plans didn't work out in the orchard.

Parking in the orchard was easy, with plenty of dirt and gravel shoulder where many a fruit-hauling truck had parked. Only a few trucks were present, on the far side of the orchard along the old narrow one-lane road. Cam parked away from all that, grabbing his notepad and donning his hat. Today's garb was locale-friendly, with denim jeans and a tucked-in work shirt. With his cowboy hat brim low and the thermos tucked under his arm, anybody spotting him would likely assume he was working there as opposed to planning a coup.

After an hour of walking the orchard, both around the tree line and into the rows of lush, shade-giving trees, Cam had nearly finished the coffee. He came upon a small clearing in the midst of the grove of trees. Looking around, he saw a few yellow flags stuck in the ground. He knew from his youth that these were common in farming, used to mark off trees that were dead or diseased for removal. The clearing was small, perhaps two trees were removed unceremoniously from a row. Under his feet, he could feel soft soil. For safety reasons, they'd backfill the holes left behind when the stump and roots were pulled out of the ground. It was unlikely they'd plant a new tree anytime soon, he figured. Using his notepad, he had counted rows and trees North and East of the road. He knew exactly where to enter the orchard's long roadside tree line to reach the little clearing without having to enter near the buildings or main driveway.

Feeling satisfied he had what he needed, he made the hike back out to the pickup. When he got back out to the road, he saw a group of laborers unloading irrigation equipment from a stake-bed Dodge truck. The old, rusty Dodge was idling away, and the radio was playing loudly, some horn-heavy jazz. Cam nodded and tipped his hat at the one man in the group who noticed him; he received a nod back, and that was that. He slid into the sun-warmed leather seat of his old Plymouth and puttered away, smiling at the successful reconnaissance.

Arriving back near town a short time later, he grabbed his change of clothes from the bag he'd brought. A man can't go to lunch with a nice woman looking like a field worker; that simply wouldn't do. He brought out gray slacks, a crisp white shirt, and a black wool vest he wore many a day. Tucking his newsboy cap under his arm and looking in the mirror, he liked the way his dress reminded him a bit of Shay. He'd almost hit noon, and it was a short jaunt back to City Hall, which he made with haste. His growling stomach had him excited for lunch, regardless of the company.

Miss McGovern, upon his arrival in the lobby of City Hall, was already purse-in-hand and heading his way. After a bit of pleasant how-do-you-do, she took his arm and tugged him back out the door. It was clear she had decided where they were heading.

"Anna, I'm famished. I hope we're going somewhere swell!" She laughed and tossed her hair a bit, smiling brightly.

"My dear man, you just wait. My sister works at the lunch counter up the street, and she'll be sure to get you fed properly. It's the best meal in town… and it's, well, you're welcome there." In the daylight, her silky black hair reflected the sunlight in an almost blue hue. Her skin was nearly olive. While she had the brightest of blue eyes, she was clearly not Irish, as her first name, Anna, might imply.

As they made their way up the block, they passed a few friendly local folks fiddling about in shop windows and twice as many folks milling about on the sidewalk. Several of them had said hello to Anna, and Cam knew he was walking with the right woman to chat up; folks here knew her, and she knew them.

Making conversation, he asked as they crossed one intersection, "Say, tell me something. How long have you been here in town, working at city hall?" She did a little math in her head before replying.

"Well, my sister moved out here a dozen years ago, and I got the clerk job in the summer of '43; my predecessor had left to fight the war. In fact, I just passed my tenth anniversary! Do you believe that? It's been ten years, and they haven't bought me a cake or *anything*! I'm going to treat myself soon, perhaps throw my own little party…" She was being sarcastic, and he was well amused.

They reached the restaurant. It was a clean, bright diner-style joint located in a long, narrow building, with a service counter running down one side and the kitchen situated in the rear of the establishment. Booths and tables took up most of the space, with a small bar and stools along one side. Familiar midwestern diner layout, and he was just about to ask where she'd like to sit. She stepped forward, leading him to a booth as she waved to a younger, equally sweet-looking girl beaming at them from behind the counter.

Shortly after they sat, Anna's sister arrived at the table in her apron and cap, quickly introducing herself before taking their order. It was lunchtime at the best place in town, and her sister Belinda had little time for conversation with her sister, much less a dark and handsome stranger in a dapper cap. Cam had noted how much alike they looked, perhaps with a bit sharper features. Cam noted her complexion was fairer than Anna's.

"She's quite a sight too, I see it's a family trait, Miss McGovern," he quipped.

Anna looked up from her menu and waved his formality out of the air; "It's Anna, if you don't mind. Miss McGovern was my mother," she said with a wink.

"Oh! I do appreciate it. I'm not usually much for formalities. Say, you have some heritage around here, yeah?" She knew instantly to what he referred.

"My mother was a Yakama native, my father was a loser from the worst little corners of Europe. My sister and I were the only children."

Cam understood the inference of 'was' in the context and reached a bit. "Am I right in understanding your folks have passed?" She nodded gently. He decided it was time to change the subject to a happier conversation.

"I sure do enjoy little towns, especially where they get a lot of workers and tourists. Fewer… small-minded folk, that's all."

"Only because there are *fewer folk*", she teased him.

Cam gazed out the window and answered with honesty, "No, it's not easy anywhere, but it's gettin' better some places."

She folded her hands in her lap for a moment. "It's better here, sure. Not that you don't get stares and a bit of disrespect, I'd be a fool to deny that. A few times, even I had…" her words trailed off as she got lost in a thought she clearly would rather not share. Cam was curious, but not wanting to pry.

"Anna, we make the best of it, day in and day out. My father taught me that, grabbing every minute you can. Not letting opportunity pass while folks hold you down. Why do you think I'm here with you right now?" He waved his hand toward the setting, a restaurant filled with smiling folk and the tremendous din of happy conversation.

She flashed a warm expression and reached for his hand, gripping it a bit. "You've got the hands of a builder, a craftsman. You're really a writer?" He squeezed her hand back, gently, and then placed his hands flat on the tabletop. It was an odd habit of his, but it put people at ease without drawing their attention to his body language.

Belinda whizzed by and dropped two colas near the edge of their table. Cam reached for his soda pop and took a big, icy-cold sip. "I used to be a real hands-on guy, sure. That was years ago, I served. Six years in, most of 'em in Europe. Got a star and all. It was… it kept me humble."

Her eyebrows raised a bit. "Oh? How would that keep a man humble?"

He took another sip, his stomach growling nearly loud enough to be heard over the prattle and clanking of the kitchen. "I had enough close calls to remind me that skill only takes you so far. I had a few buddies that I left there, a few that we sent home… great men. Family men. Smarter than me, better soldiers. It reminds an old goat that he's lucky to have whatever he has just then. Every minute is just luck, a gift."

Her expression turned from smug and curious to wistful. Looking away at the desserts in the glass case which faced the street, she took a long pause before sharing, "I had a husband, you know. Daniel never made it home. He loved flying in those bombers, watching the world scroll by underneath. He used to send me photos he'd taken while on training missions, and I would wonder what it felt like to be up there in those cold metal birds, just watching the rest of the world be so… small. He told me about Tuskeegee, about the segregated mess halls and barracks. He was convinced how great the world was going to be if we forced it to change."

"He sounds like a great man. Sorry for your loss."

She took a pause and looked around the place a bit before she continued. "Dan was a good man. Every day, I wonder what it would have been, were he still with us. Made friends anywhere he went. You know, you remind me of him."

"Because of the service?' He replied, but feeling he might want to lighten the conversation, he added, '…or because I'm as dashing as Clark Gable?"

She chuckled a little bit and shook her head. "Not only that. He was…" She reached out and grasped his forearm, drawing attention to her fair, olive hand on his dark, battle-scarred arm. "You stand like him, lean like he does. But he was a gentle soul. You carry the fight, even now. I see it in you."

Cam was quiet for a moment, realizing that his new friend might have a real insight into him. She slowly released his arm and sat back, asking, "I'm sorry, is that too forward?"

Cam winked and shook his head, "No ma'am, er… Sorry. I like it, Anna… I like the honesty."

She sipped her cola, her deep red lipstick leaving its pattern on the white straw in a beautiful pattern. He considered that it might not be a time to push with his investigation; this woman deserved a proper social parlay.

"I don't want to talk about anything you don't want to talk about. We can save my political curiosity for another time…" and just at that moment, her tallish-but-comely sister returned over the table, delivering steaming-hot pastrami sandwiches in front of each of them. Cam whistled at the spread, and Anna wagged her finger at him.

"I told you it's the best in town!"

Cam smirked before teasing back, "Let me take a bite before I give out the award ribbons… It's damn sure the *biggest*…" and with gusto, he dug in. His eyes widened; she hadn't been lying. It was the best pastrami he'd ever had, marbled rye bread, with a perfect smattering of sauces. Swallowing a lump of a bite, he admitted, "O-kay, Anna. You're right. I owe you for this, been starving all day!" and she simply nodded in agreement, as she had already taken her own impressive bite.

Wish I could cook up a plate like this… wonder if Miss Anna… oh, hell.

Cam's date ate with her fork and knife, demure but not haughtily so. He was hands-on and having a time.

"No lie, Anna, this may well be the tastiest sandwich I've ever had. Certainly, the best I've had in the States…"

"Oh, I'd love to hear about your travels, Cam."

With both of them enjoying the food and neither sure how to proceed, the meal was their focus over the conversation for a short while. They enjoyed each other's company regardless, chatting about the sights they'd seen and the trips they'd like to take. After both plates were nearly cleared, Cam teased her.

"You kept up! Hell of a sandwich. I'm glad I had the backbone to ask a lady out!"

"Suppose I'm glad you did as well. Now, I'm not the sensitive type, and I know you had some… let's say *motives* in asking me out. I'd wager you have some questions for me you couldn't answer in those dusty old files."

He appreciated her candor.

"Yeahhhh, you might be right. I couldn't turn down a bit more backstory for my piece, and I'd bet that you know more than a lot of folks I might poke and prod, so… yeah. I'd love to know anything you want to share, little lady."

"Oh, you came here to poke and *prod* me, Cameron?" She shot back with a wink.

He blushed, taken aback by her delightfully crude joke.

"Firstly, Cam, you need to understand about our, ah… your subject. He's old money here, and these folks are sure to hold their tongue about anything unseemly. You could say that they like to play it safe."

"And you don't?" he retorted.

"I'm not so invested here that I can't help you more than some folks. In fact, did you know that our friend is planning a broader political career?" She then silently mouthed *Mayor*.

He was surprised, but only a little. "No, miss, I did not."

"He let it slip in closed doors, not too long ago, a meeting with our current sad sack mayor. Seems he doesn't want to pay his fair share of taxes and fees, typical entitlement."

"Perhaps he's not as upstanding a citizen as some local folks think?"

She nodded ever-so-slightly. Her voice remained just low enough that it would be hard for a bystander to eavesdrop.

"Well, to be honest, that's not the thing that sets me on edge when he's around. A few years ago, while Daniel was deployed. I was new to the clerk position, and our man was a deputy sheriff. This was before he left for law school; it seems he didn't have the patience for small-town policing."

Cam was leaning forward, resting his chin on his palm, and listening intently. He nodded, "That's news to me…"

She hushed her tone a bit further and continued. "Don't read too far into this, but… There was some gossip surrounding the disappearance of some children back then, which persisted for a while. It didn't really register much with the locals, since all the children were farmworkers' children." Her soft cheeks turned into a bit of a drawn, sad visage. "My parents were farmers, way back. Before we relocated, anyway, these kids went missing, and nothing was ever found. It always rubbed me wrong that most, if not all, of them went missing from the orchards *his* family owned. Every few months, another sad story."

Cam nodded and stared intently. "Whatever came of that, now?"

She took a brief look over her shoulders into the now-empty adjacent booths and then continued, though she wasn't making eye contact anymore.

"Well, I was rather new at being a grown-up and didn't know the realities of living in a place like this. One morning, the man was in my office about a deed transfer filing. That's no matter. What put me off, Cameron… I *asked* him. I asked him about what they were doing to find those children, and he laughed at me. He actually had the guts to laugh!"

Cam waited, eyebrow arched and one fist clenching subconsciously.

"He said, and I swear I'll never forget these words, Cameron. He said, I will never forget his words… 'They'll turn up, or maybe not. Nobody cares; they'll just make more. Like rabbits.' He didn't care at all! Like they were *livestock*!" and her raised voice led him to raise a finger to his lips gently, in a 'shush' motion. She nodded and leaned back in her seat, closing her eyes for a few breaths to try and calm herself.

Cam had dealt with abusers before, and he knew how inhumanely they would speak when they thought nobody was listening. He'd encountered it in the Army once or twice, regarding his own troops' treatment of civilians. On more than one occasion, he'd had to lay a man out flat, to set an example when civilians and children weren't being treated with dignity and humanity.

Protecting the innocent was what brought him here to this very table in a dry little town in Nowheresville, Washington. He couldn't help but wonder how many folks were secretly disturbed about it, like Anna McGovern clearly was.

"That's a lot to swallow. You're not the first person to let me know he ain't exactly a stand-up guy, but I think you and I know that there's more to the story we won't talk about here. Am I right?"

She nodded and dried the corner of her eye as she took a big sip of Coke. Cam reached out and took her hand.

"Listen, Anna, I don't want you worrying about this business. I'm gonna do my own digging, and you should just pretend this little talk didn't happen. If I'm right, my work —my story — is going to help some folks. Be good for the world. I have a lot to write about already, honest. I appreciate you bringin' me here and opening up."

Her head cooled a bit by now, Anna turned to her sister, who was milling about, topping off coffee mugs. Beckoning Belinda back to the table, Anna was playing cool as a cucumber. Belinda saw the two embracing hands and could read Anna's face. "You *okay*, Anna Banana?"

Anna smiled softly. "We were telling some old stories, Cam was in the service like my Daniel… You know how I can get. Sweetie, can I bother you to box up a slice of that cherry pie for my friend?" Belinda cheerfully went to fetch the dessert.

Cam had already taken a crisp five-dollar bill out of his pocket and tucked it under his own plate. Anna started to protest, and he raised his hand to say, 'I've got it.'

She squeezed his hand, and he squeezed back. They sat there in silence for a few moments, eyes telling what words couldn't.

Belinda, sweat on her brow, cheerfully handed a box with nearly half a pie to Cam as they stood to leave. "On the house, soldier. Thanks for getting my little sister out of that dusty office!"

Cam took his date by the arm and tilted his hat toward Belinda, retorting, "Won't be the last time, I hope!"

Belinda reached out, exclaiming, "Hold on, your change-"

"—is *yours*, ma'am. Surely the pie is worth that much!" He offered with a goodbye nod.

Grinning, she stuffed the remainder of two dollars and forty-three cents into her apron and waved them out the door.

They strolled lazily on the walk back to City Hall. Cameron let her lead and quickly noticed they took a circuitous route.

Must have a little extra time…

"You're a good man, Cameron Wilson. I know in a few days you'll be back in Seattle, writing some exposé on my little town and *all* its secrets, and I may not cross your mind again. I'm still glad I got a chance to make your acquaintance. But…"

"There's always a *but*, ain't there?"

Shaking his arm a bit, as if to say, 'Don't be silly,' she inquired, "… you're no reporter, are you, Cameron Wilson?"

He looked down at her and saw the earnest curiosity in her face, and he wondered how deeply she was fishing for her answer.

"Just Cam, little miss. My friends call me Cam. Why would you ask that? Am I too handsome to be a journalist?"

Her stern look said it all.

She's not playing with me.

Frowning, she bit her lip for a moment and replied with a palpable hesitation. "It's not that I'm calling you a liar, Cam… It's just that I never heard of your paper, so I made a few calls yesterday, and it seems that the Seattle Park-Times Gazette? Well, it doesn't *exist*… not anywhere I can find, anyway. Stopped publishing before the war?"

He thought about making up some excuse about 'we're starting up again,' but felt sour about the idea immediately.

Nah… If I fib, she may just dig deeper and unravel things.

He stopped walking. They were near the entrance of an alley not far from City Hall. He shoved his hands into his pockets and kicked at the dirt a bit, chin down in defeat, but never breaking eye contact.

"Suppose you weren't too far off. What would you want me to say?"

He leaned slightly to and fro in the still air, like an aspen in a chilly fall breeze. This woman made him nervous in a way that was so long-forgotten it felt new again. She placed her hand on his chest. He stopped swaying.

"I wouldn't do or say a thing, Cam. I just want to know if a man is honest or not. I suppose I need to know, just for my own sake. Like you said… the truth, *always*."

He rolled his tongue in his mouth, and she waited. The words came in time.

"Anna, I don't take joy in lying, but that's sometimes the price I pay. If you'd have called that number on the card I gave you, regardless of the name you got from the other end, you'd be talkin' to a man by the name of William Bigsby. He's a damn fine private eye; me and some of my old Army pals work under his license. Think of it as being deputized into the gumshoe business. I'm here on a job, it's just not… It's not exactly what I said there in your office. That's all."

She balled up her fist and socked him in the shoulder, albeit not hard.

"I *knew* it! You had to be! That business card looked cheap, anyway. I *knew* it. You're a real Philip Marlowe! A Sam Spade! Does this make me your girl Friday? How thrilling…" she clicked her tongue; she was teasing him.

With the tension broken like cooking spaghetti in a too-small pot, they burst into laughter that echoed in the alley.

He caught his breath and grasped her shoulders gently.

"Anna, you can't go speakin' about any of this, okay? I've got work to do, and *none* of it involves you. I aim to keep it that way, keep you safe."

Still gazing in her eyes, he found them breathtaking in the single sunbeam that dashed across her face.

Leaning in, she told him quietly, "I'd never spill your secret, Mister Gumshoe. I promise."

Relieved, he chuckled a bit more.

"Okay, mum's the word. Just one last question, and I'll leave you be.' She looked up the alley toward the street as a logging truck rumbled past. When the quiet fell once more, she demurely asked, 'Is Cameron Wilson even your real name?"

He grinned a devilish grin and tipped the brim of his hat. Leaning in and giving her a gentleman's goodbye kiss on the hand, he whispered to her, "Cameron… that *is* my real name. See you 'round, lil' miss."

Before she could say another word, he spun on his heel and trotted off and around the corner. She stood there in the alley for a hundred heartbeats, waiting for the flush she felt in her cheeks to depart.

Bad Call

The phone rang in Jimmy Corker's small home. His legs were heavy with hesitation at answering; he knew exactly who was calling. He picked up the receiver and took a deep breath before lifting it to his ear. Yet he said nothing, simply waiting.

"Corker, still alive?" Cameron grunted.

"I'm here."

"So let's cut the shit. What have you got for me?"

Corker was still pale with what he had seen. He hesitated but knew he'd better respond. "I went to the cabin."

Cam hadn't expected that, but played right through. "And what's that to me, slim?"

Corker could be heard striking a match, lighting a cigarette. "I seen what you did to Steve Hardigan."

"Dunno what you're talking about, Jimmy. You making up fables?" Cam sneered back into the phone.

"I don't know what happened… I don't care, either. I just…" he took a deep drag of his cigarette. "Steve was scum, the real worst of the worst. He was the big man's number one guy. Got real into that shit, all the hunting and… and the other stuff."

Coy little sonofa…

"Don't dance around it, slim. What 'other stuff' you talkin' about?" Cameron growled.

"I just don't wanna be next, man. I know what you're doin' and I can help, or keep quiet, whatever you need. I just don't wanna be next." He sounded defeated.

Cam knew this was the time to prod. "Relax, Jimmy. I ain't here to lay everyone low. If I were, you'd still be strapped to that pole. So, I know the cabin, and now I know the motel. You got anything else for me? If it's liable to make my life easier, you can tell me now, or I'll squeeze it outta you later."

Corker thought for a bit, but his worried mind came up blank. "I'll get you dates and times. Places. I ain't gonna talk on anything if I wasn't there, but the stuff I saw? I can get all that. That's what I can do. Just gimme a little time to sort it out and put it to pencil."

Cam was pleased but didn't want to give up his hand. He kept up the intimidation tactic. "Ain't what I wanted, but that's a start. Write it all down, keep it shorthand, and seal the envelope. Keep it *with* you. I'll tell you soon where you're gonna drop it for me. Got it?"

"Sure, yeah. I can do that. I'm gonna do that for you," Jimmy cooed as he took another soothing drag of the cheap cig. He leaned back onto the kitchen door frame, shaking a bit.

Nervous folk repeat themselves… little Jimmy's quakin' in his boots.

"I'm gonna give you a job, Jimmy Corker. You'd better be ready to get this show started. All you're gonna do is wait up til one o'clock in the morning. At *exactly* one o'clock, you'll call up the big boss and tell him you got something top priority and gotta see him. Tell him to meet you at your desk in the precinct by one-thirty sharp, that's it. Then, you stay your narrow ass at home. Don't take no for an answer, Jimmy. If I call you later, it'll be two rings, then I'll hang up, and then I'll call right back. Don't answer for anyone else."

"Yeah, yeah, I can do that, I can do all of that. Just… should I say anything about the cabin?" Corker genuinely didn't know how to proceed with that crime scene he'd discovered.

Cam shot back, "Leave that mess for the buzzards and keep your mouth shut, 'less I tell you to open it," and hung up the phone with a click.

Corker took a deep breath, sighing, then he slid down to his narrow ass on the cold tile floor, where he took to sobbing. Glad that nobody could see him in such a state, he couldn't help but wonder what was going to happen after he made that call.

Miles away, Cameron was sitting on the edge of the bed, feeling excitement, pure and simple, filled with confidence about how smoothly things had gone to this point. He was surprised Corker would take any initiative and check on the cabin. He did not expect Corker to drive out there and see the grisly mess for himself. He could only imagine how scared Corker was, believing that his interrogator might be a stone-cold killer, an assassin. Cameron was barely a bloodhound these days, though he knew that idea would have Corker on a leash for now.

He's no dummy, just gotta keep him cornered. Tonight is gonna be a chore.

It was early, but he knew it would be good to hit the hay for a few hours. Cam lay there staring at the rough ceiling of the dusty room, a few cobwebs creeping out of one corner and to the lamp hanging slightly off-center on the ceiling. His mind resounded with the details of a brazen plan, thanks to Shay's planning help. Knowing that little candy-filled room existed in the motel and might be put to use anytime? Cam had been forced to accelerate the plan. This meant he'd need to get under O'Rourke's skin sooner, get him to slip up sooner. He could not risk allowing another child to be taken because he wanted to 'play it safe'. That wouldn't work.

He lay there and thought about his other option. About doing what Corker thought he was here to do, he thought about snatching that old bastard and putting him under the dirt.

That card's on the table, but I won't play that hand unless I come up bust. No... this shit needs to be out in the daylight. We need this whole network outed; we need to let these bastards know they'll never be safe again. I gotta do this, Billy's way. Stick to Shay's plan.

So, he set his little alarm clock for midnight and closed his eyes.

~

Miles away as the twilight gleamed overhead, wispy clouds streaked across the sky like the tendrils of seaweed swaying in the shallows of a glassy lake. On a small porch of a small house down a narrow street on the edge of a small town, two women sat, drinking bourbon from teacups and gazing out into the twinkling stars on the horizon.

"He's trouble, you know." Belinda Crawford offered her opinion without her sister, Anna, ever asking.

"And what's it to you?" Anna shot back with a smirk, as if to say *Don't you think I know that?*

"I'm not against trouble, of course. You said the same thing about Dan."

Chuckling, Belinda, swigged more of her bourbon and swallowed a big gulp before replying.

"Well, there's good trouble and there's bad trouble."

Leaning over and grabbing a cigarette from the soft pack on the table between them, Anna shrugged and nodded.

"Well, I can't tell you how I know this, but I'm pretty sure he's the good kind of trouble. Or, I suppose what I'm saying is, I think he's *going* to be the good kind."

She handed the pack to Belinda, who struck a match and lit each of their cigarettes in turn.

"Oh, so he's going to stick around? He seemed like a big city boy."

Anna shrugged and shook her head side to side. She spat a little flake of tobacco off her lip.

"I don't think he's going to be trouble for me. In fact, I don't know if I'm ever going to see the man again."

Belinda took a drag of her cigarette and blew the smoke across the moon over her head.

"Well, then, who precisely is he going to be causing trouble for, little sister? You should have heard those folks in the wall booths, they had some choice words about you bringing his kind in."

"Well-dressed?" Anna shot back with a sharp glare.

"Oh, you know what I mean. Don't be silly."

Nursing her own cigarette, Anna ruminated on a response for a bit before replying.

"I don't care what they think. Dan's father was mixed; they called him *melon-Johnnie*. Half your kitchen staff is from Mexico or south of there. Why wouldn't these country bumpkins want to eat next to somebody different from them? When somebody different from them prepared their food. Somebody different from them fixed their car. Somebody different from them... For Christ's sake. I'm sick of this shitty little town."

Belinda leaned forward and topped up each of their teacups from the bottle on the porch.

"You could leave anytime you want."

"Where would I go? All I've got is a little house worth practically nothing. The only thing Dan left me was a folded flag and some ribbons in a cheap tin box. He was so determined to go save the world, and he didn't care that he ruined our world."

Cradling her teacup, Belinda tapped her ash onto the creaky porch floorboards.

"You've still got me. You know you're always welcome in our home. You could move in with me and Glenn. We've got that little... we've got that in-law out back, and you can settle in and you'd never be alone."

Crossing her eyes and making a silly face toward Belinda, Anna teased her back.

"Sure, if I get kicked in the head by a horse, I might move in and be an invalid in that little cottage. But up until that day, I've got to do things for myself. And sometimes that means making sacrifices."

Belinda scowled at her sister's silly expression. "Little girl, every woman makes sacrifices. I know you sacrificed your college to be with Dan, and you know that I sacrificed having a family to be with Glenn. The doctor said there's nothing they can do."

Sneering, Ana retorted, "You never really liked kids anyway."

"Well, that's not the point, is it? You don't have to like something to want it," Belinda chided her.

Annalene was back in her rocking chair and was silent for a while. They took turns blowing smoke clouds across the moon. These little puffs, from their perspective, joined those long silvery streaks of precipitation in the sky, dancing among the bright stars.

"Beli- Do you remember Hidalgo?"

"How could I forget?" came Belinda's somber reply.

Hidalgo had been a joyous man. He was a local, a farmhand and mechanic, a regular customer at the cafe where Belinda had been working for quite a few years. Belinda and Glenn settling in this sweet, cozy little town was the entire reason that Anna and Daniel had made their way out to the middle of nowhere.

"Do you remember the day he disappeared?"

With a deep sigh, Belinda recalled the man and his smile. "No. But I remembered the day they found him."

Anna leaned forward and scooted her rocking chair just close enough so that she could place her hand on her sister's knee.

"He lost his son. That little boy just went into the... He just disappeared into the darkness. That was it. And the light left that man's face. I feel like everybody in town knew him. And then, he was just a shell. Hidalgo was gone, and this... This shell of a man was just wandering around, going through the motions, drinking his coffee, and reading the newspaper, scouring it for any clues, because nobody in our little world cared to go and look for that boy."

"That's the problem with a small town, little sister. When you know everybody, you also get to know everybody's secrets. Everybody's pain. That's just the way things are. And sometimes it's the price we pay for not having to deal with all of the big city problems."

"As if children never go missing in a big city?" Anna grumbled.

Steering the conversation, Belinda tamped out her cigarette and placed her hand upon her sister's, which was still resting upon

Belinda's knee.

"What does any of this have to do with that dapper chap in the booth today?"

Anna deflected and stared her sister deep in the eyes, pleading.

"I might not have a job soon, or maybe I can't stay where I'm at. I might need to move on. Would you come with me?"

"What would I do? Leave Glenn behind?"

With a smirk, Anna confided in her sister. "You've been bored with that man for years, and if you want children, you've got to start making some changes in your life. That's all I'm saying."

The two were quiet for a time, and each of them leaned back into their respective rocking chairs, thinking about what Anna had said.

"Where would you go? Just where would I be following?" Belinda asked in earnest; her eyes were sad, misty.

Anna gazed off into the clouds again. "When they found Hidalgo, there was no note. I remember it was just him and his rope and that little picture of his sweet child in his empty wallet. They wrote about it in the paper as if it were some kind of spectacle. That was so cold-hearted."

"He lost his wife, and then he lost his son. A lot of folks weren't surprised."

Anna didn't have an answer, but instead she offered, "What if there was some closure? What if we found out what happened to the little boy? What was his name?"

Belinda winced. "Ernesto. I served him a tiny slice of pie on Sundays after church. His little chubby cheeks..."

Anna's voice was strained. "I don't believe that anything happens in this world without the intervention of man. There's no guiding hand. There's no old bastard in the sky smiling down on us. It's just all of us little people and all the terrible things we do to each other."

"Everybody does terrible things. Dan was on the front lines. I'm sure he did terrible things."

"Yeah, and if your sad sack of a husband, Glenn, was not a flat-footed and soft-shouldered cholera baby per his *costly* doctor's note, he might have served as well. And then we could say the same about him."

Belinda, taken aback, said nothing while Anna continued.

"I'm sick of this small town and all the little vile tendencies these people have. They smile and they wave, but I know what they think of me. I know what they thought of... my friend today. And it— Beli, it disgusts me to the core of my being. I need somewhere new, and I'm going to burn this fucking place down on the way out if I'm given the chance."

With a nod and a *hmmph*, Belinda handed the pack of smokes to Anna.

"The whole world could burn if one little match were lit in just the right place."

Clinking tea cups with her sister, Anna raised hers and offered a cheers, "For Hidalgo."

Belinda raised her cup, "For Ernesto."

Surprise

Tuesday, September 20th

The clock struck one in a downstairs room, a well-furnished study with a lovely view of a lush forest. Red velour hand-carved oak armchairs framed a hewn rock fireplace where embers from the evening's fire still radiated. A long gun was neatly saddled in an ornate rack above the hearth. The massive buck's head on the adjacent wall existed silently in defiance of the weapon that took its life. Its horns were now dry, and without their short, fibrous fur, they looked more like a set of dry bramble branches casting black, contorted shadows from the reading lamp nearby.

It was a grand home telling of luxury and leisure, and the birthright of the one remaining O'Rourke child, Wallace. A phone rang out in the study to disrupt the silence. It rang once, thrice, nearly a dozen times. Eventually, the incessant ringing brought the home's sole resident tromping down the stairs in a hideous smoking jacket, two bare legs chilled by the air creeping in from the aging seals of large glass viewing windows.

The hour was inappropriate for calls, except in emergencies. Ever the politician, the dour-faced and half-asleep man yanked up the phone's receiver and, with a forced grin, simply answered, "May I help you"? He never said his name; his ego told him anyone reaching out to him better damn well know whom they're speaking with beforehand.

A soft and apologetic tone answered him. "It's James Corker, sir. Sorry about the hour, I—" and O'Rourke gruffly cut him off.

"You don't call me, shithead. I call YOU. This had better be goddamn apocalyptic." The call perturbed him, but Corker persisted.

"Sir, I… I have something to show you. It's urgent. I need you to meet me at the station in thirty minutes. It can't wait."

O'Rourke was skeptical. "You *think* it can't wait. What do you think I'll do to you if you're wrong?"

Corker shot back, "I know exactly what. Which is why I wouldn't have called if it *could* wait, sir. Thirty minutes?"

O'Rourke grunted back into the handset, "Shit. Fine, thirty," and hung up the phone. Afterward, he yawned deeply and shuffled into the kitchen to gulp whatever cold coffee might be lurking in the pot.

Not ten minutes later, the sedan in the O'Rourke driveway was slowly backing down the driveway. The house was still and silent once again, though not for long. To the trained ear, a slight rustling could be heard. The sound of a buck knife sliding under a windowpane, a small brass lock forced open. The warm, honking sound of wood burninshing upon wood as the window shunted open, letting in some cool night air and a man covered in black from head to heels.

Into the cozy, well-furnished study crept a figure, lean and tall, moving to the center of the room and taking a long, slow spin to estimate the place. With soft shoes and lambskin gloves, the intruder moved slowly and silently toward a wall of photographs. A hand reached out toward a few smaller frames of hunting and camping photos in which the participants did not smile. The men in the picture could be recognized by a longtime local, but in this case, Cameron Mason stood there recognizing the faces of only three people; all of the photos contained Wallace O'Rourke, in each photo standing tall with his chest out like a prizefighter. Two photos showed O'Rourke joined by Steve Hardigan, grimacing at the camera in disdain. He was never a handsome man; he knew the camera did him no favors. Lastly, a man Cameron recognized from a few newspaper articles he'd come across in his archival investigation at city hall, the chief of police in this town whose name escaped Cam at the moment. In the photo, the Chief and O'Rourke were younger, seeming to be drinking buddies at some rowdy bar. It didn't bode well for Cam that he couldn't trust local law enforcement to take on and apprehend Wallace O'Rourke, but he had a plan for that.

With stealth and patience, Cam began his search of the home for anything that might implicate O'Rourke. He opened the narrow closet door in the study, finding some hanging coats and a plaid bag of golf clubs. Next, he prowled through the other rooms of the house. Kitchen, bathroom, dining room… no signs of anything incriminating. Moving silently upstairs, he checked the bedrooms and closets first. Beds were made, blinds were drawn. A smell of dust and disuse hung in each room: blankets, holiday decorations in boxes, nothing of import. Even the man's bathroom was meticulously clean. The master bedroom was as fastidious as the others, save for a robe on the floor and a bed half-unmade. The indentation in the bed indicated that the man was sleeping alone on just one side, with an empty denture jar on the nightstand. Everything Cam saw spoke to this man living a compulsively clean, very mundane home life.

The attic was a dead end. Cam had ambled up the ceiling's drop ladder and found the crawl space empty. He'd used his flashlight there, but sparingly; any lights shining around inside could give a passerby cause for alarm, so he refrained and relied mainly on the moonlight and his decent nighttime vision. In his mind, the place seemed more like a home that was newly occupied. Nothing felt lived-in; there were no signs of anyone but the bachelor O'Rourke. Cam was disappointed but continued his search. "The basement", he had thought, "gotta be something there worth all this creeping around." He was moving quickly as he could while still eyeing details, as there was no way to tell how long O'Rourke might wait for Jimmy Corker to show up before returning home.

Making his way back downstairs, he went to find the basement door. He hadn't recalled seeing one before, though these old houses usually had something... he wandered the hallway, kitchen, and back to the study. No door, no way down. He peered out the window and saw a bifold-door basement hatch outside the kitchen, just off the back of the house. Common in these big estates. Now, he knew he was onto something. "No way a house this nice didn't have a stairway down. How would they've gone for firewood?" He knew something was amiss. Creeping back toward the study, he noticed something odd. There was no storage space under the stairway, which meant the basement stairs must be under the main stairs.

No way that's just wasted space...

Rapping his knuckles on the walls in the short hall around the corner and back into the study of the house, he turned the corner to find the small closet existing where a basement door should be seen in such a home. Carefully, he shifted aside the coats hanging there and moved the golf clubs out into the room. The closet was papered in a floral print, rather bland. He pressed on the rear wall of the closet, and to his expectations, it rattled a bit.

...Hinges?

Reaching for his flashlight once more, he found there was no knob. Instead, there was a small coat hook screwed into the top of the door. He tugged on it, and the door released from its place, swinging open about halfway. There was a light coming from the basement. "Now who would leave a light on in a hidden basement?" He grumbled to himself as he reached for his trusty buck knife.

He rolled his wool ski mask, which he'd been wearing like a sailor's cap, down over his face, obscuring all but his eyes and mouth. Clad in black and feeling much like a cat burglar at this moment, he took a deep breath to calm his nerves and began his descent into the basement. His left hand was out in front, guiding him down the dark stairs by the handrail. His right hand clutched his buck knife tightly, its polished blade gleaming in the reflection. When he was near the end of the wall that opened into the basement on one side, he reached the blade out and used it as a mirror to peer into the dimly lit open space without being seen. He'd hoped the little creaks in the steps had not given him away. The makeshift mirror was all he needed; he saw a room devoid of people, but could not quite make out all the contents of the room. Swallowing his fear, the man continued down the flight of steps leading into the dirt-floored basement.

As he came to the foot of the steps, he looked around the room, taking stock. On the far wall was a rack, shelves built of lumber. There were rows of banker's boxes there, each with some dates and other writing he couldn't yet make out. Along the right wall, a round stack of about two cords of firewood. Typical for this season. Along the left side were two small doors that appeared to be set into the wall of the room. In the middle, a long and stout solid-timber table that looked like it was either a woodworking bench or perhaps a butcher's table, hard to tell in this light. A few boxes of paperwork were stacked on top, but nothing significant.

He went first along the left, peering into the first small door. It was something of a dugout, a sump chamber to pump water out of the basement. Nothing special. The second little room was odd; it looked swept clean and had a chain lying across the unfinished floor. He'd seen no sign of a pet, but perhaps it was from the prior owners. Some years back, Cam had seen such dog cages in the basement of a city-block-sized U.S. armory down in San Francisco. There were also larger quarters for other animals such as horses. In the winter, even surly animals couldn't be left outside. He shrugged and moved toward the bankers' boxes on the rack as he sheathed his knife.

None of the boxes caught his eye, mostly old files and personal paperwork: taxes, vehicle service records, bland letterhead memos. Standing there peering into those dusty files in the light of the single bulb, he put his hands on his hips and let out a frustrated sigh. He felt rather silly in his mask and makeshift cat-burglary uniform.

A slight rustle came from behind, and he froze. He was confident he'd been alone in the room; he'd have heard the steps creak if anyone had followed him down. Slowly and carefully, he turned around and scanned the room. Empty. Now feeling both paranoid and frustrated, he pulled off his hot wool mask and leaned back on the table a bit while he finished rifling through the bankers' boxes with the tip of his knife.

Another rustle had him jump like a cat! He lurched back, grabbing the mask off the table and raising his razor-sharp blade. He looked around; it was just him and this large table. Now, he realized his oversight. The table was broad and long, maybe three feet by seven. Its thick top was a single slab of redwood, rough knots showing around the ends. The table underneath had been built like a box, with no shelves underneath.

Is this… is this a crate?

He saw no way of looking inside this makeshift Pandora's box, so he tried lifting the table a bit. It was damned heavy, but it gave a bit. He looked down and saw the feet of the table still on the ground. The table top was a lid, and it was hinged!

Cam stepped back and lit his flashlight. Hoisting the massive slab a few inches once again, he peered inside with his flashlight. A small hand reached up into the beam of light.

"Jesus *CHRIST!*" he yelped out in surprise.

There was a child stowed away inside the table! His instinct taking over, Cam sheathed his knife with one hand and with the other, in a feat of adrenaline-fueled strength, he slung the lid violently upward, sending the boxes of papers from the workbench crashing to the floor. The hinge of the lid ripped out of the base, the tabletop thumped to the floor, and all the papers flew every which way.

In the dim light, his stomach lurched and his eyes began to water as he saw the form of a six- or seven-year-old Mexican boy cowering in fear at the sound. The small child was wearing a tattered white shirt and denim pants that barely met his ankles; he shielded his face with dirty hands. His arms and knees were caked in mud, or possibly blood.

Cam reached down and placed his hand on the boy's shoulder,

whispering "Safe, safe… you're safe now, kid… *segura, seguro…* ". The boy was trembling, and Cameron knew the child must be terrified. Cam put away his flashlight, reached down, and hoisted the boy up as delicately as he could while whispering "You're safe, you're safe" in hopes the boy would understand.

The boy tried to wrench himself free in vain, yet he made little sound—just a squirming baby, terrified and whimpering. Cam rolled the ski mask back off his face; it fell to the floor. He could feel tears streaming down his cheeks.

As he lifted the struggling child out of the table and into his arms, he gave the child a gentle hug, holding on for some time as the boy's frantic writhing calmed to a heaving breath. After a time, as the dust swirling in the air slowly fell to the floor, the boy stopped writhing and simply went limp from defeat and exhaustion. Cam laid the child on the floor and stepped back. The frail little one had passed out completely, either from fear and shock or possibly from malnourishment. His little ribs showed through his shirt; he looked feral.

Cameron knew his only option was to get the hell out of that house and get the child to safety. His plan to surprise O'Rourke the next day had gone to hell; his only thought now was saving this tiny soul that he once again lifted and clutched tightly to his chest. He lurched up the stairs two at a time, the child's head lolling over Cam's shoulder. With his one free hand, the man drew out his silvery weapon and prepared to leave the house, whether O'Rourke had returned or not. He knew that if O'Rourke had returned, it would be a hell of a fight. No man capable of this evil would hesitate to put hot lead through anyone creeping around his house.

Cam gently laid the unconscious child down at the top of the stairs and stepped deftly out into the study. He saw no sign of O'Rourke and heard no footsteps. Reaching back and tossing the emaciated child over his shoulder like a fireman's rescue, he moved back through the study and to the window where he had entered. He lowered the boy out onto the ground outside, then crept out himself. As he was almost out of the window, he saw the closet door still open. He figured his only way of buying time might be to close that damned door. Hurrying back to the closet, he shut the stair door and tossed the golf clubs back inside. He shut the closet door and, just then, saw the headlights of what he could only assume was the homeowner returning. Those beams shone brightly through the front of the house and moved across

Cam's face. He ducked in haste and crawled back toward the window to make his escape.

Hope I didn't get spotted…

Luckily, O'Rourke was slow and plodding back from the car, audibly grumbling. He was half-asleep, and it showed. Cam held his breath. Quickly slipping back outside and once again shouldering the child, he realized he was going to have to traverse the woods a bit to return to his truck down the road. He reached for his flashlight and mask, only to realize that the mask had been laid on the table and was now lying in a pile of O'Rourke's papers.

"Shit!", he murmured. "I'm a damned fool."

He shook the idea for now, as he silently strode across the manicured lawn back toward the line of birch and oak trees along the back of the property. The moonlight was just enough to guide him safely to the treeline, but he knew that if the child woke, he might face two problems. In the pitch darkness, he clutched the head of the flashlight in his palm, his fingers covering the beam, letting a crack of light escape between two fingers —a faint glow that he hoped nobody would notice this late at night.

Slowly but swiftly, Cam carried the child to his truck. After swaddling the boy in a blanket he'd had behind the seat, Cam fired up the motor and made a U-turn with headlights off. In darkness, the truck idled away from O'Rourke's street. Cam's secret switch under the dash helped; with a pull of the hidden knob, his tail & brake light circuit was interrupted and the truck could be driven in total darkness, no brake lights to give away their departure. He'd read about the trick in a book about bootleggers from the prohibition era down South, and it was a great trick.

When they had reached a place far enough away, perhaps half a mile, Cam pulled the truck over. To his surprise, the child had woken up and was sitting there watching him intently. Cam could see the glimmer of moonlight in the poor boy's sallow eyes. Gently, Cam reached under the seat. The child flinched a bit, and Cam raised his open hand to say, "It's okay". In silence, Cam gave the small boy what little food he had in the truck: a few pieces of dry cheese and a few pieces of pull-apart bread. The boy's eyes widened at the sight of the food, and he scooped them out of Cam's hands without a peep. As the boy stuffed his mouth, Cam surveyed the situation and handed the lad a thermos of water.

"Drink slow, drink slow… *suave*… take your time, kid." The boy seemed to understand, but he didn't say a word.

The simple facts were: O'Rourke would find the child gone, but perhaps not tonight. The mask would prove that someone was there, not that the child escaped. If he were unlucky, Cam might have lost a few short, dark, and curly hairs in the mask for O'Rourke, which might give up Cam's identity if he tries to get close like he'd planned. Lastly, this child would make a poor traveling companion. He'd need to get the child to safety first and foremost.

Antsy to get back on the road, Cam waited for the boy to finish the food. It was hard to focus on the road with such a passenger; he was worried the little one might try to escape or jump out of the truck. Softly, calmly, Cam asked the boy, "English?" and waited for a response. The little boy blinked, but made no sounds. Cam asked, "Talk?" and made his hand into a puppet-like mouth, pantomiming a talking mouth. The little boy sat in silence, cowering under the blanket. Cam knew he'd need to make some calls, and he would need help with the child. An idea struck him just then.

With a tap of the brakes and a flick of the wrist, he made a turn South and back toward the main county road. "Caroline", he muttered to himself. "She'll help, no doubt".

With the boy watching Cam intently, they made their way through the dark toward Caroline Hardigan's house. Cam thought about the irony that her husband himself may have been part of this child's terrible journey. He hoped she'd not yet left town; it had only been a couple of days since he saw her. As the Plymouth carried them along in warmth, Cam tried hard to think of any Spanish words in hopes he might be able to communicate with the child. In his tired and stressed state, nearly none came to mind.

"Shit, kid, you better just wait. I'll get you more food, okay? *Mas food, uh… mas comida*, little guy. Just stay calm, you're safe."

He pointed to the road ahead. The child watched Cam, never looking away.

Arriving at Caroline's place, Cam felt immense relief when he saw lights on in the house. No cars on the street out front; it wasn't likely she had company. He parked and, as best he could, told the child to "stay here". He patted the boy on the head, and the boy seemed to understand. When he reached the door, he heard the TV on. He knocked, and in a short time, Caroline came to the door in a nightgown and an open robe.

"Hey Cam, you're back… what's going on? It's so late…" She leaned on the doorframe. He supposed he'd just woken her up from sleeping in front of the TV.

"Caroline, listen. I'm in a real spot. I've just hit a snag, and I need your help. You alone?"

She nodded sleepily.

"Good, 'cause you're gonna help me out. I gotta trust you with some things, can I do that?"

Caroline stood up straight and placed her hand on his arm.

"Come on in, Cam. It's late. What happened? You know you can trust me." Cam patted her hand and raised a finger to say 'wait here' as he jogged back to the truck. She rubbed sleep out of her eyes and tied her robe.

Cam walked softly back to the front door, holding the child wrapped in a blanket. He looked at Caroline, who had a surprised expression.

"It's complicated, let's go inside."

She stood aside for him, a grimace on her face.

Cam laid the child on the couch and turned to Caroline, who had shut the front door but was still standing there, confused. She scratched her head and piped up, "...you have a child"? To which he shook his head, and motioned for her to "come sit down" as he patted the chair cushion next to the couch.

In a haze, she walked over and sat down. The din of the TV filled the room, and the little boy climbed down off the couch and went to the TV, promptly sitting down in front of it. An episode of The Lone Ranger played on in crisp black and white, with the child enthralled.

Cam took a big breath and pressed his palms on his temples. He was wholly unprepared for how the night had gone. He sat down on the couch, turning to face his friend, who was staring at the child.

"Caroline, sweetheart, listen. You're the only person I could come to, and you can't speak a word about this to anyone, okay?"

She nodded in silence, still peering at the dirty and bruised little boy.

"I came into some bad stuff, some real bad folks. They had this kid penned up like livestock, God only knows what for. I had to get him outta there, but I can't take him right now because those men are still a threat. You understand?"

Caroline was coming out of her sleepy daze now, and she turned to Cameron, "I understand, sure... what sort of bad stuff? Does Steve know about this? Did you find him?"

Cam noticed the luggage by the front door and realized he'd caught her just in time.

"You were supposed to leave, little lady. I'm glad you didn't, 'cause here we are, but were you gonna leave like I told you?" She nodded.

He continued, "Good, 'cause I'm still looking for Steve. This kid, this is on me. I'm working on a bad case, Caroline, and this kid is the crux of all of it now. I need to keep him safe for a day… can you stick around and help me?"

She looked at her luggage and responded with worry in her voice, "What if Steve comes home? I was all set on getting away from him…"

Cam leaned over and patted her on the leg.

"I'm sure if he comes home, he'll understand. And he ain't gonna get too rowdy if you tell him I'm coming right back, okay? This is big bad stuff. I need you to take care of this kid until I can take him someplace…" he trailed off a bit, not wanting to give up all the details of his mission, "until I can get him back to his parents. Now in the meantime, you gotta clean him up and keep him fed and happy, okay?"

"I can keep him, sure, Cam. I'll bathe him, feed him, and make sure he's safe and sound, okay? But you gotta call me if you can't take him back soon. What's his name, anyway?"

Cam stood up and gently smiled at her.

"I have no idea. If you bribe him with some chow, maybe he'll tell you?"

The sound of the Lone Ranger blasting cattle rustlers with his six-shooter rang in the background.

A Nice Drive

Cam had left the kid in Caroline's safe home and returned downtown to make a phone call. He'd need to act fast; it was nearly three o'clock in the morning as Cam leaned wearily in the phone booth. He rang up Billy's home number, something he hadn't done in some time. A dozen rings, no answer. A half dozen more rings and Cam was getting tired of waiting. Finally, the sound of a receiver and a half-awake Billy Bigsby murmured "Mhmmm" into the line.

"Billy, it's Cam. I'm in a pinch. Slap yourself, wake up. We got work to do."

Billy chuckled into the receiver, "I'm awake enough, Cam, even got my notepad. Go ahead."

Cam tried not to talk too fast; Billy needed time to write. "I got some info about our big bad friend, decided to do some poking around in his den. Turns out, he had a little boy down there. Now I got the kid, he's safe with Caroline, but I gotta work fast if we're gonna get this done right, okay?"

Billy grunted in acknowledgment before asking, "...Caroline? She's... yeah, fine."

Cam continued, "She's sober enough. I'm gonna get this sonofabitch today, I mean now. What I need from you is to make sure I have backup ready when I need it."

Billy rhythmically tapped his fingers on the phone's receiver, listening intently. Over the next few minutes, Cam told Billy the story of the Motel and how he thought it could be of use. He explained his situation with the boy and what it meant if their plan didn't work. Billy assured Cameron he'd have plenty of backup "when the time was right". Cam knew Billy was full of surprises, so he let Billy get to work and let him off the line. Next, it was time to get O'Rourke out in the open.

With another dime plunked into the phone, Cam dialed up Jimmy Corker and let two rings go, then hung up. He waited ten seconds, then called the number back. After a few rings, Corker picked up the phone. "Jimmy?"

A curt voice answered, "What?" and Cam knew it was Jimmy. He couldn't take the chance that O'Rourke would go to check on Billy at home.

"You alone?" he asked, and Corker shot back, "I'm always alone, pal. What do you need now?"

"I need you to wait thirty minutes and wake that asshole up again. Can you do that?"

Corker sighed in frustration.

"Yeah, I can try. In thirty minutes, I'll call him. What should I say this time?"

"Just tell him you got held up on a job, tell him it's urgent. Tell him it's about the motel, and he'd better get to your place quick."

"Okay, fine. But this late-night shit better quit, man. I need my beauty sleep!" Cam got a good laugh and hung up the phone.

Hurrying back to his truck, he knew he had only a short time to get to O'Rourke's place again. He knew exactly how he was going to work this con to get O'Rourke right where he wanted him. Reaching under his seat, he drew out the denim coat wrapped around his sawed-off shotgun. Lifting it and setting it in his lap, he fought off an acute yawn. His watch read half-past-three, and he had no time to spare. The old pickup was alone in the streets as he made his way up the hill once again.

O'Rourke lumbered out of his house for the second time this night. His watch read four-fifteen. His very tired gait was evident as he strode toward his 1953 Oldsmobile sedan. Its chrome decorative fender ports glinted in the moonlight, and he fumbled for the keys, trying not to spill the night's second mug of cold, day-old coffee he'd brought along this time. His trying was in vain, and some chilly coffee spilled down his flannel shirt and his pants, even a little onto his bare ankles and his loafers. He cursed at himself and Corker even more, as his fumbling paid off. Unlocking the car door and sliding back into the chilly bench seat, he set the mug on the dashboard. Firing up the car, the tired and sour man leaned his head back and yawned once again.

For a moment, he was confused. A chill ran down the back of his neck. He had never felt a headrest in this car before. Reaching back, his weary hand brushed the cold barrel of a sawed-off shotgun, its wide steel barrels pressed firmly against his skin.

His adrenaline kicked in, and in that moment, O'Rourke was wide awake. Realizing he wasn't alone in the car, his first instinct was to turn around. A firm grip caught his left shoulder and held him back firmly against the seat. A low, raspy voice came from the backseat.

"Don't move, just sit. Don't turn around, don't try and peek. Listen closely and don't say a word, got it?" O'Rourke nodded but only mildly so as not to spook his captor.

"We're goin' for a ride. You're going to stay quiet, when and *only when* I say you can speak, then you speak. Understood? Nod if you understand."

O'Rourke's mind was racing at the idea that he might not see the dawn. His base instincts had set his nerves on fire with the flight response, but he gripped the steering wheel and ignored his body shouting for him to twitch, to spring an escape. He knew nobody outruns a trigger finger at point-blank range; he knew that from experience.

He softly nodded again. The voice didn't respond for a few seconds, and he felt it was a test. He resolved then and there to live through the night, and he took a deep breath to quell his nerves. The cold steel barrel was starting to warm slightly from his skin, or perhaps the chill was setting in his neck. He couldn't tell.

"Start the car, go to the cabin." O'Rourke hesitated, hands still on the wheel and the car in park. "Hardigan's cabin." The words sent a chill down the spine of O'Rourke, a man who knew now that nothing remotely good would come of this. Being in the business of evil deeds, his first thought was that this was going to cost him either business or a bribe, figuring the man would have already pulled the trigger if the endgame was O'Rourke's demise.

It was an oddly comforting thought for this scared bastard.

He slowly reached for the shift lever and set the car in reverse, whereupon they backed down the driveway. He felt the barrel resting on the seat-back now, the barrel poking between his shoulders no longer at his neck. His eyes moved to the rearview mirror to notice now that it had been removed, unscrewed from the windshield frame. Acknowledging to himself that his captor must be a professional, O'Rourke finished reversing with what was in his peripheral vision. He had been told not to turn around, and while he usually would be the sort of prick to buck any order or instruction he received? Tonight,

Wally was a good listener.

Cam was steely-eyed, his nerves as tight as a violin string. He was ready for whatever O'Rourke might try. He hoped the man would play it *smart* this night.

It was a quiet night, still and moonlit. A bit of mist in the woods brought condensation to the inside of the windows. The glow of the dashboard lights had O'Rourke's face dimly lit. Cam lifted his head just enough to see the face of the man he'd been pursuing for the past two years. He'd not seen the man in person before, and it brought Cam satisfaction to have got his work this far. It was only a matter of time before it was all over, and he could see this man's face behind bars. He felt a bit of conflict, knowing how simple it would be to bring this bastard to his knees and simply end the saga with a wad of buckshot. The idea didn't stay with him long… the new plan had Cameron feeling much more like the 'good guy' that Irish insisted he was. Leaning back and lying down on the floorboard, he switched hands on the shotgun's stock and watched the moon and stars slowly pass by the window over his head. It was a beautiful night to make the world a little safer.

Slowly, down several back roads, the Oldsmobile's powerful inline engine hummed along as its occupants rode in utter silence. The twists and turns shuffled Cam about a bit on the rear floor, and the driver was grimacing and eager to ask a thousand questions that his worried mind needed answers to. Still, they rode in silence. Cam eventually rested the shotgun over O'Rourke's shoulder, so as not to let any accidental misfire end the mission prematurely. Too many accidents happen with loaded guns, he'd seen it in the trenches and barracks back in the service. Even his trusty shotgun could be jarred enough to release the hammer, so he played it safe and simply kept it in view for his unwitting driver. O'Rourke slunk away from the barrel like a cat avoiding a petting, but he kept his calm.

Finally, they reached the turnout for the long dirt road up to the cabin. Cam was pleased it hadn't rained much recently, or he'd have had to march the poor fool up to the cabin on a muddy road. Oldsmobiles are heavy, and heavy cars will sink.

As they pulled into the driveway, Cameron reached his gloved hand over the seat and handed the driver a black sock. This confused O'Rourke, who almost asked what he should do with it, whimpering out, "A… sock?"

"Eyes", Cam grunted. O'Rourke begrudgingly stretched the

possibly unclean sock over his eyes and tied the long tube sock in the back, just as Cam wanted him to. At this point, O'Rourke still had no idea who the hell was holding him hostage, and Cam intended on keeping it that way. "Leave the keys in the dash, too." He didn't have any plans of letting O'Rourke back in control of the car after what he had planned.

"Stuff your hands down the back of your pants and keep 'em there."

His prisoner complied without saying a word.

O'Rourke's eyes now covered and his hands away, Cam slunk out of the Olds and took O'Rourke by the shoulder to walk him up to the door of the little cabin. The captive man hung his head, looking as though he was about to meet a firing squad.

"Stay," Cam muttered.

Pulling Hardigan's lighter out of his pocket (he had been saving it), he struck the flame and opened the door. The smell hit him in an instant, the mucky air of death and rot. He saw O'Rourke sneering and then making a gagging sound before murmuring something that sounded like a curse upon his assailant's head. Still, Cam grabbed him by the shoulder and reminded him, "Don't move", tapping the barrel of the shotgun on O'Rourke's abdomen as a reminder.

Turning back to the foul entryway, Cam used the lighter to check the room; same as he had left it, save for some animals gnawing away at Hardigan. He fumbled for the light switch and found it. With a flick of the finger, he was brought back to this horrible scene, which he'd hoped never to see again. He walked out and around behind O'Rourke.

Dawn was creeping up; it was nearly five in the morning, and the blue light gave everything in sight an eerie tint of moonlight mixed with the blue of the dawn sky.

"I'm gonna tell you to lift your blindfold. Just lift it, look around, put it back down. Don't take a step, don't move, just use your eyes. Got it?" He was nearly choking from the smell, and as he pressed the barrel into O'Rourke's lower back, he realized the man was shaking.

"I got it", O'Rourke replied.

He reached both hands up and was dead still for a good ten seconds. He put the blindfold back on as he lurched forward, one hand landing on the doorframe as he grabbed his stomach with the other. The smell had overcome him, and he vomited across the doorframe and onto the stoop.

After a few moments and O'Rourke panting from stomach

contractions, Cam took him by the shoulder and walked him over to the pile of ash and wood near the cabin. O'Rourke was quiet, and his face looked defeated in the bright moonlight.

Cam nudged him a bit and instructed, "Get on your knees, Wally".

O'Rourke hesitated, so Cam clapped the back of O'Rourke's left knee with the butt of the gun. The man stumbled to his hands and knees, unable to keep his balance without sight.

Cam rested the shotgun on O'Rourke's shoulder once more.

"Reach forward, dig around a bit. See if you can find the prize."

Cam prodded him with the gun, knowing he was dealing with an evil and violent man. O'Rourke fumbled with the pile of debris, his hands turning gray and brown. He picked up a log. Cam said, "Nope". He sifted around a bit, and his hands together lifted a strange and ashen-colored piece. It was the pelvic bone Cam had seen before.

"You win the prize, Wally. Lift your blindfold, just take a peek, old boy."

O'Rourke held the bone in his left hand, using his right hand and his filthy fingers to get a look at his prize. Once again, he was dead silent. Cam knew that without so much as a reaction, the kneeling man either knew the bones were there… or, more likely, had put them there himself.

Cam coyly rubbed the barrel against O'Rourke's cheek and whispered, "Eyes".

O'Rourke put his blindfold back down and spat on the ground nearby, still trying to void his mouth of the taste of bile and old coffee.

Cam stood there in silence for a minute, waiting for a word from O'Rourke. The two remained still in the slightest dawn light, and Cameron's patience waned. He tapped O'Rourke on the shoulder with the barrel of the gun.

"Now you know that I know what you and your boys have been up to. Do you know what I'm gonna do with this information?"

O'Rourke had a sour tone, rightfully so.

"Turn me in"?

"Not if you give me what I want. I don't give a shit about some folks dyin', they don't mean a thing to me. Folks die every day."

Cam knew that if he were to play the part of a bad guy well, he'd need to play the part damned mean.

O'Rourke sneered, "Money?"

"Bingo!" Cameron replied. "You're a smart man. I guess you have more sense than old Hardigan there. He didn't wanna give up the dough, so I sent him to meet his maker. Do you wanna meet your maker? Say hello to your dead grandmother?"

The man, still on his knees, shook his head in response, indicating that he did not. Cam wanted to put real fear into this man. With a booming voice, he struck O'Rourke in the back of the head with the buttstock, shouting, "I SAID, DO YOU WANT TO MEET YOUR MAKER?"

The blow sent O'Rourke tumbling forward, face-first into the pile of ash and bone. He reeled in pain, cradling his head, as he whimpered, "N...no, NO, I don't want to meet my maker, you damned... You *lunatic!*"

Cam knew he'd reached this man's senses.

"Keep your eyes shut, or this is gonna go ugly, understand?"

O'Rourke blindly uprighted himself onto his knees, but obediently never touched the blindfold. He was covered in soot like a Victorian chimney sweep.

The trembling man held his now bleeding head and, with a quaking in his voice, replied, "I won't... I won't look, I don't know you. Honest, please... just don't hit me again, please!"

He sounded genuinely frightened, but Cam had heard many times before how ill-intentioned men faked a conscience.

"I know something you don't, old man."

He tapped his finger on O'Rourke's forehead.

"What about?" O'Rourke whimpered.

With a smile, Cam stood tall and replied, "See, I know you didn't check your basement after you got home." O'Rourke went dead silent, almost waiting for the punchline. Cam knew his hostage's mind was racing with possibilities, and likely the hope that Cam hadn't stumbled onto the cage under the table.

With a laugh, Cam continued, "Yeah, I know you like to keep little kids around. I know what you do with 'em, and I know how you get 'em. I got a famished little boy tucked away right now that you might not want me to turn over to the cops. What do you say to *that*, Wally?"

He was teasing, hoping to get O'Rourke steaming. His plan worked.

O'Rourke scowled under the makeshift blindfold, his face turning an angry red as he growled out his response.

"You'll never get away with this, you goddamned ni—"

Cam interrupted him with a backhand that sent the man reeling off his knees again into the dirt. By now, the man was covered in muck and leaves.

"You ain't in a position to talk back. I got two cold barrels aimed at your head. See, I don't give a shit about some kids. I got bigger problems, and this world don't need more dirty little kids than it has. As a measure of… let's say good faith, I'll give you the kid back if you behave today. Understand?"

Cam had to nearly spit out the words, as the repulsive nature of what he was saying went against everything that made him a good person.

Nodding, O'Rourke spat out blood and coughed up "Sure, we can work something out, just… please, I don't know if I can drive… I'll pay you, just lay off me, okay?"

Cam knew the trap was set well. He took the man's arm and hoisted him upright.

"Good, you understand. Now, I'm gonna give you some real simple instructions and you're gonna follow them, okay?"

The injured man nodded in response.

Cam hoisted him by the arm and started walking him back toward the car.

"All right, good. It's real simple. You're gonna go to the bank, make a withdrawal. Can you do that?"

O'Rourke nodded his head, still blindfolded and now standing at the back of the car where Cam had led him.

"Okay, old man. You bring a *thousand* dollars to that motel of yours, out by Snake River. No cops, no bullshit. Come alone, and bring the money. Eleven O'clock sharp, no sooner and no later. You have plenty of time to do what I say, and not enough time to do anything stupid. Just you and my money, no backup, and no goddamn cops. One thousand dollars, small bills. That's my price for silence. It's a *start*, anyway. I might be callin' you down the road for more. You'll get the kid back after I count my cash, understand?"

He poked the blindfolded man in the chest.

O'Rourke was furious but nodded yes once again.

Daylight was coming, and Cam didn't want to be seen on the road, let alone let a desperate man drive the car. He opened the trunk and took O'Rourke by the arm.

"Get in."

O'Rourke blindly lurched back just a bit, knowing what Cam had in mind, asking, "Is that the trunk?"

Cam put the barrel of the rifle right up to O'Rourke's stomach.

"Wally, your choice. The trunk… or I leave here alone and sell your pretty golf clubs to line my pockets."

The implication was clear.

"All right, all right. I'll get in the trunk, goddammit."

The man blindly fumbled around until he was lying on his side in the trunk. Cam grabbed his belt, unlatching it and whipping it off with a swift motion. He bound the man's hands, and O'Rourke hardly moved. It was like abducting the willing; the man clearly understood what would happen if he did not comply, being under the assumption that Cam was a cold-blooded killer after seeing what happened to old boy Steve Hardigan.

Cam knelt to his hostage and spoke in a low and serious tone.

"We're goin' for a drive back home. *Your* home. At the end, I'm gonna leave the trunk open, just a crack. Then, I'm gonna stand by for a while. If I see you open that trunk before half an hour passes, I'll shove your ass back in and drive this sweet machine right into a lake where you can say hello to the trout and salmon. Or maybe I'll bury you under an apple tree. Wouldn't that be ironic? Otherwise, you be a good boy and be patient in making your escape, and I'll let you live long enough to get me my money. Understand?"

O'Rourke cocked his blindfolded head toward Cameron and, with a raspy, tired voice and a creeping grin, replied, "I can tell you're a professional. I'm a professional in my own right. You'll get your money, and I'll let you walk away, sure. I know you'll come back begging for more. You think you're the first bastard to blackmail me? You got this far, I think you're smart enough to know what I do to people who try to fuck with me, son. Now let's get this over with."

Cam realized O'Rourke was likely referring to the troopers in South Dakota who met an unkind fate. It figures that there was more to the story, but right now, that was all assumption. The morning light was just beginning to show between the trees. Cam knew it was time to move out and wrap up this mess. He reached down, shoving O'Rourke by the shoulders into the trunk. Unceremoniously slamming the lid, Cam slid into the driver's seat as he cranked the engine by the cold brass keys, whereupon it took to a low, smooth idle in the silent morning air.

Goddamn Oldsmobile… nice car. Maybe I should… nah.

The drive was quiet, with hardly any other cars on the road. Cam had donned O'Rourke's driving hat, pulling the brim low. The road gave him time to solidify his endgame. He knew he'd be up against some odds in a showdown at the motel, but it wasn't as though he could just walk O'Rourke into any police station. The evidence needed to be intrinsically linked to the man, which meant O'Rourke would need to be caught in his wicked little den for any of the stories to hold water.

Cam also knew that his skin might cause a bias against his evidence, regardless of his credentials. That's why he'd called Billy for backup; he knew his old friend would send some G-men his way as was customary. State lines prevented a lot of inter-agency cooperation, but Bigsby had plenty of friends in suits along the western seaboard, ready to intervene at opportune times. It always amused Cam how his old pal made so many professional connections in his years of private eye work that his portfolio had a better close rate than most police detectives.

The idea that people believe only the government should be trusted in situations like these gave Cam quite a chill. He knew why we went to war, and he knew the government liked to burn down the homes and towns of rabble-rousers. No, sir, the government was no benevolent hand.

Arriving back in the smoothly paved driveway of the house where he'd intruded hours prior, Cam was anxious. His mind raced with both anger and frustration at the scene he'd discovered there, the dirty little boy locked in a makeshift crate (or perhaps coffin). The thought nagged at Cam, how easy it would be to simply end the ordeal with O'Rourke using his trusty blade, or possibly something cleaner… maybe a garden hose from the exhaust into the trunk. He shut his eyes and leaned on the steering wheel for a moment, able to picture only his friend Shay standing there in a tweed suit, wagging a finger as though to say 'You're better than that, my friend'.

Cam's eyelids were heavy, and the car was *so* warm and comfortable.

Feeling the weight of his activities, Cameron leaned back in the car and took in the view of the headliner. He whispered to himself, "Just one more day, old man. Just one day, and it'll be time to go home."

The thought brought him much comfort, though he knew it was probably a lie he was telling himself, and he threw the car back into gear. Reversing up the drive, he drove right off the pavement and settled the sedan at the side of the house. Somewhat out of view of the road and most neighbors, Cam got out of the car and unlocked the trunk, without opening it. Tapping on the fender, he repeated to the man inside, "Thirty minutes, no less. Get to counting."

No response came from the trunk, but a slight shuffling noise told Cameron his captive audience was plenty alive and simply being stubborn. Cam couldn't care less, as he knew he'd given the man little option in how to proceed. As he walked away, he dropped the keys in the grass by the tire.

Jogging to the treeline behind the house, Cam made his way back until he was near his little truck once again. The neighborhood was basking in a misty morning with the golden light of dawn now cresting the treetops on the hills that surrounded the wealthy-looking collection of homes. Cam had noted on his first trip that the O'Rourke home was unique in its brick construction. Most of the other homes were log homes or had more modern siding. It was a pretty place, and as he walked through the backyard of a very Frank Lloyd Wright-looking home toward his truck, he wondered to himself how many other villains might be lurking just under the guise of suburban family folk.

Having seen enough of the country to know that most folks were generally decent (perhaps except in the Deep South), Cam shook his head and waved at an older lady walking past with her dog. She waved back and smiled. He climbed into the truck to head back to his motel for final preparations.

New Pals

The Eastern sky was blinding to Cam's sleep-deprived eyes. The nap the evening prior was no preparation for the exhausting work of burglary, child rescue, and a subsequent kidnapping. It had been a night from the fourth circle of hell, and this old soldier was ready to lay his head down for now.

As he pulled into the gravel drive at the Motor Inn, he saw a black Lincoln sedan parked adjacent to the office. Two thin men in sharp black suits were leaning against the car, each smoking a cigarette and each craning their heads toward Cam's truck as he arrived. He recoiled at the somewhat familiar sight.

Ah, hell. This better not be like last time... South Goddamn Dakota.

Cameron drove past the men, parking in front of his room. As he got out, he nodded toward them, and they each nodded back, but curiously, they both turned back to their cigarettes and monitored the road.

He stepped out of the truck and made long, casual strides toward the men. Walking right up to the man on the passenger side, he stopped in his tracks and stood up tall, hooking his thumbs in his belt loops. He stood there, still dressed in black and wearing a dusty, well-worn brimmed hat. The G-man looked up from his cigarette and made eye contact with Cam; he let smoke out of his nose, and his chin jutted forward as though he were trying to get a better look at this stranger.

Flicking his cigarette into the gravel, he asked, "...Mason?"

Cam smiled broadly and replied "Cam" with a shallow nod.

"Bigsby said you might stick out around here."

Cam extended his hand and responded, "Not by choice. Bureau?"

The man in the suit stepped forward a bit, firmly grasping Cam's hand.

"Bureau."

The other G-man had turned around and was peering over his glasses across the top of the car at them, blurting out, "I'm sorry, Mr. Mason. Bigsby never mentioned you were…"

"So damn handsome? I know, I know. It's a curse. The man knows all the facts, forgets all the details."

He was ribbing the G-man, as the duo was clearly not expecting a combat veteran-turned-private eye to be *colored*. He didn't mind much; it had happened before. It felt kind to Cameron that Billy didn't knee-jerk about describing color as an essential part of a man's makeup.

"He said you were a sharp, tough sonofabitch. That's all that matters."

Friendlies! Thank youuuu, Billy!

The bespectacled G-man walked around the car as the first introduced himself. "I'm Smythe, this is Harris." He motioned to his partner, who was still power-smoking a Marlboro. Cam reached out again and took Harris's hand firmly.

"Agent Harris, Agent Smythe, a pleasure to meet you both. Call me Cam. Nice to have you here."

He was still beaming at the prospect of having serious backup. Of course, Billy knew the stakes here, and so did the agents.

The two men took out their notepads almost simultaneously, and Cam leaned back onto their new Lincoln trunk a bit.

"Boys, I'll tell you now I am damned tired. It's been a rough night, you know."

Harris spoke up first, "We got here on short notice, we could use a coffee ourselves. What have you been up to since you got off the line with Bigsby?"

The man was still puffing as the cherry of his cigarette reached the filter.

Cam appreciated the straight-to-the-point nature of Agent Harris.

"Well, you know about the boy. He's safe, got him tucked away. I went back and picked up O'Rourke, took him out to the woods, and scared him with some… unpleasantness. He thinks I'm a blackmailer."

Smythe interrupted, "Why's that?"

Cam chuckled at the question. "Because I'm blackmailing him!"

Harris chortled and inquired further.

"Okay, what for? What's your plan so far? Bigsby told us to follow your lead, and that's damn odd… but he's been right in the past, and I'll give you the benefit of the doubt here. I know you're… *invested,*

Mister Mason. Bigsby made that clear."

Cam nodded and folded his arms, warding away the morning chill.

"Okay, so here's the score. The old boy has the whole day to mess this up. I bet he's gonna do three things; in fact, I'm sure of it. He's gonna get me the money because he thinks it'll buy him time. That puts you guys back in town soon, so you can verify he did that. Next, he's gonna try and take me out either when I leave or just afterward. That's a safe bet since I know enough to put him away."

Smythe tapped his pencil on his notepad. "What's the third thing?"

"He's gonna get rid of the evidence, of course. It's a tough one. Right now, he's well aware that I snatched that little boy from his basement. He thinks I'm gonna give the kid back after I get my money. Hell, he's probably counting on it. That'll be the moment, boys, when you're gonna need to come in hot and save my ass. Sound good to you?"

Smythe was nodding, but Harris seemed unsure.

"Well, what if he decides to screw it all and just take you out? Say he goes rogue on you, what's the plan?"

Cam shrugged and replied calmly, "Then you stop him, whether I make it or not. I don't think he's a tough guy, but he's mean and he's smart, so that makes him damn dangerous in any situation. You just better be ready to cover my six, okay?"

Smythe patted Cam on the arm, offering, "We've got your back, Cameron. What's the timeline on all this?"

Cam sighed in frustration. "Eleven. We've got just over three hours, that's it. Time enough for me to catch thirty in the barracks," as he motioned to his room with his thumb, "and get my ass to the O'Rourke Motel and wait for the old boy. Now, after you get some coffee, just set up on the highway nearby. Maybe put on something casual, maybe your car gets a flat. Just be close by off the south road, and listen for the signal."

Harris raised an eyebrow behind his thick black glasses' frame. "What's the signal?"

Cam stood up off the body of the Lincoln, and before he started walking toward the pickup to grab his belongings, he offered, "You'll hear my engine fire up. She's got a little juice."

He smirked at the understatement that was.

"Of course, if it goes sideways, you'll hear my Remington 12-gauge instead."

Agent Harris shrugged and reached for another cigarette. Smythe waved to Cameron, who was walking away, reminding him, "Rest quick, pal."

An exhausted Cameron stopped back at the truck, grabbing his shotgun and buck knife from under the seat where he'd stowed them for the drive home. As he went into his dusty room, he could hear the Lincoln drive off, and without taking off his clothes, he sprawled out on the bed. Reaching lazily for the alarm clock, he cranked it to a thirty-minute alarm and let his heavy eyelids close. His last thought before he slipped away into dreamland was about the sallow eyes of that poor child. He wondered if the little guy had spoken yet... the kid was so spooked. He felt a pang of guilt about even saying he'd send the child back to such a dark place, but as he mulled it over, a heavy sleep took his mind away, and he was snoring in no time.

A hot shower, a cold cup of old coffee. Cameron was back on the road toward the motel, having changed into his muddied workman's coveralls once again. He saw the need to arrive early at the motel and try to get a leg up on O'Rourke. Puttering down the road, there was just enough time to stop for fuel. Cam found himself in the same old gas station where he'd stopped earlier in the week, and the same lanky attendant came striding out to him.

"G'morning again, sir! She's thirsty, huh?" The man patted the Plymouth on the hood.

"She's always thirsty, Larry. I put more into *her* tank than I put into my own!" Cam joked, patting his stomach.

"Tell ya what, you could save a bit of gas on this baby if you just pull out half your spark plugs!" Larry joked back. He was happy to be back under the hood, where he went to check all the necessary bits to keep the old truck's big heart pumping strong.

"Listen, take your time as long as it's ten minutes. I'm hitting the payphone, be back in a jiffy!" and Larry responded with a very Midwestern 'ayuh' from under the hood.

Cam plunked a dime into the phone, calling Jimmy Corker's number from memory. After two rings, he hung up the phone. The dime fell out of the phone, and he tossed it right back down the silver slot. Waiting ten seconds, he called Corker back. Three rings, and Corker picked up the receiver.

"Jimmy boy, it's your best pal."

"Better be good. I'm goddamned tired, buddy. I think the boss has called me twenty times since this morning! I almost picked up once or twice, you know."

"Dammit, don't worry about him. I've got something in the works that will take him out, and I mean *today*. Did you mean what you said about wanting to help?"

Corker paused, then relented. "I'll do anything, anything at all. I just want this over with. Do you… d'you think I can get immunity?"

Cam reassured him, "I can get you taken care of, sure. I know all the right folks. Listen, lemme ask you something and I need an honest answer, okay, Jimmy?"

"Sure, anything you need, pal. Listen, all I care about is being free of all this. I know you want the best for Caroline, I'm hoping that maybe after all this, there's still a chance I can…" he trailed off, sounding defeated.

Cam changed the subject. "Do you know anything about a Mexican boy being delivered? This one was recent. Real recent, I'm thinking."

Corker hesitated again. "I guess… I mean, I heard about it. I wasn't there. The boss wanted something else done; this was recent, sure. Why, what happened? Christ, did he kill… is… is the boy still alive?"

Corker stuttered a bit, sounding borderline frantic.

Cam, hearing Corker so exasperated, changed the subject at first to give Corker some good news to ease his mind. "Caroline didn't leave yet, Jimmy. She's good; she doesn't know about Steve. She'll never know about all this if I have my way. The boy is safe as well; she's got him now. Don't worry, I'll handle keeping them safe. Stay home, and I'll come by tonight to introduce you to some Fed friends who can help you out, okay?"

Corker breathed a relieved sigh and whispered 'hallelujah' under his breath before responding, "I'll be here, buddy. Don't let me down, I can't go on like this."

"No sweat, Jimmy," Cam replied and hung up. He felt good about keeping Corker on board. He knew that while Corker would likely be facing some consequences for his involvement, it could be mitigated by working with the prosecutors when O'Rourke went before a jury.

Realizing he was taking too long, he jogged back to the truck to find the service station attendant lying under Cam's pickup, only his legs protruding and splayed out. Cam knocked on the tailgate, and his attendant hollered out from underneath in surprise.

"Gah! Hey, pal, I'm almost done. Just checking her seals, see. Watch your feet!" and with a grunt, Larry rolled out from underneath on a wheeled mechanic's creeper, his face covered in road grit and a happy grin,

Cam leaned over and offered the man a hand, helping him to his feet.

"I'm just pleased as punch you came back, I wanted a little more look-see at that Hemi-head of yours! I have a second cousin who works at Chrysler in Detroit; he's a whiz. He keeps hassling me, saying I need a new car when they visit for fishing trips. Might be about time, sure."

He motioned toward a beaten, rusty, and homely 1938 Ford, sitting nose-out on the pavement between some tire stacks.

Cam laughed at the forlorn old car and nodded.

"Keep it, someday you'll regret it if you don't."

"Sure, you're likely right. Fuel's a buck and a half, service on the house. Say, what sort of work are you doin' around these parts?" He looked Cam over as he asked.

Cam handed him two paper dollars and hopped into the truck. "I clean up messes!" he laughed as he roared off toward the highway. Larry waved him goodbye, and Cam rolled his window down to let in the morning air; he felt a second wind and a lighter burden than he'd had in some time.

After a spirited drive, he was nearing the motel. Rumbling down the old highway, he noted his watch was nearly ten o'clock. "It's almost over", he thought with excitement. The truck was pulling like a stallion; he knew Larry must have tinkered with the carburetor jets or the timing advance. That little Plymouth had never felt so brand new, at least not since Cam had newly shoehorned the hot engine under the hood.

Slowing his pace as he came to the last miles before the motel, he saw a broken-down, hump-roofed Divco milk delivery van halfway in the roadside ditch. It was empty. He considered that it would be an excellent cover for Smythe and Harris. "No, they'll probably still use the Lincoln. Those G-men ain't as creative as me or Irish".

Sure enough, another quarter-mile up the road, there was the Lincoln, one back tire an inch off the ground with the jack stand comically teetering under the chrome rear bumper.

Easy getaway. Huh. Clever.

The two men were dressed in fishing gear, with Smythe in waders and Harris wearing the most ridiculous shorts; each of them had also donned a river hat and the requisite boots. Cam nodded at the sight, but chuckled to himself and hardly made any acknowledgment of their presence. This was, after all, an undercover mission.

Passing the Lincoln, only another eighth of a mile remained before he reached the O'Rourke family's Five-Star Motel. On Cam's arrival, the lot was empty except that busted old Chevrolet slowly rusting away in the gravel. As he pulled up and parked nose-out near the main office, his head was on a swivel. It was down to the last minutes here, and his mind was coming up with all sorts of scenarios about how this could go smoothly or turn south. Reaching under him, he gripped the shotgun and brought it up onto the seat. He turned it over just so, knowing how best he could take the gun in hand if he needed to. He gripped the buck knife's hilt, brought it up from under the seat, and tucked the leather sheath into his boot. His pant leg barely fit over the bulky knife, but he managed to make it work. He also made a mental note that it wouldn't be quick to grab, were he to need it in a pinch. It was a compromise, but better than being wholly without.

"Ain't the day to be slow, old man." He reminded himself.

As he climbed out of his truck, he surveyed and listened. Not a soul seemed to be around. After finding the main office door locked and nobody answering a gentle rap of the knuckles, Cam set out around the property to try to find the old man he'd seen some days prior. He figured being under the guise of dim-witted 'Charlie Ford' might help him lay low until O'Rourke arrived with the money. For a moment, Cam considered what he might do with a grand in his pocket. Reminding himself he had far more than that amount in his bank savings, plenty to retire with, he snorted at the thought of taking that wicked bastard's blood money.

His footsteps in the gravel and dilapidated walkways crunched with an echo. No cars passed by, and no industry filled the air with machinery hum. The only sound he could hear was the light breeze in the eaves and the hum of the 'No Vacancy' neon sign on the street. It was a dry, depressing place, and he knew its ugly secret. Walking around the rear of the building, Cam took note of the fact that there was no good cover around the perimeter. No good place to hide on the property. He'd need to compromise and find an unoccupied room to stay in until the time came.

Finding nobody in sight, Cam went to the back window of room 1C, one room to the left of 2C and one wall away from the spot where Cam hoped he'd have enough evidence to send O'Rourke up the river for a long time. After finding a slit in the curtains and peeking inside the room to see it was empty, Cam crouched down to retrieve his knife from his pant leg; he would need to bust the window open.

Just then, a fierce blow from behind rattled his head and sent him sprawling. In his daze, he looked up to see the old man who ran the place standing over him with a menacing grin. The old bastard had somehow managed to sneak up behind Cam and swung a splintered piece of lumber to deliver a near-knockout blow.

Luckily, Cam had always had quite the resilient noggin. He lay there for a moment, considering his options, as the old man pressed the stout wood beam into Cam's ribs to pin him down.

"Jesus Christ, you gonna kill me? I'm just here workin' on the windows, you fool! It's me, Charlie! Charlie Ford!"

Cam plastered on his best acting combination of frightened and pissed. In reality, this man sprawled out with his hands up was as cool and calculating as ever. The spike of adrenaline had Cam seeing clearly through the haze of getting his bell pretty well rung, and now all his muscles tensed in preparation to spring on the old man the moment the chance was there.

"The hell are you doin' back here sneakin' around, boy? You got no reason to be back here. I spoke to Wallace the other day and he said he ain't ordered no window work. What reason you got to be back now? I could crack your skull and plant you in the woods." The manager poked Cam hard in the chest with the wood beam.

It was clear that he was still looking down on Cam as some lowly maintenance man, and Cam knew he wasn't discovered just yet.

"Sir, sir, I am so sorry. It ain't Mister O'Rourke had me out here, it was Bailey down at the packing plant. Remember? I swear I said so! Finley Bailey! He sent me up here 'cause I was doing his weather seals too! Please, sir, please let me up?"

His façade was working, as the old man relaxed a bit.

Lifting the beam from Cam's ribs, the old-timer stepped back half a step and glared down at his unwanted visitor.

"Get your ass up and get back to work, dammit. Wasting the day, that's what you're doing! Well, what the hell are you waitin' for, another crack on the head?"

Cam rolled onto his side and stood up swiftly. Standing there in front of this man whom he so desperately wanted to lay out with a good punch, instead Cam held out his hand and smiled innocently.

"Keys, sir?"

The man grunted at him, then fumbled around in a pocket for a set of keys to hand his worker. 'Charlie Ford' smiled broadly, despite a terrible ache and that ringing echoing through Cam's head.

"Sir, I'll make quick work of it all, thank you, sir. I won't be no trouble!"

Before he finished the sentence, the old coot was already walking away. Just as he had expected, playing the fool worked yet again.

Cam was rubbing the knot forming on the back of his dome as he grumbled to himself, "I wonder if I'll ever go a day without bein' underestimated?"

Walking back around toward the truck, Cam followed the old man. He reached the truck bed just as he shouted, "Sir, one moment, sir. Can you show me the windows in the office?"

The man peered at him incredulously as though this window guy was the dumbest cus in the land.

"You got keys, boy. Use 'em!" He barked back.

Cam grinned and shook his head.

"It's your spot, sir. I just need a minute of your day, sir. I just wanna make sure I do good!" The old man grumbled an epithet that Cam could hear and started pacing toward the office door. A grinning Charlie Ford reached into the truck and retrieved his *particularly* heavy coat, as well as a roll of tape from the bed, before following the old man into the office.

The faded lamp over the sign-in log flickered a bit while flies buzzed around a half-eaten sandwich on the desk. The room smelled of musty carpet and unwashed rump. The old man shuffled from the main office reception into the smaller room behind the only door and pulled the chain hanging in his face to turn that light on as well. The old coot was still grumbling to himself as he heard the door creak when the handyman stepped inside. After taking a sip of swill from the filthy mug on the desk, he slowly turned around to face a shadow in the doorframe from the bright midmorning daylight outside. His eyes not yet adjusted, he stepped forward into the main reception booth and found himself not two feet from the rough-cut steel rims of two stout shotgun barrels aimed directly at his sternum. All else he could see were two bright and very focused eyes gleaming in the dim office lamp's glow.

"What in the... Boy, are you out of your goddamned mind?" the man insisted.

This foolish and lowly handyman, he knew, must be stupid or crazy or perhaps both.

"I oughta kick your ass, quit aimin' that thing at me!" His voice cracked, nervous.

"Sit in that chair, oldtimer."

Cam motioned to the seat behind the desk in the main room.

"Sit your old ass down, or I'll give you a hundred little reasons to listen better."

He nodded toward the shotgun, and its twin shells eagerly ready to send a spitfire of lead and grit through the innkeeper.

The man, now realizing this was a serious exchange, nodded and raised his hands a bit as he sat down. Cam set the roll of tape onto the desk and smiled.

"Any other day, you would've been a meatball by now. Today, old man, I'm feelin' generous. Tape your arm to the chair. Three times around, good and tight."

He rested the shotgun barrels on the desk, aimed just above the old man's head.

"Just what in the blue hell do you think you're doing? You think just because I smacked you with a little stick, you got a right to tie up a white man and embarrass him? I know the lawmen around here, you're gonna be begging them for mercy by the time we're done, boy."

His grimacing face looked almost ghastly in the dim light, but Cameron would not be dissuaded.

"Tape your mouth, then your arm. Then you sit still, and I'll finish the job. Do as I say, or you'll be tasting more than those ugly words."

He tapped the gun barrels on the counter.

"Anyway, Mister O'Rourke is on his way already. Believe me when I say, Wally ain't gonna be surprised to see you like this. Hell, he probably thinks I'll be killin' you anyway, and that's fine with me."

As the man taped his own forearm to the chair's arm, he glared at Cameron with that same hateful expression tainted with sheer confusion.

"You talkin' some nonsense, boy. I'll see to it they string you up, just you wait."

Cam chuckled a bit at those comically run-of-the-mill threats. Becoming impatient with the slow-moving septuagenarian, Cam leaned forward and snatched the tape away from the man's free hand. Pulling off a strip nearly a foot long, Cam stretched it tight across the mouth of his second hostage in a dozen hours.

"I'm tired of your words. Sit tight and you might live long enough to see the inside of a cell, old man."

He finished taping the man's other arm to the office chair and finally wrapped the man's hands in tape, so he couldn't reach for anything handy to free himself. With a huff, Cam dragged the man, fully bound to the chair, into the smaller back office, shutting the door soundly.

Dusting off his hands and grabbing his shotgun, he tucked the weapon back into the coat he'd brought and walked outside, whistling a tune as though it were any other day. Now, feeling relatively free from prying eyes, Cam took to the truck and grabbed his thermos and the bag of tools he kept in the bed. It was a gritty burlap sack, with a few handy implements inside, such as rope, hand tools, and some painter's drop-cloths that would come in handy should he need to either appear to be a handyman… or perhaps craft a makeshift interrogation hood. Taking confident strides back to room 1C, he was sure this would be a good place to hide and wait for O'Rourke to show up for the party.

Unfinished Business

Peering at his watch, Cam Mason saw it was quarter-to-eleven and he had just enough time to calm himself and get a cool, damp towel on his now-throbbing skull for a few minutes. Room 1C was quiet, as virgin as ever. He was sure that it never got rented due to its proximity to the room they used to quell the frantic children whom O'Rourke and company had undoubtedly stowed away. Tossing his bag on the floor behind the door, Cam grabbed the edge of the bed and dragged it to the front of the room, where he could sit on its edge and peer out the window. With his perch set up, he went to the washroom and soaked a clean but surprisingly scratchy white hand towel to cool the lump on his head. He went to the bedside and took a seat, adjusting the blinds' angle just perfectly to give him a view outside without giving anyone a view inside. He knew that if he waited for the perfect moment, O'Rourke wouldn't see him coming, and he could get the upper hand.

A few minutes passed, almost exactly fifteen. Cam's watch showed 11:03 when O'Rourke's 1953 Oldsmobile cruised into the drive, replete with muddied fenders from the prior night's cabin visit. Cam watched and waited as O'Rourke parked directly in the center of the lot and sat in his car. Five minutes passed, no sign of the blackmailer, O'Rourke stepped out of his car and lit a small cigarillo to pass the time. He was wearing an unusually tight golfing shirt and some light slacks. There was no good place to hide a gun, and he couldn't hide his paunch either. He stood with his arms folded, looking over his shoulder and appearing generally impatient. Cam took a long sip of cool water from his thermos. It still held the tinge of old coffee, but Cam paid no mind.

Ten minutes passed, and O'Rourke thought better of his position; Cam chuckled as O'Rourke fired up the Oldsmobile and pulled it into a parking spot four rooms away, nose-in and looking casual. O'Rourke went into the trunk and withdrew a small black vinyl pouch, the sort that a bank might use to transport money. O'Rourke clutched the bag and sat back on the trunk of the Olds, tapping his foot and checking his watch to see that it was eleven-twenty, and still there was no sign of his faceless abductor/blackmailer.

Eleven twenty-five and O'Rourke got impatient. He saw no sign of the man he was awaiting, so he took a short walk and went to the little yellow 1937 Plymouth pickup resting coolly in the lot. He poked his head inside, seeing nothing of import. Then, much to Cam's amusement, Wallace O'Rourke walked straight back across the lot from the office toward room 2C. He stopped at the Oldsmobile, taking a set of keys out of the dashboard glovebox. Cam could hear the man cursing his blackmailer's tardiness and spitting some blue words about the situation. Cam was nearly giddy with excitement about what was going to happen next.

He *loved* this subterfuge shit.

O'Rourke keyed himself into the room directly left of Cam's current hideout. Cam heard a door shut and then listened to the restroom door inside 2C shut with a slam.

Sounds like you're gonna be a minute…

With stealth hardly matched in the world, Cam crept out of his room and shut the door most of the way, leaving the deadbolt poking out to stop the door from latching shut. He may need fast entry for cover. His trusty shotgun in hand, he took out the keys and, in slow and steady-handed, near-silent movements, unlocked O'Rourke's room door and crept inside. The toilet flushed in the bathroom, so Cam stepped aside from the bathroom door and raised the shotgun to just about eye level. Then, he waited.

With a creak, the bathroom door swept open, and a flustered, impatient O'Rourke stepped out into the room. He hadn't even seen the man standing in his peripheral vision until it was too late. Instinctually, O'Rourke swung around and fumbled with the black pouch. Upon seeing the sawed-off shotgun aimed at his face, he promptly dropped the pouch and froze in his tracks. Had he not just used the bathroom, he might have needed a change of pants just then.

"You didn't even wash your damn hands." Cam chided him.

Cam's black-clad silhouette must've looked out of place surrounded by all the toys, the candy… all those bright, cheery things, and Cam better matched the dark truth hidden in plain sight.

Feeling confident, Cam grinned widely at the scared-motionless man standing in front of him. Now Cam had the upper hand and caught O'Rourke in a deception that was somewhat predictable.

"That's a heavy bag for a stack of bills. You thought I'd let you draw on me? You ain't so smart, are you, Wally?"

Face-to-face with his previously faceless abductor, O'Rourke stared into Cameron's eyes with a hatred that could not be summed up in words. His face contorted into absolute rage, though he remained still in the face of the double-barreled option.

"You son of a bitch. How DARE you try to fuck me? I know your face now, you're not gonna be safe no matter how far you go. I promise you that."

His hands balled into fists, and Cam knew the man was not thinking straight. Not wanting a fight, Cam lowered the gun and extended it, poking O'Rourke in the belly.

"Don't get excited, I'm only here for the cash. You'll be fine once I hit the road, Wally. Don't go makin' this blackmailing into a murder, understand?"

His two hands on the gun, cam motioned toward the pouch on the floor.

"Pick it up slow, Wally-walrus, and dump it on the bed."

O'Rourke's eyes told that he was calculating his chances, and in a beat, he had come to the conclusion he'd better do as he was told. His hands unclenched, and he slowly crouched down to pick up the vinyl pouch with one hand as he raised the other like a good hostage. Slowly turning toward the bed, he never took his eyes off Cameron while he reached out and unzipped the envelope, shaking the contents onto the cheap print quilt. A small revolver bounced off the mattress and clattered to the ground. Aside from that, a stack of crisp green bills fell to the side. It sure looked like a thousand dollars to Cameron.

"Nice… now we are gonna do this the smart way, Wally the Weasel. You're gonna sit in the corner in that little pink chair, and I'm gonna take this gun *and* this money. Understand?"

O'Rourke nodded, still holding a visage of pure rage. Cam almost laughed at how silly the man looked, sitting in the tiny children's chair with his knees drawn up to his chest, red-faced and huffing.

Cam picked up the pistol, stuffing it into his pocket. He flipped through the cash, not counting it. He felt he had a moment now to extract a bit of truth from a man who believed Cam to be a true villain.

"Wally, tell me something. All this shit, all these kids, what's the deal? Are you a pervert? Do you like messing around with little kids?

You don't *look* like a sicko..." he baited the man well.

Wallace O'Rourke gripped the arms of the chair he sat in, looking away in what appeared to be a deep shame.

"I ain't a sicko."

Cam knew he could prod a bit more.

Shotgun still aimed in O'Rourke's general direction, Cam "If you ain't a sicko, and you don't seem like some serial killer, what's all these kids for?"

O'Rourke lifted his head and shrugged a bit.

"I sell 'em, I just *sell* 'em. After that, ain't my problem. Now, go get me my goddamn product you—"

The fat man neglected to finish his sentence, not wanting to goad his well-armed captor.

Cam wanted more answers, but decided Wallace had given him a good start, and the feds would question him later. He needed the agents to see this man in this environment; he needed them to apprehend O'Rourke amid his criminal enterprise. He considered the best way to proceed.

Stick to the plan, old man. Stick to the plan.

"You want the child that bad, huh?" O'Rourke simply glared. "Okay, Wally. You got it. I got a couple of associates from Chicago holding him nearby. You ain't the only game in town for moving people around, see? So I'm gonna get my boys and come back with the little cus. You gonna wait right here?"

O'Rourke looked around the room pensively. His reply wasn't what Cam wanted to hear when he responded, "I might not."

Nobody wants to be a caged animal.

Cam lowered his gun a bit to put the man's mind at ease.

"Look, Wally, if I wanted you dead, you'd be ice cold layin' over Hardigan. I can't come back for more grease in my palm if you're dead, can I? I don't wanna have to use your own piece on you for bein' short-sighted. Don't take it so *personal*."

O'Rourke seemed to be wising up. Cam knew how he would convince the man of his position.

"Sure. I'll stay put. For a few minutes, anyway. Don't *fuck* with me, boy."

"You're a businessman and so am I, Wally. I'm gonna go wrap up that little kid in a bow and bring him back. As a show of good faith, you can keep half the cash 'til I come back."

He peeled off about thirty crisp, sequentially numbered twenty-dollar bills, then tossed the remaining twenty-or-so bills back onto the bed.

"Now, when I get back, you better not do anything foolhardy. This is just business, it ain't personal. You understand?"

Wallace nodded, begrudgingly.

Cam stepped closer to him and insisted, "I want to hear you say it, Wally. You gotta be *clear* on this!"

With the man looming over him, gun in hand, O'Rourke leaned back a bit and put his hands in the air passively.

"OKAY! Okay. I'll be here, waiting. You better not be going *far*."

He just had to get the last word in, but Cam knew it was a safe bet O'Rourke wouldn't do anything until he had the little boy back in his possession. He knew the kid *must* be able to ID O'Rourke; all it would take was a competent bilingual and a one-way mirror.

Walking out the door, Cam said, over his shoulder, "Five minutes."

He knew it would be less than that. Walking out across the lot, he carried his shotgun with a smile on his face. It was almost over.

He fired up the Plymouth, and after a moment to let the oil pressure build a bit, he was grinning like a child; this was his favorite part. He stepped on the brake halfway, then threw the truck into gear. He beeped his truck's loud horn twice, then mashed his right foot into the gas pedal. In a flash, the big V-8 engine roared to life in a cacophony of booming noise from the mufflers, and two Firestone tires spun up into a smoky, shrieking torrent of gravel from under their tread. His front tires dug in under the brake, and the ass end of the truck shook and shrieked like it was possessed as the tires dug into the ground and the springs clamored to find traction. After a few moments of concussive noise from the yellow beast, he let off the gas and sat there in the cloud of dust kicked up from the plump tires.

Sounds like those Navy boys' makeshift dragstrip back in Alameda. Fun times.

With the blood in his head pounding both from the noise and the thumping he'd received not an hour earlier, he stepped out of the truck and waited. Not two minutes went by, and the black Lincoln rolled hastily into the lot. The two agents, Smythe and Harris, stepped out of the sedan still dressed casually in their river hats. Cam walked to meet them and made a 'stay low' hand signal. Both agents nodded, and neither withdrew their firearm. The unusual trio of good guys walked three abreast. Cam made a bladed hand toward room 2C.

The curtains shifted slightly in the window, and Cam knew

O'Rourke had peeked out; by now, he would have seen that there was no child in sight. Cam knew he had already disarmed the man, and he knew there was no window in the room through which O'Rourke could escape. As they reached the stoop of the door into the room, Cam lurched back and, with all his might and his size-twelve boot, kicked the door squarely inward.

Inside, a now-terrified O'Rourke shouted "Jesus Christ!" as he dove behind the bed.

Cam stood in the doorway, stepping into the room with the shotgun gripped in both hands and the butt of the stock against his hip. He was prepared in case O'Rourke got any funny ideas. The agents stepped in just behind him, but quickly maneuvered around him. These men were professionals to the letter. Harris jumped onto the bed, and Smythe went around Cam's left side, both of them with pistols drawn, only to find a cowering and nearly sobbing O'Rourke curled up on the floor.

Cam was elated as he watched the two G-men hoist the trembling O'Rourke to his feet and slap a set of heavy steel cuffs on his wrists. Smythe read the man his rights as Harris swept the room for threats.

Cam stepped out into the sunshine as the agents dragged O'Rourke out and toward the car. Wallace was cursing up a storm toward the men and toward Cameron, who was so bemused a the situation that he couldn't hold in a laugh. That sent O'Rourke into a further blue-faced tirade about what a dirty scoundrel Cam was, and how he'd need to watch his own back for years to come.

Cam remarked to him, "Yeah, good luck. You don't even know my name!" That didn't help, and O'Rourke cursed Cam's mother and his family all the way to the backseat of the Lincoln sedan.

Smythe slammed the door shut on a now-quiet O'Rourke, fuming in the car as Harris began making a sweep of the property.

Cam remarked, "Hey, Harris, you'll need these. The old man in the office is… well, I got him on tape. You'll see." Cam tossed him the master keys.

Harris caught the keyring, twirled it on his finger, and made a 'shooting' gesture to Cam behind a lopsided grin.

"Smythe, tell me something. How long will I need to stay until all this gets sorted? I'm a little homesick, y'know?"

Agent Smythe patted Cam on the arm and shook his hand. "Sir, I feel like you give me the day, and we can all head to Seattle to debrief. From there, you can head home with whatever expenses I can get covered for you. Full tank of gas for your hot rod, too. Sound good?"

Cam shook his head, "Billy pays me just fine. You save your gas money to come and visit me out in California sometime, yeah?"

He was half-joking, and Smythe laughed knowingly.

A short few minutes later, Harris had cleared the property and was in the office dealing with the old man. Smythe had returned to the room to take evidentiary photographs, while Cameron kept an eye on O'Rourke. He was still holding his shotgun, loosely. He wondered if he should toss it back in the truck. Feeling a bit idle, Cam walked back to the sedan and leaned in the half-open passenger side window, as O'Rourke fought the cuffs and the chain that tied his cuffed wrists down to the backseat.

"Hey Wally, you know I forgot to mention, but you ain't as big and bad as you thought. I turned one of your men; I'll find the rest. Seems like you're gonna go away for a while, maybe I'll send a cake." He started to walk away.

Wallace O'Rourke looked genuinely confused. "One of my men?"

A confident Cameron turned back toward the car and shot back, "You didn't think you could keep a jittery guy like Corker under your thumb, did you? He flipped easy."

O'Rourke, looking surprised, replied as he stared off toward the dashboard, "Corker doesn't... he doesn't work for *me*..."

Cam stepped forward, demanding, "What the *fuck* do you mean by that?"

Cameron Mason's confusion was interrupted by an explosion of glass and a red mist filling the car, spattering his face. The shock of it sent him reeling, and he ducked under the fender of the car, hoping it might shield him from whatever the hell that was.

After a moment of catching his breath, he peered just over the door and into the car. The rear windscreen was shattered but intact, and a small, clear hole of daylight shone in. The slumped-over body of Wallace O'Rourke was a mess, half of his head eviscerated from the bullet that someone had precisely aimed through the car window. Cam ducked back down, realizing O'Rourke had just been assassinated. He was still clutching his shotgun, now with both hands in preparation to use it.

Moments later, having heard the noise, Smythe came running out of room 2C with his pistol drawn and his camera dangling off his wrist like a tourist. He was crouched low and shouted "MASON!" in a growl.

Cam raised his hand over the fender and barked back, "I'm okay!" as he checked himself for glass shards, though he found only red grease and chunks of brain matter strewn across his face and coveralls.

Another moment passed, and a familiar sight came into view for Cameron. The milk delivery van he had seen abandoned on the roadside earlier went whizzing by in a blur. There appeared to be two men in the front seats, but it happened so fast that Cam could hardly tell.

There was no time to fire a shot, and at that distance, it would have been a waste of ammunition. Smythe ran across the lot to the car, coming around the side where Cam had been ducking.

"I don't think they hung around, pal. Let's follow that truck!" Cam directed Smythe.

Smythe popped up and shouted, "Harris! Recall! We have a situation!" just as Harris was running out of the office.

Seeing the scene and realizing what had happened, Harris shouted back, "Go! I'll stay behind!" and darted back into the office, likely to secure his prisoner.

Cam and Agent Smythe ran to the Plymouth and jumped in. With a flick of his wrist, Cam fired up the Hemi, and they peeled out into the street, kicking up gravel and road dust into the air. Cam handed the short shotgun to Smythe as they blasted down the road.

"Shells in the glove box, man. Get ready!" Cam shouted.

Smythe opened the dashboard glove box and pulled out a box of shells.

As Cam stomped the gas, it pinned the men to the seat springs of the pickup.

Smythe, in surprise, shouted, "The *hell* is under this hood, pal?" and Cam laughed.

As Smythe checked the barrels and set aside two more shells, Cam navigated the winding road headed east. They were near Snake River, and the old rickety highway was rough but passable. As they crested a hill, they spotted the milk van some distance ahead. Cam was closing the gap quickly, as Smythe held the doorframe for dear life.

"Jesus, Mason, you've got a real talent for this!"

He was joking to cover his nervousness as the frighteningly fast pickup swayed and yawed over the hills.

The milk truck was less than an eighth of a mile ahead, and Cam saw an opportunity. The road straightened for a stretch, and there was a levee on one side with railroad tracks perched atop it. Cam figured if he could get the truck aside, Smythe could take out a tire or possibly the driver. Throwing the Plymouth into second gear, the engine raced past 5,000 RPM, and the truck's rear tires lost traction for a moment, spinning in place as they reached nearly 80 miles per hour. Trees and signposts blurred as Smythe sat up and leaned out the passenger window, bracing the gun with both hands.

Forty yards quickly became thirty. Cam held the wheel steady and came up directly in line behind the truck, waiting for his moment to lunge past them. His tachometer clocked 6000 rpm, and the motor was screaming, spitting exhaust and flames out of the tailpipes like a P-51 Mustang fighter plane. The milk van was sputtering along, trying to outpace the Plymouth in vain. Cam could see a face reflected in the side mirror; the driver was a white man with a ball cap tucked low and a thin mustache. Twenty yards closed, and Cam kicked the truck into third gear as he jerked the wheel left. Correcting in a flash, the car was now overtaking the milk truck on the driver's side. Smythe let one barrel out, a shot that blew apart the side mirror on the Milk van and shattered the window.

The soft-handling old Divco van swerved and rocked a bit, nearly clipping the fender of the Plymouth, but held steady, and its motor could be heard struggling to rev faster. Cam tapped Smythe on the arm and shouted to help direct the agent's next shot.

"TIRE!"

Smythe raised a hand to acknowledge before aiming low for the next shot. With another percussive BANG, the shotgun sent its wad into the driver's side wheel and tire of the getaway truck. The tire blew out, and Cam stomped the brakes as the milk truck swerved hard left.

What happened next was so unexpected that Cam panicked and jerked the wheel himself, causing the old pickup to skid sideways to a stop in the middle of the highway. Cam felt his heartbeat in his throat as he watched, the destruction unfolding before him in an adrenaline-fueled slow motion.

The getaway driver had jammed his brakes and jerked the wheel hard left, still moving along at over seventy miles an hour. In his haste, the driver hadn't noticed the road's outlying features; a railroad bridge passed overhead, its concrete abutments standing strong and stoic in the mid-morning sun. As the milk truck swerved hard, it left the road and, without slowing, cannonballed directly into the ten-foot-wide solid concrete bridge abutment.

In a deafening blaze of shattered glass, twisting aluminum, and exploding debris, the milk truck collapsed into itself, flattening against the wall. With a last shriek, the metal box truck settled into the roadside gully, and the horrible scene came to a complete rest. Cameron had already stepped out onto the pavement as Smythe climbed out of the Plymouth's window, not able to take his eyes off the wreck.

Five seconds had passed, with two righteous men hurrying toward the wreckage to try and retrieve the assassins. Five seconds of pierced fuel tank and a pool of high-test gasoline had spilled just enough for the sparks of the carnage-frayed wiring to ignite it.

With a flash of heat and a deafening boom, the air beneath the twisted truck erupted in a ball of fire. Cameron and Agent Smythe shielded their faces as the truck and all its contents boomed ablaze. The shockwave of the blast sent them reeling.

"Holy hell, pal! We lost 'em!" Smythe exclaimed, dryly and with his hands shielding his face from the heat.

Cam turned to Smythe with hands on his hips, retorting, "He should've buckled in".

Smythe burst into laughter, an uproarious and ridiculous guffaw. Through his teeth, he managed to make out a sentence. "Jesus... you can't... you can't just *say* that shit, pal!" and Cam took to laughter as well.

Despite the heavy circumstances, both men were relieved that they'd survived the ordeal. Their nerves had brought them to fits of laughter as a defense mechanism for the insanity they'd just witnessed. Neither of them could keep their eyes off the blaze as it engulfed and decimated the mangled truck body,

It took nearly twenty minutes for the flames to die down before they could get close enough to inspect the truck through the shattered, baked-brown windows and blown-apart doors among the crushed tin can that was once a van body.

After estimating that they wouldn't be able to salvage much evidence aside from the gun and perhaps dental records, they took the pickup back to the motel to call in the wreck to the local lawmen. On the drive back, Cam was deep in thought. Smythe was still jittery from the chase, but he was a perceptive man.

"Cameron, what's on your mind? You're not satisfied." He was right.

Cam figured out the words before responding. "It's damn odd, all this work, and we find out O'Rourke probably wasn't running the show. It's like he was just another cog in a machine, that's all. Nobody just *takes out* the boss."

Smythe nodded, feeling the air on his face.

"Well, it's a good cog to have gone. You saved that little boy, you know. What was the last thing O'Rourke was saying to you?"

Cam glared at the road ahead.

"He said, Corker didn't work for him. Which means…" and he stomped the gas, sending the truck hurtling down the road back toward the Five Star Motel.

Just a few minutes later, Cam spun the truck into the gravel driveway and came to a jarring stop. Without saying a word to Smythe, Cam ran into the motel office. With the phone to his ear, he impatiently tapped his fingers on the counter as he dialed Caroline Hardigan's number.

Three rings, seven rings. Ten rings later, and he was ready to hang up. "Why do folks let the damn phone ring so long?" he muttered, just as she answered the phone.

Caroline answered sweetly, "Hello? Hardigan residence"

Cam, biting his lip, calmly inquired, "Hey, Caroline. It's Cam. How's everything there? Is the kid okay?"

She answered with her honey southern drawl, "Ohhh, Cam, everything is just dandy. Jimmy came by and explained everything!"

Cam was getting concerned."Is Jimmy still there?"

She was playing with the phone cord as she replied, "Why no, Cam? He's already on his way to see you!"

His patience was wearing, but not wanting to alarm Caroline, he replied, "Where? Where did he say he was headed?"

She clucked her tongue. "Oh, he didn't say. But, he's got the little boy with him, just like you asked. He's all cleaned up and happy. I even sent him along with some candies for the road. Strange, the little guy didn't say a word, but he sure didn't seem happy to see Jimmy. I think he was hoping to see you again, seeing as you saved him. Not that I could really *ask* him… Won't you all come to see me before you leave?"

Cameron's heart sank, and he barely replied, "Sure, Caroline… sure. See you soon."

Hanging up the phone, he folded his arms on the counter and rested his head on them. Leaning on the counter, he felt his knees begin to buckle. Corker had played him for a fool, and now a child was gone. Cam had held the little man in his arms and promised him everything would be okay.

At this moment, the weight of sleepless nights and driving hours on end, the fight of it all drained him thoroughly. He turned his back against the counter, sending the phone clanging onto the ground with a backhand. His chin sank to his chest, and he realized now this wasn't over. He would not go home; he may never. Sitting there on the floor of the grimy little motel office, Cam looked at his palms. They were caked in blood and dirt, lacerations from shards of the car's window glass decorated by small bits of rough gravel that were clinging to the blood.

He felt *old* once again.

With a heavy sigh, he fell nearly limp in exhaustion as Agent Smythe walked back into the dingy office, Harris in tow. The feeling of defeat was crushing. Cam didn't even lift his head to meet the men who had helped him stop the man he foolishly thought was the root of all this evil.

Smythe knelt there and patted Cameron on the shoulder.

"I'm sorry, pal. He's… was it Corker? Uh… you need a beat?"

Cam could barely respond, but he spat out the words.

"Corker, he took the kid. He's in the wind. He's out there, and I told him *everything*. I let him hoodwink me, you see? I thought I had him outfoxed… and now that little boy is gone, just… gone."

Smythe stood up and turned to Harris, who was drawing on another cigarette with a scowl on his face.

"Harris, we've got work to do." Harris nodded, turning toward the parking lot to wait for local lawmen. Before Smythe could step out of the office, he felt a hot palm on his shoulder. The G-man turned around to meet eyes with Cameron Mason. Cameron stood there towering over the man, his eyes ablaze in rage and purpose.

"Yeah, Smitty. *We* have a lot of work to do."

One Little Match

Monday, April 23rd, 1956

Uneven footsteps echoed throughout the barren hallway. The hideous spattered-green asbestos tiling on the floor absorbed no sound and, more unfortunately, no impact. Hard-soled shoes met the ground with misfortune at the placement of every heel, and a slip underfoot every time a toe lifted. This sort of flooring wasn't designed with comfort in mind. No, this sort of flooring was designed with ease of maintenance in mind. It was easy to mop. It was inexpensive and plentiful. When you have to cover the flooring in a multiple-thousand-square-foot facility? Price becomes a concern.

Perhaps worse than the flooring was that god-awful, baby-shit-beige paint lazily rolled across all of the walls. It was like a house paint, but not exactly. It had this weird watered-down quality to it, so you could see where some of the walls used to be a different color, or there used to be some sort of signage painted on the walls that was run over with that roller. This tacky hue was applied on top with only the slightest effort at uniformity.

The ceiling tiles were made of fiberboard and showed various drips and stains that soaked right through and made the ceiling perhaps more unappealing than the rest of it, but nobody really looks up in a place like this. The lighting is harsh, and those damn fluorescent tubes like to flicker just outside what the eye can see. It becomes nauseating. Perhaps even depressing. One thing it was, Most certainly, was oppressive.

The people who built this facility spent as little as possible on decoration. They certainly spent a lot of money on locks and fasteners and heavy doors, but the reason for *that* was apparent. At least it was evident to anybody who had spent any time in the upper levels. Now, in a place like this, not everybody gets to see the real inner workings. In a place like this, many people are relegated to the pleasant lower floors, where there might be nice, bright white walls and even a pretty silk plant in the corner of any given office. Desks faced away from each other and out a window where one could see what gorgeous scenery that surrounded the place. Not upstairs.

No, upstairs there were no windows. That was very much also by design.

Those aforementioned uneven footsteps continued echoing throughout the hallway as the owner of those tired feet, in hard-soled dress shoes, trudged along toward today's task.

Head hung low and an empty box swinging in one hand, Jimmy Corker thought about the strange sensation of his thighs rubbing together in those cheap polyester pants he had bought simply because his other pairs no longer fit. Now, as he gained weight and got some meat back on his bones, he chuckled to himself about how they don't mention the side effects of medication, how they just like to hand you pills and tell you to swallow them and kick your ass out the door, no matter the consequences.

"It's not going to take much time to take effect, so you'd better be ready for some changes."

That's what the smarmy son of a bitch sitting across from Jimmy had said when he was handed his first batch of those little green pills.

That shithead doctor was right. I feel like a pregnant woman. Am I waddling? I think I'm waddling.

Jimmy swung the box over his left shoulder and grabbed the door handle with his right hand. Sweeping it open wide and peering inside. Another one of those unfortunate flickering fluorescent tubes lit the room in a putrid glow. The room was empty. Well, it was devoid of occupants anyway. On a steel table in the far corner of the room, there was a small rumpled-up pile of clothing and next to it a shaggy blue blanket that had been washed too many times, causing the edges to become frayed.

Unceremoniously, Jimmy slid the box under the edge of the table and swatted the clothing and the blanket inside. The smell hit him first. It was sickly sweet, like someone had thrown up after drinking a belly full of fruit punch. It was acid, sugar, and rot.

Fucks' sake. That's nasty. Gotta get one of those spics up here to run a mop.

He turned to leave and saw that, just behind the door in the adjacent corner, there was still a pile of sick on the floor.

"Ah, fuckin' hell… Hope I didn't get any on my shoe." He complained to the air as he let the spit collect in his mouth.

He didn't want to swallow that foul odor. He hurried out of the room and slammed the door shut.

In short order, Corker made his way down to the maintenance room. Inside, next to a row of about a dozen industrial washing and laundry machines, a commercial incinerator stood proud; its exhaust pipe resembling a galvanized steel tree trunk that shot straight up through the ceiling.

He tossed the box on the floor in front of the incinerator and stood there for a moment with his fists upon his hips, considering the situation. Bobbing his head side to side as he talked, he imitated his superior and the instructions he had received earlier.

"James, you need to put some work in around here. I need you to clean up all of the rooms on level 2 that don't have a white tag next to the door—every single room. I want them empty, and I want all of the personal items disposed of. We want the blankets separated, and please, whatever you do, don't throw away any equipment. You dumb idiot."

He kicked the box and sneered.

"Also, I want you to bend over and grab your ankles so we can screw you right in the ass. Right in your big fat ass. Yes. We want you to drive that little shitbox Studebaker and show up every day and clean up like you're some kind of fucking janitor. That's what you do now, Jimmy. That's what you do, and you're going to like it."

He was getting himself worked up, making a mockery of the instructions he'd been given earlier.

"Also remember that we own you, so you can't go home, and you can't have any money, and you have to live in a little ramshackle fucking cottage in the middle of nowhere, and you will lick our boots. Grab those ankles, fat boy. Fucking fat fuck!"

He spat on the box and snatched the swinging door open on the incinerator. It must have been two feet by two feet, six or seven feet deep. Large enough to burn just about anything. It looked like something you would see in a mortuary, but far more streamlined and severe. It looked like something from NASA—real high-grade equipment.

Jimmy Corker didn't care in the least. He slammed the door open and grabbed the box by a corner, tossing the entire thing into the incinerator as he cursed his boss.

"Fuck your blankets and fuck you and your stupid glasses, Dwayne. I'm not separating laundry like I'm some kind of fucking Mexican maid. You want laundry done? You have one of those fuckers do it. I get paid to clean up messes, and today I'm cleaning up messes *my* way."

Just as he reached for the door to slam it shut, Somebody cleared their throat, and it sounded like they were standing right behind him.

"*Mister* Corker, do you believe you performed an adequate job separating the items you removed from J2?"

Corker spun around on his heel to find that stern-faced old crow, Miss Schulz, staring down her nose at him. She was all of five feet tall, and this woman terrified Jimmy. Hell, he's pretty sure she terrified everybody.

Jimmy looked back to the box sitting there on the grid steel inside the incinerator and then back to Schulz. She was dressed in a white canvas Uniform with a bleach-stained brown sweater over top. In one hand, she clutched a heavy binder, and in the other, she held a Ring of keys that would make the janitor at any high school fully turgid.

"I, uh… The blanket was real tattered. I didn't— I didn't think it was serviceable anymore."

She scowled at him, pausing for far too long before she responded.

"I must have misheard. It sounded like you were unhappy with performing your duties today. Is that the case? Shall I spend my day finding other… *tasks* for you to perform?" She had a stiff German accent, but it was tainted with something else, possibly British. Her tone was educated and superior at all times. Jimmy was sure she had teeth, but he had never seen a smile.

"I'm sorry. I'm sorry about that. I just… It's these pills. This medication. It's making me a little… I think it's making me moody. I can do better." He sheepishly stuffed his hands into his pockets and shrugged.

"I see. I am not surprised by the side effects of a hormonal shift, *James*, but let's be sure that your quality of work does not diminish, no?"

"No, miss Schultz. Missus. I'm sorry."

As she turned to leave, she remarked to the air, "*Schultz* is adequate," and she left him in the room to finish his work.

Fucking kraut… He thought to himself, suddenly finding himself afraid to utter a blue word out loud.

He separated that little blanket and tossed it into the adjacent washing machine. He then gingerly closed the door on the incinerator and set both levers before pressing the large red button to initiate the incineration cycle.

He peered down at his wristwatch and saw it was nearly four o'clock. Quitting time. He'd been trudging around those halls since seven in the morning, and his feet were swollen tight in his shoes. He made a slow, plodding trek down to the locker room to retrieve his coat and lunch box. He made his way through the lobby and toward the small parking lot adjacent to the facility. Warm sunshine on his face made him feel a little less exhausted. A little bit more enthused to have made it through another day.

And it's just fucking Monday…

He walked around the building to the even smaller lot hidden behind a row of trees. It was the parking lot where less essential employees left their vehicles. While some of the facility was dedicated to the in-house resident staff, He was one of the ones who got to go every day and make his way some six miles out to the company-owned housing. On this day, for some reason more than other days, he stopped in his tracks on the grass that ran alongside the building and stared up at the mountains that sprawled out in front of him and continued, seemingly endless, into the distance.

Late April in this part of British Columbia, Canada, meant that there would still be snow on all of the mountains, but the ground was clear, and there was plenty of moisture in the air to amplify that sunshine. Not quite enough to give you a sunburn, but enough to warm your shoulders through your coat and remind you that it was recently very cold indeed. Holding a few birds were chirping, but it was enough to bring a slight smile to the face of this otherwise miserable and exhausted man.

Fuckin'… fucking mountains. Fucking birds. Fucking fat feet.

He peered down at his feet and wished he had brought some more comfortable shoes to change into. Maybe some of those canvas athletic shoes. Something with a soft sole. Hell, he even thought about walking through the parking lot barefoot. But the last thing he needed right now was any more talk about him. Rumors and gossip in a facility of some four dozen people. It spread quickly, and it almost always made its way back around to the subject of said rumors and downtalk.

Jimmy Corker took a deep, cool breath and slowly lurched toward the very back of the far lot, the very last space that was practically his assigned space. He had the ugliest, most run-down little car, even compared to the muted beige and brown sedans that the facility owned and parked in the front area of that lot. There were also a number of company panel wagons; they were black and somehow ominous, all parked in a perfect row nose-out, ready to dispatch.

After what felt like an eternity, Corker arrived at the back bumper of his little brown rusty Studebaker sedan. The rear window glass was cracked from a branch falling on it this past winter. He didn't want to spend the money to replace it, so he just taped it up with box-packing tape; they didn't pay him well enough to make any fundamental changes in his life, so right now, he had to grin and bear it.

He withdrew his key and slid it in the door lock, wiggling it as one must when the lock starts to wear out from oxidation and use. He finally got the door unlocked and grabbed the door handle, swinging the door wide with a nasty creaking sound.

"Fucking car. Fucking old piece of shit." He grumbled to himself, although he felt the urge to look over his shoulder to make sure that *Schultz*, the bitch-in-chief who seemed to run the whole show, wasn't looming behind him to catch him complaining again.

With two stomps on the accelerator pedal to prime the carburetor, he cranked it and let it whine until the ignition caught a good spark in a cylinder.

URR-RURR-RURR-RURRURRURRRRURRRR BRRRUUMMMBUMBUMBUM…

The engine grumbled to life, just like he grumbled to himself. A little blue smoke chuffed out of the tailpipe while the engine idled, running a little higher rpm until it warmed up, and he could let off the choke to idle down the six-cylinder, which was shaking like a spastic and desperately clinging to life underneath the rusty hood.

While he waited, he opened his lunch pail and peered inside. A half-empty pack of cigarettes was all that remained now. That and a little glass jar with the remnants of a few grapes in the bottom; he left the brown ones, the mushy ones. He couldn't stand them.

Sitting there waiting for his engine to warm, he tapped the base of the box of cigarettes on the dashboard of the car to knock loose any leaf tobacco that might be wanting to otherwise crackle out of the cigarette and leave burn holes in his clothing when he went to light the end. He struck a cigarette and took a deep breath of poorly filtered smoke. The smoke swirled around him as he exhaled in the car, and he wished right then that the little heater hadn't quit working a month ago. Sure, the engine got warm, sometimes too warm, but the fan that pushes the air through the heater had conked out on him, and he was so far from any town that he didn't know when he might be able to buy a replacement.

Fucking car. This fucking car is going to bring my cancer back.

He took another drag and stared out the side window at that mountain range that stood so silently over the little, carved-out valley where this facility was hidden away.

Fucking Canada.

By the time he finished the cigarette, the engine had warmed up. Now he was safe to push in the choke cable on the dashboard and let the engine idle down. Slipping off his shoes in the footwell was a pleasure, and then he put his hole-ridden socked feet on the worn-smooth rubber pedals to mash the clutch and head home.

He watched the road intently as this was a very wilderness-heavy area and there would often be wildlife skittering across the road. He tried to avoid them when he could, but he couldn't swear that he hadn't ended the lives of at least half a dozen squirrels in recent memory.

It was only a dozen minutes or so before he arrived at the little quiet gravel street where some ramshackle homes had been put up. Once again, his was the last house on the row. He had no neighbors, either.

Idling the little car slowly down the gravel road, he swung wide and pulled into the driveway, which was on a slight hill. He had made a little game of it; he knew just when to cut the engine, where it would roll up and come to a stop on its own in the driveway, without even touching the brakes. Just rip the parking brake when she got to her tire grooves in the gravel driveway.

Those little idiosyncratic habits of his were some of the few things that brought him a semblance of joy in this new life. No matter how bad things were back in the Dakotas, at least back there, he had a lady he could get a little frisky with, and there were stores where he could buy good booze, and there was work that paid him enough to buy a decent meal. Hell, there was even decent national news and storytime radio, and he truly enjoyed that; he missed it every night.

Out here, all they picked up were forestry service channels and the occasional weather alert service. The only thing Jimmy Corker had to look forward to when he walked into that place was a stack of books left by the previous tenant. A stack of books on Entomology and the African continent, and various other historical and cultural crap that he couldn't give two shits about.

He was purely miserable, and it was only Monday.

Corker killed the engine at the perfect point in his arcing turn, coasted that little car into the driveway, and pulled the parking brake as it came to a stop. Just as he reached for the door handle, he heard a Foreign and very unfamiliar sound.

HISS-CRACKKKLE

"The hell—"

He spun the radio knobs, but they were dormant.

"Hey, Jimmy! Jimmy fucking Corker, is that you?"

The voice sounded mute and distant. It was coming from a speaker somewhere in the car.

Jimmy froze and did not move for fear of what might come next.

"Come on, Jimmy, pick up. Reach under your seat and pick up the radio," the voice goaded him.

Fuck. Fuck me. I do not need this... Jimmy thought, but with little hesitation, he reached under the seat, and his hands grasped a boxy, square metal object.

He felt an antenna and realized it was a handheld two-way radio.

"I can see you sweatin', Jimmy. Just pick up the radio. Come on, we need to have a chat."

He peered outside and in his rearview mirror, but he saw nobody around who might be talking to him through the radio. The voice was oddly familiar.

His mouth suddenly dry, he had to push his lips off his teeth with his tongue to speak. Slowly and deliberately, he brought the olive green army-issued radio up to his mouth and, with his thumb, cautiously pressed the transmit button.

"Whoever this is, you're fucking dead. I don't like pranks."

There was a little static and a crackle from the other side before the response came.

"Oh, now, this is no prank, Jimmy Corker. Can I just call you Jimmy? I used to call you Jimmy, and I think I'm going to stick with that. You seem like a Jimmy. I mean, you seem like a sweaty fat bastard who maybe ate some guy named Jimmy. So... close enough, huh?"

Shit. Can he see me?

Corker looked around once again, and once again, he saw nothing out of the ordinary. Just his shitty little cottage house and the trees that began a few dozen yards from the end of the gravel street.

"You've got me at a disadvantage. Who am I speaking with?" He asked, doing his best to muster bravery in his voice.

"Oh, come on now, Jimmy, don't you remember? Don't you remember that sweet little cigarette we had in your basement? Don't you remember the way I smelled? Don't you remember how you figured out I was colored even though you couldn't see shit?"

The fucking... gumshoe. The fucking... That Cameron sonofabitch. Corker felt a lump in his throat form in an instant.

"Okay, mister detective, you found me. I know you can't be too far away because these radios don't have that kind of range in the mountains. So why don't you just come out and we do this face-to-face?"

There was silence on the other end. An uncomfortable, eerie, unbearably long silence. It must have been five seconds, maybe six. Jimmy's stomach tied itself in a knot.

"You know, I thought about that. I thought about confronting you like a man. And then I thought about all the shit that you've done. And I realized that you ain't much of a man. So I figured I would do it this way. You know, have some fun with you."

Jimmy squirmed in his seat and started leaning to step out of the car.

"AH! Don't do it, Jimmy. Don't you step one foot out of that goddamn car. You never know what else I have waiting for you. I might have some surprises in store. Shit, I might even have something fun under the hood of the car where I could just press a little button over here and you would be gone in the blink of an eye. Vaporized."

Jimmy cleared his throat and reached for another cigarette with a trembling hand. He wasn't going to let the voice on the radio browbeat him.

"Oh, so you're one of the *clever* ones. Didn't seem that way when I met you. From what I recall, I played you like a fool. Played you like a goddamn jazz piano. Don't you people love Jazz?"

On the other end of the radio, Cameron Mason stifled a chuckle. "Yeah, *we people* love those things. We are a musical people. We are a beautiful people, and you don't seem to appreciate that. I'm heartbroken over here, Jimmy! Whatever am I to do without your approval?"

The confidence and sheer mockery in Cameron's tone set Jimmy Corker's teeth on edge.

"Well, you found me. Now you tell me what you want, because I've had a long day and my feet hurt. So, you can have whatever you want. I will tell you whatever you want to know. Just... Stop fucking with me!"

Another hiss and crackle from the other end before the response came.

"Jimmy, your feet hurt because you're fat. I remember you looked like skin and bones, but now you look like a goddamn donut. You move out to the woods just to eat yourself to death?"

"Listen, not that it's any of your concern, but I'm recovering. I've got new medications, and they said this was a side effect. Besides, I'm still man enough to kick the spit out of you. Hell, I could have done that when I was skinny."

The cigarette was calming his nerves, and he was finding his gumption again.

"Heh. You might be right. I guess it really doesn't matter. See, right now, you belong to me. You're not going to do a goddamn thing because I could spark your ass up at any given time, and no one in this world would miss you. Not even Caroline. Shit. *Especially* not Caroline."

Jimmy squished the cigarette between his fingers, causing it to crumble apart into the carpet.

"Yeah, I figured you'd ruin a good thing. What did you tell her?"

"Oh, come on, Jimmy. I didn't have to say a damn thing. Those friends of mine, the ones in the black suits, they told her everything. They sat her down and gave her the rundown. You know, that cabin... Steve made a mess of things. Just a little bit of digging around, and they found all kinds of nasty shit up there. I was more than happy to guide them once I had those federal boys by my side. And they figured out a lot of what you boys were up to. They figured out what a disgusting piece of filth Steve was. What a sick, twisted villain he had become. The things he did to those children. Now I've got to wonder, are you like that? Do you like to mess with kids that way?"

The anger in Cameron's voice came through clearly over the radio.

Jimmy lay his head back on the seat and sparked up the last cigarette in the box.

"You know, I didn't lie about everything. What did I tell you about Steve Hardigan? That was true. That man had a sickness. I don't know what it was, but yeah. Steve went too far. He was like a rabid dog... Like a shark that got the scent of blood, he stopped treating those children like human beings. I mean, yeah, they're just dirty little shits, but that doesn't mean I don't have humanity. Someone was going to put him down. I think it's hilarious that it was you. Everything else I saw of you, you're fucking incompetent."

Cam took a beat while Corker power-smoked his cigarette.

"Now, Jimmy, that's not very nice. Would an incompetent man track you down to the wilderness of another country? Would an incompetent man pin you down in your little rusty car where you're too afraid to step out and walk into your own house? You think it's a coincidence that the little car started leaking gasoline out of the carburetor a few weeks ago? And you're the one who's too incompetent to tighten the nut on the fuel pump hard line..."

Jimmy recalled that recently ever-present waft of gasoline.

He's going to fucking kill me.

"Okay, I'll give you that one. Like I said, you're one of the clever ones. So what do you want? What do we do now? I think if you wanted me dead, I'd be dead, especially since you've clearly been skulking around for a while. I hope you froze your black ass off out there in the woods."

"Jimmy, Jimmy, Jimmy. I was on forward reconnaissance. My boys and I used to live out there in the fields and woods, and in whatever gully we could shelter in for the night. This ain't hardship. In fact, I sort of like it out here. You know, if it wasn't so full of... well, people like you. It might be a real pretty country."

Jimmy Corker felt defeated. He was staring at the slightly stained and faded headliner of the car, halfway done with his cigarette, and contemplating what mistake he might have made that he wound up back in the crosshairs of this overly determined man.

"Like I said, Cameron, just tell me what you want. I figure you know what I'm doing up here, and so I figure you might know at least a little bit of what's going on in the facility. And if you don't, I'm willing to help you with whatever mission you have in mind—Christ's Sake. I'm just a fixer. I'm a handler. I don't... I don't have any power. I've got three bosses and nothing in my pockets but smokes and lint. So whatever you want, just fucking say it. I'm too tired for your games today, Mason."

The wait for a response was the worst part of it. Jimmy Corker hated that about conversations. He hated that about simple people. He hated people who took their time trying to find the best words to get their way. His parents had called him *unsociable*. They called him a lot more than that when they booted him out at 16, but that doesn't matter now.

"Okay, *Mister* Corker. I told you way back that I was going to put a stop to all this. Now you're going to help me do it. Otherwise? Those federal boys know where to find you as well. So you go ahead and walk your lard ass into that house, and you soak your feet with some Epsom salts if you've got it, and I will ring your phone *if* and *when* I see fit. Until then, you just play it cool and do your lackey-bullshit job. I figure you have a routine, so you'd better stick to it. You tell anyone about this, and you know there will be consequences. Am I clear?"

Jimmy let out a long sigh punctuated by a whistle at the end.

"Crystal clear, *boss*. Boy, I sure pulled the wool over your eyes last time. I hope you learned your lesson because this time, I think the stakes might be a bit higher. Just tell me one thing. What happened to Caroline after you broke the news?"

"Oh, she's a strong woman. She got over Steve lightning-fast, and she got over you even quicker. I don't think your little pink pecker did much for her anyway. I think she just liked the cocaine you used to push. Anyway, I've got her stashed at a nice little Craftsman Home by the Sea. She's taken up knitting, and I must say, Caroline is a talented girl. I think she also joined a new church. The stuff she went through? Man, that will change your life. Anyway, don't you worry about her. You just get yourself some rest, because I want you bright and bushy-tailed in the morning. Capiche?"

With a smirk, Jimmy imagined Caroline sitting on a couch somewhere with sunshine coming through the window, casually knitting away, pretending like she wasn't his little cocaine-addled world-class cocksucker back in the day. Jimmy might have been a villain, sure, but he had a soft side.

"Capiche." He sneered into the radio and then tossed it onto the car seat before leaving everything behind and stomping barefoot into his little cottage. He plodded up to the icebox and swung it open wide.

"Fucking cheese. Fucking bread. Fucking moldy bread. Damn it." He picked up the block of sharp cheese and turned it over in his hand, looking for signs of mold he'd cut off before eating it straight off the block like a little rat in a matinee cartoon.

He stood there, barefoot and sweating, shaking from adrenaline for a while. It might have been half an hour… He'd finished the block of cheese, and his stomach had already begun to ache.

RINGGGG

"Oh, what the fuck now…" He seethed as he spun around and snatched the daisy-yellow plastic phone off the kitchen wall.

"WHAT!" He shouted into the handset, half question and half exclamation.

"Say, Jimmy?"

That voice.

He dropped the rind of cheese on the floor as Cameron's voice crackled across the phone line.

"Y—yeah?"

"That little boy, that poor little beautiful baby boy you stole from Caroline. That little child that you went and stuffed in your trunk and handed over to your labcoat nazis up here? Up here at 'Fenster-Pratt Institute of Advanced Medical Research'? Yeah, I know a lot more than you might think, considering I'm 'incompetent'. I don't need shit from you. You're a *nobody*. A stain on my boot. But I wanted to give you a little bit of hope."

"Hope?"

"Yeah. Hope like that little boy had when I rescued him. Hope like he had when Caroline kissed him on his forehead and handed him off to you. Hope when she waved goodbye as though it was Easter Sunday. Hope like he held onto up until the moment you vile sons of bitches locked him in a white room and started injecting and cutting and all of that shit they do. I just wanted to give you that taste of hope before, well, *you know*."

A bit of piss trickled down the front of Corker's polyester pants. It was already cold when it reached his thigh as he stammered for the words to respond.

"B— Before what? Before WHAT?" His throat cracked like a pubescent boy.

"Jimmy, Jimmy… oooooh, Jimmy. Yeah, my unit was forward reconnaissance, but you never asked if I had any specialist training in the service."

Cameron was savoring this moment; he could feel butterflies in his stomach. It was two years of muck and mire to get to this point, but Cameron Mason was a dog with a bone. This shit felt *good*.

A long pause hung in the air until finally a meek voice peeped out, "I don't… I don't wanna ask."

"*Heh*. Yeah, figured. But I'm gonna tell you anyway, Jimmy-boy. It was demolition… incendiaries, napalm. All the real fun stuff."

Jimmy Corker's knees turned to custard as he heard a clicking noise emanate from behind the gas stove, and he murmured his last word, "Demoli—"

KRAKOOOOOOOOM

As a fireball consumed the house, splintering every wall into a million shards, the roof blew up like an umbrella in a bad storm. The gas lines blew, and a raging blue flame churned up the center of the hellfire. Detritus and burning embers rained down for a hundred yards around, sizzling and hissing as they met cool earth and foliage. The glow of white-hot flames glinted off the tired pupils of a weatherbeaten but determined man standing not fifty yards away in the tree line. He stood still as an aspen tree, holding a pair of binoculars and wearing a green canvas tarpaulin. Thin electrical leads ran from the telephone in Cameron's hand to the telephone switchbox a few yards away.

Cameron Mason never blinked as rubble scattered and smoke bellowed.

He smirked when Corker's ratty old Studebaker caught fire, and he chortled as the tires half-melted and then exploded as their gases expanded hot enough.

He observed in silence as the timbers of the house burned down into skinny little blackened matchsticks.

Eventually, the tired old dog leaned back against a tree to rest as the rubble churned into embers. The roar of combustion broiled and groaned, and it warmed him in a place deep down. As the fire diminished, so too departed a small portion of the man's guilt and grief for what happened to that little boy. He had visited death upon this wicked perpetrator—death, arguably the only *true* closure.

Yet what remained was a hollow inside of Cameron that now only fire and fury could fill, and he knew this path well. He spat on the ground, cursing this place and knowing this was just the start.

"Say hello to Steve Hardigan."